LOOK
BOTH
WAYS

Books by Carol J. Perry

Tails, You Lose

Caught Dead Handed

LOOK BOTH WAYS

CAROL J. PERRY

KENSINGTON PUBLISHING CORP.
http://www.kensingtonbooks.com

KENSINGTON BOOKS are published by

Kensington Publishing Corp.
119 West 40th Street
New York, NY 10018

All Kensington titles, imprints and distributed lines are available at special quantity discounts for bulk purchases for sales promotions, premiums, fund-raising, and educational or institutional use. Special book excerpts or customized printings can also be created to fit specific needs. For details, write or phone the office of the Kensington Special Sales Manager. Kensington Publishing Corp., 119 West 40th Street, New York, NY 10018. Attn: Special Sales Department. Phone: 1-800-221-2647.

Kensington and the K logo Reg. U.S. Pat & TM Off.

ISBN-13: 978-1-61773-373-4
ISBN-10: 1-61773-373-3
First Kensington Mass Market Edition: November 2015

eISBN-13: 978-1-61773-374-1
eISBN-10: 1-61773-374-1
First Kensington Electronic Edition: November 2015

10 9 8 7

Printed in the United States of America

For Dan,
my husband and best friend

ACKNOWLEDGMENTS

The flicker of an idea for *Look Both Ways* came from my memories of the many happy and productive years I spent as advertising manager of a wonderful old New England department store (which may or may not have been haunted), augmented with knowledge gained from writing lots of nonfiction articles for antiques and collectibles publications. But those tiny sparks grew into a book only, as Lennon and McCartney wrote, "with a little help from my friends."

Special thanks to fellow writers Liz Drayer and Laura Kennedy for ongoing friendship and support, along with exceptional reading and editing skills.

Much appreciation to Dana Cassell of the Writers-Editors Network for years of encouragement and good advice.

Thanks to my dear friend and Emerson College graduate, Jacquie Luke Hayes, for generously sharing her theater arts background with Lee.

Loving thanks to my husband and BFF, Dan, for caffeine-fueled, after-midnight "driving along the beach" brainstorming sessions.

Writing can be a solitary pursuit, and I'm a big fan of writers' organizations. The companionship of other writers not only improves our skills but also keeps us reasonably sane. I belong to several. Much gratitude to the Bay Area Professional Writers Guild (BAPWG), the Pinellas Authors and Writers Organization (PINAWOR), the Florida Freelance Writers Association (FFWA), Mystery Writers of America (MWA), and Sisters in Crime (SinC).

Once again, Esi Sogah at Kensington proved the incalculable worth of a fine editor.

"Looking glass upon the wall, who is fairest of them all?"

The Evil Queen in "Snow White,"
Grimm's Fairy Tales

CHAPTER 1

"Maralee, come here. You won't believe this!"

I hurried from my sparsely furnished bedroom to the kitchen, where Aunt Ibby sat on an unpainted and slightly wobbly wooden stool. She pointed to the new TV, which was propped against a carton of books on the granite countertop.

"Look," she said "It's exactly the same, isn't it?"

I pulled up a faded folding beach chair and peered at the screen. "You're right," I said, watching as a tall, gray-haired woman opened and closed the top drawer of an oak bureau. "It looks just like mine. What show is this?"

"*Shopping Salem,*" she said. "It's new. The WICH-TV reporter goes around the city, interviewing shop owners. You should go right over there and buy that bureau before somebody else grabs it. Lord knows, you need furniture. Sitting out there on the new fire escape would be more comfortable than this thing." She rocked back and forth on the wobbly stool.

I sighed. "I know."

My sixty-something, ball-of-fire aunt had recently

turned the third floor of the old family home on Salem's historic Winter Street into an apartment for me. I was delighted to have the private space, but selecting furnishings had become an unexpected challenge. Who knew that deciding between red and blue, modern and traditional, oak and walnut could be so bewildering?

So far all I'd bought for my spacious new digs was a king-size bed, the television set, a coffeemaker, and a scratching post for our resident cat, O'Ryan—supplemented with assorted temporary seating brought up from the cellar.

I'm Lee Barrett, née Maralee Kowalski, aged thirty-one, red-haired, and Salem born. I was orphaned early, married once, and widowed young. I was raised by my librarian aunt, Isobel Russell, in this house, and I returned home, to my roots, nearly a year ago.

"You'd better get going," Aunt Ibby said. "A handsome bureau like that will get snapped up in no time. The shop's called Tolliver's Antiques and Uniques. It's on Bridge Street. Won't take you but a minute to drive over there." She tossed her paper coffee cup into the recycling bag next to the sink. "And you might pick up some proper coffee cups while you're there."

I had a special reason—besides my obvious dearth of furnishings—to want this particular piece. An identical one had long ago adorned my childhood bedroom and had later been relegated to the attic. Sadly, it had been destroyed by a fire that pretty much ruined the top two floors of our house. The damage to the structure had been nicely repaired, but the contents of the rooms, including my bureau, had proven pretty much irreplaceable.

"Do you suppose hers has little secret compartments like mine did?" I wondered aloud.

"It does," she said. "The shop owner said that it has six and that she'll give whoever buys it directions on how to open them."

"It's been a while, but I think I can remember all of them," I said. "But maybe that one is different."

"Only one way to find out," she said, and within minutes I was driving along Bridge Street, convertible top down, enjoying the bright June morning and looking forward to adding one more piece of furniture to my apartment, and reclaiming a happy childhood memory at the same time.

Tolliver's Antiques and Uniques wasn't hard to find. The shop's weathered silvery-gray exterior featured a purple door. Bright pink petunias in purple window boxes added more color, and the lavender shield-shaped sign suspended over the doorway spelled out the name of the place in black Olde English lettering. I parked on a hot-top driveway next to the building and hurried inside. A bell over the door jingled a welcome, and the gray-haired woman I'd seen on television stepped from behind beaded curtains, right hand extended.

"Hello. I'm Shea Tolliver," she said, "Welcome to my shop." Her handshake was firm, her smile genuine, and the gray hair clearly of the premature variety.

"Hello," I said. "I'm Lee Barrett. I saw you on television this morning. I'm interested in that five-drawer bureau."

"Yes, a lovely piece. It was made by a little known Salem cabinetmaker back in . . ." She stopped mid-sentence and looked at me intently. "I've seen you on television, too. You were the psychic medium on that *Nightshades* show before it got canceled."

She was right. I'd worked in television, one way or another, ever since I graduated from Emerson College. I smiled and held up both hands in protest. "That was me," I admitted. "But I promise I'm not a psychic—just played one on TV. These days I'm teaching TV Production 101 at the Tabitha Trumbull Academy of the Arts—better known around here as the Tabby."

She laughed. "Quite a switch. From soothsayer to schoolmarm."

"You're right," I agreed. "But teachers get the summer off, and I'm planning to spend some of this one furnishing a new apartment."

"Well, you couldn't go wrong with that bureau," she said. "Good looking, useful, and secret compartments to boot."

"I know. I had one exactly like it when I was a kid. Mine burned up in a fire."

"No kidding. What a shame. The cabinetmaker made only three . . . that we know of. If yours is gone, there may be only two left—mine and one I saw in a New York shop, where the dealer showed me how it worked. I'd never have figured it out by myself." She parted the beaded curtains. "I found this one at an estate sale, and I don't think the owner even knew about the secret spaces. Come on back here and take a look."

I followed her into a back room. What a nostalgia rush! It was as though my own bureau had been magically restored, every curlicue and drawer pull exactly as I remembered. I reached out and stroked the polished top.

"This is it," I said. "How much?"

The price she quoted was steep, but not unreasonable.

"If you'll throw in those white ironstone coffee mugs over there," I said, remembering Aunt Ibby's plea, "you've got a deal. Is a credit card okay?"

"It's a deal, and a credit card is fine."

"Will you hold on to the bureau for a day or so, while I round up a truck and some extra muscle to help me get it home?"

I wasn't sure where the truck was going to come from, but I knew police detective Pete Mondello would be ready and willing to lend the muscle. Pete and I had become kind of a steady item since I'd come home, and I was pretty sure he was looking forward to me having a place of my own as much as I was!

"No worries about that," she said. "My delivery guy is due here any minute. You'll have your bureau by this afternoon, no extra charge. You're sure you remember where all the compartments are?"

"I think so." I touched each spot that I thought might hide a tiny compartment. "That's where mine were. Is it the same?"

"Sure is." She handed me a blank index card. "Just write down your address. And in case you forget, I'll put the directions for opening all of them in the top drawer."

"Perfect," I said. I did as she asked and handed back the index card. She tucked it into the cash register drawer.

I swiped my credit card while she wrapped four mugs in lavender tissue, put them in a purple bag, and handed it to me. "Come back again soon, Lee."

"You can count on it, Shea."

"I will." She smiled. "By the way, there is one thing I guess I should tell you."

"What's that?" I asked.

"The estate your bureau came from . . . A kind of famous murder happened there. That doesn't bother you, does it?"

"Murder?"

Shea dropped her voice. "The Helena Trent murder."

I shrugged. "Sorry," I said. "Doesn't ring a bell."

Her eyes widened. "Really? It was all over the news. In the papers for months."

"I've been away from Salem for quite a long time," I said. "Like about ten years."

"Oh. That would explain it. Anyway, they caught the guy. It was her husband, Tommy Trent. I just thought you should know your bureau came from a house where somebody got killed. That's all."

"I'll ask my aunt to fill me in about that murder," I said. "She's a reference librarian, and she knows something about darned near everything. But it won't affect my love for the bureau," I promised. "Was there anything interesting in the secret compartments?"

She grinned. "Naturally, I opened them all as soon as I got it into the shop."

"And?"

"Nothing valuable, but sort of interesting. You'll see. I left everything just the way it was so the new owner— I guess that's you—can enjoy the discovery." Shea walked with me to the purple door. "I just wanted to be sure you don't mind about . . . you know . . . the murder, what with all the psychic stuff you did on TV."

"It was just a job," I said. "No big deal." I took another look around the store, noticing a Tiffany-style lamp, a pair of Victorian brass candlesticks, and a really pretty cut-glass punch bowl. "I'll definitely be back soon to shop some more."

"Good," she said. "I can use the business."

"Slow, is it?"

"Not too bad." She shrugged. "Tourist season hasn't really started yet. It'll get better. It's just that I had a partner who kind of took off with a chunk of our joint bank account."

"Sorry," I said, stepping out into the sunshine and pausing on the top step. "Someone you really trusted, I suppose."

"Yep. That's the worst of it. But I'll land on my feet. Always have."

"Just like a cat," I said, thinking of O'Ryan, our big, yellow-striped boy. "Well, good luck. I'll head for home and wait for my bureau."

I parked the convertible in the garage behind the house, picked up the purple bag, and headed through the garden to the back door. Low bushes of "almost ready for picking" blueberries lined the path, and the thought of Aunt Ibby's famous blueberry pies and muffins reminded me that I'd skipped breakfast. I let myself into the back hall and was welcomed by a big, soft cat doing figure eights around my ankles.

"Is that you, Maralee?" My aunt's voice came from the kitchen. "Did you get it?"

I bent to pat O'Ryan and pushed the kitchen door open. "Sure did. It'll be delivered today. You were right. It's exactly like mine, and in even better condition."

"I can hardly wait to see it," she said. "You know, I've

always been surprised by how clean and modern the lines are, and how cleverly the compartments are disguised."

"Shea Tolliver—that's the owner's name—says there may be only two of them left in the world. This one, and one in New York. The cabinetmaker made only three that she knows of. Of course, we know what happened to the third one."

"The fire. What a shame." A momentary look of sadness crossed her face, and then she smiled. "But what luck that you are blessed to own two of the three."

"Lucky for sure," I agreed. "Guess I'll call Pete and invite him over to see it. He doesn't know about the secret compartments. I'm going to wait until he's here to open them."

"Any idea what's in them?"

"Not really. Shea says it's nothing valuable, but she left them as they were when she bought it. It'll be fun, anyway. Besides, Pete will be glad I've finally bought a piece of furniture. He thought I'd never get started."

"Can't blame him for thinking that," she said. "Have you had anything to eat, Maralee? You ran off without breakfast. Want an English muffin?"

"Love one," I said as I punched in Pete's number. "And look." I put the purple bag on the counter. "I got some coffee mugs."

She smiled her approval and popped an English muffin into the toaster.

Pete answered on the first ring. "Hi, Lee. I was just thinking about you."

"Good," I said. "What were you thinking?"

"Just wondering how the furniture shopping is going."

"You'll be proud of me. I bought a bureau this morning."

"Good for you." I could hear the smile in his voice. "I have tonight off. Can I come over and see it?"

"Absolutely. I was calling to invite you to dinner."

"Great. I'll be there. Around six?"

"Yep. I'll cook dinner on my new stove."

"Got dishes yet?"

"Nope! I'll figure something out." O'Ryan streaked past me toward the front door. "Oh, oh, there goes O'Ryan. The deliveryman must be here already." The cat always knows when someone is coming—and which door they're coming to. I heard the chime. "Gotta go. See you tonight."

There are two entrances to our house. The front door opens onto Winter Street, and there's a back door facing Oliver Street. The latter one opens onto a narrow hall, with one door leading to Aunt Ibby's kitchen and another leading to a stairway that goes up two flights to my apartment.

I headed for the front hall, while Aunt Ibby ladled homemade strawberry jam onto the hot English muffin. I opened the door and signed a slip, then dashed back into the kitchen and took a couple of bites of my belated breakfast while two very large men hefted the quilt-covered bureau from a truck marked BOB'S MOVING AND DELIVERY. They lifted it onto a dolly, placed a wooden ramp over the front steps, then wheeled it into the foyer.

"That was fast," I said. "Thanks."

"No problem. Ms. Tolliver said to make this my first stop," said the taller of the two. "Where do you want it?"

"I hate to tell you this, but it's going to the third floor."

If the news of the two flights of stairs bothered them, neither one showed it.

"Want to lead the way, miss?" The tall mover had "Bob" embroidered on his shirt pocket.

I hurried upstairs, with O'Ryan racing ahead of me, opened the door to my apartment, and waited for the men to catch up. After carefully removing and folding the quilt, one man taped the drawers shut, while the other ran a piece of tape across the top, securing a center panel that, if I remembered correctly, lifted to reveal a small mirror. Then, without the slightest grunt or groan, they started up the stairs, one man at the base of the bureau and the other at the upper end.

It took the men only a few minutes to wrestle my bureau up the stairs, through the almost empty kitchen, and into my bedroom, where they placed it carefully in the spot I'd reserved. Tape removed, it looked even better than I'd expected. The movers and I stood there for a brief moment, admiring it.

"Nice," commented the one named Bob.

"Sturdy," said the other man. "They don't make 'em like that one anymore."

"It's a beauty," I agreed, watching as O'Ryan judged the bureau's height, then leaped and made a perfect soft landing on top of it.

"Big cat," said Bob.

"Nice," said the other mover. They turned and headed down the stairs, O'Ryan and I tagging along behind. I slipped Bob a generous tip, while O'Ryan sniffed at the folded quilt, then watched as the men headed back to the truck.

Aunt Ibby appeared in the bedroom doorway. "It's

even more beautiful than I remembered. The lines are so classic, and the raised panels between the drawers are so delicately carved. They look like tiny flowers, don't they?"

"They do," I agreed. "It looks perfect up there, and nobody would ever guess there are hiding places all over it. Shea Tolliver said she thought the person she bought it from didn't even know they were there."

"They're well hidden," she said. "If Grandmother Forbes hadn't shown them to you when you were a little girl, you might never have found them, either."

"Shea put the directions in the top drawer, in case I forget."

"That was thoughtful," she said. "Pete will get a kick out of the secret spaces."

"I know. And I promised to cook him dinner, too."

"You don't have dishes yet," she said. "Maybe you should have looked for some when you bought the nice mugs."

"You're right." I looked at my watch. "It's not too late. I think I'll go do a little china shopping."

"Good idea."

"Oh, Aunt Ibby, remind me when I get back to ask you about a murder that happened while I was in Florida."

"A murder? What murder?"

"Somebody named Trent. Shea mentioned it. I'll tell you what she said later."

It occurred to me as I backed out of the driveway that I'd much rather have vintage dishes than new ones. Maybe Shea Tolliver would have some nice old Fiestaware. Within minutes I was once again headed for Bridge Street. I parked the Corvette in the same space I'd used earlier, and headed for the purple door.

I stepped aside quickly when the door burst open and a tall blond man rushed past, jostling my arm.

"Watch where you're going!" I exclaimed, my redhead's temper flaring for a moment.

"Sorry," he said and broke into a run.

The bell over the door tinkled a welcome as I stepped inside.

"Shea? You here?" I called.

No reply, but I saw her.

At least, I saw her feet. Sensibly shod toes pointing up, they stuck out from behind the counter. I had a very bad feeling as I slowly rounded the corner. Sightless eyes stared upward, and a trickle of blood issued from her mouth.

It was Shea Tolliver, all right, and I didn't need to touch her to know that she was dead.

CHAPTER 2

I backed away, thoughts jumbled. *Call 911.*

Yes. Calling 911 was what people did in a case like this. With my eyes still focused on Shea's feet, I reached into my purse and pulled out my phone.

Don't touch anything.

Right. That's important. I punched in the numbers.

A calm, unemotional voice answered. "What is your emergency?"

I glanced around, avoiding looking at those still feet. The cash register drawer stood open. It looked empty. "Emergency," I repeated, hardly recognizing my own voice. "I found a dead woman. On the floor."

"What's your location please?"

Location? I don't know the address.

"I'm . . . I'm on Bridge Street. It's an antique shop. Tolliver's Antiques and Uniques. There's a purple door. The owner, Shea Tolliver, she's the one who's dead. On the floor."

"Are you sure she's dead? Did you check?"

"No. I didn't touch anything. She . . . she looks dead."

"All right. Help is on the way. What's your name?"

"Lee Barrett. I'm a . . . customer."

"All right, Ms. Barrett. Are you safe where you are now? Is there anyone else in the building?"

I looked around the room. I hadn't thought about that. Could anyone else be here? Was someone hiding behind the beaded curtains?

"I . . . I don't know, but I think I'll get out of here." As I moved quickly toward the entrance, I heard the wail of sirens. "The police are already here. Thank you." I pushed the door open and stepped gratefully into the sunlight. In seconds there were three police cars, red, white, and blue lights flashing, in front of the building, along with an ambulance.

Two uniformed officers, guns drawn, ran toward me, shouting, "Police!"

I didn't know what I was supposed to do, so I put my hands up.

"Did you call 911?" asked one of the cops, while the other, gun still drawn, approached the shop. "Reporting a body?"

I dropped my hands, stepped aside, and pointed wordlessly to the purple door. Three more uniforms, followed by two EMTs, crowded into the place. One officer remained beside me, eyes watchful.

"Just wait right here, ma'am," he said, his tone courteous but firm. I leaned against the rough clapboards of the shop. The gaily painted window boxes with their bright blossoms seemed out of place as the horror of what I'd just seen behind the counter crowded my senses.

I need to call Pete. Can I just reach into my purse and pull out the phone? Uh-uh. Bad idea.

I didn't have to think about it for long. Pete's unmarked Crown Vic pulled up right onto the sidewalk.

Tall, broad shouldered, his dark hair curling just a little in Salem's early summer humidity, his suit coat unbuttoned, Pete strode toward me.

"You okay, Lee?" he asked.

I gave a weak smile and nodded. Then, with what I always called his "cop face" firmly in place, he proceeded to take control of the situation.

"Escort Ms. Barrett to my car," he told the officer. "The ME and the CSI team are right behind me." The purple door stood open, and Pete went into the shop, barking orders as he entered. "Let's get the crime-scene tape up while a couple of you search the building."

Once inside the cruiser, I couldn't hear his voice anymore. The officer stood respectfully, watchfully, beside the vehicle. Soon the EMTs left, and the ambulance pulled away—empty, confirming my certainty that Shea was dead. By then yards of yellow plastic tape announced that Tolliver's Antiques and Uniques was officially the scene of a crime. Before long two men carrying a folded stretcher went inside, followed by the medical examiner, with his ever-present black bag. I recognized him. We'd met less than a year ago, when I was the one who'd discovered a body floating in Salem Harbor. It was the same day I'd met Pete Mondello.

More sirens. The CSI team arrived, strangely alien looking, masked and booted in shiny white jumpsuits. It seemed like hours before Pete emerged from the place, notebook and pen in hand, dismissed my vigilant guardian officer, and climbed into the backseat next to me.

"You discovered the body, Lee?" he asked, cop face still in place.

"Yes."

"What time was that?"

"I don't know exactly. I called 911 as soon as I saw her."

"Okay. Was anyone else in the room?"

"No. But I saw a man leaving. He was in a hurry. Bumped into me before I opened the door."

"Can you describe him?"

"I think so." I searched my memory, trying to picture the man.

"Good. Begin with when you arrived at the store, and tell me exactly what happened. Don't leave anything out."

I closed my eyes. "I parked the Corvette in the driveway next to the shop," I said. "I walked to the door. I'd just started to reach for the doorknob when a man came rushing out." I frowned, remembering my annoyance when he bumped my arm. "I said something like 'Watch it,' and he said, 'Sorry,' and ran away."

"Did you see where he went? Did he get into a car?"

"I don't know," I said, opening my eyes. "But he ran that way." I pointed west. "Maybe toward the parking lot over there."

"What did he look like?"

"Tall. A couple of inches taller than you," I said. "Around forty, I'd guess. Thin. Dark blond hair. Receding hairline."

"What was he wearing?"

"Jeans," I said, eyes closed once more. "Faded jeans and a short-sleeved tan shirt. No hat. Sneakers, I think."

"Carrying anything?"

"Not that I could see."

"You know anything about this Shea Tolliver?" he asked. "Family? Enemies or anything like that?"

"Pete," I said. "I just met her this morning. We spoke for a few minutes. That's all. Mostly about the bureau I bought."

"I understand," he said. "But think about it. Did she say anything at all that might help us out?"

"Wait a minute. She said she had a partner who'd ripped off some money."

"Any name mentioned?"

"No."

"Anything else?"

"Well, the bureau's already been delivered. Maybe the deliveryman saw something. The truck said Bob's Moving and Delivery."

Pete scribbled in the notebook. "Good observation, Lee," he said.

I smiled at the compliment.

A wheeled gurney rolled past, and the techs lifted their stretchered burden onto it. Shea was mercifully encased in a blue body bag. I bowed my head as the men maneuvered the gurney past my window, followed by the ME.

"Excuse me, Lee," Pete said, putting the notebook in his pocket. "I need to speak to the doc." He climbed out of the car, leaving the door open, and spoke in low tones to the doctor, then turned to me. "Can you follow me down to the station in your car? We'll finish up the official stuff, and then you can go along home." He smiled. "Are we still on for dinner?"

I was glad to see that familiar smile. "Of course we are. How do you feel about paper plates?"

CHAPTER 3

I followed Pete's car, driving extra carefully, gripping the wheel more tightly than necessary. After all, it isn't every day that I get summoned to the police station to talk about a dead body. I was entitled to be a little nervous about it.

Pete parked next to the Corvette and opened my door. "You might want to put the top up and lock it," he said. "You never know who might be hanging around here."

"Okay," I said. The laguna-blue Corvette Stingray had been my dream car for years. My late husband, Johnny Barrett, had been a rising star on the NASCAR circuit, and during our too-short time together, I'd learned to love fast cars. Now that I finally had one, I sure didn't want anybody messing with it. I put the top up, locked the car, then followed Pete into the station. We headed for the glass cubicle that served as his office.

"If you don't mind," he said, offering me a seat opposite his scarred desk, "I'm asking a stenographer and a sketch artist to join us."

"Fine with me," I said. "I guess you'll be looking for that guy who bumped into me."

"Right." Pete stood as a pretty brunette stenographer, pushing a wheeled stenotype machine, entered the cubicle. A man carrying a laptop sat next to me. "If everybody's ready, let's get started." Pete resumed his seat. "Lee, I've already asked you a few questions, but let's go over it again. From the beginning."

I repeated everything I'd told him earlier—how I'd approached the shop and encountered the man who'd bumped into me, how I'd seen Shea's feet and then her face. I said that the cash register drawer had been open and had looked empty. The stenographer clicked away on the machine as I tried to recount those terrifying moments before help arrived. Then it was the sketch artist's turn to ask questions.

"How about the man's age?"

"Older than me," I answered, recalling his face. "Maybe in his forties."

"The shape of his face? Round? Square jawed?" He turned his laptop so that I could see a variety of featureless face shapes on the screen. "Like any of these?"

I selected a narrow outline. He continued his questions, and while I searched my memory, a face emerged on the screen. After about thirty minutes, and several changes, a clean-shaven man with receding hair, sparse eyebrows, and slightly protruding ears stared back at me.

"That's him," I said. "I think that's him."

Strange. He doesn't look particularly sinister. Doesn't look like my idea of a killer.

Pete had another question for me. "You said the man spoke to you. Can you describe the voice?"

"Hmmm. A voice is much harder to describe than a face," I said. "He spoke only the one word. 'Sorry.'"

"A gruff voice? Hoarse? High pitched? Deep?" Pete prompted.

I thought about it for a long moment. "His voice was soft," I said finally. "Soft and serious. I felt as though he meant it when he said he was sorry he'd bumped into me."

Pete raised one eyebrow, the way he does when he's doubtful about something, but said nothing. He thanked the stenographer and the sketch artist. I thanked them, too, and after they left the room, Pete leaned across the desk.

"Are you thinking that the guy might have walked in and seen the body, the same way you did, then just beat it out of there?"

"Maybe," I said. "Yes, I guess that's the way it could have happened."

"Things aren't always the way they seem," Pete said as we walked toward the parking lot. "You should know that as well as anybody."

I knew he was right. Pete and I had been involved with unexplained deaths before, and no one knew better than I did that sometimes the very people you think you know best have a dark side you'd never dreamed existed. Once we were outside, away from that intimidating building, with all its trappings of suspicion and questions and doubts, I felt a little better.

"Guess I'll put the top down again," I said and unlocked the car door. "Some fresh air might help clear away this feeling of sadness. I didn't know her, but . . . poor Shea." I blinked away a sudden rush of tears.

"I understand. Wish I could help," he said, leaning

in for a quick kiss. "I'll be at your place around six. I'm looking forward to trying your cooking."

I'd learned enough from Aunt Ibby to be pretty confident about my talent as a cook. I climbed into the car, put the top down, fastened my seat belt, and headed for the grocery store. I didn't actually have to pass by Shea's building to get to the nearest supermarket, but I did it, anyway. The yellow police tape gave the front of the place a sinister look, and the CSI van was still there. One officer stood outside the purple door. I slowed down and tried to peek into the windows of the place, past the pink petunias, past the sparkling colored bottles and china teapots on the glass shelves.

What am I looking for? What do I expect to see?

Maybe I was hoping I'd see Shea Tolliver, alive and smiling, waving to me, inviting me inside. Maybe I was wishing none of the horror of the morning had really happened.

I shook my head and stepped on the gas, passed the municipal parking lot where I'd told Pete the blond man might have gone, took Highland Avenue to Shaw's Market, and began some serious food shopping. Twenty minutes and a couple of shopping bags later, I was headed home. When I turned into our driveway, I felt my whole body relax. It was almost as though I'd been holding my breath for hours.

I hurried past the garden, where tall sunflowers nodded their cheerful greeting. As usual, O'Ryan was waiting right inside the back door to greet me. Knowing when someone is coming to the door is the least of the big cat's talents. He'd once belonged to a practicing witch—some say he was her familiar—and in Salem a witch's familiar is to be respected, and sometimes feared. At any rate, he's surely not your ordinary house cat, and he'd proven that many times since coming to live with Aunt Ibby and me.

I hadn't stopped to call my aunt about the morning's sad happenings. No point in worrying her unnecessarily. I'd ignored the fact that my very tech-savvy aunt would probably know all about it between Facebook, Twitter, and possibly the noon news.

She did.

She rushed to greet me. "Maralee, you've been gone for such a long time. Did you hear about that Shea Tolliver woman being killed? They think it was a robbery."

"I know," I said, putting my grocery bags on the kitchen counter. "Actually, I was the one who called the police."

She sat abruptly on a tall stool next to the counter. "What do you mean?"

I explained, as gently as I could, what had happened. "Afterward, I had to go to the police department and help an artist sketch the man I saw leaving the shop."

"My dear child, how frightening for you. Why didn't you call me?"

"Pete was with me almost the whole time. I was perfectly safe. I didn't want you to worry."

"Well, you're right. I would have. Did you tell Pete what Shea told you about the bureau and the Trent murder?"

"Why, no. I didn't even think of it. But that couldn't have anything to do with what happened today."

"I guess it doesn't. It's just interesting," she said. "I remember the whole tragedy, of course, but I looked up the facts on the Helena Trent case while you were gone."

"I'm going to run upstairs and put these groceries

away," I said. "Want to come up and tell me all about my bureau's mysterious past?"

"Of course I do," she said. "I've printed out a few old newspaper articles for you. I'll get them and meet you upstairs in a few minutes."

O'Ryan was ahead of me on the stairs and raced into the apartment as soon as I opened the door. He jumped onto the beach chair, turned around a couple of times, and fixed golden eyes on the wooden stool.

"You're right," I told him. "Not only don't I have proper dishes, but I also don't have any place for us to sit while we eat dinner, do I?"

The cat closed his eyes and pretended to be asleep. While I arranged the groceries in my almost empty refrigerator and totally bare cabinets, I thought of the card table and the folding chairs Aunt Ibby used for her mah-jongg group. I asked for permission to use the furniture and was offered my choice of tablecloths, as well. That problem solved, and with the makeshift dining arrangement quickly in place in my kitchen, my aunt and I adjourned to the bedroom and sat on the bed, facing the bureau.

"It looks just perfect there, Maralee," she said. "Now, with some bedside tables and lamps and maybe a chaise longue, this could be quite a pleasant room."

"Maybe its previous home wasn't so pleasant," I said. "Tell me about Helena Trent and how she came to be murdered."

"Poor Helena," my aunt began. "Her husband was quite an unsavory character, it turns out. Everyone thought he married her for her money in the first place."

"Money? She was wealthy, then?"

"Oh, yes, indeed. Helena came from a prominent

North Shore family. Then she married into an even wealthier Salem family. United two old fortunes, so to speak. Her first husband, John David Hampton, Jr., died. . . . He was quite a bit older than she was. But everyone said they were a truly devoted couple."

"So she married Mr. Trent after that?"

"Not right away, of course. But Helena was quite beautiful, and nobody expected that she'd stay single for long. She had no children of her own, just her husband's grown son from his first marriage."

"A confusing family tree."

"It is. And it got even more so after she married Tommy Trent. Tommy brought a woman named Daphne—who, he *said,* was his sister—to live with them, and Helena befriended her. Bought her expensive clothes, included her on trips. But it turned out that Daphne was really Tommy's girlfriend."

"What a rat!"

"I know. Anyway, Tommy was really the only suspect in Helena's death. He copped some kind of a plea, and a judge found him guilty of voluntary manslaughter. Ten years in prison. I think that means he can get out in five or six, if he behaves himself in jail." She shook her head. "Of course, he still claims he's innocent. Says some intruder did it."

"Sure. Don't they all say something like that?"

She spread several sheets of copier paper across the bedspread. "Look. Here are a few articles about the trial from the *Salem News.* I'll make us a pot of coffee while you read them."

I chose one of the articles at random. The headline read SOCIALITE DIED FROM SINGLE GUNSHOT WOUND. The accompanying photo showed a pretty woman in jeans and a turtleneck, standing in what looked like a vegetable garden. According to the paper, Helena Trent's body was discovered by her stepson, John David Hampton III, known to his associates at one of Salem's most prestigious investment firms as Tripp Hampton. The article said that he found his stepmother dead in her bedroom when she didn't appear as usual for lunch. She'd been shot in the back of the head at a fairly close range with a nine-millimeter projectile. I shuddered at the thought. When her stepson found her, Helena surely wasn't pretty anymore. Burglary was given as a possible motive. Her jewelry box was found open and empty, and her bureau drawers and her closet had been ransacked.

I put the article down when Aunt Ibby reappeared, a new ironstone coffee mug in each hand. "Here you go," she said, handing me one. "Did you get to the part about the girlfriend yet?"

"Nope. Sill trying to get past the gunshot wound in her head."

My aunt nodded and sat next to me. "I know. Messy business, wasn't it? Poor Tripp must have had nightmares for months."

"You know him?"

"Oh, yes. He's on the board of directors of the library. So was Helena. Very civic minded, the whole family. Helena was president of the garden club, too, and one of the founders of Friends of Strays. The list goes on and on."

"What about the husband? Tommy?"

"Not so much, although he was somewhat involved in Helena's fund-raising efforts for her various charities."

I took a sip of coffee. The handle of the white mug fit perfectly in my hand, and the thick rim was smooth against my lips. "Mmm. Good," I murmured, picking up another article. MURDER WEAPON FOUND IN HUSBAND'S MERCEDES. The photo on that page was of Tommy Trent—a handsome, smiling man in tennis wear, holding a trophy. "Guess finding the gun in his car must have been pretty convincing to the jury." I looked again at Helena's photo, then back at Tommy's. "They must have been a beautiful couple. I wonder what went wrong. Seems as if they had it all."

"Everybody wondered that at first. A gorgeous home, fine cars, a yacht, the best country clubs, fabulous jewelry."

"So why did he kill her? Why not just a divorce if they were having trouble?"

She pulled a sheet of paper from those scattered on the bed. "Here. Read this one."

The headline read MONEY PROBLEMS BESET "GOLDEN COUPLE." The article went on to detail unpaid taxes, maxed-out credit cards, canceled club memberships because of unpaid dues, a repossessed automobile. . . . The list went on.

"Wow. What a mess." I put the paper down. "'Follow the money,' they always say. Guess that's true in this case. But still, how would Tommy benefit from Helena's death?"

She shrugged. "That's a puzzle. Helena's stepson had control of whatever's left of the family fortune, and there was a prenup, so it doesn't seem as though Tommy would actually benefit financially from her death." She lowered her voice and looked around the sparsely furnished room, as though someone might be listening. "But, of course, there's the pink diamond."

At that moment, O'Ryan strolled into the bedroom and jumped onto the bed, scattering papers in every direction. Stretching a big yellow paw next to one of the pillows, he rescued a page from sliding to the floor. Then, tilting his head and fixing those golden eyes on my green ones, he uttered, "Mmrrup," which the way he does it, always sounds as though there's a question mark at the end.

Aunt Ibby and I had each lifted our mug out of harm's way just as O'Ryan had made his perfect soft landing, so the new bedspread was spared coffee stains.

"What was that all about?" my aunt asked, reaching for the paper still under the cat's paw. "You think we should read this one, boy?"

I could see the headline from where I sat on the edge of the bed. "How does he *do* that?" I asked before reading it aloud. WHERE IS HELENA'S PINK DIAMOND? queried the bold print. "Whoever heard of a cat who could read?"

My aunt shrugged. "Nothing about this cat surprises me anymore."

She was right. The cat, who'd once belonged to Ariel Constellation, my ill-fated predecessor on the *Nightshades* show, had shown unusual behavior from the first day he arrived at our house.

Aunt Ibby passed the paper to me. "As I was saying, there's the missing pink diamond."

I scanned the article. Apparently, Helena Trent's first husband had given her an enormous pale pink–colored diamond pendant. I'm pretty sure ten carats qualifies as enormous in the diamond world. Anyway, the report said that until John Hampton's death, the necklace was locked in a safe, and Helena wore it only on special formal occasions. But after his passing, she began to wear it quite casually. The reporter noted that some of the members of the garden club were astonished to see Helena wearing the precious gem on a simple leather thong around her neck while digging up tulip bulbs. Others said that she often wore it that way, usually with jeans and a black turtleneck.

My aunt had picked up the scattered papers, and I took another look at the photo of Helena. "She's wearing some kind of necklace in this picture. Do you suppose it's the diamond?" I asked.

"Quite likely," she said.

"What's it worth, anyway?"

"The paper said several million dollars."

"Insured?" I asked.

"Sure. The insurance company is still looking for it."

"If they had money problems, I wonder why she didn't just sell it."

"They say Tommy wanted her to. But her friends said she just loved wearing it. Her thought was, 'Why have beautiful things locked away in a safe? It makes more sense to just enjoy them every day.'"

"Can't say I disagree with the philosophy," I said.

"It's generally a good one," Aunt Ibby said. "I'm heading for the library in a few minutes. You sure you don't need anything else for your dinner date with Pete?"

"I'm almost all set, I think. Except for dishes. I never got a chance to pick any out today."

"Please help yourself to any of my china," she said. "You know I have extra place settings."

"Thanks. May I use the ivy pattern ones?"

"The Franciscan Ware? Of course. It was always your favorite when you were little."

"Thanks. I still love it."

"All right then. I'll see you later."

I followed her downstairs, picked up two place settings of the green-and-white dishes and a couple of serving pieces, and hurried back to my apartment. There were several more newspaper articles I wanted to look at, but I decided to put them away until I had more time. I looked around the room. *Put them where? Aha!* I now had a bureau. I pulled open the top drawer. Just as Shea had promised, there was an envelope marked DIRECTIONS TO SECRET COMPARTMENTS. It made me sad to think that putting the envelope in my bureau drawer might have been one of Shea's last actions. I closed the drawer and lifted the center panel on the bureau's top.

If this one is just like my old one, there should be a mirror under here.

There was a mirror, all right. But what I saw there made me slam the panel shut in a hurry. Oxidation or moisture or something had turned the glass almost entirely black—and shiny black surfaces meant bad news for me.

CHAPTER 4

I'm apparently what's known in paranormal circles as a "scryer." My friend River North calls me a "gazer." River happens to be a witch, and she knows all about such things. Anyway, I'd found out fairly recently that I have the weird ability to see things in shiny black objects—things that have happened or are happening, and even things that could happen in the future. River calls it a "gift." I don't think of it that way. It had come in handy a couple of times, but mostly all it had ever shown me was death and dying. I'd learned a little bit about controlling a vision once it started, but I much preferred that it didn't start at all. River and Aunt Ibby were the only people who knew about the gazing thing. I hadn't even mentioned it to Pete yet. Didn't know how to without sounding crazy and scaring him away.

I ran down the stairs to my old second-floor bedroom and grabbed a white lace runner from the top of a maple dresser. I hadn't meant to use anything from that room, pretty as it was; I wanted a totally different look for the apartment. But covering the mirrored panel with the runner would make it go away, and that was all I wanted just then.

Enough pots and pans had come with the new kitchen, so I was well prepared for dinner in that area. I planned to broil a great big sirloin steak, bake the Idaho potatoes in the microwave, and serve them with sour cream and fresh chives from Aunt Ibby's herb garden. A healthy salad with fresh greens and home-grown tomatoes would round out the meal, and dessert would be hot apple pie with vanilla ice cream, both from the grocer's frozen dessert department.

I double-checked the items I'd bought for dinner, then, satisfied with the menu, poured another cup of coffee and turned on the TV. WICH-TV was showing a roundup of local news stories. Field reporter Scott Palmer stood in front of Tolliver's Antiques and Uniques, speaking in hushed tones. "This morning, Shea Tolliver, the owner and manager of the shop behind me, was found dead, apparently the victim of a robbery. Ms. Tolliver suffered a fatal blow to the head. Police are looking for a man who may have information about the matter." The sketch artist's rendering of the man who'd bumped into me filled the screen. "Police chief Tom Whaley has released a statement saying this man is a person of interest in this case. If you can identify him, please contact the Salem Police Department." A phone number in bright green appeared above the drawing.

"I hope my description is good enough for someone to recognize him," I told the cat, who'd found a pleasant square of sunshine on the hardwood floor and was busily grooming his whiskers. The rest of the news broadcast consisted of a rundown of recent happenings at city hall, the local weather, a feature on kids' summer camps, and some footage of a sidewalk sale on Essex Street. No more than twenty minutes had passed before my cell phone buzzed. Caller ID showed Pete Mondello's name.

I hope he doesn't have to work tonight and cancel our dinner.

"Hi, Pete," I said. "What's up?"

"Just wanted to tell you that your description of that blond guy was so good, we had an ID on him right after the drawing aired on TV."

"No kidding? Who is he?"

"Name's Gary Campbell. Seems he was Shea Tolliver's ex-business partner. We've already picked him up. He admits to being in the store. His fingerprints were on the doorknob and on the counter. Shea had a restraining order on him, so we're holding him right now on a violation. Can't charge him with anything else yet."

"A restraining order? Did he abuse her?"

"Verbal threats. Serious enough for a judge to grant one."

"Poor Shea."

"I know." His tone was sympathetic. "Gotta go, babe. Just wanted to tell you how that ID worked out. See you tonight."

"See you," I said, but he was gone.

I checked my watch. Now would be a good time to pop the frozen apple pie into the oven, and it was late enough in the day to call River North. She'd taken over the time slot of my canceled show, *Nightshades.* . . . Now it was *Tarot Time with River North*. Being on camera until two in the morning meant sleeping in the daytime, so I never phoned her until the afternoon.

Pie centered in the spotless new oven, timer set, I dialed River's number. She sounded just a tad sleepy when she answered. "Oh, hi, Lee. I've been thinking about you. You okay?"

That's usually an easy question for me to answer, but today . . . not so much. "Ummm. I guess so," I said. "It's been an unusual day."

That woke her up. "What's happening? Wait a minute. Let me get my cards. I'll read you while you tell me all about it." There was a short pause. "Okay. Shoot."

"That was fast. Do you sleep with the tarot cards under your pillow?"

"Sure do. Now, tell me what's going on."

"All right, but first, have you watched the news today?"

"Of course not. You know I never do. Too depressing."

"Well, then, it's going to be a long story." I began with how we'd seen the bureau on TV and how I'd hurried to Shea's shop before someone else could grab it. I told her about having one just like it when I was a kid.

"I know you got the bureau. I can see it here," River interrupted. "The Six of Cups. It's right here beside the Queen of Wands. That's you. But listen, Lee. You'd better let me come over and check on where the bureau is. Proper feng shui, you know."

"What?"

"Feng shui." She pronounced the words carefully. "F-u-n-g S-h-w-a-y balance and harmony. Furniture placement is important."

"I've heard of it," I said. "And you know you can come over anytime. But what about the Six of Cups? What does it mean?"

"Enjoyment and pleasant memories coming from the past."

"You're exactly right," I said. That bureau did remind me of happy childhood days. River's accuracy with her cards used to amaze me every time. But I was beginning to get used to it. "Pleasant memories, for sure, and I'm going to enjoy having someplace to put my clothes."

"Still not enough furniture, huh? Go on. Tell me more."

"The rest of it is not good news," I said and described how I'd gone back to Tolliver's to look for china and how the blond man had bumped into me. Once again, she interrupted.

"I see him. The Seven of Pentacles reversed. He's impatient for success. He's anxious about money he owes to someone."

"You're probably right about that, too," I said. I told her how I'd found Shea dead and called 911, how Pete had come to the store, and how I'd worked with the sketch artist and helped to capture Shea's ex-partner.

She didn't comment right away, and I could hear the swish of the cards. "I'm sorry you were the one who found that woman. The Nine of Pentacles reversed. Danger from thieves. Was she robbed?"

"It looks that way. The cash register drawer was open."

"She felt safe among her possessions." River sounded sad. "I'm sorry," she said again.

"I liked her."

"I can see Pete, too," she said, her voice brightening "He's the Knight of Swords. His card moves closer to yours every time I read you. How's that going?"

"He's coming over tonight. I'm cooking him dinner."

"Uh-huh. Get a bed yet?"

"River, you're terrible!" I felt my face coloring.

"No, I'm not. You know you're thinking about it."

She was right about that. I'd been thinking about it for quite a while. Had even refilled my birth control prescription, just in case.

"To answer your question, yes. I have a bed. King size, pillow top, Egyptian cotton sheets."

"Sounds nice. Be sure the bed doesn't face an open door. Bad feng shui."

"It doesn't," I told her.

I could hear the smile in her voice. "Good. Have a *really* pleasant evening, then. Talk to you later. Bye."

CHAPTER 5

The oven timer buzzed, and I took the perfectly browned pie from the oven. The apartment was filled with a delicious smell—if not much else. I'd exchanged shorts and a T-shirt for my favorite Hawaiian-print halter dress and strappy sandals. There wasn't too much I could do with my red hair—humidity made it too curly—so I just pulled it back with a silver barrette and hoped for the best.

The table looked pretty good with Aunt Ibby's white linen tablecloth, and a small bunch of lilies of the valley in an ironstone mug added a summery touch. I'd brought my wedding gift sterling silverware with me from Florida, and it looked nice with the ivy pattern Franciscan Ware. I wished I'd taken those candlesticks I saw when I bought the bureau.

I'd told Pete he could use the entrance at the back of the house and come upstairs that way instead of coming to the front door, as usual. Aunt Ibby had thoughtfully provided me with a separate entrance from that side. "So you can come and go as you please," she'd said, handing me a pair of bright new keys.

I left the pie cooling on the counter, passed by the bedroom, and entered the totally empty space designated to be my living room. I checked to be sure the door to the back stairway was locked. I'd come in that way only a couple of times, still in the habit of using the downstairs backyard entrance to Aunt Ibby's kitchen or the familiar front door on the Winter Street side.

At exactly six o'clock the vintage chimes over my apartment's living room door played "Bless This House," and I hurried to let Pete into my sparsely furnished new space. O'Ryan was already waiting by the door, sniffing along the sill and purring a resonant welcome. Pete stood grinning in the narrow hall, balancing a vase of yellow roses and daisies, a bottle of wine, and a gift bag with CONGRATULATIONS ON YOUR GRADUATION in sparkly letters.

"It smells great in here," he said, leaning forward for a quick but awkward kiss, which landed on my forehead. He glanced around the empty room. "Where can I put this stuff down so I can try that again?"

"Follow me," I said and led the way to the kitchen.

Pete put his predinner offerings on the counter, next to the still-hot pie, pulled me close, and delivered a lovely, slow, satisfying toe-tingling kiss, followed by another with a lot more urgency behind it than usual.

Note to self. Inviting a man to dinner at your own apartment may turn out to be quite different from inviting the same man to dinner at your aunt's house.

I think we were both surprised by the intensity of that moment. Holding my breath, looking up into those dark eyes, I took a tiny step backward. "Pete," I said, my voice ragged, "I think . . ." I wasn't sure what I was going to tell him, because O'Ryan chose that instant to scratch on the door leading to the front hall.

"Cat wants to go out," Pete said, his lips still close to my ear.

"I'm going to buy him a cat door tomorrow," I murmured as I reluctantly, and maybe wisely, stepped out of that mind-altering embrace. I let O'Ryan out and watched as he trotted toward the stairway, a cat smirk on his fuzzy face.

Pete had moved next to the counter and held the bottle of merlot in one hand and the gift bag in the other. "Here," he said, offering me the bag decorated with mortarboards and rolled diplomas. "They didn't have any that said 'Congratulations on Your New Apartment.'"

"Graduation is close enough," I said, laughing as I reached into a nest of gold tissue paper. "And June is the right month for it." I pulled a corkscrew from the bag, followed by a pair of crystal wineglasses. "Perfect," I said. "How did you know that I didn't have either one?"

He smiled, looked around the sparsely furnished kitchen, reached for the corkscrew, and began opening the bottle. "Just a wild guess." He filled one glass and handed it to me. "Cheers," he said and filled his own. We clinked our glasses in the traditional way and sipped the fruity crimson liquid.

"Going to show me the famous new bureau?" he asked.

I was about to say, "Sure," then thought about where the thing was situated, right across from the big, soft bed I'd so recently described to River. "Later," I told him. "Here. Sit down, and I'll tell you about it first." We sat opposite one another at the card table, where my simple bouquet of lilies of the valley shared space with the roses-and-daisies creation.

I began with, "Aunt Ibby was watching television this morning. . . ." I described how she'd recognized the bureau as the exact one that my grandmother Forbes had given me when I was a little girl. "The cool thing about it was, it looked like a regular antique bureau, but it had secret compartments," I said. "And so does the one I bought today."

"Is there anything in them?" I could see the interest in his face.

Of course he's interested. He's a detective.

"Yes. And it's all still there. I haven't opened them yet. I was waiting for you."

"Really? You have no idea what might be in them?"

"Well, Shea told me a little about it. 'Nothing valuable,' she said. But it'll still be fun to open them."

"I wasn't going to mention Shea Tolliver tonight," he said. "But since you brought her up, I want to say how well you handled . . . well, everything that went down today." He reached across the table and took my hand. "It couldn't have been easy for you."

"No. Not easy."

Understatement of the year. Those sad feet sticking out from behind the counter. And Shea's dead face. Dear God. Her face.

I shook away the thoughts. "But I still want to tell you what else she said about my bureau. It came from a house where there was a murder. A really famous one."

He picked up his glass and took a sip. "Let me guess. Helena Trent, right?"

"Right. How did you know?"

"The 'really famous' part. Chief Whaley said he hadn't seen that much ink and airtime used on one murder around here since the Beryl Atherton case back in the fifties. How did Shea get the bureau, anyway?"

I shrugged. "Estate sale, I guess. She said the owner didn't even know about the secret compartments."

"So the missing pink diamond wasn't in it? Bummer."

"Afraid not. But after dinner I'll show you how to open all the secret compartments. Want to watch TV while I start cooking?"

"No thanks. I'd rather watch you."

That was just what he did, too. Chin on his fists, elbows on the table, he watched quietly as I put the steak under the broiler, dumped the plastic bag of mixed greens into a Franciscan Ware bowl, and sliced tomatoes on top. Sour cream with fresh chives went into another ironstone mug. I popped the potatoes into the microwave, and miraculously, everything was done at the same time. Steak, medium rare. Salad, crisp and pretty. Potatoes, white and fluffy with golden skins. I served my first dinner in my new apartment proudly.

The pie was still warm enough to melt the vanilla ice cream; the after-dinner coffee with a tiny dash of Baileys was hot and delicious. Pete leaned back in his chair, smiling broadly, as I put the silverware, the dishes, and the bowl in the dishwasher and rinsed our coffee mugs.

"Ready to see my prize purchase? Even if there's no treasure hidden in it?"

Pete patted absolutely flat abs. "Don't know if I can move. That was a perfect dinner, babe. And the apple pie was just as good as your Aunt Ibby's."

I refrained from giving credit to Sara Lee, glad that

the telltale box had already gone into the recycling bin . . . and silently vowing never, ever to repeat his remark to my aunt.

"Thanks," I said, with all the modesty I could muster. "Glad you liked it."

Pete stood, gave me a quick kiss—on the cheek, nothing like the earlier version—and, with one arm around my waist, said, "Lead me to this fine piece of furniture."

"Okay. Come on." I pushed the bedroom door open and clicked on the overhead light. With a dramatic Vanna White gesture, I indicated the bureau. "Ta-da! The furnishing du jour."

Pete switched his attention from me to the bureau. He moved from one side to the other, not speaking, not touching it, just looking. He crouched, sitting on his heels, studying the graceful embellishments on each of the bureau drawers, peering closely at the triangular frames around the keyholes. He stood up again. "May I touch it?" he asked.

I sat at the foot of the bed, watching him. "Of course. It's not delicate. It's lasted over two hundred years."

"Remarkable," he said and ran his hand down the paneled right side of the bureau. He looked at me, smiled, and gently tapped a spot close to the back edge. "Is one of the hidden compartments right about here?"

"Wow," I said. "That's amazing. You're right. If you press it slightly, it will move sideways." I stood closer, watching him. "Go ahead. There are two tiny pockets behind there."

"Do you know what's in them?"

"Nope. I told you. I haven't even peeked. Waited for you."

He put his arm around my waist again and pulled me close. "Thank you," he said, then, following my directions, pressed the spot he'd selected.

Nothing happened.

He frowned. "Did I do something wrong?"

"I don't think so. Let me try." He stepped behind me, still holding me close, but with both arms around my waist now.

I'm pretty sure he's not totally focused on the bureau anymore.

I pressed the panel, just the way Grandmother Forbes had taught me to so many years ago. The wood, which had appeared seamless, gave under my pressure, and a section that was about two inches by four inches slid aside. "See?" I said. "It's easy. Shall I close it again so you can do it?"

"Are you kidding? No. Let's see what's in there."

I laughed as Pete's concentration returned to the bureau. A compartment with two shallow square pockets, side by side, had been revealed. Each one contained a tissue-wrapped object. "Shall we each take one?" I asked.

"Okay," he said. "You go first."

"All right." I stuck my index finger into the space on the left and pried the article carefully from its hiding place. "Your turn."

"My fingers might be too big," he said, letting go of me completely and poking at the tiny shape in the remaining pocket. "This is fun. Like a treasure hunt at a kid's birthday party."

After a few stabs at it, the little parce fell into his

hand. We looked at one another, each holding a slim tissue-wrapped package. "Shall we open them together?" He smiled broadly.

I had to laugh. "You look as though you really *are* at a kid's birthday party. Okay. One, two, three . . . open 'em!"

Mine was a shiny 1951 Benjamin Franklin half-dollar. His was a tarnished brass Salem, Massachusetts, dog license.

"Cool," he said. "But yours is more valuable. Real silver."

"I like yours better. It's a remembrance of a pet somebody loved."

"True. Shall we do another one?" he asked, still smiling.

"Did you figure out any more of them?" I asked. "The panel you found is one of the most difficult."

"It's the only one I spotted. A tiny indentation in the wood. Did you say you have directions?"

"I do. I left them in the top drawer where Shea put them. Want to get them out while I pour us another cup of coffee?"

"Okay."

I headed for the kitchen, while Pete spread one of the pieces of tissue paper on the bed and carefully arranged our treasures on it. When I returned with the coffee, Pete was facing the bureau, his back to me.

"I don't see them, babe," he said. "You sure this is where you left them?"

He stepped aside, and I saw that instead of opening the top drawer, he'd removed the lace runner and lifted the hinged center panel, exposing the black mirror. I wanted to scream, "No!" and race across the room and slam it shut, but instead I managed to place the mugs calmly on the floor and walk over to where he stood. I reached out and closed the thing—but not before I saw the little cloud, then the flashing lights and swirling colors that always preceded the damned visions.

Not now. Not tonight. Not in front of Pete.

"N-n-no," I stuttered. "Not that one." My hand shook as I tugged at the half-moon–shaped wooden drawer pulls. "In here."

"Lee. Shhh. Come here. Sit down." He led me to the bed. "You're as pale as a ghost. What's wrong?"

"Nothing," I said. "Really. I'm fine."

"No," he said. "You're not. I shouldn't have come tonight. You've been through so much today, finding Shea . . . the way she was, and going through all that questioning." He sat beside me and held both of my hands. "Listen. Why don't we finish going through your bureau another time, okay? Now, you just get ready for bed. I'll let myself out." He kissed my forehead. "Dinner was great. You get some rest now. I'll call you tomorrow."

CHAPTER 6

Pete picked up the abandoned coffee mugs from the floor and carried them to the kitchen. I heard water running and knew he was rinsing them out. Probably would put them in the dishwasher, too.

What a guy.

I closed my eyes and pretended to be asleep when he walked past the bedroom and headed for the back door. I lay there, unmoving, until I heard his car start. I got up, retrieved the lace runner, and plopped it back on the bureau. Then I went into the kitchen, grabbed the new vase of flowers, carried it into the bedroom, and put it right in the middle of the center panel, trusting that would deter anyone, including me, from lifting the thing up and revealing the damned mirror.

Hoping that Aunt Ibby would be at home—she'd been dating lately—I went out my kitchen door and down the stairs to the first floor. "Aunt Ibby? You here?" I called.

She answered from the den. "I'm here, Maralee. Has Pete left already?"

I walked into the room and sat beside my aunt on the couch as she hit the mute button on the TV. "He's left," I said, surprised by my own dejected tone of voice. I tried to sound more upbeat. "Oh, the dinner went just fine. It was after dinner that didn't quite work out as planned."

She leaned forward and patted my knee. "Oh dear. You didn't quarrel, did you?"

"Nothing like that," I reassured her. "Not at all. It was the darned mirror."

She frowned. "Mirror? What mirror?"

"I guess I didn't tell you. Remember the mirror inside the top section of the bureau that used to be in my room?"

"Of course. There's one in the new bureau, too, isn't there?"

"Yes. But this one is discolored. Tarnished so badly, it's actually black."

She smiled. "We can get it repaired. Don't worry. I know a furniture restorer. . . ." She stopped in mid-sentence, and her smile disappeared. "A black mirror. Oh dear. You mean you saw something . . . unpleasant in it?"

"No, thank God, I didn't. Pete picked up the panel, and as soon as he did, I saw the flashing lights and the colors." I shook my head. "I guess I kind of panicked. I hurried across the room and banged it shut. Probably scared the poor guy."

"What did he say? You didn't tell him about that . . . *thing* you do, did you?"

"Of course not. But he knew something was wrong. He thinks it's because of my finding Shea and having to go down to the police station and all."

"Well, my dear," she said, "that's enough to upset anybody."

"Anyway, he was so nice about it. Told me to get some rest and he'd call tomorrow."

"Fine then. It'll be all right. No need to upset him with all that gazing foolishness."

"Do you really think so? That it's okay to keep all that from him?"

She cocked her head to one side, the way she does when she's weighing a problem. "Hmmm. Not forever, of course. Maybe just for now. He's got this new case on his mind, and you're justifiably upset about it, too." Again, the confident smile. "Don't worry. You'll know when it's the right time."

I hoped she was right, and turned my attention to the still-silent TV screen. I sat up straight, pointing. "It's him. That's the man who bumped into me in front of the antique store." I grabbed the remote and quickly hit the volume button.

We listened to the announcer's voice as we watched the man, still wearing the faded jeans and the tan shirt I'd described for Pete, being assisted into a police car.

"Gary Campbell is described as a 'person of interest' by Salem police in their investigation into the death of antique shop proprietor Shea Tolliver. Mr. Campbell was at one time Ms. Tolliver's business partner, but reports say that the two became alienated more than a year ago." The picture on the screen changed to Campbell's mug shot. The announcer continued. "A police spokesperson emphasized that Campbell is not at this time being detained in connection with the death and is cooperating with authorities. He was arrested this morning for a violation of a court order, but he has posted bond and has since been released."

"What does Pete think about all that?" my aunt asked.

"I have no idea," I said. "We haven't talked about it since he called this afternoon to tell me that my description of that man had been good enough to get him picked up. You know Pete hardly ever discusses police business with anybody."

"That's as it should be." She nodded affirmatively. "He's a good man, Lee. Your, uh, friendship seems to be developing nicely." She raised one eyebrow with an expectant look. I chose to ignore the unspoken question.

Is it developing "nicely?" Where is it leading? I don't know.

I changed the subject. "Talked to River today."

"Oh, how is she? I like that girl."

"She's fine. Read my cards, as usual. Nothing dire there, apparently. We talked mostly about furniture."

"That seems to be the topic of the day. Did you and Pete get to open the secret compartments?"

"Just one," I said.

"What was in it?" She leaned forward, eyes sparkling.

"It was the double-pocket compartment," I reported. "Two little tissue-wrapped items in it."

"Well? Don't tease. What did you find?"

I laughed. "You sound like a little kid. Okay. I'll tell you. We each picked one. Mine was a nineteen fifty-one Benjamin Franklin silver half-dollar."

"That was nice. What did Pete find?"

"Pete's was an old Salem dog license tag."

"That's kind of touching, isn't it?" she said. "A remembrance of a loved pet is something a sensitive person would value."

"We thought so, too."

"So you didn't open the other compartments?"

"No. I'm not going to do it until he can come back and open them with me."

"Good for you. I'd be much too curious to wait even another minute to see what else is in there," she said. "But, Maralee, you look tired. Why don't you do as Pete suggested and get some rest?"

"You're right. I'm beat. It's been a long, strange day." I looked around the room. "Where's O'Ryan? He scratched on the door to get out right after Pete arrived. Did he come down here?"

As though he'd heard his cue, the big yellow cat strolled into the den and sat in front of me, golden eyes fixed on mine. "Mmrupp," he said, then turned and headed for the front hall.

"I guess he's ready for bed, too," I said as I followed him. "Good night, Aunt Ibby. I love you."

"Love you, Maralee. Get a good night's sleep."

I climbed the stairs and opened the door to my apartment. Taking a long look around the kitchen, I decided that a proper table and chairs to replace the folding variety would be my next purchase. I'd buy some vintage dishes of my own, too.

I guess I'd better get River to show me how to arrange them all for balance and harmony.

O'Ryan had already gone into the bedroom. I tagged along behind him. Smoothing the rumpled bedcovers, I picked up the piece of tissue paper, along with the treasures Pete and I had unwrapped.

"Guess I'll put these back where we found them," I said aloud. Talking to O'Ryan as though he was a person and could respond had become a habit. I'd noticed that Aunt Ibby did it, too. I wrapped the coin, then looked around for the other piece of tissue paper. "Where did the other one go?"

O'Ryan darted under the bed and returned, batting a wadded-up white ball of paper.

"Good boy," I said. "Saves me from crawling under there." As I flattened it out and put the dog tag in the center, I noticed that one edge was torn unevenly. "Did you chew on this, boy?"

I was rewarded with a grumpy cat face and an "Are you serious?" look.

"Okay, okay, no need to get huffy," I said. "Maybe the other one has a raggedy edge, too." I unwrapped the coin and looked closely at the tissue paper. The two halves matched. Someone had torn one sheet of tissue paper in half. "So," I said in my best Nancy Drew fashion, "these two items were placed in the bureau at the same time."

"Mrruff," O'Ryan said, obviously bored with the game, as he curled up at the foot of the bed and closed his eyes. I rewrapped the coin and the tag, replaced them in the bureau, and slid the panel closed. Pete was right. There was a tiny indentation in the wood at the spot hiding the double cubbyhole. I made a quick inspection of the spots that I knew hid secret compartments. No more flaws or dents.

Yawning, I kicked off the sandals, hung up my dress, took a quick shower, and pulled on one of Johnny's old Indianapolis Speedway T-shirts.

I joined the sleeping cat on my big, new, soft, properly placed, and much too empty bed.

CHAPTER 7

It was barely light out when I woke up. I looked around, a little disoriented. Until very recently I'd been sleeping downstairs, in my old bedroom. There a clock radio with a lighted dial on a handy bedside table had kept me aware of the time and, with a push of a button, had brought me soothing music or the latest news. Now I was in a room that was still a bit strange to me, empty except for my bed and the bureau. O'Ryan, perhaps sensing my momentary discomfort, moved from his spot at the foot of the bed and settled himself on my shoulder, purring loudly and rhythmically into my ear.

"Dear cat," I whispered, which caused the purring to increase in volume. I knew that my watch was on the top of the bureau across the room. I'd put it next to the vase of roses and daisies. But did I want to get up and look at it? Did it matter what time it was? It was summer. I was on vacation. I had no plans for the day. That in itself was a strange feeling.

I've always been a busy person. Had had full-time

jobs on television ever since I graduated from Boston's Emerson College. I'd been a weather girl, a shopping channel show host, and even a phone-in psychic. My new job, as an instructor of TV production at the Tabitha Trumbull Academy of the Arts in downtown Salem, was interesting and I really liked it, but having a two-month vacation was an entirely new experience for me. Even the online criminology course I'd been taking wouldn't resume until August. I planned to finish furnishing the apartment, but that was hardly a full-time project.

"What do you think, O'Ryan? Look for a summer job? Volunteer someplace? Get a hobby? What?"

O'Ryan rolled over, eyes still shut, and assumed a pose that meant "Scratch my tummy." I obliged.

"I know," I told him. "Two months of cat petting would be fun, but let's think of something more productive. Come on. Get up. It's time for coffee."

I padded into the kitchen, still not looking at the watch, not really wanting to touch the top of the bureau. O'Ryan stretched, yawned, and followed me. I poured some kitty kibble into his bowl and started a fresh pot of coffee for myself.

I retrieved a mug from the dishwasher and a jar of powdered creamer from the cabinet. Then I took a pen and a pad of paper from the junk drawer Aunt Ibby had so thoughtfully started for me, poured myself a nice cup of that fully caffeinated, life-giving fluid, and began to make a list.

1. Buy china, table, and chairs.
2. Buy bedside table and clock radio.
3. Furnish the living room.

That was as far as I got on the first cup. I was halfway through the second one when I thought of number four.

4. See if Mr. Pennington needs help.

Rupert Pennington was the executive director of the Tabby. Not only was he my boss at the school, but he'd also been dating my aunt pretty steadily. Although I had no classes to teach during the summer months, the Art, Dance, and Theater Arts Departments were still in session, and there was a new sound and lighting studio being built there, too. Maybe he could find something for me to do.

"Okay, then, that's four things," I said, more to myself than to the cat. "I'd better get dressed and get started on one of them." Most of my clothes were still downstairs, in my old bedroom, so I showered in my new bathroom, tossed on a robe, made my bed, and opened the door to the front hall. O'Ryan scooted out ahead of me and headed down to Aunt Ibby's part of the house. The tantalizing smell of bacon and home-made bread wafted toward us from her kitchen.

"Oops. Forgot my watch." I hurried back to the bed-room, grabbed my watch from the top of the bureau, then paused, looking at the lace runner–covered center panel.

Why did I see the swirling colors and the sparkling lights in the brief instant when Pete lifted the panel? I wondered.

Is there something I'm supposed to see in there? Something important?

This scryer thing, this gazing ability I seem to have, isn't anything I've ever wanted. According to the books

I'd read since I learned that I actually have this weird ability, a scryer can see things in shiny, polished surfaces, and in my case, they apparently have to be black. It was less than a year ago that I discovered this "gift," as River called it, although Aunt Ibby had known about it most of my life. River thinks I should use it as much as possible. She says it's a blessing, something that could help people, the way she helps with the tarot cards. But River didn't see her parents die in a fiery plane crash, watch her mother's silent scream. She didn't see a woman being murdered, unable to do anything about it. True, one of the visions had probably saved my life once, but I was still terrified of the whole creepy process.

I reached again toward the top of the bureau, then pulled my hand away. I hurried from the room and raced down the stairs, heading for the warmth and safety of Aunt Ibby's kitchen. O'Ryan was already there, enjoying a second breakfast from his own red bowl.

"Good morning, Maralee," my aunt called. "You're up bright and early. Sit down and have some bacon and eggs and nice warm homemade bread. Where are you off to today?"

I poured myself another cup of coffee and sat at the round kitchen table. "I've thought up four things I need to do," I told her. "I haven't decided which one I should start with." I recited the list, counting each item off on my fingers.

"All worthy ideas," she said, "and I'm sure Rupert will be happy for the help. He mentioned to me just yesterday that he was looking for a volunteer property manager for the summer theater program. Someone to find stage props for the plays they'll be producing this summer."

I nibbled on a piece of crisp bacon. "I can do that."

"Of course you can. They have a really slim budget, though, so you'll have to prowl around in thrift stores and beg, borrow, and steal from friends, I imagine, but it might be fun."

"Okay," I said. "I'll go to see Mr. Pennington first thing. I hope he hasn't already found somebody else."

"I doubt that he has. Volunteers aren't as easy to find as they once were. Lots of people who'd like to offer to help have to bring home a paycheck these days."

"I know. I'm one of the lucky ones. I have a lovely home here with you, a job I like at the school, and enough money so that I don't need to worry."

It was true. Between an inheritance from my parents and Johnny's insurance, I was quite well set financially. That was another thing Pete didn't know about me yet. The list seemed to be growing.

Within the hour, dressed in conservative black cropped pants and a crisp white cotton blouse, with tummy full and to-do list reprioritized, I backed the Corvette out of the garage and headed downtown to offer my services to the Tabby.

Mr. Pennington was in his office, behind his massive old oak desk. He rose to greet me, smiling broadly. "Ms. Barrett, what a delightful surprise. I'd just been thinking of calling you . . . asking a favor of you, so to speak." He gestured toward the one comfortable chair in his office. "But please sit down. What brings you here this fine morning?"

"Thank you." I sat as directed. "My aunt told me that you might be in need of a property manager for the theater group."

"How perfectly serendipitous, my dear! The very favor of which I spoke."

"Really? Well, then, if you think I can handle the job, I'm happy to volunteer."

"Oh, you're perfectly suited to the task, Ms. Barrett. With your extensive background in television production, your familiarity with set design, and with your innate exquisite taste . . . why, I couldn't have found anyone better. I've been trying to fill the position myself, gathering together a few things for our first production, but . . ." He spread his hands in a helpless gesture. "But my executive plate is very full, so to speak."

Mr. Pennington had been an actor in his youth and was given to long, flowery speeches. He looked the part, too, always impeccably dressed, with flawless manners. He and Aunt Ibby had started dating some months earlier. They are both film buffs, and it was fun listening to them try to top each other when they recited lines from old movies.

"Glad to help," I said. "What's my job description?"

"We'll be doing three plays during the summer," he said. "I'll give you the script of each one, along with the general set outlines, so you can see how the onstage action should flow."

"Sounds like a fun challenge. When do you want me to start?"

"How about tomorrow? I'll speak with the Theater Arts Department people." He scribbled on a large desk calendar, then frowned. "I suppose you realize that our budget is . . . shall we say . . . somewhat limited?"

"Aunt Ibby made that clear."

"Ah, yes. Miss Russell is a remarkably astute woman." Again, the broad smile. "Will tomorrow at ten be convenient?"

"I'll look forward to it," I said, shook his hand, and

left the office, mentally checking off number four on my list.

The Tabby was housed in Salem's old Trumbull's Department Store. Even after considerable renovation, the building had kept its retail-store look. There was a wide staircase leading from the main floor to the upper stories, and even some of the original store fixtures had been repurposed. An old rolltop glass counter housed student awards, and the elevators still had the old directory in them, showing floors marked MILLINERY, MENSWEAR, BEAUTY SHOP, and the like. My classroom was housed on the mezzanine, between the first and second floors, in the old shoe department, and was complete with vintage Thonet chairs and campy mid-century display pieces. I couldn't resist taking a peek at it as long as I was in the building.

The lights were out; the TV monitors, dark; and the desks, bookshelves, and tabletops, empty—just what I'd expected to see in a classroom vacated for the summer. I took a few steps closer. Something was missing. In fact, quite a few somethings were missing. Most of the vintage chairs were gone, along with the old shoe department display pieces. Where was the cute tin cutout of Buster Brown and his dog, Tige? Where was the framed picture of the scarlet macaw advertising Poll-Parrot shoes for children? Where was the 3-D patent-leather pump that used to hang on the wall behind my desk? Not that I'd ever be sorry to see that particular shiny black object disappear.

I guessed I'd learn the answers when I reported for my new job in the morning, and set out to check off number one on my list.

Buy china, table, and chairs.

CHAPTER 8

Finding the perfect set of dishes was a lot easier than I thought it was going to be. I stopped at the first antique store I found after leaving the Tabby. Although an OPEN sign was in the window, the door was locked. I shook the knob a couple of times and was ready to walk away when a smiling woman appeared, threw the door open, and said, "Welcome to Jenny's Antiques! Sorry about the lock, but, well, we've all been kind of nervous ever since Shea Tolliver . . . you know . . . died."

"Understandable," I said. "That was a terrible thing. Are you Jenny?"

"I am," she said, locking the door again. "I peek out to see who it is before I open up. I know it sounds paranoid, but I can't help it."

"Glad I passed inspection," I said, trying to lighten the mood. I didn't want to talk about or even think about Shea Tolliver.

She smiled and waved a dismissive hand. "Of course you did. Anybody can see that you're honest!"

I thought about the times I'd been wrong about people in the not too distant past. Looks can be deceiving. I didn't comment on that, just returned her smile.

"How can I help you today? Something special or just browsing?"

"I'm looking for a set of dishes," I said. "Something vintage, on the casual side."

"Sure. Come on back here. I'll show you what I have." I followed her into a long sunny room where a dozen or so tables each displayed various place settings of china, along with serving pieces, flatware, and coordinated crystal.

"Just look around. Take your time." Jenny lowered her voice. "I need to get back and see if anyone's at the door. Can't be too careful these days." She turned back toward me. "Did you know Shea?"

The question caught me off guard. "Me? No, not really. I bought a piece of furniture from her recently. Seemed like a very nice person."

"Shea was a peach." She nodded vigorously. "I always kind of liked Gary, too."

"Gary?"

"Shea's partner. The guy they arrested. Ever run into him?"

Yeah, I did "run into him."

I gave a kind of noncommittal "uh-uh" and picked up the closest teacup, barely looking at it, hoping to change the subject. "This is pretty."

"Noritake. Azalea pattern," she said. "I don't think he killed her."

"Excuse me?"

"Gary. I don't think he killed her."

We clearly weren't going to avoid the topic of Shea Tolliver, so I figured I might as well listen to what this woman had to say about Shea's erstwhile partner. "Why is that?" I asked, keeping my tone neutral and picking up a beige plate with a shell on it.

"Franciscan Ware. Sea sculptures," she said. "Because

he was trying to get back together with her. She told me so."

I remembered what Shea had said about a partner taking off with a chunk of their money, and I remembered, too, what Pete had told me about a judge granting a restraining order against Gary Campbell because of threats he'd made. That didn't add up to the partners "getting back together" in my book.

"Seems to me I heard somewhere that he'd threatened her." I replaced the plate on the table.

She nodded and handed me a pale green cereal bowl. "Russel Wright. Iroquois. Nineteen fifties. Gary owed somebody a lot of money. He was desperate to get cash. But he wouldn't have hurt her. Not him."

I started to put the bowl back, then turned it over and looked at it more closely. "This is nice. What makes you think he wouldn't hurt her?"

"I have it in four colors. I've known Gary for years. A real pussycat. He got in with a rough crowd, though, a while back. Drinking heavily, too, I guess. But he's straightened out. I'm sure of it."

"Hmm. People can change, I guess. Can I see the other colors?"

"Sure. Come on over here by the window."

She led the way to a small bay window where a square table of clear Lucite sparkled in the sunlight. Four varicolored place settings of the fifties-style piece I still held in my hand were arranged on the glass top. Four Lucite chairs with padded tan leather seats completed the picture.

"Wow," I said. "Are the table and chairs for sale, too?"

"Sure," she said. "Mid-century modern. Nineteen seventies. You want the whole works? Dishes too?"

"Oh, yes," I breathed. "I surely do. It's perfect. Do you deliver?"

"I use Bob's Delivery," she said. "Most of us dealers do. He's good."

"Yes," I said. "He delivered the bureau I bought from Shea." I ran my hand across the curvy back of one of the chairs. "I suppose I should ask how much this is going to cost."

She mentioned a price in the four-figure range, and I nodded my agreement. "Was that the bureau she got from the Hampton estate?" she asked.

"Yes," I said, surprised. "How did you guess?"

"I was with her when she bid on it. She bought several things from there. Kinda high price she paid for that bureau, I thought. I mean, I thought so until I found out about the secret compartments." She shook her head. "Shea and Gary were both high rollers when it came to getting good merchandise. Too rich for my blood. I guess you paid a pretty price for it?"

I nodded. "I did. But I wanted it because I had one just like it when I was a little girl."

I followed her to the cash register and made out a check. She cocked her head to one side and, with a half-smile, asked, "So, was Helena's pink diamond inside?"

That made me laugh. "I'm afraid not. Shea looked in all the compartments before I got it. No diamonds."

Delivery of my table, chairs, and dishes was promised for the following day, and as I shook hands with Jenny and left the shop, I mentally checked off number one on my to-do list. *Not bad. Two down. Two to go. Enough shopping for one day.* I headed for home.

I parked the 'Vette in the garage, noting that Aunt Ibby's Buick was missing. That wasn't surprising.

Although she's semiretired from Salem's main library, she still put in several hours a week there, helping out and training staff. O'Ryan greeted me at the back door entrance with happy "mmrupps" and playful claw-sheathed taps on my ankles.

"Well, you're in a good mood," I told him. "Me too." The big cat scampered up the stairs ahead of me and sat patiently beside the door to my apartment while I fished the key from my purse.

Once inside, O'Ryan and I hurried through the empty expanse of my living room, my heels and O'Ryan's claws tap-tapping on the new hardwood floors, and emerged in the kitchen.

"Guess I can return the borrowed table and chairs and make room for my new ones," I told the cat. "Wait till you see them. Clear Lucite. You won't be able to hide underneath. We can see right through it."

O'Ryan stuck out a pink tongue and strolled into the bedroom, then looked back at me from the doorway. I knew what he was thinking. As soon as I said "see right through it" out loud, I'd thought of the same thing—the blackened mirror glass under the center section of the bureau. The swirling colors and the pinpoints of light were waiting beneath the hinged panel, and I knew there was a message there that I was supposed to see—whether I wanted to or not.

I followed the cat.

The roses in the bouquet Pete had given me were just beginning to open. I inhaled their fragrance as, with O'Ryan walking behind me, I carried the vase to the kitchen and put it on the counter. Then together the cat and I returned to the bedroom and faced the bureau. I tossed the lace runner onto the bed.

"Here goes," I said and lifted the panel.

The colors and the lights swirled, then quickly faded. I saw a long sandy beach. Waves lapped gently at the shore, and in the distance I saw a crumbling stone wall. Beyond that, far down the beach, I could make out the figure of a woman. Her back was to me as she picked up a stick and tossed it. A small gray dog ran ahead of her and retrieved it. She knelt in the sand, patted the dog, and tossed the stick again. The action was repeated several times, until the woman and the dog were reduced to tiny, faraway dots.

"Is that all?" I said aloud. The image disappeared abruptly, and I found myself looking once again at the ruined mirror.

I closed the panel and sat on the foot of the bed, staring blankly at the bureau and wondering about what I'd just seen. What had I just seen? It certainly was by far the most pleasant scene my gazing "gift" had ever presented. But what did it mean? Who was the woman? She was too far away for me to tell if she was anyone I knew. Where was the beach? It could be anywhere. Here in Salem? Back in Florida? Maybe not Florida. No palm trees. But then again, I hadn't seen any trees—just sand, water, a crumbling wall, and a woman and a dog.

At that moment I wished there was someone with me . . . someone I could share this experience with, but I was alone in the big house, except for the cat. Actually, I knew there were just two people in the whole world I *could* share it with. Aunt Ibby and River were the only ones who knew about the gazing thing. Aunt Ibby was at the library, and it was still too early in the day to call River.

I wandered into the kitchen and heated a mug of leftover coffee in the microwave. The refrigerator yielded only a wilted salad and half of the apple pie. I chose a slice of pie, gave it the microwave treatment, added a scoop of vanilla ice cream, and told myself that the combination of fruit and dairy equaled a healthy snack. Hours of the day stretched ahead of me. I didn't feel like watching TV and hadn't brought any books upstairs yet. I wasn't in the mood to tackle any more items on my list, so what to do? I could do some grocery shopping, but that didn't hold much appeal at the moment, either.

Newspaper clippings! The articles from the *Salem News* that Aunt Ibby had given me were in the top drawer of the bureau. I'd spend my time learning more about the former owners of my bureau.

O'Ryan was already heading for the bedroom by the time I swallowed the last bite of pie. *How does that cat know what I'm going to do before I do it?* I retrieved the sheaf of articles from the bureau and returned to the kitchen. After heating up another mug of coffee, I sat at the table and began to read the first article in the pile, dated five years earlier.

The headline read POLICE SEEK TRENT'S GIRLFRIEND. *A woman known as Daphne Trent, alleged to be the girlfriend of accused murderer Tommy Trent, is wanted for questioning by Salem police. Lead detective Pete Mondello announced this morning that Daphne Trent, who for several years had been accepted as Tommy Trent's sister, may have information relevant to the murder of Helena Trent. Mondello emphasized that Ms. Trent is not suspected of wrongdoing relative to the death of Mrs. Trent. Ms. Trent, whose last known address was the Trent family estate, is believed to still be in the Greater Salem area.*

So Pete was lead detective on the case. He didn't tell

me that. Did they find Daphne? What did she know about Helena's death?

"This is like reading a mystery novel," I told the cat. "Except it all really happened, right here in Salem."

O'Ryan, with a warning "mrrow," leapt into my lap and, putting his front paws on the edge of the card table, seemed to study the paper in front of us. One paw shot out, and he moved the top page aside and revealed the next article. This one had a color photo of Helena and Daphne standing together at a Junior League fashion show where the two had modeled evening wear.

"What pretty women," I murmured, looking from one to the other. Helena wore a low-cut, formfitting pink sequined gown. On a gold chain around her neck was what I guessed must be the famous pink diamond. Daphne wore a similar sparkling blue dress, which complemented her blond good looks.

My gaze wandered to the headline—ALLEGED KILLER'S GIRLFRIEND CLAIMS FRIENDSHIP WITH VICTIM. *Daphne Trent responded this morning to a request by the Salem Police Department to answer questions regarding the death of Helena Trent. According to sources, Ms. Trent denied any knowledge of the circumstances leading to the death of Helena Trent, or of the murder itself. She claimed that she and Helena Trent were the best of friends, despite her secret relationship with Trent's husband. 'I loved Helena,' she said, 'and I hated that Tommy and I were always lying to her. She was so kind to me. Even after she found out about Tommy and me, she said she didn't hate me.' Salem police reiterated that Daphne Trent is not suspected of any wrongdoing in the matter. Several witnesses have verified that on the evening of the murder Ms. Trent was at a charity fund-raiser, in the company of Mrs. Helena Trent's stepson, John David Hampton III.*

I put my coffee mug down beside the stack of papers. "I wonder if Pete was the one who questioned her." I spoke aloud to the cat on my lap. Sometimes it seemed as though he understood every word, and sometimes, in his own way, he *did* answer questions.

This was one of those times.

Out shot the paw again. This time he flipped a couple of pieces of paper onto the floor, seemed to study the one he'd revealed, then curled up on my lap and began to purr. It took me a moment to find the short paragraph near the bottom of the page.

I read the headline—AIRTIGHT ALIBIS FOR ALLEGED KILLER'S GIRLFRIEND AND HAMPTON HEIR—before glancing down the page. *According to Salem police detective Pete Mondello, Daphne Trent and John David Hampton III were present at a charity auction sponsored by the North Shore Patrons of the Arts on the evening of the death of Mr. Hampton's stepmother, Helena Trent. Numerous witnesses have verified the presence of the couple at the event. Tommy Trent, the husband of the deceased, is at present the only suspect in the case and remains in police custody on suspicion of murder. Trent is being held on one million dollars bail.*

"He could have told me that he was lead detective on that case when we talked about it," I complained to the apparently sleeping cat. "Why does he keep things from me?"

I knew the answer, of course. *He's a cop. He's supposed to keep quiet about police work.* What was my excuse?

CHAPTER 9

Late afternoon shadows had stretched across my windowsills and spilled onto the floor when Aunt Ibby's gentle *tap-tap* sounded on my door. "Maralee? Come on downstairs and have a bite of supper with me."

I opened the door and hugged her. "I'd love to," I said. "I have such a lot to tell you."

We walked downstairs together, O'Ryan leading the way. It felt good to enter the dear familiar surroundings of my childhood home after leaving the stark setting of my own new living space.

"I hope I can make my apartment as attractive as this," I said, arriving in the long fireplaced living room, with its tall windows facing Winter Street. "Everything looks so perfect."

"Nonsense," she declared. "That's just because there are fond memories attached to the old place. The couch needs reupholstering, the carpet is frayed, and O'Ryan—that naughty boy—has been sharpening his claws on the wing chairs." She shook her finger in the direction of the cat, who calmly groomed long whiskers. "You're looking at it through the eyes of love,

Maralee. Once you get things organized in your place, you're going to love it just as much."

"I hope so," I said. "Anyway, I have a new table and chairs and dishes coming tomorrow. I think that'll be a good start."

"Come on into the kitchen and tell me all about your day," she said. "I've made a lovely antipasto and your favorite veal Parmesan. We'll have a nice glass of wine first, and you can tell me everything."

That was exactly what I'd wanted to do all day. I hardly knew where to begin. "Okay," I said. "I'll start with my visit with Mr. Pennington."

"I do hope Rupert was able to help you. Was he?"

"He sure was. I start tomorrow as property manager for the summer theater stage productions. They're doing three plays, and just as you said, I'll be working with a pretty slim budget, but I'm looking forward to it."

She smiled and poured white wine into delicate stemmed crystal glasses. "You always did enjoy a challenge, dear. You'll be a wonderful property manager."

"Darn," I said, sipping the wine. "I should have bought glassware, too."

"Tomorrow," she said. "Now tell me more."

I told her about my visit to Jenny's Antiques and about the Lucite kitchen set and the Russel Wright dishes. "Jenny was apparently acquainted with Shea Tolliver," I said, "and she knows Gary Campbell, Shea's ex-partner, too."

"Really? What does Jenny think about this Gary person being in the shop just before you found the poor woman dead?"

"I didn't tell her I was the one who found the body. She can't believe he'd hurt Shea. Says that Shea told her Gary was trying to get her to forgive him . . . to take him back into the business."

Aunt Ibby gave an unladylike snort. "What a nerve! Imagine. After threatening her severely enough so that a judge granted a restraining order. They don't hand those out easily, you know."

"I know they don't. And I don't know what to think about Gary Campbell. I guess we just have to trust the police to figure it all out."

"Does Pete say anything about the man?"

"No. But you know Pete. He doesn't make small talk about police business. Did you know he was the lead detective on the Helena Trent case? I read it in one of those articles you gave me. He never even mentioned it when I told him about the bureau that came from Helena's house."

My aunt began to serve the colorful salad. "He might have thought it would sound like bragging if he told you."

"I guess that's true. He doesn't talk about himself much at all." I thought about that for a minute and sipped my wine. "And I certainly don't tell him everything about myself, either."

She frowned. "Like about the gazing?"

"Exactly. And it happened again today. I looked into that blackened mirror and saw . . . something."

"Oh dear." She opened the oven and transferred the cutlets to a serving plate. "Was it anything . . . frightening?"

"Not at all," I said. "Actually, it was quite a pleasant scene. I just haven't the slightest idea what it's supposed to mean."

She put the steaming platter on the table and sat down. "Tell me about it."

I described the beach and the waves breaking on the shore. I told her about the crumbling wall and the woman and the small dog in the distance. "The woman threw the stick, and the dog retrieved it. Then she knelt and patted him and threw the stick again. The same action was repeated again and again, until they were little, faraway specks. Any idea what it might mean?"

"Not a clue," she said. "Could you recognize her? Anyone we know?"

"She was too far away. Anyway, she had her back to me. I couldn't see her face at all."

"Maybe River can help you figure it out. You should call her."

"I will. This is delicious." I felt relaxed and happy there in the familiar kitchen, sharing a meal with the woman who'd raised me. "Pretty soon I'll invite you to my place for dinner."

"I shall look forward to it," she said with a smile. "Now, tell me some more about your visit with Rupert."

Aunt Ibby and Rupert Pennington had begun "keeping company" the previous winter. At first I hadn't been thrilled to see my boss and my aunt dating, but they seemed to have a lot in common, and they were each obviously happy in the relationship.

"Well, as I told you," I said, "the summer theater group will be presenting three plays in the student theater at the Tabby. Mr. Pennington said that he had me in mind for the job of property manager all along."

"That must please you. What plays are they planning to do?"

"I don't know yet. He's going to give me the scripts and general set outlines tomorrow. He said he's been gathering up some props for the first play himself, so that gives me a head start."

"I'm sure you're about to have a truly productive summer, Maralee," she said. "Now, how about some nice strawberry ice cream for dessert?"

"Sounds good. And I'm going to take your advice and call River."

We cleared the table and loaded the dishwasher together. "I think I'll sleep in my old room tonight," I said. "I'll set the alarm. Don't want to be late on the first day of my new job."

"Good idea. Why don't you just spend the evening here? Rupert and I are going to a poetry reading later, but I'll be back early, and you can tell me what River says about your new vision."

I glanced around at the comfortable surroundings, thought about the near-barren space upstairs, and decided to do as she suggested. Besides, O'Ryan was already curled up on a needlepoint cushion on the window seat. "I think I will," I told her. "O'Ryan and I will just play couch potatoes in your living room."

Aunt Ibby went to her room to change for her date, while I opted for my trusty old gray sweats and a seat on the couch, which may or may not have needed reupholstering. O'Ryan ran for the front door before the bell chimed, announcing Mr. Pennington's arrival. Aunt Ibby, looking lovely in gray silk, waited as usual for him to ring twice so that she wouldn't appear anxious. He stepped inside the foyer and the two, looking so darned cute together, peeked in at me through the arched living room doorway.

"I won't be late, Maralee," she said. "You and O'Ryan have a pleasant evening."

"Have fun, you two. See you in the morning, Mr.

Pennington." I picked up the cat, and we watched from the window as the school director's brown Lincoln pulled away from the curb.

We'd just resumed our spots on the couch when my phone vibrated. The caller ID showed River North's name. "I was just about to call you," I told her.

"What's going on?" she said, sounding a bit uneasy. "You've been on my mind all afternoon, so I read the cards again. A couple of cards turned up next to yours that haven't been there before."

"Is that a good thing?"

"Maybe. I'm not sure. The Ace of Wands is close to you. It means the beginning of an enterprise. Like something of a creative nature might be offered to you. Does that make sense?"

"Sure does. What else?"

"Okay. This one's not so clear. The Knight of Wands is there, too. He's a man, usually with blond hair and blue eyes. Ring a bell?"

I immediately thought of Gary Campbell. "I guess I know lots of men who fit that description," I admitted. "But yeah, there was a recent, um, encounter with one."

"You mean the blond guy who bumped into you at the antique store? Possible, but this one might be a friend of yours. He can be generous, but he can be cruel or brutal."

"That's one of those cards that can mean practically anything."

She sighed. "I know. But listen. Just be careful around blond, blue eyed men, okay?"

"I'm careful around all men, River. You know that."

"True. Anyway, tell me about the creative opportunity."

"I don't know how to handle all this free time, so

I've been looking for something to do during school vacation," I said. "Mr. Pennington offered me a chance to work as property manager for the plays the summer theater classes are producing."

"Creative for sure. Congratulations. Now, what were you going to call me about? Please tell me you've opened all those secret compartments. I'm dying to know what's in that bureau!"

"To tell you the truth, so am I. But I kind of promised Pete we'd open them together and um . . . he had to leave early."

"Wow. You have a lot more self-control than I do. I would have had those little guys emptied out ten minutes after the thing was delivered."

"Yeah. But I promised. What I wanted to tell you is that . . . a gazing thing happened today."

"Really?" Her excitement was obvious. "Tell me everything."

I explained about the messed-up mirror and how I'd seen the lights and colors while Pete was in the room. "I kind of freaked out, I guess. That's why Pete left before we'd opened any more of the compartments," I told her. "I knew there was something I was supposed to look at, but I waited until this afternoon to do it."

River sighed. "So I guess you didn't have the enchanted evening I was visualizing. You're such a chicken. When are you going to tell that man what you can do?"

"I don't know." Deep sigh. I really didn't know. Would I ever work up the nerve to tell Pete the truth?

"Never mind that now. So, what did you see?"

I closed my eyes and saw the picture again in my mind. "It was a pretty scene. Calm. Not frightening at all, like most of them have been. There's a long beach.

Waves along the shoreline. There's a wall. It's old, crumbling. In the distance I see a woman. Her back is toward me, and there's a little dog with her. She throws a stick, and the dog retrieves it. She pats him on the head and throws it again. They move down the beach. She's throwing. He's bringing the stick back to her, till they're just tiny spots in the distance. That's all." I took a deep breath. "Any idea what it means?"

"Is the dog happy?"

"Seems to be. He's having fun chasing a stick. Why? Does that mean something?"

"If it was a dream, it would mean social activity. Good times. It's probably about the same for a vision, I guess."

"I like that. How about the beach? And the woman?"

"Have to look in the dream book for that one. Hold on a sec."

I waited, heard pages being turned. O'Ryan moved to the back of the couch, with his head next to my shoulder, ears up straight. I knew he was listening, too.

"Okay. Here it is. A long beach can mean you're looking for a change in your future. Make sense?"

"Oh, River. Everybody has changes in their future. Doesn't mean a thing. How about the woman with her back to me?"

"Okay. There's a lot here about backs. Is her back naked? Like in a bathing suit?"

"Don't know. Maybe? She's too far away for me to see clearly."

"If it is, you're keeping secrets from those in your life, it says here. You fear that the secrets may be revealed. Your subconscious wants you to come clean. Wow."

"Wow, what?"

"Don't you get it? Your subconscious wants you to tell Pete your secret!"

"Come on. She might be wearing a burka, for all I know. I think you'd better stick to the cards."

She laughed. "You're probably right. Anyway, I'm glad it wasn't a scary vision. Talk to you later. Got to get ready for the show."

"I'll watch you, if I can stay awake that long."

After we hung up, I couldn't get what River had said about revealing secrets out of my head. I wished she hadn't looked in that dream book. Maybe it was a scary vision, after all.

CHAPTER 10

It was still early when Aunt Ibby returned from her date, just as she'd promised. O'Ryan ran for the front hall, and moments later the lights from Mr. Pennington's car reflected in the window as he drove away.

"Aunt Ibby?" I called. "That you?"

"Of course it's me, dear." She peeked into the living room. "I'm going to run upstairs and change into something comfortable. Then I'll come back down, and we can chat."

"Shall I make tea?"

"That would be lovely."

I headed for the kitchen, filled the kettle with water, and put it on the old gas range to boil. I picked a red teapot from Aunt Ibby's collection and tossed four Earl Grey tea bags into it. Aunt Ibby always uses loose tea, but I've never quite mastered that art. By the time my aunt appeared in the kitchen in a blue chenille bathrobe and bunny slippers, the tea was ready, and I'd arranged a few slices of homemade marble cake on a red plate.

I put the teapot, the cake plate and a couple of

bone china teacups on the round oak table and we sat opposite one another. "How was your date?" I asked. "Poetry reading, was it?"

"It was quite delightful. I was surprised when Rupert went to the podium and read a poem he'd written. Did you know he was a poet?"

"Mr. Pennington is a constant source of surprises." It was true. Some of the school director's "surprises" had been quite pleasant. Others, not so much. But I could tell from my aunt's happy countenance that she definitely approved of his poetic efforts.

She took a sip of tea. "Well, don't keep me on pins and needles. What did River have to say about your latest vision? Could she figure out the meaning of the beach and the woman and the dog?"

"She wasn't much help with the vision," I admitted. "She tried looking up the symbols in a dream book, but it didn't make a lot of sense. We agreed she's much better with the cards."

Aunt Ibby smiled. "I watch the readings she does on her show sometimes, and it surely seems as though there's something to it. Did she read your cards again?"

"She did. She saw an offer of something creative—I'm guessing that's the property manager position—and she told me to be careful around blond, blue-eyed men."

She raised an eyebrow. "Any particular reason for that?"

I shrugged. "Kind of vague. He could be a bad guy. I told her I'm careful around all men."

"Good answer! Say, speaking of bad guys, did you read today's *Salem News?*"

"Not yet. Why?"

She leaned forward. "That Tommy Trent is out of

jail. You remember. Helena's husband? I guess his sentence was reduced for good behavior. Anyway, he's out after only six years. I'm surprised Pete didn't tell you about it."

"No reason he would, I guess. Other than the fact that I have a bureau that came out of the Trent's house, he'd have no reason to think I'd be interested." I helped myself to a piece of cake.

"True enough. The paper says the reporter asked Pete what he thought about Tommy getting out of jail, on account of him being the detective on the case back then, and he just said, 'No comment.'"

"Sounds like Pete, all right," I said. "Want to watch River, as long as we're up?"

"Might as well," she said.

A few minutes later we were comfortably seated on the couch, teacups and cake plates arranged on the coffee table and the television set tuned to WICH-TV. The late news was just winding up, and my old coworker Scott Palmer wore a serious expression. "Convicted killer Tommy Trent was released from prison over the weekend," he intoned. "When asked by this reporter what his plans for the future were, he said, 'No comment.'"

"Seems to be a lot of that 'No comment' going around," I said, watching as the image of Tommy Trent emerging from behind prison gates and getting into a waiting automobile flashed on the screen. He faced away from the camera, and a baseball cap shaded his features. "He looks thinner than he did in that newspaper photo."

"Probably prison fare is quite different from what he was used to," Aunt Ibby said, reaching for a piece of cake. "And I think I've read that men in jail do a lot of exercising. Muscle building and that sort of thing."

"I've heard that. Look. Here's River." Our friend appeared on-screen while her theme music, *Danse Macabre,* played in the background. Her dark red sheath, shot with silver threads, glistened under the studio lights, and a spray of silver stars woven into her long black braid accented her exotic good looks.

"Good evening, friends of the night," River said, smiling. "Our film tonight will thrill and delight you, I know. Prepare to be scared. But first, let's see what the strange and beautiful tarot cards will offer us with their miracles of psychological insight, wise counsel, and accurate divination."

She leaned back in her rattan fan-backed chair, bowed her head, and placed the deck of cards in front of her on the round table. A telephone number appeared at the top of the screen, and a moment later River spoke to her first caller, asked for his birth date, and chose a card to represent him. An overhead camera focused on the King of Cups, which she'd placed in the center of the table. While she delivered a rapid-fire explanation of the horoscope method of reading tarot cards, River arranged twelve cards in a circle around the first one.

"The cards are quite beautiful, aren't they?" My aunt leaned closer to the screen. "Like lovely little paintings."

River's reading seemed to please the caller, and her running explanation of what she was doing and what each card meant kept the audience interested in the process. But when she announced the movie du jour— *I Walked with a Zombie*—I wished my aunt a good night, carried my teacup to the kitchen, and headed upstairs to my childhood bedroom.

I prepared for bed, wearing one of Johnny's old DAYTONA RACE WEEK T-shirts. It was faded, soft, and comfortable, as only a well-aged T-shirt could be. A determined scratching at the door announced that O'Ryan didn't want to watch zombies walking, either, and he joined me on the French Provincial bed. I looked across the room, toward a matching bureau. It had five drawers, like the one in my apartment, but no hidden mirror, no hidden compartments. Just a pretty, ordinary piece of furniture, with no secrets, no past, no memories of death . . . or murder.

What's in the other four spaces? River is right. I'm dying to open each and every one. But I promised Pete. . . .

I knew that Pete was probably curious, too—after all, he'd wanted to open them all before dinner. "I'll call him tomorrow," I told O'Ryan, "and tell him he *has to* come back tomorrow night."

That matter settled in my mind, I set the alarm for 8:00 a.m., turned out the light, and with large cat purring beside me, fell asleep in minutes.

Anyone would think that after the jam-packed and eventful couple of days I'd had, I'd sleep like a . . . well, like a well-fed yellow-striped cat. That was not to be. Maybe the dream was the result of River's foray into the dream book. Maybe it was because of the vision in the black mirror. Maybe it was because of all those old newspaper clippings. Whatever the cause, it was one of those disturbing dreams that could linger in the mind for a very long time.

I was on a beach. The sand beneath my bare feet was cool and pebbly, not like the sand on Florida beaches. I heard the sound of waves and looked around, wondering where I was. The water was calm and blue, gently lapping at the shoreline. I paused and picked up a large white clamshell. It seemed important that I should keep it, that I should put it in my pocket. I looked down and realized that I was wearing a bathing suit. So I held the shell in my hand, palm up, looking at it intently as I walked. The scene seemed to change then. The sky grew cloudy, and the waves began to crash on the beach. I felt cold. I heard a voice. "Follow me, Lee!" Someone was far ahead, running. I had started to follow when I heard barking. A small gray dog stood in my path, teeth bared, growling. I dropped the shell and began to cry, because it had broken open. I picked it up and saw the sparkling pink diamond inside.

CHAPTER 11

My cheeks were still wet with tears when the buzz of the clock radio's alarm woke me. I don't usually remember dreams, but this one was very clear. I'd read somewhere once that you should write down a dream while it's still fresh in your mind, before it fades away. I wiped my face on my sleeve and padded over to my desk, pulled a sheet of college-ruled paper and a pencil from the drawer, and began to write. *Beach. Seashell. Growling dog. Diamond. Running.*

It was certainly far too early to wake River up with dream questions. Our study was just a few doors down from my room, and I was pretty sure I'd find a dream book there. I had time to grab a book before I needed to get ready for my first day at the Tabby.

"Come on, O'Ryan," I said, picking up a few more sheets of paper and the pencil. "Let's go look up a dream."

He stretched, opened his mouth wide for a long, luxurious yawn, hopped down from the bed, and followed me down the hall to the study. Floor-to-ceiling bookshelves lined every wall, and a small computer rested incongruously on top of an old-fashioned wooden card catalog. Our books are arranged according to the Dewey decimal system, courtesy of my librarian aunt, so it took me only a couple of minutes to find what I was looking for. Number 154.63, *999 Dream Symbols*.

I carried the book back to my room and tossed it onto the bed. Trying hard to resist the strong temptation to take just a tiny peek at the index, I opened the closet and picked out a pair of faded jeans and a yellow TABITHA TRUMBULL ACADEMY OF THE ARTS T-shirt. I'd gathered from my conversations with Mr. Pennington and Aunt Ibby that I'd probably be prowling around in thrift stores, at yard sales, and even in attics and cellars in my pursuit of cheap or free props, so casual dress seemed appropriate.

I dressed and sat on the edge of the bed to tie my sneakers, that darned book just lying there, begging to be read. I'd just flipped it open when O'Ryan appeared and, with one of his cat flops, completely covered the pages.

"Okay, okay," I grumbled. "I'll read later. Get up so I can make the bed."

The cat jumped down and waited next to the door, watching me as I made the bed, tucked the book into my handbag, and pulled my hair back into a ponytail. Then the two of us followed the smell of coffee down to Aunt Ibby's kitchen.

A quick breakfast of scrambled eggs and toast, along with a to-go cup of coffee, and I was headed out the back door to the garage. I backed the Corvette out onto Oliver Street and headed for the Tabby. It felt good to have a destination. A job. A productive way to spend summer hours.

Traffic was heavy, normal for a popular summertime tourist destination like Salem. In front of the Witch Museum, tour buses discharged their cargoes of chattering, camera-toting visitors. Across Washington Square, inside the wrought-iron fence surrounding the Salem Common, the popcorn man welcomed a line of customers, while women with babies in strollers walked along tree-shaded paths or sat on long wooden benches, watching the bigger kids toss balls around.

When I pulled up in the parking lot beside the Tabby, I was surprised and pleased to see that my old parking space once again bore the RESERVED sign with my name on it. I parked and locked the 'Vette, and with one backward admiring glance at the blue beauty, I walked to the big glass front doors and stepped inside. Bypassing the elevator, I hurried up the broad staircase to the second floor and Mr. Pennington's office.

"Ah, Ms. Barrett. What a pleasure to see you once again." Mr. Pennington rubbed his hands together. "Ready to get to work?"

"Yes, sir. Looking forward to it."

"Well, then, let us proceed." He stood and motioned for me to follow him.

Although I'd taught classes in TV production at the Tabby the previous school year, other than a brief tour during orientation week, I'd never spent much time in the Theater Arts section of the sprawling building. A rudimentary stage had been built in the area which had long ago encompassed Trumbull's furniture department. Sharing that space was Scenery, with rows of painted backdrops, piles of assorted doors and windows, along with what looked like a forest of artificial plants. Make-up occupied the former beauty shop;

and Costume, complete with whole families of 1950s-era mannequins in various periods of dress, was housed in the old S&H Green Stamp redemption center.

"Come along, Ms. Barrett." Mr. Pennington took my arm and led me into a square room with an ancient-looking freight elevator at one end. The walls were of rough bare wood. An irregular-shaped pile covered with sheets loomed like a lumpy ghost in one corner. A small desk with a straight chair stood in another corner. A gooseneck lamp and an empty in-out box rested on top of the desk. The director made a sweeping gesture. "Behold! Your new domain."

"Uh, wow," I said, at a momentary loss for words.

"You see," he explained, "the freight elevator easily transports large items from the warehouse at the rear of the building up to this very useful space. So as you unload your truck—"

"My truck?" I interrupted. "I'm sorry, Mr. Pennington. I don't have a truck."

"Oh, we have one for you. Not to worry. As I was saying, as the various and sundry items you find on your search for properties are unloaded from your truck, they are sent up here via elevator, where they can be refurbished or painted as necessary." He beamed. "Then, when all is in readiness for the performances, we'll just send them down to the first floor and carry them into the student theater and place them on the stage."

I nodded my understanding. The Tabby's student theater was a beautiful little venue, accessible from the main floor of the school and also from a public Essex Street entrance. During the fairly short time the school had been open, the theater had gained a reputation for presenting some professional-quality plays.

"What are the three plays you've decided on for the summer performances?" I asked. "I think you said you'd give me copies."

"I did indeed," he said. "First will be *Hobson's Choice*. We'll be giving it a 1930s setting and I've already begun gathering props for that one." He pointed to the sheet-covered mound in the corner. "I didn't have to go far." He beamed. "The action takes place in a cobbler's shop, so all I had to do was raid your classroom of shoe-related memorabilia."

"I wondered what had become of it all," I said. "What's the next one?"

"The easiest one of all. *Our Town*. Virtually no scenery at all! All we need is lots of chairs and a few boards."

"And the third?"

"It's another period piece. Takes place in the nineteen forties. *Born Yesterday*. Know it?"

"I've never actually seen it performed onstage, but I'm sure Aunt Ibby has the movie. I'll watch it."

"Fine, fine. Come along, then, down to my office, and I'll give you the plays to study." He took my arm once again and steered me past the wooden cage that served as a freight elevator. "I'll give you the keys to your truck, too. It's not a pretty thing, but serviceable. It must have belonged to one of the Trumbull boys, I guess. The engine is good, and the air conditioner works."

"I have my car here, you know."

"Of course. You'll just need the truck for transporting large items once you locate them. You can leave it inside the lower-level warehouse when you're not using it."

"Sounds good. I guess finding props for the third play will be the most challenging. But I'm sure there's still plenty of nineteen forties stuff around Salem. Actually, there's probably some at our house."

"I have every confidence that you'll find everything we need." He smiled, then shook his head and sighed. "I'm hoping that I, too, will succeed in finding everything I need when casting these shows."

"You don't have all the casts in place yet?"

"Almost. *Hobson's Choice* is already in rehearsal, and *Our Town* is nearly ready. There's only one part that has me a bit flummoxed, I'll admit. It's the part of Billie Dawn, you know, the Judy Holliday part in *Born Yesterday*."

I didn't know but silently vowed again to watch the movie. "Well, I'm sure it'll all work out just fine." I followed the school director down the stairs to his office, where a stack of three slim playbooks had been placed on the polished surface of his big desk.

That desk had originally belonged to the store's founder, Oliver Wendell Trumbull. Next to the plays, an oblong silver tray with the monogram O.W.T. held a pen and an inkwell. It had once held a silver letter opener, too, but I guessed that the opener might still be in the Salem Police Department's evidence room. Not too many months ago I'd had to use that sharp, slim little device to save myself from a killer. I looked away from that sad reminder and picked up the paper-covered books Mr. Pennington had indicated.

"I'll take these up to my new, um, office and get started."

"Excellent, my dear. You'll find paper, pens, etcetera in your desk, and feel free to ask for anything else you

might need, and here's the key to your truck." He
handed me a Ford key on a key chain with a yellow
plastic smiley face attached. "It's down in the warehouse. I started it myself this morning, so I know it's in
good running condition."

"I'm sure it'll be fine," I said, with more confidence
than I felt.

Minutes later I sat at my new/vintage desk. I placed
the three plays on the scarred surface, then reached
into my handbag, pulled out the dream book, and put
it on top of the pile. After a tiny hesitation I pulled my
phone from the handbag, too, and punched in Pete's
number.

He answered on the first ring. "Lee? You okay? I've
been worried about you."

"I'm fine, and sorry about all the drama," I said.
"How about a do-over tonight? I'll send out for pizza,
and we can tear into that bureau."

Long pause.

"Well, babe. I'm sorry. Can't do it tonight. Something, um, came up. Maybe another time. Okay?"

Another long pause. This time on my end.

"Uh, all right . . . okay. Talk to you later."

"Sure. And look, I know you're dying to see what's
in the secret compartments. Why don't you just go
ahead and open them without me?"

"I'll think about it," I said, my tone a little too frosty.
"Maybe I will. Bye."

I hung up, then stared at the phone in my hand for
a long moment before I put it back in the handbag. I
moved the dream book to one side and picked up
the first play, *Hobson's Choice.* I honestly had never

even heard of this play, so I checked Wikipedia for information. I began to read.

Hobson's Choice *is a play by Harold Brighouse, the title taken from a popular expression, Hobson's choice—meaning no choice at all* . . .

CHAPTER 12

By noontime I had read the entire script of *Hobson's Choice* and had unveiled the sheet-covered blob in the corner of my so-called office. The action of the play, as Mr. Pennington had explained, takes place in a 1930s-era shoemaker's shop A dozen or so of the Thonet chairs from the shoe department had been carefully stacked in the corner, and Buster Brown, the Poll-Parrot macaw, and the giant patent-leather pump, each one tissue paper–wrapped, had been arranged atop one of Trumbull's old wooden counters. It seemed that Mr. Pennington had done a good job so far, but I'd need to find some old-fashioned shoes and boots and maybe an iron shoe last and cobblers' tools. The costume department might have 1930s dresses and suits. I made a note to check on that and tossed the sheets back over the blob. I started a list and then moved on to the second play in the pile.

My phone buzzed, and I reached for it eagerly, hoping it was Pete calling to explain his strange behavior. Caller ID revealed River North's name.

"Hi, River," I said. "I was going to call you later."

"You were? Any new visions? Advances in the romance department?"

"No visions, and the romance department might be moving in reverse. I had a weird dream, though. Want to hear about it?"

"Sure I do. But first, what's up with you and Pete? Is he coming back to open the secret compartments?"

"Guess not. He says he has something else to do tonight."

"Nothing odd about that. He's a cop. He always has stuff to do. How come you sound so down about it?"

"I'm not sure," I admitted. "It was more the way he said it, not what he said. Know what I mean?"

"Not really. I'll read your cards. Now, what about the dream?"

"I have an idea," I said. "Why don't you come over to my place around five o'clock? I'll send out for pizza, and we can analyze my dream and open all the secret compartments."

"Me? Really? I'd love to. And while I'm there, I can help you figure out your *bagua*."

"My what?"

"Your *bagua*. It's a feng shui thing. To help you relate the areas in your house to the aspects of your life."

I had to laugh. "Isn't my life complicated enough already? Let's stick with the cards for now."

"You need all the help you can get, girlfriend. I'll see you at five. Bye."

The second play in the pile, *Our Town*, was, as Mr. Pennington had said, the easiest one to stage. The

Thornton Wilder classic required only the simplest of props, and we already had a lot of those on hand.

My tummy, rather than the clock, told me it was lunchtime. After tucking the *Born Yesterday* script, along with my props list, into my handbag, I headed downstairs to the diner, which had become one of Salem's favorite eateries for both students and the public alike.

I pushed open the chrome-trimmed glass door that led directly from the Tabby's main floor into the diner. A quick glance told me that all the high-backed, red vinyl–upholstered booths, with their tabletop jukeboxes, were occupied, but there were a few chrome bar stools available at the counter. I hurried across the center aisle and claimed one. I looked around the long room, fully expecting to see some familiar faces. After all, I'd been teaching at the Tabby since the first of the year. I was surprised to find that, other than a couple of instructors I knew only by sight, I'd be lunching among strangers. I shrugged, realizing that summer students and teachers were likely to be an altogether new group, propped *Born Yesterday* against a napkin dispenser, ordered an egg salad sandwich on whole wheat and a Dr Pepper, and began to read.

> *This happens in the sitting room of Suite 67D, a large part of the best hotel in Washington, D.C. It is a masterpiece of offensive good taste, colorful, lush and rich . . .*

What the heck is "offensive good taste"?
I read on and decided that I'd be on the hunt for ornate furnishings, with plenty of satin, velvet, and gilt. That pretty much crossed Aunt Ibby's house off the list,

but there'd surely be some likely prospects in Salem's many thrift stores.

I thought of my bureau. With its simple lines and smooth patina of age, it was far from opulent. What was the rest of Helena Trent's home like? Would a ten-carat diamond be considered "offensive good taste"? Maybe Helena thought so. Maybe that was why she treated it so casually after her first husband's death. The diamond reminded me of my recent dream, so I snapped the play shut and tried to think about something else.

But the only something else that came to mind immediately was a handsome Salem detective. Why had I been so snippy on the phone? River was right. Pete is a cop. He always has cop stuff to do—stuff he can't discuss with me.

I'm probably just on edge because of discovering Shea's body. I should call him and apologize.

I reached for my phone, and it buzzed just as I took it from my handbag.

"Hello?"

"Ms. Barrett? This is Bob, from Bob's delivery service. I have your table and chairs and dishes from Jenny's on the truck, and I can deliver them to your house at around four o'clock, if that's convenient."

I told him I could be there at four, put the play and the phone back into the handbag, paid for my lunch, and returned to the school. I still had a couple of hours before I needed to leave to meet the delivery truck. I put the idea of calling Pete aside for the moment. What could I say, anyway? That I'd behaved like a bad-tempered brat? He had so much on his mind, he probably hadn't even noticed my snarkiness.

This would be a good time to get acquainted with my new truck. I headed for the exit that led into the warehouse garage behind the old store. Mr. Pennington was right. The 1980s vintage truck wasn't pretty—just a plain old, dull, tan-colored regular-cab Ford F-150 pickup. The remnants of a faded DUKAKIS FOR GOVERNOR sticker still clung to the rear bumper, contrasting with the bright new Massachusetts license plate. The tires seemed okay, and when I climbed inside, the interior looked clean enough. I turned the key, and the engine cranked to life immediately. So far, so good. A garage-door opener rested on the dashboard. I pressed the button and watched as the wide aluminum door slid open. I was ready to take my new wheels for a spin around Salem.

I drove slowly onto what had once been Trumbull's Department Store's warehouse receiving lot. I rounded the building, emerged in the Tabby's parking lot, and with one regretful look toward my own beautiful blue Corvette, pulled out onto Essex Street.

I headed down Washington Street, past the post office. I turned onto Margin Street, trying to tell myself I'd chosen that route because there'd be less traffic that way—that it was just a coincidence that the police station was located there.

It's still lunchtime. Maybe I'll see Pete.

"Be careful what you wish for," Aunt Ibby always said.

I slowed down when I saw a familiar Crown Vic pulling out of the station's driveway. It was Pete, all right. But who was that blonde sitting beside him?

CHAPTER 13

I saw Pete glance at the truck, but of course, he didn't recognize it. Or me. I'd turned my head away as we passed one another, then immediately regretted it, because I hadn't been able to get a good look at the blond woman.

I took Jefferson Avenue all the way down to Salem State University, probably driving a little too fast, before I turned the truck around and headed back to the Tabby. What was the matter with me? I was acting like a silly teenager. Getting snippy with Pete because I didn't like his tone of voice, then being upset because he had a woman in his car. She was probably a fellow police officer, or maybe even a shoplifter he'd just arrested.

Preferring, although doubting, the latter explanation, I stopped at the market on my way back, picked up a bottle of wine to go with tonight's pizza, then drove straight to the warehouse garage. I parked, locked the truck, and walked back into the school. Mr. Pennington's office door was partially open, so I knocked gently and entered.

"I've just taken a ride in the truck, sir," I said, "and I think she should do fine."

"Excellent, my dear," the director said, pulling his top desk drawer open. "Here's a credit card for you to use in the acquisition of properties." He extended the card toward me, then hesitated. "You understand, I'm sure, that our budget is *extremely* limited."

"I do," I said, "but it would be helpful if I knew exactly *how* limited it is. Could I have a dollar figure to work with?"

"We think seven hundred and fifty dollars total would be a good figure."

I accepted the card and tucked it into my bag. "Probably doable if I can borrow some of the furniture and get lucky at thrift stores and yard sales."

"We have every confidence in you, Ms. Barrett." He smiled, stood, and shook my hand. "Of course, the gasoline for the truck is included in the seven-fifty."

"Of course," I said. "That's only fair. Guess I'll get started shopping right away, and thanks again for this opportunity." I gave him a big smile and headed down the broad staircase to the Tabby's first floor.

I wonder exactly how much offensive good taste I can get for seven hundred and fifty bucks?

I still had some time to spare before I was supposed to meet Bob at the house on Winter Street, and checking out a thrift store or two would give me some idea of what I might expect to find in my conservative price range. I left through the parking lot exit, climbed gratefully into my own car, and headed for the closest Goodwill store.

I have to admit that for the next hour or so I happily mixed business with pleasure. I bought a plump blue velvet–upholstered chair complete with ecru crocheted antimacassars on the arms and back for thirty dollars. It looked eminently suitable for suite 67D. Even better, I found a great-looking Biedermeier-style bedside table for my own suite. It was antique white, and the curvy lines had just the look I wanted for my bedroom. I put the chair on the Tabby's card, the table on my own, and promised to pick up both pieces with my truck the following day.

I hope the table has the proper feng shui. Even if it doesn't, I'm keeping it.

I found myself humming happily on the way home. I was off to a good start on my summer job, and I'd already acknowledged to myself that I was undoubtedly imagining problems in my relationship with Pete, problems that had absolutely no foundation in fact.

By the time I pulled into the garage back home, I was feeling pretty darned good. It was still a few minutes before four, so I'd be right on time to welcome Bob and my new kitchen furniture.

I paused in the back hall, deciding between the two doors facing me. One led to Aunt Ibby's kitchen; the other, to the narrow flight of stairs leading to my third-floor apartment. The wonderful smell issuing from the kitchen made the decision easy. I knocked, pushed the door open, and called, "Aunt Ibby? It's me."

"Come in, Maralee." My aunt, wearing a red-and-white-striped apron, with KISS THE COOK in black letters, waved me inside. "You're just in time to do a taste test on Tabitha's Joe Froggers."

Aunt Ibby had been working for several months on preparing a cookbook of Tabitha Trumbull's recipes. She'd discovered a loose-leaf notebook full of them while helping my class with research on the Trumbull family. Proceeds from the sale of the book would benefit the ongoing construction of a state-of-the-art sound and lighting studio in the old building's basement.

Big, plump, round, dark, and fragrant, the cookies were displayed on square racks. "They smell great," I said, reaching for one of the still-warm goodies. "What's in them?"

"There's molasses, the dark kind. Some ginger and clove and nutmeg. Salt water and a healthy shot of rum," she said. "Sit down and pour yourself a glass of milk to go with it, and tell me what you think."

I did as I was told. One bite, and I closed my eyes, leaned back in my seat, and gave her a silent thumbs-up. "This one's a keeper," I said. "No doubt."

"Thought so." She smiled. "They have a bit of history. The fishermen in Marblehead used to take Joe Froggers to sea because they never got hard. That's because of the rum and salt water."

"Smart fishermen." I looked at the clock. "Almost four," I said. "Bob's Delivery should be along any minute. I'd better go up and unlock my door."

"Oh, it may already be unlocked," she said. "I was up there earlier, planning a couple of little surprises for you. Hope you don't mind my going in uninvited, but I'm going to a concert with Rupert this evening, and I wanted to get things in place before I had to leave."

"Of course I don't mind. What's the surprise?"

"Oh, you'll see soon enough. Look, there goes O'Ryan, heading for the front door. I'll bet that's Bob arriving now."

She and O'Ryan were right, and before long my new table and chairs had replaced the folding ones. The borrowed dishes were back downstairs in Aunt Ibby's sideboard, and the Russel Wright china was safely housed behind my glass-fronted cabinet doors. Bob and his partner returned to their truck with a check for the safe and prompt delivery of the furniture, along with a brown paper bag full of Tabitha Trumbull's Joe Froggers.

I found one of Aunt Ibby's surprises immediately. A brand-new cat entrance had been installed in my kitchen door. I'd promised Pete I'd get one, so I was pleased because it was there, but felt a little guilty because I hadn't done it myself.

The cat door made me think of Pete, which made me think of the yet unopened compartments, which made me think of River, which made me think of pizza. I looked at the clock and grabbed my phone. River would be here any minute, and she'd probably be hungry. I called the Pizza Pirate and ordered a large pizza, half with extra cheese and half with pepperoni— since I didn't know which River might prefer. I gave the Pizza Pirate the Winter Street address—a lot easier to find than my "Oliver Street, back door, through the garden, up two flights" location. I hurried down the aforementioned two flights and unlocked the Oliver Street door for River, climbed back upstairs, put new plates on the gleaming surface of my table, took the two wineglasses Pete had given me from the cabinet, and sat down for a minute to catch my breath. Then I opened my kitchen door so I'd be sure to hear the front doorbell when the pizza arrived. O'Ryan sat there in the hall, head cocked, tail swishing, eyeing the new cat door, apparently debating whether or not to use it.

"It's okay, boy," I told him. "Brand new and just for you."

He stood, stretched, ignored the new entrance, stalked into the kitchen the old-fashioned way, and hopped up onto one of the new chairs. Downstairs, the Winter Street doorbell chimed "The Impossible Dream," while at the same time the bell at my own back steps played "Bless This House." Hot pizza at one door, River at the other. I stood on the third floor landing. Which way to go?

Aunt Ibby appeared downstairs and admitted the pizza guy, so with a quick wave over the railing to my aunt and a hasty "Thanks," I raced through the apartment to the door in the empty living room, and greeted my friend with a breathless "Come on in."

"Where are you going in such a hurry?" she asked.

"Trying to be in two places at once," I gasped. "Make yourself at home while I run downstairs and pay for the pizza."

She looked around, laughing. "Make myself at home? Where?"

"Follow me," I said, dashing to the kitchen and pointing toward the table. "Have a seat." I grabbed my purse, raced downstairs, paid the bill, thanked Aunt Ibby again, and returned to find River standing in the middle of the kitchen, holding a compass and turning slowly in a circle.

"Looks pretty good so far," she said. "Love the Lucite. Is the stove electric or gas?"

"Gas," I said. "Why? Does it matter?"

"Sure. It's the fire mouth." She put the compass into her pocket. "Yours is okay. It's separated from the dishwasher, so there's no clash between fire and water."

"Cool," I said. "Glad to hear it. Want some wine?"

"Of course. Listen, you need to hang a picture of fruits and food right there." She pointed to the wall next to the sink. "And I brought a wind chime for your bedroom. To encourage passion." She handed me a bright pink bag.

"Thank you," I said. "That might be just what I need." I put the pizza box on the counter, took the wine out of the refrigerator and the corkscrew out of the drawer. "Should I open it now?"

"The wine? Or the present?"

I laughed. "Both, I guess."

"Open your present while I open the wine." She picked up the corkscrew. "We'll figure out exactly where to put it when we go in the bedroom to check out that bureau."

River's gift was really lovely. Delicate crystals dangled on silver threads from a gracefully shaped piece of driftwood. Tiny silver dragonflies tinkled, bell-like, as I lifted the wind chime from its pink tissue paper cocoon.

"I love it, River," I said. "It's just perfect."

"Glad you like it. It encourages passion, keeps a man in your life." She handed me a glass of wine. "Or puts some life in your man. Whichever."

"Oh, there's life in the man, all right," I said. "I was just having a few minutes of doubt about how he feels about me. That's all. Silly stuff."

"Why? What happened?"

I put two slices of pizza on each plate—one of each kind—and River and I sat facing each other. The new chairs were not only beautiful but also comfortable, as O'Ryan had already discovered. The big cat lifted his head and sniffed the air. I saw River slip him a piece of pepperoni, and he lay back down on the seat cushion. Eyes still open, ears straight up, he seemed to be listening to the conversation.

"I guess you already know that I was upset because he said he couldn't come over to open the compartments tonight. I thought he was as curious about them as I am. Then—I hate to admit this—I saw him today with a blond woman. She was in the front seat of the car with him, and I felt a little . . . um . . . suspicious."

"Jealous?"

I shrugged and took a sip of wine. "I wouldn't call it that. Anyway, I'm over it. She's probably just a coworker."

"A pretty blonde? Short, curly hair? Big boobs?"

"I didn't get a good look at her. I think the short, curly hair is right, though. Why? Do you think you know who she is?"

River took a big bite of pizza. "Probably just Daphne. They ask her to come in every once in a while to talk to them about her low-life boyfriend—especially since he just got out of jail. I know all about it because she calls me for a reading once in a while." She shook her head. "Poor kid."

"Daphne?"

"Yeah. She goes by Daphne Trent, but that's not her real name. Got mixed up with that low-life murderer years ago. She says that the cops think she might know where a big gazillion-dollar diamond is. There's been some stuff in the paper about it lately." She helped herself to another slice of pizza and slipped O'Ryan another piece of pepperoni. "Pete was probably just driving her home so she wouldn't have to take a cab. It's really sad. You'd think they'd figure out that if she had a giant diamond, she could afford to buy herself a car."

"Wait a minute. You know my bureau came from the lowlife's house, don't you? We are talking about

Tommy Trent, aren't we? Daphne's boyfriend who killed his wife?"

"That's him, all right. You mean, your bureau came from Trent's house?"

"Uh-huh. That's where Shea Tolliver told me she got it."

"Oh, oh." She drained her wineglass and stood up. "That might be bad karma. Bad *bagua*. Especially since it has that mirror thing, too. You'd better let me take a look at it right away."

O'Ryan had already jumped down from his chair and stood waiting at the open door of the bedroom. River and I followed the cat into the room. I sat at the foot of the bed, while River stood, hands on her hips, facing the bureau.

A long silent moment passed. River reached into her pocket and pulled out the compass. She turned slowly, as she had in the kitchen. She walked to the window, looked out, returned to the center of the room, and turned again, this time in the opposite direction.

"Well?" I said. "What do you think?"

"It's a really nice piece of furniture," she said, putting the compass back in her pocket. "It would be a shame to get rid of it just because of where it used to be." She waved a hand toward the window. "And the furniture placement so far is fine. You could use some plants in here. I think I'll just try a cleansing spell on the bureau after we look inside the compartments, okay?"

"Whatever you say."

"Good. Got any red candles?"

"I've got one of those candles in a jar that makes the place smell good. Cherries Jubilee. It's red."

"That'll do. And next time you go shopping, get a

big mirror. Put it where you can't see yourself when you're in bed."

"Big mirror. Okay."

"Speaking of mirrors . . ." She frowned, facing the bureau once again. "Can I get a look at the black mirror please?"

"All right. Just lift the top section there. You'll see it." I turned away from the bureau and closed my eyes. "I won't look, if you don't mind."

I heard the creak of tiny hinges as she lifted the panel. "I don't get it, Lee," she said. "Looks like an ordinary mirror to me."

Reluctantly, I opened my eyes. I stood and walked across to where River stood, her hand still holding the panel upright. She was right. It looked like an ordinary mirror to me, too. A bright, shiny beveled edge, a perfectly clear mirror, without a trace of tarnish or a spot of blackness anywhere.

CHAPTER 14

I moved closer, peering over River's shoulder. "It's not the same mirror," I said. "But how can that be?"

"If it's a different mirror, someone replaced the old one," River said with perfect logic.

"Aunt Ibby," I said, remembering her promise of surprises. "She said she knew a good furniture refinisher who could fix it."

"You must be relieved. At least you won't be seeing visions in your own bedroom."

I thought about that for a long moment. "I guess so," I said, looking at my reflection in that clear, unblemished surface. "But still . . ."

"You want to know where the woman and the dog were going. What they were trying to show you."

"I think you're right," I admitted. "I must be nuts. I've been complaining about this gazing thing from the minute I learned about it, and now, well, I was kind of getting used to having it."

"Don't worry. I'm sure there are plenty of black, shiny objects around here that will work just as well. Let's open those compartments. Okay?"

"Okay." I knew she was right. "Here we go. Shall I open the one Pete and I opened first, so you can see the coin and the dog license?"

"Yes, please. I want to see everything."

I pressed the tiny indentation in the wood that Pete had spotted and pointed out the compartment with two pockets. "You go ahead and take them out if you want to."

"Oh, I want to." She reached into the first one and unwrapped the coin. "Real silver," she said, placing it on the bed, just as Pete had the evening before, and followed it with the tarnished dog license. "That's nice that somebody saved it to remember a dog they loved."

"That's just what Pete and I thought," I said. "Well, let's get started on the rest of them." I pulled out the top drawer, tossed the envelope containing the directions and the sheaf of newspaper clippings onto the bed, and tapped the back of the drawer gently. "Watch this. There's a false back in this one." It took a bit of prying, and one broken fingernail, but a smooth section of wood soon moved upward, revealing a narrow hiding space.

"Holy cow!" River leaned forward. "Is there anything in it?"

I slid my hand gingerly into the opening and grasped a slim, flat tissue-wrapped item between two fingers. I pulled it out and placed it on the bed. "Want to do the honors?" I asked my friend.

"Really? Me?" River removed the tissue paper, revealing an ordinary composition book, the kind with a speckled black-and-white cover and lined pages inside. She opened the cover. Neat, childlike handwriting covered page after page with rounded cursive letters. Here and there items had been pasted in—postcards, ticket

stubs, and the like. It reminded me of notebooks I'd
kept when I was a kid.

"Some of it looks like poetry, the way the lines are
spaced," River said. "Want to read it now or keep
opening?"

"Open now. Read later," I said, putting the clippings
and the directions back into the drawer, replacing
it, and laying the composition book on the bed. I
smoothed the tissue paper and laid it carefully on the
bolster in front of the headboard. I moved around to
the same side of the bureau where Pete had found the
first compartment, and knelt on the floor. "Here's another one," I said, pointing at a spot a few inches above
the floor. "This is my favorite. It works from a spring
inside." I pressed on the spot and watched as a small
section of wood slid silently to one side, revealing yet
another tissue-wrapped item, this one much smaller
than the previous one. "My turn to open."

I unwrapped the package, trying not to tear the
tissue paper, and revealed a silver picture frame holding a faded color photo of an elderly gentleman. He
stood, smiling, in front of a rustic-looking cottage,
holding a large fish at arm's length. "A nice big cod.
He looks really proud of it. I wonder who he is." I
turned the frame over. Written in pencil on the cardboard backing was the word *Grandpa* and the date *1974*.
"Somebody's grandpa," I said, putting the frame next
to the notebook and the tissue paper on the bolster.

"This is fun." River's eyes sparkled with excitement.
"Could I open a compartment? Will you show me how
it works?"

"Sure. The next two are on the back. Help me
move it away from the wall. I'll show you." Together,
we pulled and wiggled the bureau far enough so that

we could both fit behind it. "You have to sort of pry this one a little. Wait a minute, until I get a kitchen knife or a nail file or something. I've already broken one fingernail today."

I hurried back to the kitchen, grabbed a small paring knife, went back into the bedroom, and handed it to her. "There. See that seam between the boards? Stick the knife right about here." I pointed to the spot, which I remembered from my childhood.

"Wow! Look. It's moving!" I smiled at my friend's delight as yet another secret compartment was revealed. This one held a small, tissue-wrapped blue velvet jewelry box. River gave me a questioning look. I nodded, and she opened the lid. She frowned. "Do you think this is the box the pink diamond used to be in?"

"It could be," I said. "Is that a card in there?"

"Yep. Looks like it." She removed the ivory-colored oblong and carried it over to the window, where the fading late afternoon light was better, and read aloud. "For my darling Helena, the sparkling gem of my life. With all my love, from John."

"Ohh," we chorused.

"How sweet," River said, replacing the card in the jewelry box.

"A real love story," I said.

"So, where's the diamond?" River asked. "Do you think Shea found it, after all?"

"I don't know. It's possible, though, isn't it? It could have been in the jewelry box. I ought to tell Pete about this."

"You think he might want to check for fingerprints?"

"Probably not. We know Shea touched it. She said she'd opened all the compartments and left everything the way it was for the new owner. But I'll tell him about it for sure."

"The new owner. That's you." She handed me the velvet jewelry box.

I reached over and gently closed the bureau's top panel, hiding the mirror once again, and then put the jewelry box on the bed and the tissue paper with the others. "Okay. Five compartments, counting the double one. One more to go. Want to take a guess at where it is?"

"You said there were two on the back, so we're probably looking at it. Right?"

"Right."

She knelt and ran her hands up and down the smooth wood. After a few minutes she sighed. "I give up. Show me."

"I don't blame you. This is a tricky one. Watch." I leaned down beside her and pointed to the spot where the leg met the body of the bureau. "Press hard at the top edge of the leg."

She did as I said, and gasped when a tiny drawer slid open. We both leaned forward and looked inside.

I reached into the little space with thumb and forefinger and pulled out a small unsealed envelope. I opened it carefully. Another photo. This time of a dog. A pretty little gray schnauzer. "The dog on the beach," I said, slipping the photo back into the envelope and placing it on the bed. "It has to be."

River sat back on her heels, then stood. "It's kind of like Christmas morning, after all the presents have been opened, isn't it?" she said.

"Exactly like that," I said, closing the drawer, standing, and pushing the bureau back into place. "I guess there's no doubt that the bureau belonged to Helena. I suppose it came from her bedroom."

"You're thinking the woman in your vision is Helena," River said.

"It would make sense."

"And maybe the little dog in the photo is the one the license belonged to."

"I'll bet it is."

"And you're wondering what Helena and the dog are trying to tell you. Right?"

"Right. But I guess I'm going to have to find another magic mirror somewhere if I'm ever going to find out what she wants me to do." O'Ryan stepped daintily over the picture of the dog, sat on the bolster, beside the pile of tissue-paper wrappings, and looked at me expectantly. "But did you notice that the tissue the coin and the dog license were wrapped in was torn in half."

"Are you talking to me or to him?" River whispered, pointing at O'Ryan.

I laughed. "Both, sort of. But I have to admit, I do talk to him quite a lot."

"Does he ever answer?"

"No. Not exactly. Maybe," I answered weakly. "It's sort of hard to explain."

She held up both hands. "Stop. Never mind. Listen. Get that red candle and put it on top of the bureau. I'm going to try a quick spell."

I did as she asked, lit the candle, and watched as she faced the bureau, raised her arms, palms up, and bowed her head. She spoke quietly, with a chanting rhythm. "May the powers of the stars above and the earth below bless this place and this time and this woman and I who am with you."

Then she turned, facing me, and smiled. "That should help. Thanks for the pizza and the grand opening. It was fun. I have to get going if I'm going to grab a nap before I have to go to the station."

"Thanks for coming over," I said. "I love the wind chime, and I appreciate the spell. I'll try to watch your show tonight. What'll it be? Zombies again?"

"Nope. An oldie but goodie. *The Curse of the Cat People.*"

"Great. O'Ryan will love it."

I let my friend out through the living room door and watched as she headed down the stairs to the backyard.

CHAPTER 15

After River had left, and I'd cleaned up the kitchen, I went back into the sweet-smelling bedroom and stood silently, just looking at the things spread out on the white bedspread. Helena's things. After a moment O'Ryan strolled into the room, put his front paws on the edge of the bed, and appeared to be studying each item.

"Well, boy, what do you think? Is it just a random collection of odds and ends, or does it all mean something?"

He jumped onto the bed, so carefully that nothing was disturbed, and picked his way between the coin and the license, the book and the jewelry box, the envelope and the picture frame, sniffing at each item without actually touching any of them. Then, with barely a backward glance in my direction, he hopped down to the floor and left me alone with my jumbled thoughts and erstwhile treasures. A slight creaking sound from the kitchen let me know that he'd deigned to use the new cat door, after all.

I gathered up all the things we'd found, and put

them carefully into the top drawer, along with the tissue paper. In the flickering candlelight, I glanced at my watch. Time for the evening news. I reluctantly blew out the candle, choosing safety over *bagua*, and left the bedroom.

I sat at the kitchen table, poured myself another glass of wine, and clicked on WICH-TV. The familiar face of the station's longtime anchorman, Phil Archer, filled the screen. "Antique dealer Shea Tolliver, whose lifeless body was found two days ago in her Bridge Street shop, was the victim of a robbery. Ms. Tolliver sustained a fatal head wound. The cash register was found open and empty. An attempt had been made to break into a locked display case, but the perpetrator apparently fled the scene without gaining access to the contents. Police have determined that the killer may have entered and left the store through an unlocked back door. The shop had been open for only a few weeks, and although video surveillance equipment had been installed, it had not as yet been activated. The public is asked to call the Salem Police Department with information about any unusual activity two days ago in the area of Tolliver's Antiques and Uniques shop."

A phone number flashed on the screen. There was no mention at all of Gary Campbell. I wondered why.

I wondered, too, whether I ought to call Pete and tell him about the things River and I had found. O'Ryan wasn't around to give an opinion, so I decided all by myself. I turned off the TV, grabbed my phone, and punched in Pete's number. He answered on the first ring.

"Lee? You okay?"

"Sure. I'm fine. Just came across something you might want to know about, that's all. Got a minute?"

"For you? Always."

Oh, that warm, sexy voice.

"River and I opened the rest of the compartments in the bureau."

"I'm so sorry I couldn't be there for that, babe. Chief's got us hopping around here, between the Tolliver murder and an old case. Anything good turn up in the secret hiding places?"

"It looks as though the bureau must have belonged to Helena Trent," I told him, "and we found a jewelry box with only a card from Helena's husband in it. The first one."

"What else was in the bureau?"

Warm and sexy gone. Cop voice activated.

"Just an old picture of somebody's grandfather holding a fish, and a kid's composition book. Oh, and another picture. One of a little gray dog. A schnauzer, I think," I said. "But I thought the jewelry box might be important."

"Might be," he agreed. "The old case the chief's dug out of the files is the Trent murder. He still thinks Tommy Trent and his girlfriend have that diamond stashed somewhere. Trent's out of jail, you know."

"I know. Saw him on TV."

Saw you with the blond girlfriend, too.

"I should be out of here in a couple of hours," he said. "Would it be too late for me to come over and take a look at that jewelry box? Chief might want to see it, too."

"No problem," I said. "I'll be here. Just come up the back way." I wanted Pete to get into the habit of using my private entrance. I'd even fantasized quite a bit about giving him the extra key.

"I'll be there as soon as I can. Want me to bring anything?"

"I don't think so. I still have a couple of slices of left-over apple pie," I said, "and I know where there are some great molasses cookies."

"Sounds good. See you soon."

"Okay. See you." I put the phone on the table and turned the TV back on. Phil Archer was still there, the same video I'd seen before of Tommy Trent leaving prison playing as Archer intoned the same information I'd heard on the previous broadcast. This time I paid more attention to the vehicle picking him up. It was a black Mercedes, and a blond woman was driving it.

Daphne Trent? But she doesn't have a car. Or is she driving Tommy Trent's Mercedes? The one where they'd found the murder weapon?

I had at least an hour to kill before Pete would arrive, maybe more. It might be a good idea to take a shower and put on some clean clothes. I'd had the same faded jeans and school T-shirt on all day. I headed down to my old room, picked out some newer jeans and a much more attractive T-shirt, showered, and washed my hair. Within a half hour, feeling re-freshed and looking pretty good, I ran down to the first floor, with the intention of grabbing a few cookies, in case Pete was really hungry. Aunt Ibby had already gone to her concert, but she'd left the big brown glazed cookie jar on the kitchen table. I returned to my apartment with a plate full of Joe Froggers and with O'Ryan tagging along behind me.

I didn't feel like watching TV anymore, and I hadn't brought any books upstairs yet. I felt like kicking myself because I'd left the dream book on my desk at the school. Bored, I looked around the room for something to do. I put fresh water in the vase for the roses and daisies, cleaned the already clean countertops, then wandered into the bedroom and turned on the overhead light.

Note to self. Get some soft, subtle lighting in here. That thing works like a spotlight on the bed!

I smoothed out the white bedspread, centered the bolster against the headboard, then stood in front of the bureau, just looking at it. I moved the candle to the edge of the top and lifted the center panel—not all the way, but enough to peek in. The new mirror looked like exactly what it was. A new mirror. I lifted the panel all the way and moved closer, not so much inspecting my own reflection as trying to look past myself, expecting to see . . . what?

I knew from the fairly extensive reading I'd done about scrying ever since I learned that I had been blessed—or cursed—with this "gift" that scryers throughout the centuries had used all kinds of reflective surfaces to see the kinds of things I'd been seeing. Nostradamus had used a bowl of water. Jean Dixon had used a crystal ball. My "magic mirrors" had always been black, shiny objects—first my little Mary Janes when I was a child and later a black obsidian ball I'd found on the set of *Nightshades*. When I'd started work at the Tabby, it had been a giant patent-leather pump in a vintage shoe display; and most recently, the tarnished mirror in Helena's bureau.

Will a shiny, brand-new beveled-edge mirror in a murdered woman's two-hundred-year-old bureau work just as well?

I got an answer immediately. My reflection was still

there, but it looked like a pale, floating etching of my face superimposed on another picture. I saw the sandy beach and the crumbling wall, too, but this time there was a cottage in the background. I moved even closer to the mirror and squinted, trying to focus better, to see more details in the scene. As I did so, the cottage door swung open and a white-haired man stepped out onto a flagstone path.

At that moment the back door chimes rang out, and the vision—if that was what it was—blinked away. Nothing there but a reflection of me. I smoothed my hair, closed the hinged panel and hurried to let Pete in.

It was clear that he'd come straight from work. His suit coat and tie looked professional, but not too comfortable for a warm summer evening.

"Hi. Missed you," I said.

"Missed you, too. A lot."

We shared a lovely, long, luxurious kiss; then, with arms around each other's waist, we walked through the empty living room into the comparatively well-furnished kitchen.

"Hey, I like the new table and chairs," Pete said. "That's Lucite, isn't it? My grandmother had a coffee table made out of it."

"Glad you like it. O'Ryan likes the chairs. Not sure how he feels about the see-through table yet. But look. He has a cat door." I pointed to the new addition to the front hall entrance.

"Thanks for remembering that," he said, pulling me close once again. "No more cat interruptions."

I felt bad enough about taking credit for the pie, so I ducked his kiss and told him the truth about the cat door. "I was going to get it done, but Aunt Ibby beat me to it," I admitted. "It was all installed when I got home from work today."

"Good for Aunt Ibby." He laughed, and his kiss landed on my forehead. "Smells good in here. You been cooking?"

"Afraid not. It's just a nice-smelling candle." I decided against telling him about River's cleansing spell.

"Smells good," he said again. "But tell me about the job. Do you like it so far? And what's up with the old truck?"

Surprised, I took a step backward. "You saw the truck? I mean, you knew it was me?"

"Sure. Can't miss that red hair. Didn't you see me?"

"Uh, yes, I did," I said. "I just haven't figured out where the horn is. I would have beeped at you."

The part about the horn is true. But would I have beeped it? Not a chance.

"So why the truck? I know you haven't traded the 'Vette."

"Part of the job," I said, glad to be back on solid ground, telling the truth. "The Tabby provided it. I'm supposed to be rounding up props for the three plays they'll be doing this summer. A lot of it involves furniture."

"Well, speaking of furniture, want to show me what the bureau yielded? Especially that jewelry box. I told the chief about it, and he's real interested." He pulled a pair of rubber gloves and a plastic bag from his pocket. "See? Evidence bag. He's serious about looking for that missing diamond."

"Come on." I led the way to the bedroom and clicked on the glaring overhead light. "Do you think it

could have been in the bureau all these years? And that
somebody found it there? Shea Tolliver maybe?"

"I think that's a possibility. But the chief still thinks
that Tommy Trent and his girlfriend have it stashed
somewhere, and that now that Trent's out of prison,
they'll go get it."

I pulled open the top bureau drawer, and Pete
reached across, pointing to the slim blue velvet case.
"That it?"

"That's it."

He pulled on the gloves, picked up the case, and
opened it carefully. "Did you pull up the insides of
the case, look underneath?"

"No. Never thought of doing that. You mean the
diamond could have been hidden under there?"

"It's a possibility. But it doesn't look as though it's
been tampered with." He snapped the case shut and
deposited it in the plastic bag. He pulled out a Sharpie
pen, scribbled on the bag. He put the pen back into his
breast pocket, and slid the plastic-bagged case into an
inside pocket of the jacket. *It must be handy, having all
those nice pockets. If girls had them, we wouldn't need our big
handbags.*

"There," he said. "Mission accomplished. Now want
to show me the rest of the loot? And what's the little
pile of tissue paper for?"

"Just the tissue paper the things were wrapped in.
I'm not sure why I saved it."

He pointed to the notebook. "Anything interesting
in the book?"

"I don't know," I admitted. "I haven't had a chance
to read it yet. Looks like a kid's notebook. Maybe a
journal of some kind. Some of it looks like poetry."

He nodded and touched the picture frame. "Who's the old gent? Any ID on that?"

"Just 'Grandpa.'"

"Pleasant-looking fellow," Pete said.

I picked up the frame and examined the photo. Was this the same old man I'd seen in the doorway of the cottage?

CHAPTER 16

"Did you say something about apple pie?" Pete asked as I replaced everything in the top drawer.

"Sure did," I said. "And there're a couple of slices of leftover pizza, too, and samples of Aunt Ibby's newest cookie offering from Tabitha Trumbull's recipe collection. I'll put the coffee on."

O'Ryan was waiting by the refrigerator when we came back to the kitchen. "He must have heard me say there's pizza. River slipped him a few pieces of pepperoni, and he's probably hinting for more."

Pete took off his suit coat, hung it on the back of a chair, and loosened his tie. "He may have to fight me for it. Chief had us working right through dinner."

"Sorry. This is pretty slim pickin's. Haven't had much time to cook." I started the coffee, then popped the leftover pizza under the broiler until the cheese began to bubble. "How about a glass of wine with the pizza? And coffee with pie and cookies for dessert?"

"Sounds great. If there's still some vanilla ice cream left, I think that'll cover all the food groups." Pete leaned back in his chair, hands clasped behind his head. "I feel as though I should get up and help, but to tell the truth, I love watching you."

"Now that I know you're watching, I'll probably drop something," I said. "And yes, there's plenty of ice cream."

"Lee, can I ask you something?" His tone of voice had changed. He sounded serious.

I slid the hot pizza onto one of my new plates and poured a glass of wine. "Of course," I said, hoping his question would be one I could answer completely honestly. The half-truths were wearing on my conscience. I put the plate and the glass on the table and took the seat opposite him. "What would you like to know?"

"It's about last night," he said, reaching across the table and taking my hands. "When I opened the top of that bureau and you got so upset. You actually turned pale. I was afraid you might be about to faint. I thought at first it was because of finding Shea. You know, all the questioning and identifying Campbell. But I've been thinking about it all day. It was something else, wasn't it?"

I'm not ready for this. No. Pete's not ready for this. But I don't want to lie to him.

I couldn't meet his gaze. I looked down through the clear tabletop A pair of golden eyes looked up into mine. O'Ryan, the witch's cat, almost imperceptibly shook his head. *No.*

Pete spoke again, his voice soft. "It has something to do with that bureau, doesn't it? I'm only asking because I care about you. My God, Lee. Helena Trent owned that thing, and she's dead. Murdered. Then Shea Tolliver owned it. Now she's dead. Murdered. Now you own it. Is it any wonder that I'm worried about you?"

I hadn't ever considered the bureau's history in quite that way. When Pete connected it to two murders, I had to rethink my own situation. "I've never thought about it," I admitted. "But you're right. The two women who owned it before me were both murdered. But they were killed years apart. You think my bureau is connected to those murders, and now it's connected to me?"

"I think they were connected by a pink diamond on a gold chain." He held my hands more tightly. "There's something about the bureau that you haven't told me. It may be important in solving one of the murders. Maybe even both of them. Mostly, though, I want to be sure nothing happens to you." His voice broke. "Will you tell me what frightened you last night, when you saw me looking into the top of your bureau? Was there something in there I wasn't supposed to see? Do you think you know where the damned diamond is?"

I pulled my hands away. "Is *that* what you think? That I'm hiding a stolen diamond? That I'm mixed up somehow in a couple of murders?"

"Of course I don't think that. I'm just afraid that someone . . . someone out there somewhere . . ." He waved toward the open window. "Someone else might think that. After all, you were the first person on the scene at the antique store. You ID'd Shea's partner. And now you have the bureau and everything that was in it."

His words were chilling. I looked down through the table top again, but the cat had moved back over to Pete's side of the table, probably hoping for pepperoni. No help there. "Pete," I said, meeting his eyes. "There was something about the bureau that scared me last night. But please believe me, it has nothing at all to do with Helena or Shea or the diamond. It's something about the piece of furniture itself. Something that goes all the way back to when I was a little girl and . . . something bad happened. The tarnished mirror behind the top panel reminded me of it. I hated looking at it. That's all. And Aunt Ibby had the mirror repaired today, so I'm not afraid anymore. Okay?"

The tiniest flicker of doubt crossed his face before he smiled. "Okay. I guess you're not ready to tell me what it was that happened when you were a child. But remember, Lee, I'm always here to listen whenever you feel like talking to me about anything. Anything at all."

"Thanks for understanding," I said.

"I didn't say I understand." His smile was tender. "But I believe you. And if you don't mind, I'll be keeping a very close eye on you, anyway."

I returned his smile. "How could I ever mind that?"

"Okay then. If we're through with the serious stuff, how about that pie and ice cream?"

Relieved, I heated what was left of the pie, added a hefty blob of ice cream, put a couple of Aunt Ibby's cookies on the side, and served it with a flourish—along with a cup of coffee and a dash of Baileys.

Pete wasn't kidding about being hungry. He polished off that sugar-laden dessert with obvious pleasure. O'Ryan, who apparently had no interest in apple pie or molasses cookies, returned to my side of the table, curled up and went to sleep at my feet. On my feet, actually. I sipped my coffee, enjoying the company of both cat and detective.

"Are you still interested in NASCAR races?" Pete asked, looking up from the empty plate. "I mean, if that brings back sad memories, forget that I asked."

"No sad memories," I said. "Just good ones. I still love automobile races. Why?"

"Chief scored a couple of tickets to the Sprint Cup at the raceway in New Hampshire. He says I can have them. Want to go with me?"

"You bet. Love to," I said. "Just let me know when."

I was interrupted by a sudden motion under the table. I reached down to pat the cat and felt the muscles tense beneath his fur. He streaked toward the cat door, pushed it open, and disappeared into the hall.

I followed and opened the door a crack. I motioned to Pete to join me. "He's heading down to the front door," I whispered. "Someone must be coming."

"He always does that, doesn't he? And why are we whispering?"

I shook my head, laughing. "I don't know. Come on. Let's see who it is. I don't think Aunt Ibby is home yet."

Together we walked down to the second-floor landing and looked over the railing. O'Ryan was poised, ears alert, with hind legs on the floor and front paws against one of the narrow windows on either side of the front door. I waited for the doorbell to ring.

Instead, I heard a key scraping in the lock and Aunt Ibby's voice. "Thanks so much for the ride. Do come inside and have a cup of tea. It's early yet." She appeared in the doorway, stooped and patted O'Ryan, and then stepped aside as a tall, slender man wearing white slacks and a navy-blue blazer entered the hall. I knew that my aunt had left to go to a concert with my boss, the director of the Tabby—and this man was definitely not Rupert Pennington.

CHAPTER 17

Aunt Ibby looked up and saw us standing there. "Oh, Maralee. And, Pete. Come meet an old friend. He rescued me when Rupert had to leave suddenly."

We hurried down the stairs.

"Is Mr. Pennington all right?" I asked.

"Oh, yes, he's fine. Had to rush over to the school. Some sort of plumbing problem. He may stop by later." She linked arms with the man beside her. "This dear fellow is Tripp Hampton. Tripp, my niece, Lee Barrett, and her friend Peter Mondello."

Tripp Hampton extended his hand first to me and then to Pete. "How do you do? I'm so very pleased to meet you, Ms. Barrett. Your aunt speaks of you often. And, Detective Mondello, we met many years ago. Perhaps you don't remember. It was under such sad circumstances."

"I do remember you," Pete said, grasping the man's hand. "Tragic circumstances. You'd just lost your mom. How are you?"

"I'm well, thank you. Life goes on. Although I still miss her every day."

Hampton. Tripp Hampton. This tall, handsome guy with Aunt Ibby is Helena Trent's stepson?

That annoying "It's a Small World" song from Walt Disney World started playing in my head. Helena's bureau was in my bedroom. The lead detective on her murder case was standing beside me. A sheaf of newspaper articles about a woman I'd never met was in my top drawer, along with some of her belongings, and now her stepson was in my house. Small world indeed.

"Come along, everybody," my aunt said. "Into the dining room. I'll make some tea while you all get acquainted."

Dutifully, we followed her into the pretty hexagonal-shaped room and sat at the round mahogany table. There was a moment's awkward silence while we just looked at each other. Then we all spoke at once.

"Miss Russell is such a delightful person," said Tripp Hampton.

"How was the concert?" I asked. "Did you have to leave early?"

"Where'd the cat go?" Pete looked around the room and under the table.

Our laughter relieved the tension of the moment, and before long we were chatting easily, making small talk about the weather—perfect for the tourists; the concert series, Tripp had season tickets—and my new job as the Tabby's property manager, since Tripp had some old furniture he'd be glad to donate.

Aunt Ibby reappeared with a tea tray, O'Ryan following along behind her. After she placed the tray on the table, I stood to help with the cups and saucers, while Pete put the plate of cookies in the center of the table. Tripp pulled out a chair for my aunt and stood until she was seated.

"Well, then, isn't this nice?" she said, pouring tea for each of us from her best Reed & Barton silver teapot. "Maralee, I told Tripp how pleased you were to find the duplicate to your own childhood bureau. He's interested to know what you found in the secret compartments. Aren't you, Tripp?"

"Of course I'm curious." His smile was gorgeous, testifying to either great genes or a talented orthodontist. "I never even knew the compartments were there. When I learned about them, I felt rather like Monsieur G——, the prefect of the Parisian police in Edgar Allen Poe's 'The Purloined Letter.'"

It took a moment for the reference to register. Of course, it was Poe's master detective C. Auguste Dupin who found the missing letter in a cabinet's secret compartment.

No wonder Aunt Ibby likes this guy. He's a fellow bibliophile.

"No compromising letters, I'm afraid," I said. "The things we found were more on the sentimental side."

Pete nodded his agreement. "That's right. An old dog license, a kid's school notebook, things like that."

"Yes. I called Ms. Tolliver as soon as I heard about the bureau she'd bought from me having secret compartments," Tripp said. "She told me the same thing. The insurance company had already checked with her, too."

"The insurance company?" Aunt Ibby asked. "Was that about Helena's diamond necklace?"

Tripp Hampton sipped his tea slowly. "They're still looking for it. It's probably worth well over twice what it was insured for."

"No kidding. If they find it, then the insurance company gets all the money?" I asked.

"That's the way it works," Pete said. "If the insurance company has compensated the owner and then they find the item, it belongs to the insurance company, right, Mr. Hampton?"

"Right, Detective."

I wondered whether Tripp Hampton had accepted the compensation or had held out for full value, in case the missing diamond turned up. I didn't voice the question—none of my business—and neither did anyone else at the table. Aunt Ibby deftly changed the subject.

"I remember going to some delightful events at your home, Tripp. Helena was a remarkably inventive hostess. Do you recall the spiderweb party?"

"I do indeed! It took the whole day to set that one up. I was home from college, and Helena let me help spin the web," he said, a little wistfully.

"A spiderweb party?" I asked. "What is it?"

"It was elaborate," Aunt Ibby said. "I think it involved every room in that huge estate, didn't it, Tripp?"

"It did. Forty rooms and eleven bathrooms." Tripp leaned toward me. "There were big piles of red silk cord, the thick, soft kind, one for each guest. Helena attached a gift to the end of each length of cord and hid it somewhere in the house. Then we wandered around, tangling the cords from room to room, weaving them around furniture and lamps. We did one for every guest, of course—I think there were around twenty or so—and the result was an enormous spiderweb. You were handed the other end of your cord, with a name tag attached, as soon as you entered the front door, and you had to follow it all the way to the end to get your gift." His perfect smile was blazing full blast.

Aunt Ibby nodded. "And that involved a lot of

bumping into other guests, crawling around on the carpet, or reaching up over someone's head. It was a fabulous icebreaker!"

"Yes, that was a good one, all right," Tripp said. "Helena loved that kind of thing. Even my birthday parties always involved some kind of puzzle or riddle or treasure hunt. She was a trickster, Helena was." He looked in Pete's direction. "Did you ever meet my stepmother, Detective? She liked mysteries. You two would have gotten along swimmingly."

"I met her once," Pete said. "A generous lady. She used to donate to the Police Athletic League every year. She came out to the hockey rink to present a check to the kids on the team I was coaching. Paid for new uniforms for every kid there."

"She was an angel," Tripp said, looking down, smile gone. "An angel."

An awkward silence was broken by O'Ryan streaking toward the front hall.

"Rupert must be here." My aunt hurriedly pushed her chair back and stood. "Excuse me."

"I didn't hear the bell," Tripp said. "Did you?"

"They don't need a doorbell here," Pete said. "The cat always knows when someone's coming. I didn't believe it, either, at first. But I've seen him do it so many times, I'm convinced. Lee says it's because he used to be a witch's cat."

Tripp chuckled. "A witch's cat, hmmm? Thought they were always black."

Aunt Ibby and O'Ryan were right, of course, and Mr. Pennington joined us in the dining room. "Good evening, all," he said, taking a seat beside my aunt. "Sorry I had to be called away like that."

"Is everything all right at the school?" I asked.

"Yes indeed. All is well, my dear. Thank you for asking."

"What was the problem?" Pete asked.

"Someone phoned in a false alarm, Detective. Nothing of concern at all."

"I'm so pleased to hear that, Rupert." Aunt Ibby poured a cup of tea and placed it in front of him. "I'm sorry you had to leave us, but Tripp and I had a nice chat on the way home. Renewing an old acquaintance is always pleasant."

"I'm afraid I'll have to be leaving now, Miss Russell." Tripp stood and bowed slightly toward my aunt. "Thank you so much for the tea. Enjoyed meeting you, Ms. Barrett." Another bow in my direction. "Please let me know if I can help with any of the props for the plays. There's plenty of furniture and odds and ends at my place. Here's my card. Call me anytime." He handed me a card.

"Pete, would you see Tripp out, please?" Aunt Ibby said. "You know how to set the alarm after he leaves, don't you?"

"Sure do." Pete and Tripp left the room together, and I turned toward Mr. Pennington. "I did a little prop shopping today," I said. "I'll be using the truck tomorrow."

"Good for you, and do take young Hampton up on his offer of furniture and such. I'm sure that old mansion must be full of interesting artifacts. The more things we can get donated, the better."

"I will," I said, "and to tell the truth, I'm looking forward to seeing inside a house that has forty rooms and eleven bathrooms!"

"Of course, it's been many years since I was in there," my aunt said, "but it's a beautiful old building, and quite homelike for such a huge place. Helena had exquisite taste in furnishings, too. I understand, though, that Tripp has had to sell quite a few things. The upkeep on a place like that must be an enormous expense."

"That must be why he sold my bureau," I said, looking at the card Tripp had given me. "Jenny said that Shea had bought several antiques from him, things that were too expensive for Jenny to bid on."

"Do you know Jenny? The antiques dealer with the shop over near the Tabby?" Pete asked, resuming his seat at the table.

"I wouldn't say I really know her," I said. "But I bought the Lucite kitchen set and my new dishes from her shop."

"No kidding. Jenny's going to be doing the appraisal of all the things in Shea's shop, once we get through in there," Pete said.

"What's going to become of Shea's merchandise, Pete?" my aunt asked. "Did she have family?"

"She had a sister, but there's a problem with the merchandise—and with the business, for that matter."

"What's the problem?" I asked.

Pete reached for another cookie. "It'll be in the papers soon enough. The problem is Gary Campbell. Seems that he and Shea had a reciprocal will. If one dies, the other one inherits the whole works."

"Oh dear. That makes things messy, doesn't it?" Aunt Ibby poured more tea into Pete's cup. "Quite messy."

"Business should be transacted in a businesslike manner," Mr. Pennington intoned.

"Sydney Greenstreet to Humphrey Bogart in *The Maltese Falcon*," Aunt Ibby recited. "That one was too easy."

Aunt Ibby, looking pleased with her quick response to Mr. Pennington's quote, turned her attention back to Pete. "It would appear, then, that Mr. Campbell would benefit substantially from Shea Tolliver's death, wouldn't it?"

CHAPTER 18

I knew Pete wasn't about to answer any more questions about Shea Tolliver's murder. With his cop face in place, Pete politely thanked Aunt Ibby for the tea and cookies and said good night to Mr. Pennington. "Lee, we both have busy days tomorrow. I'd better be going along. Want to walk upstairs with me so I can get my jacket?"

"Of course," I said. "Good night, Mr. Pennington. See you in the morning. Talk to you later, Aunt Ibby." I followed Pete toward the front hall.

We started up the stairs together. "Looks like O'Ryan's been waiting for us," Pete said, pointing to where the cat sat in the middle of the second-floor landing. "He looks impatient."

"Funny how that cat has real facial expressions," I said. "And you're right. He does look impatient. I bet he'd be tapping his foot if he knew how."

When we reached the landing, O'Ryan trotted along between us up to the third floor, then darted inside the apartment via the new cat door. By the time Pete and I entered, the cat was sitting, alert, with ears straight up, in front of my bedroom.

Pete put an arm around my shoulders. "Look at that. I think your cat is planning to keep an eye on you just the same as I am."

"Then I have nothing to worry about, do I?" I said, snuggling into his embrace. I felt his muscles tense, and he pulled me closer. "Do I?"

He relaxed his grip then. "No. Of course not. I guess I'm a little overprotective where you're concerned. Just . . . be careful, okay?"

"You sound like River," I said. "Always warning me about something or other. And you don't even read cards. Really, Pete, is there something you're not telling me?"

"Yeah. Maybe. Okay, here it is. Sit down for a minute."

I sat at the table, and he took the chair opposite me. "Remember when I told you on the phone that something had come up?"

"Sure. Why? What was it?"

"There was a break-in over in South Salem. In one of those warehouse districts."

"Uh-huh. That's nothing new, is it?"

"I was especially interested in this one, because it was in a place I'd heard you mention. Bob's Moving and Delivery."

"Really? That's the company that delivered the bureau. And the kitchen set, too."

"I know. And, Lee, the strange thing was, it looked at first as though nothing had been stolen, even though there were computers and fax machines and printers all out in plain sight. Besides that, there was plenty of stuff to be delivered. Furniture and stereos and even TVs."

"You said 'at first.' That means you found something missing, after all."

"Right. Bob noticed it. It was a manila file folder that held all the bills of lading, the work orders, for the week, including the day Shea was murdered. He said he'd left it on his desk, and it was gone."

"Then thát means . . ."

Pete reached across the table and took my hand. "Right. That means that your name and address was on one of them."

"But mine wasn't the only one. I mean, there must have been plenty of other deliveries that day." I squeezed his hand. "Jenny told me that Bob delivers for just about everyone."

"True. And maybe I'm just being a little paranoid. But, please. Be careful. Keep your doors locked. Be aware of your surroundings. If anything, anything at all, looks strange, call me. Promise?"

"Yes, of course, I'll be careful," I said. "You're scaring me."

"Maybe I'm the one who should be worried," Pete said, smiling. "Maybe I should be jealous."

"Jealous? About what?"

"About the big, good-looking blond guy with the five-hundred-dollar sport coat hitting on you tonight."

"Hitting on me! You're nuts! He was not."

"Come on. He didn't take those big blue eyes off you for a minute."

Blond man. Blue eyes. River's warning. Tripp Hampton and Gary Campbell. That's two.

I stood up, walked around the table, tugged on Pete's hand, and pulled him toward me. The good night kiss I gave him should have convinced him that he had nothing to worry about concerning Tripp Hampton.

Pete was right about each of us having a busy day ahead. Otherwise, that evening might have stretched far into the night. Or who knows? Maybe into the morning. But it didn't. We said good night at around eleven, and I reluctantly locked the living-room door and slid the dead bolt into place behind him, listening to his footsteps as he hurried down the stairs and out into the backyard. I thought about what he'd said about locking doors. Would Aunt Ibby remember to lock the back door and the door to her kitchen? Of course she would.

Wouldn't she?

I felt as though I had to check, just to be sure. The fact that somebody had stolen my name and address from Bob's worried me more than I'd wanted to admit to Pete. I couldn't very well go back downstairs and cut through the dining room to the kitchen without intruding on Aunt Ibby and Mr. Pennington. After all, it had occurred to me that my sixty-something aunt and my seventyish boss might have something more than a platonic friendship going on . . . the idea of which sort of creeped me out a little . . . but, hey, they say sixty is the new forty.

O'Ryan had followed us and sat in the center of the empty room, grooming his whiskers. "Okay, boy," I said. "We'll go down the back stairs, check and see if the kitchen is locked up, dead bolt the back door, and set the alarm. Come on."

I unlocked my door, tiptoed into the hall, and headed down the narrow staircase. "Never noticed before how creaky these stairs are," I told the cat, who said, "Mrow," which I guessed meant something like "Uh-huh" in O'Ryanese. We rounded the corner onto the second floor, and I looked down into the dimly lit entry hall. O'Ryan looked up at me, then moved ahead and started down the final flight. "Dear cat," I said, "thanks for leading the way."

Making a mental note to replace all the lightbulbs with a lot more wattage, I pulled on the kitchen door, determined that it was secure, then opened the one leading to the yard. Pete had pressed the button in the doorknob, locking it, but the dead bolt and the alarm weren't engaged. The streetlights from Oliver Street cast long shadows across our garden, making the tall row of sunflowers, bowing silently in the breeze, look like alien things, while the leaves of the maple tree whispered against the side of the garage. The cat stepped outside, looked from left to right, then up at me. Apparently satisfied that all was well, he returned to the hall and started up the stairs. I clicked the dead bolt into place, set the alarm, and followed him, hurrying back to my apartment.

I put on my pajamas, turned on the TV, and sat at the kitchen table, mentally adding "buy TV for the bedroom" to my to-do list. I caught the last half of the late news, tuning in just in time to see a close-up shot of Tommy Trent emerging from the courthouse. The news anchor, sounding just a tad surprised, announced that Trent had engaged an attorney and was attempting to regain "certain personal possessions" that had been left in his rooms in the Hampton mansion at the time of his arrest for the murder of his wife.

"Wow. What a nerve," I said aloud, assuming that O'Ryan was listening, even though his eyes were closed. I peered more closely at the image of the man, who'd somehow acquired a tan since his release from prison. He was handsome, no question. I could see why Helena had been attracted to him. Sun-streaked blond hair and the tan made his confident smile very white.

Another blond man? What about his eyes?

The camera moved in. *Yep. Blue, no doubt.*

That makes three.

CHAPTER 19

The next day, I got an early start for the Tabby and decided to have breakfast in the diner. I parked the 'Vette, picked up a copy of the *Salem News* from the vending machine outside the restaurant, and chose a seat at the counter. I'd just ordered coffee and a bagel and started to read page one when I heard my name called.

"Ms. Barrett? Lee?"

I turned and saw the smiling face of Jenny, the antiques dealer. "I thought that was you," she said. "Did you get everything okay?"

"Sure did, Jenny. Thanks. I'm enjoying them already. Here. Won't you join me?"

"Love to." She slid onto the stool beside me and ordered coffee. "I read about the break-in at Bob's and just wanted to be sure all my stuff got to where it was going all right."

"I heard that nothing was taken except some paperwork," I said. "Kind of strange, isn't it?"

"Is that right? The paper just said nothing of value was missing."

Oops. Maybe the information about the work orders is confidential.

"Well, I know my delivery was on time and intact. I'm sure your others were, too."

"Hope so. Listen, I got some good news yesterday."

"Really?" I was pretty sure I knew what her good news was, too, but I was careful not to blurt out any more information Pete had shared. "Tell me about it."

"You know I'm a licensed appraiser. No? Didn't I tell you that? Well, I am. And I got picked to do the appraisal of the contents of Shea Tolliver's shop." She bobbed her head briefly and took a sip of coffee. "May she rest in peace. Anyway, I guess I told you business was slow, but this job will pay enough to keep everything afloat for quite a while."

"That is good news," I said. "It looked to me as though there's an awful lot of inventory in that little shop."

"There is," she agreed with a smile. "Should keep me busy all summer."

"What will become of it all?" I asked. "Do you know?"

She looked from side to side and lowered her voice. "Keep this under your hat, but I heard that Gary Campbell is planning to take it over, lock, stock, and Wedgwood. He's even going to move into Shea's little apartment up over the shop."

"Really? Makes it kind of awkward for him, doesn't it? I mean with him being a 'person of interest' in her death, and then being the one person to benefit from it."

"I know. But, like I told you before, I'm sure he didn't do it. The cops will figure it out." She left a tip on the counter and stood up. "Got to go open my place now. Nice to see you. Stop in and see me sometime."

"I will," I promised. "I need a lot more furniture."

"That's what I like to hear." She waved and headed out into the sunshine.

I finished my breakfast and took the side exit into the main lobby of the Tabby. Since the school had once been a major department store, there was a wide-open feeling to it. High ceilings and a broad staircase leading to the second floor gave the place a sense of luxury, and assorted plaques, banners, and trophy cases testified to its current academic status.

I took the elevator up to the third floor and walked through the colorful Theater Arts Department to the drab little domain that had been assigned to me.

The dusty, sheet-covered ghost blob in the corner containing the items Mr. Pennington had selected for *Hobson's Choice* needed attention. I decided to make a list of exactly what was there and then to finish the list I'd started yesterday of the things I'd need to complete the stage setting. I could tell from the collection of shoe store–related props Mr. Pennington had already assembled that he wanted a realistic setting for that play. I pulled the sheets from the pile and began my list.

Around a dozen Thonet bentwood chairs.
One Poll-Parrot sign.
One Buster Brown sign.
One black pump display piece.

I examined each chair for condition, unwrapped each of the signs and the black pump. At first I tried not to look directly at the big patent-leather shoe, still afraid of what I might see there.

Go ahead and look at it. How bad can it be?

Holding my breath, I glanced, then looked, then stared. There were no swirling colors, no pinpoints of light, no visions. That hurdle overcome, I relaxed, put a check mark next to the words *chairs, signs and shoe* on my list and covered the pile once more with the sheets. I'd need a few more things to create the illusion of an old time cobbler's shop. I added an antique cash register, and some more worn-out old shoes to the list. I was pretty sure from what I'd observed in the costume department that plenty of appropriate clothing for all three casts was already on hand.

I skipped *Our Town* and moved on to *Born Yesterday.* The only thing I'd found so far for that production was one blue velvet chair. I started a new list. Hotel suite 67D would need a 1940s-type bar, couches, tables, bookcases, lamps, an old-style telephone—just about everything mentioned in the script. This could take a while. If I was going to get all this with my slim budget, I'd better get started.

I pulled the *Born Yesterday* script from my handbag and returned it to the top of the desk, then replaced it with the *999 Dream Symbols* book, promising myself I'd take the time to consult it later.

Turning to the classified section of the newspaper, I looked under *antiques, yard sales, estate sales, vintage clothing,* and *used furniture.* I circled a couple of possible addresses and headed down to the warehouse, shopping lists in hand.

The Ford coughed and wheezed a couple of times, then started. I let it run for a minute and pulled slowly into the big, empty lot behind the school. I was just about to move out into traffic when my phone buzzed. I stopped, put the truck in park, pulled out my phone, and looked at the caller ID. I had to look twice to be sure I was reading correctly. My early morning caller was Daphne Trent.

I offered my usual business salutation. "Hello. This is Lee Barrett. May I help you?"

The answering voice was breathy, almost childlike. "Ms. Barrett, you don't know me, but I really need to talk to you. I mean, maybe you need to talk to me. What I really mean is, well, I'm kind of worried about you. Oh. I'm Daphne, Daphne Trent." A nervous giggle. "Will you meet me someplace?"

"Well, um, Ms. Trent," I stammered. "I'm at work right now—or rather, I'm, uh, kind of on the road. Out of the office. What do you want? I mean, can you be more specific?"

"No. I don't want to say anything about it on the phone. Just pick someplace where we can talk. I don't have a car, but I can take a cab. I'll meet you wherever you say." A sharp intake of breath. "Oh, oh. I have to hang up now. I'll call you back."

I sat there for a long moment, staring at the phone in my hand.

What the hell was that all about?

My first instinct was to call Pete. Why was a murderer's girlfriend calling me? The same murderer's girlfriend who was riding around with Pete just yesterday. And why was this particular murderer's girlfriend worried about *me?* So I called him.

Pete's phone rang several times. Then it dumped me into his voice mail.

"Pete, it's Lee. Listen. Daphne Trent just called me, wanting to meet up. She hung up before I could get any more information. She says she's going to call back. What should I do? Oh. And she says she's worried about me."

I didn't see what else I could do at the moment, so I put the truck in gear, rolled out onto Washington Street, and headed for a neighborhood garage sale over in North Salem. The sale on Dearborn Street looked like a big one, with nearly a whole block full of driveways crowded with tables and hanging racks. I put the phone in my pocket, my handbag over one shoulder, and one of Aunt Ibby's canvas grocery shopping bags over the other and set out on a hunt for bargains. I hadn't really expected to find a shoe last among the baby clothes, books, and mismatched glassware, but at the third house I went to, I spotted half a dozen old shoe forms made of wood, marked five dollars each. Excited by such a find, I gathered them all up in my arms and approached the woman who seemed to be in charge.

"I'll take these," I said. "Do you have any more?"

"Nope. That's it," she said. "My dad used to collect them. He said cobblers in the old days used them to make handmade shoes."

"Perfect," I said. "Just what I needed." I fished in my handbag for cash. I'd forgotten that yard sales didn't usually take credit cards. I'd have to stop at an ATM pretty soon. Another driveway yielded a great pair of men's black-and-white wing tips, and before long I was headed to the next stop on my list, encouraged by the morning's yield so far.

The first classified ad under the "estate sale" heading directed me to an address on North Street. It promised "two rooms full of Grandma's furniture. Old stuff, but clean." If I was going to buy furniture, I'd surely need more cash, so I pulled up to the ATM at the next bank I saw. I was still in the bank parking lot, putting cash in my wallet, when the phone buzzed. It was Pete.

"Lee? Glad I caught you. What's all this about Daphne Trent?"

I repeated the brief conversation I'd had with the woman. "What do you want me to do? Should I meet her? I don't even know her."

Long pause. "If she calls you back, arrange to meet her in a public place. Maybe the diner at the school."

"All right. If you think I should. But why would she be worried about me? That bothers me."

"Bothers me, too," he said. "And I need to tell you that Bob from the delivery service called me right after you did. Seems he's found that missing manila file with the bills of lading in it. It was in his Dumpster out back."

"That's good," I said.

"Not exactly. There was one sheet missing."

I knew what he was going to say.

"It's the one with your name and address on it." His voice was ragged with concern. "I don't like it."

"That's not good," I said. "I suppose somebody thinks something special is in the bureau."

"Looks that way. I turned the jewelry box over to the chief. It's possible that whoever it is thinks the missing diamond was in that little velvet case."

"Maybe it was at some point," I said, reasoning it out. "But when?"

"I think it was there, too. So does Chief Whaley. But did it disappear after Shea bought the bureau? Or has it been missing since Helena died? That's the question. That's why I want to know what Daphne has to say."

"You said that the chief thinks Daphne and Tommy

Trent know where it is. That they'll go and get it now that's he's free."

"He does. And nine out of ten times he's right about stuff like that."

"You know her, too, don't you? What do you think?"

"Sure. I know Daphne—"

A brief ringing sound interrupted that thought. Call waiting. I peeked at the screen. "Daphne's calling back, Pete," I said. "I'll call and tell you what she says."

"Good girl. Let her do all the talking. You just set up the meet."

I clicked off with Pete and waited for the phone to ring again. "Hello. Lee Barrett speaking."

"Ms. Barrett, this is Daphne again. You know, Daphne Trent?"

"Yes, Ms. Trent," I said. "How can I help you?"

"I think maybe I can help you. That's why I called. Will you meet me someplace where we can talk?"

"Do you know the diner beside the Trumbull building on Essex Street?"

"Sure."

"I'd planned to have lunch there around twelve thirty," I said. "Will that be convenient for you?"

"I can grab a cab and be there easy," she said. "But how will I know you?"

"Look for a tall redhead in a yellow T-shirt," I said. "Or would you rather I picked you up?"

She dropped her voice and spoke quickly. "Oh, no. You can't. He might see you. I'll be there. At the diner." The line went dead.

As I'd promised, I called Pete. "We're going to meet at the diner at twelve thirty," I told him. "I offered to pick her up so she wouldn't have to take a cab. She sounded almost frightened. She said that 'he' might see me. I suppose she's talking about Tommy Trent."

"Probably," he said. "Just listen carefully to what she has to say. Okay? I'll check with you later."

I looked at the clock on the dashboard. I'd probably have time to take a quick peek at the estate sale with two rooms full of Grandma's furniture before my lunch date. I turned the truck around and headed for North Street.

It turned out to be a good move. Grandma had been a veritable pack rat. She could easily have been featured on one of those hoarders' shows on cable TV, except that this hoard was remarkably clean and well preserved. The two rooms referenced in the ad were overflowing with offensive 1940s good taste. A chrome and white-leather bar with a blue-mirrored top was the first thing I spotted. There were a dozen or more Heywood-Wakefield honey-blond pieces and cabinets full of chrome cocktail shakers and ice buckets.

I left with a truckload of Grandma's castoffs. The estate-sale dealer happily accepted my school-issued credit card, and I headed back to the Tabby, having spent more than half of my budget on the bar, an atom-shaped clock, an armchair with a base shaped like the Eiffel Tower, a blond end table, and a carton full of barware. I pulled the truck inside the warehouse, backed it up to the freight elevator, and closed and locked the warehouse doors. I'd need some help with the unloading from the Tabby's burly crew of stagehands, but I figured that could wait until the afternoon. I walked around the back of the building to the street beside the diner and punched Mr. Pennington's number into my phone.

"How is our project coming along, Ms. Barrett?" he

asked. "Any progress in assembling the various and
sundry articles that will bring our productions to life?"

"I think you'll be pleased and surprised with my
morning's discoveries, sir," I said. "I can hardly wait to
show them to you. You're really going to like what I've
found for *Born Yesterday*."

"I look forward to the unveiling, so to speak," he
said. "I have every confidence in your ability."

"Thank you, sir. I'll see you later this afternoon,
then."

"I shall look forward to it. Good-bye."

It was almost twelve-fifteen by then and I was lucky
to find one of the diner's smaller booths vacant. I
chose the seat facing the front door so that Daphne
would see me when she came in, ordered a cup of
coffee, and told the waitress that I was expecting a
friend to join me for lunch.

The nagging dream and the mirror visions were still
fresh in mind. Feeling a little silly, and at the same
time curious, I pulled the dream book from my handbag and flipped to the index. Mostly, I wondered about
the old man, the shell, and the diamond. I already
knew, from River's interpretation, about the beach and
the dog.

"An old man in your dream represents wisdom or
forgiveness," I read when I turned to the page indicated in the index. "He may be offering you guidance
on some problem."

I can always use guidance, I guess.

I flipped over to the *D*s in the index, looked up
diamond. "The diamond signifies commitment and
dedication. You may find clarity in matters that have
been confusing you," I read.

Like a nice clear mirror in place of a dark, cloudy one?

The text continued. "Conversely, it may signal that you're distancing yourself from others."

Pretty darned vague.

Rapidly losing confidence in dream interpretations in general, I turned to the word *shell* and found the page.

"You have an inner desire to be protected. You are closing yourself off emotionally, keeping things inside," I read. Finally, one that made a little sense. Was I distancing myself from others? Closing myself off emotionally? Did I need some guidance in daily problems?

I put the open book facedown on the table and looked out the window facing the street. I recognized Daphne Trent as soon as she stepped out of the cab. Blond curls bobbing, she tugged at her denim miniskirt and adjusted the hot pink crop top. She arranged a huge white handbag over her shoulder and walked toward the diner with the easy confidence of a woman who probably wore those four-inch heels every day without ever tripping or tottering. Not many of us can pull that off. *Chalk up a point for Daphne.*

She stepped inside, spotted me right away, and gave a little pinkie wave as she approached the booth. "Hi, Ms. Barrett. Can I call you Lee?" She slid onto the seat opposite me and flashed a smile so sincere that I couldn't help liking her at once.

I returned the smile and told her that Lee was fine with me. "Shall we order lunch now," I asked, "and discuss whatever it is you called about while we eat?"

"Sure thing," she said, adding dimples to the smile. "I'm starving. Have you eaten here before? What's good?" She picked up the laminated menu but didn't look at it.

"I eat here pretty regularly," I said. "Work right

next door, at the school. I usually get a salad, but the burgers are great, too."

"I guess I'll try a cheeseburger, then, with a Dr Pepper. You work at the school, huh? You a teacher?"

I gave the waitress our orders—a burger and a Dr Pepper for her, chicken salad for me—and asked for one check. "I'm a teacher during the school year," I said. "Television production. But right now I'm working with the summer theater program."

"Wow. I'd love to go to that school. I heard it's kind of expensive."

"Kind of," I agreed. "You interested in television? What sort of work are you doing now?"

"I'm collecting unemployment right now." She looked down at the table, smile gone. "The restaurant I was working in let me go. When Tommy got out of jail and my picture was in the papers again, they said I was attracting too much 'negative attention.' That's what they called it. 'Negative attention.'" The blond curls bobbed as she shook her head. "Can you beat that?"

Our lunches arrived, and Daphne attacked her burger. "You're right. This is great."

"Glad you like it," I said. "Maybe you can use this time off to find something you'd like better than restaurant work." I tried to sound encouraging.

"Maybe." Her expression brightened. "Anyway, the summer restaurants are hiring. I'll find something soon. But listen, Lee. I know you want to hear why I called you."

"Why did you?"

"It's about Tommy."

"Tommy Trent? What about him?"

"Well, the thing is . . . I need to know. Have you got something going on with him?"

I nearly laughed out loud. "Me? With Tommy Trent? What on earth gave you that idea?"

"I was snooping around in his stuff. I know I shouldn't do that. It isn't nice." She shrugged and reached for the white handbag. "But I found something. A card with your name and address on it. So I guess you know him, right?"

I'm not speechless very often, but I was at that moment. Maybe Daphne took my silence for assent, because she started talking again, her tone urgent. "It's okay if you are. Seeing him, I mean. I know how he can sweep a girl off her feet. But I just wanted to warn you. He's . . . he's not as nice as he seems to be. Especially if you've got money." She leaned closer, giving me an appraising look. "And you look like money to me."

I glanced down at my yellow T-shirt and generic-brand jeans.

"Oh, it's not the clothes. When you hang around rich people as much as I have, you get so you can spot money a mile away. And Tommy likes money."

I started to interrupt, to deny this crazy idea that I was somehow involved with Tommy Trent, but then I remembered Pete's admonition: *Let her do all the talking.*

"I found this at the bottom of his sock drawer," she said, pulling a white card from her bag. I recognized it right away. It was the card I'd filled out with my name and address at Shea Tolliver's shop the day she was murdered.

CHAPTER 20

I tried hard not to change my expression, not to betray the feelings of shock and, yes, fear that welled up inside me then.

How did Tommy Trent, convicted murderer, get the card I'd filled out in Shea Tolliver's shop, unless he'd taken it from the shop on the day Shea was murdered?

Daphne kept speaking, but I barely heard what she said. My mind raced, trying to make sense of what she'd already told me. *Focus.*

"So I just want you to know. I'm not jealous or mad at you. But I think you need to know he's bad news when it comes to women, even though I'm pretty sure he didn't really kill Helena." She paused, looked at me, clearly expecting some kind of response.

It took a moment, but I finally found some words. "But he admitted it, didn't he?"

"Had to. This is a death penalty state, you know. His lawyer said he didn't stand a chance with a jury. Everybody knows Helena was an angel. Everybody loved her. Even me." She sipped on her drink and shrugged. "Nobody really likes Tommy. He's a con man. He'd already spent most of Helena's money, anyhow. So he lied. Said he did it. Better than death row."

"Daphne, I've never even met Tommy Trent," I said, some common sense returning. "So you don't need to worry about that. But I'd like to know how he got my name and address, and why he'd even want it."

Again, she shrugged, a slight lift of one shoulder. "I don't know. Maybe I could find out for you."

"I don't want to get you into trouble over this," I said. "Especially if he's as, um, unpleasant as you seem to think he is."

"Unpleasant." She laughed softly. "That's funny. That's what a rich girl would say. You're so polite. He's a rat, no doubt. But he'd never hurt me. Don't worry about that."

"Thanks for telling me about this. I really appreciate it." I reached for the card, but Daphne snatched it away.

"Uh-uh. I have to put it back where I found it," she said. "Can't let him know I've been snooping in his stuff."

We both fell silent then, concentrating on our lunches. My thoughts were spinning. I wanted to pull out my phone and call Pete right away. He needed to know that the card I'd filled out for Shea had somehow wound up in Tommy Trent's sock drawer. I was so involved in my thoughts, as disagreeable as they were, that I didn't notice Mr. Pennington as he approached our booth. I was startled when he spoke my name.

"My dear Ms. Barrett," he said. "I had no idea! However did you manage this? When you said I'd be pleased with what you'd found for our *Born Yesterday* presentation, I didn't dream of this treasure! I am overwhelmed!"

He stood beside the table, a folded newspaper

under his arm, hands clasped, smile beaming, his voice
fairly shaking with emotion. Had he been to the warehouse and inspected the contents of the truck already?
Were my morning's bargains deserving of so much
adulation?

"I'm g-glad you're pleased," I stammered. "I hoped
you'd agree with my selection."

"Agree?" His voice rose, so that nearby diner patrons
turned to look in our direction. "Agree? How could I
not? She's perfect! How can I thank you enough?"

"She? Who?" I followed the director's gaze. He was
looking straight at Daphne Trent.

"My dear. You are Billie Dawn incarnate!" He
reached for Daphne's hand. "What is your experience?
Surely you've played her before. You must read something for me." He pushed the newspaper in her direction. "Speak, my dear. I must hear your voice."

Daphne pulled her hand away, cocked her head to
one side, those Shirley Temple curls quivering, pouted
prettily, and said, "I don't read papers."

"Fabulous," sighed Mr. Pennington. "'I don't read
papers.' The last scene at the end of act one, when
Billie is talking to Paul Verrall. Am I correct?"

Daphne looked at me, jerked a thumb in Rupert
Pennington's direction, and stage-whispered, "Who's
this dude? And who's Billie? And what the hell is he
talking about?"

"Uh, Daphne, this is Mr. Pennington. He's director
of the Tabitha Trumbull Academy of the Arts. Mr. Pennington, please meet my, uh, friend Daphne Trent." I
hadn't thought about it before, but just then I could
see what he meant about Daphne playing Billie Dawn.
Although I hadn't yet seen the 1950 film, I'd checked
out the black-and-white trailer for it online, and

Daphne's blond good looks and baby voice would surely work for the part.

"I am honored," the director said.

"Howdjado?" Daphne said, sticking out her hand. "You're the head of the school, huh?"

"I am. May I sit down, Ms. Barrett?"

I slid aside, making room on the red vinyl–covered seat. "Of course. But I don't think you understand. Miss Trent—Daphne—isn't an actress."

Daphne glared in my direction. "Who says so? I could be an actress if I wanted to. Tommy always says that. How do you think I made Helena think I was . . . you know . . . his sister, for God's sake?"

It was Mr. Pennington's turn to look confused. He hadn't let go of Daphne's hand. "You aren't here to audition for the lead in *Born Yesterday,* Miss Trent?" He shot an accusing look in my direction. "This adorable child is not the amazing find you spoke of?" His downcast expression was worthy of Hamlet. "I am devastated, distressed, totally and utterly shattered. She is perfection. I must have her. The play must have her."

Daphne hadn't pulled away from his grasp this time. Instead, with her other hand, she patted his and leaned forward. "Don't be so sad," she said. "I'm kind of between jobs right now. I could try acting. What's the pay?"

I knew that there was no pay involved, at least for me and the cast, though the lighting crew guys surely were being compensated for their work. The stagehands and the ticket-sales people, too. I sat back and watched, wondering how Mr. Pennington would handle the situation, pretty darned sure he'd figure out how to get what he wanted. And what he wanted was Daphne Trent to play Billie Dawn.

With his free hand, the director waved away all doubts. His expression brightened, and he gazed into Daphne's eyes. "Have no fear, my dear," he said. "There are significant scholarship grants at my disposal, as well as a sizable budget designated for miscellaneous production costs. Shall we repair to my office and get down to business? We begin rehearsals next week." He nodded in my direction. "Ms. Barrett? You'll excuse us?"

"Of course," I said.

By the time I stood up, the two of them were halfway across the diner, arm in arm, headed for the school entrance. Daphne turned and gave me a nod and a wink over her shoulder. I nodded back, then paid the check, left a tip, and walked outdoors.

I crossed Washington Street and found a vacant bench in the little park on the corner, right in front of the life-size statue of Samantha of *Bewitched* fame. There, with a bronzed and smiling Elizabeth Montgomery looking over my shoulder, I called Pete's number. He answered on the second ring.

"Hi. What did she have to say?" he asked. "Did you find out why she was worried about you?"

"I did," I said. "And now I'm worried about me, too."

"Why? What did she say?"

"Well, first, she wanted to know if I had something going on with Tommy Trent. Can you beat that? Me? With Tommy Trent? Anyway, she wanted to warn me that if I was seeing him, I should know that he isn't really a nice guy."

"I guess you convinced her she didn't have to worry on that score."

"I did. But, Pete, here's the thing. She thought I was

involved because of what she found at the bottom of his sock drawer."

"Which was?"

"A card with my name and address on it. In my handwriting."

I could almost see his cop face frown. "Where did that come from?"

"I filled out that card in Shea Tolliver's shop when I bought the bureau. The last time I saw it, Shea was tucking it into her cash register drawer on the day she was killed."

"You didn't tell Daphne that, did you?"

"No. I told her I had no idea how he got it."

"Good. Do you have the card now?"

"No. Daphne said she had to put it back in his sock drawer. So he wouldn't know she'd been snooping."

"Too bad. I can talk to the chief about getting a search warrant and just going over there and grabbing it, but that won't prove how the thing got there in the first place. Trent will just say that Daphne planted it on him. Maybe she did. Did she say anything else?"

"She did, but it doesn't have anything to do with murder, if that's what you mean," I said. "Want to hear about it?"

"Of course I do. Sometimes the tiniest bit of information, something that seems unimportant, turns out to be huge. So tell me."

"Okay. This was so strange. You know I told you I was shopping for props for the plays. Well, I found some really good stuff, especially for the set for *Born Yesterday.* Did you ever see it?"

"Sure. American Movie Classics. Judy Holliday. Dumb blonde turns out to be not so dumb, right?"

"Right. That's more than I knew about it until I read

it and watched the movie trailer," I admitted. "Anyway, I phoned Mr. Pennington when I got back from shopping and told him I thought he'd be happy about what I'd found for *Born Yesterday*. So who came wandering into the diner while Daphne and I were having lunch but Pennington himself."

"And was he happy about what you'd found?"

"Oh, he was happy, all right. He was ecstatic." I smiled at the memory. "But he thought I'd been talking about something other than furniture. He thought—"

"Let me guess. It was Daphne. He thought you'd found him the perfect dumb blonde for the part!"

"Boy, you're good. Did anyone ever tell you you'd make a great detective?"

"Nope. Never." I could hear the smile in his voice. "What did she have to say about being in a play?"

"She said she could do it. Even mentioned how she and Tommy had fooled Helena with the brother and sister act. She asked how much the gig paid, and she and Mr. Pennington walked off arm in arm."

He laughed. "Good for her. You're right. That probably doesn't have anything to do with murder. But I don't like the idea that Tommy Trent has your name and address. And I haven't forgotten that somebody else might have it, too, from Bob's missing paperwork."

I hadn't forgotten any of that, either. "How scared should I be about all this? Tell me the truth."

"I can tell you this much," Pete said. "I'm going to get in touch with Tommy Trent's probation officer and ask him to keep close tabs on Tommy—which I'm sure he's doing, anyway. Tommy won't move an inch without my knowing about it."

"I don't want Daphne to get into trouble," I said. "Tommy isn't a man you'd want to tick off."

"I'll keep her out of it," Pete promised. "And maybe you shouldn't mention the card with your address on it to your aunt just yet. Okay? It's her address, too, you know, so we'll be watching the house. And I want you to let me know exactly what your schedule is. We'll be keeping an eye on you, too."

"Thanks. I'll get back to you right away with that schedule, and I'll try to stop worrying about all this. Bye."

I feel a little better. But I'm still scared.

CHAPTER 21

Keeping Pete informed about my schedule wasn't as easy as it had sounded at first. I could give him a general idea of what I was doing and where I'd be, but a minute-by-minute rundown of my day was impossible. We settled on a general outline. In the morning I'd tell him what time I'd leave the house for the Tabby and what time I'd pick up the truck to go on my daily "prop hunt." I'd check with him at lunchtime and let him know what time I expected to get home after work. I found time to do some serious furniture shopping for the apartment, and between a few of the traditional furniture stores, Jenny's shop, and the occasional yard sale, I began to fill up the empty spaces quite nicely.

The collection of properties for the plays was growing, too. By the time rehearsals for *Hobson's Choice* were in full swing, nearly all the necessary paraphernalia for an old-time cobbler's shop was in place on the third-floor rehearsal stage. Mr. Pennington and I stood together at the rear of the darkened space and listened as the players spoke their lines.

"It's coming along swimmingly, don't you agree,

Ms. Barrett?" he whispered. Then, not waiting for an answer, he continued, "We open in less than a week, you know. The carpenters have the backdrop in the downstairs theater nearly ready to receive the final stage setting. Do you anticipate adding any more items? The shop looks quite complete to me."

"We need a cobbler's bench. They were quite popular as coffee tables at one time, so I'm hopeful I'll find one. I'm still looking for an antique cash register to complete the picture, you know, one that will make a nice loud ringing sound when Hobson reaches into the drawer to steal some drinking money."

"Of course. One of those wonderful old ones with the handle on the side and numbers that pop up. Capital idea, Ms. Barrett. Any leads on such a treasure?"

"Buying one is out of the question given our budget constraints. But I know where there is one," I said, picturing the great-looking brass machine I'd seen in Shea's shop when I bought my bureau. "It's possible that we might be able to borrow it, but just now there's a question about who the actual owner is."

"Just do your best, Ms. Barrett. I have every confidence in you."

I'd already asked Jenny about the status of Shea's inventory, and the possibility of the school borrowing the cash register for the seven-day run of the play. She was weeks away from finishing her appraisal, so the shop would remain closed for the time being. Unfortunately, though, there was a strong possibility that the owner of the cash register and everything else in the shop—"lock, stock, and Wedgwood," as Jenny had put it—was Gary Campbell. It seemed pretty unlikely to me that he'd want to do any favors for the woman who'd identified him as "a person of interest" in Shea's murder, whether he was guilty or not. According to the *Salem News*, and to some tiny tidbits of information Pete had shared with me, it was beginning to look as though Campbell had walked into the shop after the murder, just as I had. With the opening of *Hobson's Choice* only a few days away, I needed to know if it was okay for me to talk to Gary Campbell or not. I went into my office, closed the door, and called Pete.

"Hi. Look, I don't want to bother you at work," I said, "but there's some stuff I need to know about. Can you come over tonight so we can talk?"

"Are you okay? Is anything wrong? I'll come right now if you need me."

"Oh, Pete. I'm sorry. I didn't mean to sound as though it was something urgent. It's just that I have some questions. Mostly about Gary Campbell."

Relief showed in his voice. "Oh, that guy. Sure. It's no secret that he's lawyered up big-time. We might not have a case against him, after all."

"So you'll come over after work? I'll pick up Chinese."

"I'll be there. Can you get some of that crab Rangoon?"

"Absolutely. See you around six."

Topic, time, and menu settled, I opened my door and returned to the rehearsal area. The actors and Mr. Pennington had left, so I felt free to wander onto the stage. I inspected the props I'd selected, feeling rather proud of myself. The wooden shoe forms, the shelves full of random pairs of worn shoes I'd found at thrift stores gave a look of authenticity to the set. The bentwood chairs and the brightly colored vintage signs Mr. Pennington had pirated from my classroom looked just right. The giant patent-leather pump had been placed just above the spot on the counter where I planned to put a cash register—hopefully the brass, hand-cranked beauty I'd discussed with Jenny.

The shoe was tilted just a tad, and I reached up to straighten it, wondering as I touched its gleaming black surface whether it still held visions. Or had the new mirror in my bureau replaced this shoe, as this shoe had replaced the obsidian ball on my old *Nightshades* set? Or had it? It occurred to me with sudden clarity that it was possible that they all still held visions for me—the mirror, the shoe, the black ball, the childhood Mary Janes, all of those and more.

I sat in one of the Thonet chairs and stared up at the giant black pump. After looking around the room, making sure I was alone, I spoke softly.

"Go ahead, shoe. Show me what you've got."

The answer came swiftly. First, the twinkling lights, the swirling colors, and then I saw the beach. The woman was there in the distance, facing away from me. She was alone this time. No little dog. She turned and faced me for just the briefest moment before she disappeared around a corner.

There was no doubt now about the identity of the woman. I recognized her immediately from the newspaper photos I'd seen. It was Helena Trent, alone on the long, empty beach, and this time she was weeping, carrying something in her arms.

The picture faded away as quickly as it had appeared, and I found myself staring at the black pump. Just a harmless old display piece from a long-ago store's shoe department. I went back and sat at the beat-up desk in my office, trying to process this new idea. Apparently, like some of the scryers I'd read about, I could see visions in more than one object. I'd already figured out that I could usually turn the visions on and off whenever I wanted to.

It's entirely possible that if I can learn some more about how this whole thing works, I might someday overcome my fear of it and actually embrace it.

"Yeah, maybe," I said aloud. "Not yet. I still don't like it."

I picked up my handbag, took out the key to the truck, and headed down to the warehouse. I still had props to find, primarily two fur coats for Billie Dawn. Real fur coats had been a no-no in Massachusetts for so many years that they were hard to come by, even in the vintage clothing stores. I'd checked with Costume, and they didn't have any furs—and didn't really want any. We could use fake fur, of course, and Daphne Trent already personally owned several of those coats.

Yes, Daphne had landed the part of Billie Dawn and, according to all reports, was a natural in the Judy Holliday part. Mr. Pennington thanked me at least twice a day for "discovering" her.

A used clothing dealer over South Salem had called to tell me he had an old full-length mink coat, and the woman at Goodwill had said she had a fox jacket and a mink stole she was holding for me. In the interest of on-stage authenticity, and in keeping with the rest of the decor in suite 67D, I hoped we could use the real thing, and I set out on my own private fur-trapping expedition.

"You ain't planning to wear this, are you?" asked the used clothing dealer as I tried on the glossy brown mink coat. "People will throw red paint on you, you know."

"I know," I assured him, shrugging out of the coat

and feeling a little guilty about how much I enjoyed the luxurious feel of it. "It's for a play. Just wanted to see if it will fit the actress who'll be wearing it."

"It's only fifty dollars," he said. "Somebody paid big bucks for it back in the day. Where's the play?"

"I'll take it," I said. "The play's going to be at the Tabitha Trumbull Academy of the Arts. They're doing *Born Yesterday.*"

"Oh, yeah. I heard about that. Is it true about the wife killer's girlfriend being in it?"

For such a sprawling city, Salem still has some definite small town aspects, the gossip mill primary among them.

"I don't do the casting," I answered coolly and handed him the school's credit card. "Just props. Thanks for calling about the coat."

After paying for the mink, I tossed it over my arm and, hoping there was no one with red paint lurking around, went back to the truck. I stuck the coat behind the passenger seat and headed for Goodwill. The fox jacket was kind of ratty looking, but the Autumn Haze stole was nice, so I bought it for seventy-five dollars. That finished Billie Dawn's wardrobe and darn near finished off my prop budget. I was going to have to start begging from friends and looking closely at curbside trash on collection days.

When I got back to the Tabby, I secured the truck in the warehouse, dropped the furs off at Costume, and returned to my office. I'd just started checking off recent purchases on my properties lists when I became aware of an unfamiliar sound. I put down my pen and swung around in my chair, trying to focus on where the noise was coming from. It didn't sound like anything I'd heard before.

A grinding, clanking, whirring, buzzing noise. What the hell is that?

I stood and, walking slowly, almost on tiptoe, moved in the direction of the sound. I realized almost at once what it was. The ancient freight elevator was on its way up from the warehouse. I peered through the wire gate to where a pair of woven steel cables moved in unison—one moving up, the other down. After less than a minute the sound grew louder and the cagelike top of the elevator appeared. There was one person inside. It was a man, and from my vantage point, I saw that he had a small bald spot on the top of his head. After a few more clanks and whirrs, the elevator stopped. I stepped back as the wide door slid open and the man stepped out. I recognized him as one of the stagehands I'd seen around the building. A look of surprise crossed his face when he noticed me standing there.

"Oh, jeez. I'm sorry, miss. I didn't know anyone was up here."

"That's okay," I said, gesturing toward the elevator. "Noisy, isn't it?"

"She's an oldie but a goodie," he said. "I'm just checking her out before we start carrying the stage stuff down to the theater." He wiped his right hand on his coveralls, then stuck it in my direction. "Hi. I'm Herb Wilkins. I know who you are. You used to be on television. That psychic show."

I shook his hand. "Lee Barrett. Glad to meet you, Herb."

"Likewise. What do you say? Want to take a test run with me? I'll show you how to operate her."

"Well . . ." I hesitated. "I don't know."

"Oh, come on. You never know when you might

want to take something heavy downstairs. Or when Mr. Pennington might want you to." He leaned forward, as if studying my face. "You are over sixteen, aren't you?"

I laughed out loud. "Yes. I sure am. Does it matter?"

"Yep. Have to be sixteen or over to operate one of these babies."

Since I couldn't think of any reason to refuse, I said, "All right. I'll go," and as Herb held the door open, I stepped inside the freight elevator.

"See? Here's the control panel." He pointed at a vertical board with four round black buttons on it. On the edge of the board, printed with black marker, were the numbers THREE, TWO, and ONE and the letter B. "We're on three now," he explained. "Now watch while we go down to two." He pushed one of the buttons. I watched as directed, then reached for a handhold on the chain-link enclosure as we bumped to a sudden halt. A door outside the cage was marked TWO.

"Looks simple enough," I said.

"Okay. You try it." He stepped aside and pointed to the button marked ONE. "Take 'er down." I did as he said, and the elevator resumed its downward journey. Again, we stopped abruptly.

"You get used to that after a while," he said. "Now we'll go down to the basement. That's the warehouse where your truck is. Okay? Push the B button."

I gave the B button a tentative push, and we headed down. It was a rough landing, but I managed to stay on my feet.

"Good job," he said. "Want to take her back upstairs?"

"I'll watch while you do it," I said.

He pushed a button, and the elevator began to move upward. "See? It's easy. Anyone over sixteen can do it." We reached the floor marked THREE, and Herb held the door open for me. "Got it?"

"Got it," I said. "Thanks for the lesson."

On the third floor once again, I returned to my checklist duties but found my mind wandering to the vision I'd seen in the giant shoe. I knew that the shoe had shown me Helena Trent. No doubt about that. But why was Helena carrying a package? What was in it?

But what had me puzzled was the apparent change in my gazing "gift,"—my sudden ability to see visions in more than one object, whether I wanted to or not. I remembered reading that such a thing was possible. Jean Dixon could do it, and so, apparently, could I.

At least I'd learned how to turn a vision off when I didn't want to look at it. Like when Pete was in the room. That thought brought me back to the question I'd been asking myself for a long time.

How do I tell Pete that I'm a scryer? That I can receive messages, however scrambled, from dead people?

CHAPTER 22

Paperwork, inventory, and play reading filled the rest of my day at the Tabby, and by five o'clock I was ready to leave. I'd secured the truck, straightened up my desk, and phoned in my order for Chinese food. I was heading across the parking lot to my car when I heard my name called. I didn't have to look to know it was Daphne. She sounded more like Billie Dawn every day.

She ran toward me, high heels making staccato clicks on the pavement, the large white handbag bouncing along at her side. "Hey, Lee. How about a lift?"

"Sure. Come on." I unlocked the Corvette and held the passenger door open.

"Wow. Sweet ride," she said as she slid into the cushy seat and ran a small, red nail-polished hand across the leather dash. "Is it really yours?"

"All mine," I said, listening to the hum of the engine starting. "It was my dream car for years, and now I finally have it."

"Must have been awfully expensive, huh?"

"Yes, but it's worth it to me. Where to?" I didn't want

to get into a discussion about money. I don't have any worries in that department, but it isn't something I talk about to anyone except my bank.

"I have to go to my place to pick up a couple of things. Then I'm going over to Tommy's apartment later. Just head out as if you're going to Marblehead. I'll show you where to turn."

"Did you get a chance to, um, replace the card with my name and address on it?"

"Not yet. I'll do it tonight, when I'm over there."

"I don't want you to get into trouble over this."

"Don't worry. Anyway, it's just your name and address. What harm could it do? Maybe it was already in the drawer from the last tenant."

I hadn't thought about that.

I'll tell Pete about it, though. All I know is I gave that card to Shea on the day she was killed, and somebody took it out of the cash register.

"That's probably it," I said. "He probably doesn't know anything about it. How's the play coming along? Are you enjoying acting?"

"Loving it. Old Pennington says I'm a natural." She pulled down the visor and leaned close to its mirror, moving a little finger across one eyebrow, then the other. She ran her fingers through the blond curls, deliberately giving her hair a tousled look, then snapped the visor back into place. "There. Funny how some guys like you to look as though you just got out of bed, isn't it?"

"I don't know about that," I admitted. "In this humidity I have a hard time keeping mine from just looking frizzy."

"You kidding? You always look perfect. Take this next left. That your natural hair color?"

I turned, as she'd directed, onto a narrow side road. Tall trees formed a long archway, and the afternoon sun shone through the leaves, making dappled patterns on the pavement. "Yes, it is. Red hair runs in my family. My mother had it, too. So does my aunt." I drove slowly, looking from left to right. I didn't see any houses on either side. "You're really kind of out in the woods here, aren't you?"

"Oh, don't you know where we are? This is the private road to the Hampton place. You'll see the big house in a minute. See? There it is." She pointed toward a massive gray-stone building looming in the distance.

Thoroughly confused, I faced her. "You live here?" I pointed to the house. "There?"

"No. Not in there. I live in a little guesthouse out back. Come on. I'll show it to you. You'll see the road just ahead." She jerked her thumb to the right. "Here. Turn here."

"Okay," I said, curiosity overruling good sense. "Just for a minute. I have to get back to my place. I invited company." The road she had indicated, which was more like a long, curving driveway, led to a one-story cottage made from the same gray stone as the main house. Ivy climbed the walls, and a row of hollyhocks gave color to the front of the place.

"It's charming, Daphne," I said. "But . . . ?"

"But how did I wind up staying here after what I did?" She shrugged. "After Helena found out about Tommy and me, she told him he'd have to leave. She knew I had nowhere to go, so she said I could stay here until I found a place. Then she got killed. Tommy was still packing up his stuff to move, and then he got arrested and went to jail. Nobody told me to get out, so

I just stayed here. Tripp doesn't care. He doesn't even charge me any rent." Again, the pretty shrug and more hair tousling. "He kind of likes having me around sometimes—if you know what I mean."

I was pretty sure I knew what she meant, but I didn't want to go there. "I just sort of figured that when Tommy—Mr. Trent—got out of jail, you'd be staying with him."

I parked the 'Vette in front of the guesthouse and we climbed out. When we reached the front door of the guesthouse Daphne pushed it open.

No key? She must feel pretty secure here.

"Come on inside for a sec. It's really a cute place. Yeah, I've been spending a lot of time with Tommy. I missed him when he was away for so long, you know? Tommy's place is nice, too. Tripp even checked it out with the rental guy to make sure I'd be in a safe neighborhood and all, but I've kind of gotten used to having my own space. I like it."

"I know what you mean," I said as we stepped into the cottage. "Say, this is really cute. No wonder you like being here." The living room had a cozy, rustic look, with wood-paneled walls and overstuffed furniture in bright prints.

"Helena fixed it up like this, and I've just left it the way it was. It's kind of old-fashioned. There's even a pink Princess phone in the bedroom. But I like it. I still miss Helena. She was an angel."

"I've heard several people say that about her. I'm sorry I never got to meet her."

"She would have liked you. Well, thanks for the ride, and thanks for getting me that part. I really like being Billie Dawn."

"Mr. Pennington says you're a natural."

"You know, in the play, how Paul helps Billie out with how to talk proper and read books and all? That's how Tripp is with me. I mean, he tries to make me into . . ." She gave a little giggle. "Into a lady. So in a way, I *am* a natural for the part."

"I'm looking forward to seeing you in it. I've been working on getting just the right props for the set."

"I know. And thanks for finding those furs. I love wearing that coat." She smiled briefly, then frowned. "But Helena would have hated it. She loved the animals so much, she never would have worn furs. Never." The blond curls shook vehemently. "You should have seen her with that little dog of hers. Tommy always said she cared more about Nicky than she did about him."

"Nicky?"

"Yeah. A cute little gray schnauzer. It about broke her heart when he died."

CHAPTER 23

I made my way down the long driveway, looked back at the guesthouse in the rearview mirror, and wished I had more time to ask questions. About the gray dog. About Helena Trent. And, with some guilty curiosity, about Daphne Trent's peculiar lifestyle.

I picked up the crab Rangoon, egg rolls, veggie delight, and two kinds of rice and had barely enough time to dump them from the cartons into bowls and stick them into the warming drawer before my doorbell chimed. Pete was right on time, as usual.

"Come on in," I said, returning his warm kiss. Then I turned, facing into the living room. "Look. Furniture!"

My recent shopping forays into furniture stores, antiques shops, and yard sales had provided the essentials for a contemporary living-room arrangement. By no means complete, it still lacked what Aunt Ibby would call "character," but at least it was equipped with the basic necessities. There was a nice Oriental rug, a black leather couch with one matching chair, and an offbeat wing chair in a bold zebra print. Jenny's shop had yielded a great-looking vintage glass-fronted barrister's bookcase, which I had yet to fill with books. I hadn't hung any wall art, and the room needed some lamps, but I thought it was a good beginning.

"What do you think?" I asked. "So far, so good?"

"I like it," Pete said. "I like it a lot. When you get through here, maybe you can come over and help me with my apartment. It's mostly my mom's old castoffs and some stuff my sister picked out. Nothing matches."

Is this sort of an invitation to Pete's apartment?

"I'll be glad to," I said, maybe a little too enthusiastically. "And things don't have to match. I like it better when they don't."

"It's a deal, then. Do I smell Chinese food?"

"Sure do. Come help me set the table. I just got here. You won't believe where I've been."

In the kitchen, I handed Pete the plates and silverware, and while he set the table, I retrieved the food from the warming drawer.

"I promise I'll believe you." He smiled. "Where have you been?"

"I gave Daphne a ride home. She lives in a guesthouse behind the Trent place. But you probably already knew that."

"Yeah. Chief's keeping an eye on her and on Tommy, too. Did she have any trouble sneaking that index card back underneath his socks?" He pulled a chair out for me, and we sat together at the Lucite table.

"She hasn't done it yet. But she thinks maybe the previous tenant left it in the drawer. Did you check that possibility?"

"We did. The place had been vacant for over a year. The landlord's daughter was the last tenant, and she moved out before you came to Salem. Dead end there. Daphne have anything else interesting to say?"

I passed him the crab Rangoon and thought about the brief conversation I'd had. "She likes being an actress, and she's apparently been living in that guest-house rent free since before Helena died."

"Did she say anything at all about Tommy?"

"Just that she's been spending a lot of time with him, but that she enjoys having her own space."

"I think you do, too. Mind if I have another egg roll?"

"Help yourself. I do like having this apartment, and I like being close to Aunt Ibby at the same time. She's getting on in years, although she'd never admit it, and I'm the only close family she has."

"I understand. Now, what was it you wanted to ask me about Gary Campbell?"

"I know you can't talk about police business," I said, "but I'd really like to know if he's going to wind up with Shea's inventory."

"It looks that way. I can tell you this much. The DA isn't going to charge him with her murder. Her time of death doesn't match up, and there's apparently no motive there. They were actually planning to get back together—business-wise—and Campbell can prove it." He frowned. "Why do you ask?"

"You'll probably think it's silly, but there's something in the shop I want to borrow for one of the plays, and I didn't know whether or not it was okay for me to approach him about it."

"What's that?"

"The cash register."

"Do you want to know if it's safe to approach him? Or just if it's appropriate?"

"Both, I guess. If you think it's a bad idea, I'll just use a cash box or something." I was beginning to regret this whole conversation. It sounded petty, even to me. After all, Pete had important things to think about, and finding props for an amateur play performance suddenly seemed trivial.

"No. It's not that it's a bad idea," Pete said, evidently taking my question seriously. "Of course he'll probably recognize you as the redhead he bumped into on his way out of the shop and realize that you're the one who fingered him."

"I'd thought of that. Never mind. I'll use a cash box. Forget I asked." I pulled open the flaps of a little folded take-out container that had come with our meal. "Want a fortune cookie?"

"I'll have one if you will." We each selected a cookie, and Pete's expression turned serious once more. "You have a pretty good relationship with Jenny, don't you?"

"I think so. Why?"

"It might be a good idea for you to see if she'll make the request. Then, if he says no, you're out of the picture. If he says yes, you get the very cool cash register for the show. Make sense?"

I nodded. "It does. Thanks."

"I'd just as soon you stayed away from him, Lee. He seems like a reasonable man right now, but remember, he once threatened Shea with some really bad stuff." He reached for my hand. "I don't exactly trust him. Don't get involved with Campbell. Okay?"

"Okay. I promise. Let's see what our fortunes say. You first."

He broke open his fortune cookie, read the slip of paper inside, then laughed. "This is good advice for anyone. 'It never pays to kick a skunk.'"

"No doubt about that," I agreed. "Let's see what mine says." I pulled the strip of paper from my cookie, smiling. "Here's another truth, at least in this household. 'Dogs have owners. Cats have staff.'"

"O'Ryan sure doesn't have any worries with you and your aunt pampering him," Pete said. "Where is he, anyway? He usually meets me at the door."

As though on cue, the cat door opened, and the big yellow boy strolled in and sat, ears straight up, directly under Pete's chair.

"There's your greeting," I said. "A little late, but sincere."

Pete reached down and patted the cat. "Maybe he thinks I am part of the staff and don't need to be checked out before I come inside."

"I think you're right. It's true about cats. They don't have owners, like dogs do. I hadn't really thought about it before, but Ariel never really owned O'Ryan. And I'm pretty sure Aunt Ibby and I don't, either." I paused. "Speaking of dogs, did you know Helena Trent once had a dog? A gray schnauzer named Nicky. Daphne said Helena was heartbroken when the little dog died."

Pete looked thoughtful. "Must be the dog in that picture you found. I wonder if the license we found in the bureau belonged to him."

"I'll bet it was his."

"Did Daphne happen to mention when the dog died?"

"No. Why? Is it important?"

"Maybe. Could I take another look at that license?"

"Sure." I couldn't think of any reason why Helena's dead dog would be important, but I got up, put the dishes in the sink and, with Pete following, headed for the bedroom.

"More furniture here, too," Pete said. "Looks good." He was right. With the addition of the white Biedermeier bedside table, a new TV, and a cute antique writing desk, the bedroom had lost its stark, empty look. I pulled open the top drawer of the bureau, unwrapped the dog license and handed it to him.

"No more mirror troubles, I hope," Pete said, nodding toward the closed center panel. He took a pen and a small notebook from his pocket and copied the number from the tarnished tag.

"No problem." I spoke a little too heartily, but he didn't seem to notice. He replaced the license in the drawer and pushed it closed. "Do you have time for coffee?"

"Always time for coffee," he said, slipping an arm around my waist and propelling me back toward the kitchen.

CHAPTER 24

We had our coffee, I packed up the Chinese leftovers for him to take with him, and once again, we parted early. Pete had promised to pick up his young nephews for hockey practice. He'd invited me to come along, but I'd declined, with a promise to attend one of their games soon. We shared a prolonged good-night kiss and walked, single file, down the two narrow flights of stairs. I waved a reluctant good-bye as he crossed the yard to his car. I double-checked the lock, secured the dead bolt, then crossed the foyer and knocked on Aunt Ibby's kitchen door. She opened it immediately.

"Come in, come in. I'm dying to hear how your day went. Did you find some good props? Rupert says he's delighted with what you've done so far. Have you eaten yet? That was Pete leaving, wasn't it? Is everything going well between you?"

"Whoa. Slow down." I laughed. "You're full of questions. Yes, I found some good stuff today. Pete and I had Chinese for dinner, and everything is fine in that department."

"I'm pleased. Let's go into the living room and have a nice chat. I just made some iced tea. Want some?"

"Sure. Sounds good." I waited while she poured sweet tea from a frosty pitcher, and then, carrying my tall glass, I followed her to the living room. O'Ryan was already there, curled up on his favorite needlepoint cushion on the window seat.

"Now then," my aunt said, leaning forward in her chair expectantly. "Tell me all about your day."

"It's been a busy one, that's for sure. I hardly know where to begin."

"At the beginning," she said. "Go on."

"The first thing that happened was I found out that that old black shoe display piece at the Tabby still works."

She frowned. "What do you mean, it works? It showed you a . . . vision?"

I nodded. "It did. Just a brief picture. Nothing scary. Just a woman's face. And, Aunt Ibby, I'm sure the woman on the beach is Helena Trent. I recognized her from the newspaper pictures."

She leaned back in her chair. "I thought it might be. I'm glad she didn't frighten you. What else?"

I thought back, trying to put things in order. "I needed two fur coats for *Born Yesterday*. I had two leads, and both of them paid off." I described the mink coat and the stole. "Oh, and I learned to operate the freight elevator today. I'll take you down in it sometime, but I warn you, it's going to be a bumpy ride."

"Bette Davis," said my aunt. *"All About Eve."*

"Huh?"

"Oh, I'm sorry, my dear. I'm so used to trading movie quotes with Rupert, it's becoming automatic whenever I hear one. The 'bumpy ride' line is from a nineteen fifty film."

"Now that you mention it, I think I knew that. But

speaking of nineteen fifties movies, do you have *Born Yesterday*? I promised Mr. Pennington I'd watch it."

"I do. I'll give it to you tonight, and you and O'Ryan can watch it on your new TV."

"The props for that play are coming along nicely, but I still need a couple of things for *Hobson's Choice*. A cobbler's bench and an antique brass cash register."

"Cobbler's benches were quite the fad as coffee tables at one time," she said. "Shouldn't be too hard to find one of those. But the cash register might be tricky. And probably expensive."

"I know where there's a beauty I'd like to borrow," I said. "With the pop-up numbers and a bell that rings when you pull the handle. That's what I wanted to talk to Pete about tonight." I explained about the one in Shea's shop and that Gary Campbell would probably be the person who wound up owning it.

"That Campbell person doesn't seem very nice," she said. "Perhaps you should avoid contacting him—cash register or not."

"That's what Pete thinks, too. I'm going to ask Jenny to see about our getting it for the play."

"Good idea. You listen to Pete."

"I will," I promised. "Something else pretty interesting happened today, too. I gave Daphne a ride home. Guess where she lives."

"I have no idea. But I do know that Rupert is delighted with her portrayal of Billie Dawn."

"She lives in the Hampton guesthouse. She's been there since before Helena died. Without ever paying any rent."

"That's an odd arrangement, isn't it? Whatever is Tripp thinking?" She put her hand to her mouth. "Oh, dear. You mean Daphne and Tripp Hampton . . . may have some sort of relationship?"

"Could be, I guess. None of my business. But, anyway, Daphne told me that Helena had a little gray dog named Nicky. Did you know that?"

"Now that you mention it, I do remember seeing a small dog when I went to that spiderweb party. Helena had dressed him up as a spider in a gray sweater with little gray velvet legs sticking out. So cute."

"I think Nicky is the dog in my vision," I told her, "and Pete thinks the dog license we found in the bureau belonged to him. Pete copied the numbers from the tag tonight, but he wouldn't tell me why they might be important. What do you think?"

"There are several things he can learn from those numbers." She put down her glass of tea and counted on her fingers. "The license bureau will tell him what kind of dog it was, the dog's name and age, if he'd had all his shots, and in what year he died." She shrugged and picked up her glass. "Of course, I have no idea why any of that would be important now."

"I don't, either. Well, if you'll lend me that movie, I'll do my homework and watch it. Thanks for the tea." I stood up. "Come on, O'Ryan. Let's go home."

"I'm so glad you're thinking of the apartment as home," she said. "It's beginning to take shape nicely. A few more books, some pictures on the walls, some lamps and plants, and a few little tchotchkes, and it'll be a perfect reflection of you."

"Speaking of reflections, River says that for proper feng shui, I need a large mirror in the bedroom, placed so that I can't see myself in it from the bed. I know I need a full-length mirror in there, anyway, but I'm getting kind of skittish about mirrors in general."

"There are mirrors everywhere, dear. I doubt that very many of them are . . . special." She stood and crossed over to the long bookshelf under one of the bay windows where her collection of DVDs was filed alphabetically. "Here you go. *Born Yesterday*. A great film. Enjoy."

O'Ryan and I did enjoy the movie. At least I did. O'Ryan stayed awake through the whole thing, which I took to mean he liked it. I was glad I'd kept my word to Mr. Pennington about watching it, and when I saw him at the Tabby the next morning, I was able to sound a lot more knowledgeable about the production. After seeing the movie set, I was happy about my prop selections so far, and I could definitely see why Daphne Trent was a natural for the Judy Holliday part.

"Would you like to watch Daphne in rehearsal, Ms. Barrett?" the director asked. "We've moved the *Hobson's Choice* set downstairs to the theater, and the *Born Yesterday* set is ready up here."

"I'd love to watch. Thank you."

"Bear in mind, though, that she's just in the process of learning her lines, so don't expect perfection . . . yet. With a little more practice, her performance will be smooth as silk." He looked at his watch. "She'll be here in an hour or so. I'll let you know when to come over to the rehearsal stage."

"I'll be in my office," I said. "My aunt is contacting some of her Twitter friends, in search of a cobbler's bench for *Hobson's*, and I'm still working on getting an authentic cash register."

"I have every confidence in you, Ms. Barrett," he said, with one of his courtly little bows. "Every confidence."

I'd left a few small items in the truck overnight, nothing too heavy for me to carry by myself, so I took my first solo trip down to the warehouse in the freight elevator. It was, as I'd told my aunt, a bumpy ride. I wondered if, with a little more practice, to quote Mr. Pennington, my elevator performance would be "smooth as silk." The ride back up to the third floor wasn't much better than the ride down, and I had to steady a couple of cartons with one hand while pushing buttons with the other. I was relieved when the wooden cage shuddered to a stop at the far end of my office space. I picked up one of the cartons and stepped out onto the floor. My relief at landing there safely was short lived.

Over the top of the corrugated brown box, I looked straight into the flushed and angry face of Tommy Trent. I looked around the room. Nobody else there. I was alone with a convicted murderer—and from the look on his face, I was alone with a very angry convicted murderer.

"What do you want?" My voice came out as a squeak. I took a deep breath and tried again. "Please leave!" That sounded stronger, but pretty stupid under the circumstances.

"What the hell is this all about?" He waved a wrinkled index card close to my face. I was glad to have the carton between us and clutched it more tightly to my chest. I recognized the card, of course. It was the one with my name and address on it. The one that was supposed to be safely reposing in the murderer's sock drawer.

"Where did you get that?" I tried to match his angry tone. Shifting the carton to one arm, I reached for the card with the other. "I gave that card to Shea Tolliver. It's none of your business. Give it to me!"

He pulled the card away and took a step back. "Look, lady, I don't know what your game is, but I caught my girlfriend sneaking this into my bureau last night. Who the hell are you, and what does Shea Tolliver have to do with it? Who put Daphne up to this? She's too friggin' dumb to think anything up all by herself."

I took a chance and turned away from him, walked as steadily as I could manage to my desk, put the carton down, and sat in my chair, back to the wall. At least now the desk was between us, and my phone was right next to my hand. He had followed close behind me and now stood on the opposite side of the desk, jaw thrust forward, blue eyes narrowed.

I tried to remember exactly what I'd packed in the carton that now formed a flimsy barrier between me and Tommy Trent. Was there anything in it, near the top, that would serve as a weapon if this scene turned really ugly? If I risked a quick glance down at the box, would he guess what I was thinking? I was pretty sure he wouldn't have a gun. A convict so recently out of jail wouldn't have one, would he? What about a knife? They were easy enough to come by. There was a chrome cocktail shaker in there. I was sure of that. A pretty heavy one. Could I reach it in time to disable a murderer?

This frightening thought process was interrupted by the ringing of my phone. I grabbed it and yelled, "Help!"

CHAPTER 25

Running feet, loud voices, slamming doors. In an instant my office was full of people and noise.

"What's going on?"

"Are you all right?"

"Who's this guy?"

Tommy Trent, his expression changing from anger to surprise, held his hands over his head—probably a reflex action from years in jail, since no one was aiming a gun at him. Mr. Pennington was at my side, murmuring comforting words. My elevator friend, Herb Wilkins, and one of the very large stagehands had positioned themselves on either side of Tommy, while Daphne, on tiptoe, resplendent in Autumn Haze mink, reached up and grabbed the index card from his upraised hand and then shook a finger at him.

"Tommy, you big jerk! I told you she doesn't know how that thing got there. I figured maybe you were fooling around with her. Now look what you've done. You probably scared poor Lee to death!"

"You want me to call the cops, Ms. Barrett?" Herb Wilkins asked. "Did this guy hurt you?"

"No," I croaked. "I'm okay. He just . . . startled me. He was in here when I got off the elevator."

"No cops," Daphne said. "He's on probation, and he didn't do nothing wrong. Mr. Pennington, don't let them call the cops, okay?"

"Anything. It's 'anything wrong,' my dear," Mr. Pennington replied, correcting her gently. "And if Ms. Barrett has suffered no ill effects from this unfortunate encounter . . ."

"I'm fine. No problem." My voice had returned by then, along with a certain amount of reason. Either Tommy Trent was as surprised to find the card in his bureau as he seemed or he was an even better actor than Daphne. Either way, he hadn't actually threatened me or attempted to harm me. "I was just frightened, seeing him standing there when I got off the elevator," I said.

Daphne came around to my side of the desk. "I'm sorry, Lee," she said. "He's such a big jerk. I tried to talk him into staying away from you. But he wouldn't hurt a flea. Honest." She handed me the index card.

I wasn't sure about the safety of fleas or anything else around the convicted murderer, who had lowered his hands and now looked cocky and sure of himself, but I agreed that the situation didn't merit a call to the police. I had the damned card back. I'd give it to Pete, and he could take it from there.

One by one the people who'd crowded into my office, who'd answered my cry for help, and who'd each assured me that it was no trouble at all returned to the rehearsal area. Tommy Trent left with them, but not without a backward, unsmiling glare in my direction. It was clear that he didn't like me one bit, and I was sure my returning look told him that the feeling was mutual.

Mr. Pennington popped back into the room. "We're about ready for rehearsal. Do you still want to watch?"

"I certainly do," I said. "I'll be there in just a minute."

I called Pete and was surprised when he answered on the first ring. "Lee? You okay? I was just going to call you. Tommy Trent's been spotted hanging around the Trumbull building."

"Yes, I know. We've already met."

"He's there?"

"Not now. Don't worry. I'm fine. He'd found the card with my name and address on it and wanted to know what it meant. Says he caught Daphne sneaking it into his drawer," I said, trying hard to sound calm. "I have the card now."

Long pause on Pete's end of the phone. I waited.

"So Tommy claims he didn't put the card in the drawer?"

"Not in so many words. He just wanted to know what was going on and who had put Daphne up to planting the card there."

"Did you believe him?"

"No. Yes. Maybe. I'm not sure. I was really scared, Pete. I was just getting out of the freight elevator, and there he was, waving the card around. He sounded so angry. Maybe he really didn't know anything about it." Another thought popped into my head. "If he didn't have the card in the first place, where did Daphne get it?"

"I don't know. Looks like it may be time for another long talk with Miss Daphne. You sure you're all right?"

"I'm good. Really. You don't have to worry. Tommy's gone, and I promised Mr. Pennington I'd watch a rehearsal. Gotta go. Talk to you later."

"Okay. If you're sure you're all right. I'll call you tonight."

"I'm sure. Bye."

I wasn't sure at all, and Pete, good cop that he is, probably knew it. But I put on a happy face, pushed open the office door, and walked—head up, shoulders back—to the darkened area in front of the rehearsal stage where Mr. Pennington waited.

"Ah, Ms. Barrett. I think you're going to be pleasantly surprised by the progress we've made so far." He motioned to one of the stagehands. "Lights, please." The stage was instantly illuminated. Not all the furniture I'd bought for suite 67D was in place yet, but the general effect, from the blue velvet chair to the chrome and white-leather bar to the gilded telephone, was offensive good taste, no question.

The male lead entered first, inspecting the room. "Not bad, huh?" he said.

Daphne followed, looking absolutely gorgeous. She wore the mink coat and carried the stole, a large box of chocolates, and an armful of movie magazines. She walked around the blue chair without enthusiasm and gave a pretty shrug. "It's all right."

Some of the players still peeked at their scripts as they spoke. It was, after all, still quite early in the rehearsal schedule. But Daphne moved through the scene with ease, taking suggestions from the director, even helping other actors with a whispered prompt on occasion. I could see why Mr. Pennington was so enthused about her. She was, indeed, a natural.

At the close of the first scene, when the director called for a lunch break, I was surprised to hear a burst of applause and a shrill whistle from the darkened recesses of the performance area.

"Good job, honey! You'll knock 'em dead!" I turned and saw a beaming Tommy Trent rushing toward the stage. Daphne ran into his waiting arms.

"Don't mess up my make-up," she warned, lifting her face for a long kiss. "Did you really like it?"

"You're fabulous, doll," he told her. "I always told you, you can do anything!"

This from the man who'd just said, 'She's too friggin' dumb to think anything up by herself'?

The pair headed, arm in arm, for the stairs.

This was a much different Tommy Trent from the glowering, threatening man I'd encountered less than an hour earlier. As they passed me, the stage light blinked off, just glinting for an instant on the two blond heads, hers against his broad shoulder.

What a beautiful couple, I thought. Then I remembered saying the same thing about a photo of Tommy and Helena. That hadn't worked out well for Helena, and I felt a momentary chill of fear for Daphne.

"Well, what do you think of your discovery, Ms. Barrett? Is she not a gifted actress?" Mr. Pennington watched as the elevator door closed behind the couple. "Of course, we're just at the beginning of the production. It will continue to improve."

"She's your discovery, Mr. Pennington," I said. "I just made the introductions. But yes, she's a wonderful Billie Dawn."

"Have you quite recovered from this morning's unpleasantness, Ms. Barrett?" he asked, concern evident in his expression. "You appeared quite distraught. Perhaps you should take the afternoon off."

"Thank you, sir. I think I'll take you up on that."

"You go right ahead," he said. "By the way, any progress on finding a cash register for *Hobson's?*"

"Still working on that," I told him. "I haven't given up hope."

"Hope is a good thing, maybe the best of things, and no good thing ever dies." Mr. Pennington paused and gave me one of those quizzical looks he gets when he expects someone to identify one of his old movie quotes. I'm afraid I responded with a blank look and a helpless gesture.

"Oh, my dear, your aunt would have had that one in a second! Morgan Freeman in *The Shawshank Redemption,* 1994."

"Of course," I said, snapping my fingers. "I should have had it. I'll be leaving now. Thanks so much for inviting me to the rehearsal. Enjoyed it."

I hurried out to the parking lot, stopping in the doorway for a moment to look around for Tommy Trent's Mercedes. I didn't see it, or him, and climbed quickly into the comfort of my beloved Corvette. I snapped the locks down, pulled out onto Washington Street, and headed for home.

I found a blue sticky note pasted onto the door of my apartment. Aunt Ibby's neat, round-lettered handwriting informed me that she'd received a tweet from Tripp Hampton offering a cobbler's bench coffee table, if I still needed one for the play. She'd jotted down his telephone number. I pulled the note from the door and carried it into the apartment, where O'Ryan sat looking up at me, head cocked, golden eyes bright.

"What do you think of that, cat?" I asked. "Should I

call Mr. Hampton the Third and take him up on his kind offer?"

O'Ryan moved his head from side to side, which could mean "No" or "I don't care" or "A flea is biting the side of my neck." I chose to interpret it as "I don't care," tossed my handbag onto the new living-room couch, sat down, and called the number on the blue square. It rang several times, and I was about to hang up when Tripp answered.

"Hampton residence. Tripp Hampton speaking."

"Hello. Tripp? This is Lee Barrett. You left a message for me with my aunt? Isobel Russell?"

"Of course, Ms. Barrett. Lee. I understand you have a need for an old cobbler's bench coffee table."

"Sure do," I said. "My aunt says you have one we could borrow."

"That's right, and you're most welcome to it. I'd happily deliver it to you, but I don't have an appropriate vehicle at the moment."

"No problem. The school has provided me with a truck. It's not a pretty thing, but it'll do the job. When would be a convenient time for me to pick it up?"

"I have quite a busy schedule," he said. "Let me check my calendar." There was a short pause before he returned to the line. "Could you possibly make it tomorrow evening? Around seven o'clock? I have meetings with investment clients all week, but most evenings are free."

"I'm sure Mr. Pennington won't mind if I use the truck after business hours. Yes. Sure. I can do that."

"Excellent. Do you know where I live?"

Oops. Do I admit that I was there very recently, when I gave

*Daphne a ride home? Or would she rather he didn't know
about that?*

I sidestepped the question. "I have your address. My
GPS will get me there. Never fails."

"Good. I'll look forward to seeing you tomorrow
evening. Sevenish?"

"See you then," I said. "Thanks again for the offer."

O'Ryan jumped up onto the couch and sat beside
me. With a large yellow paw, he batted at my handbag,
then finally worked his head into the unzipped side
pocket that held the dream book. I laughed at his
antics.

"O'Ryan, you big silly. Do you know how goofy you
look doing that? Get your head out of there. What do
you want? The dream book?" I reached into my bag
and pulled out the copy of *999 Dream Symbols*. "Okay.
There it is. What about it?"

He prodded the book with his nose, pushing it
against the armrest. Then, with one delicate flip of
his paw, he popped it open to a page headed with a
capital *D*.

"You want me to look at the dream symbols that
begin with *D*, I guess. We've already looked up *dog* and
diamond. What else is there?"

He did a cat flop onto the open book, and his pink
nose came to rest on the paragraph headed *Dog Growling*. "If the dog is growling," I read aloud, "it indicates
some conflict within yourself. It may indicate betrayal
or untrustworthiness."

"How did you know the dream dog was growling?" I
asked the cat. "And what am I supposed to do with this
information, anyway? I already know I'm loaded with
inner conflict. Besides that, how do I know who's a
betrayer? Who's untrustworthy?"

And why am I holding a conversation with a cat?

I hastily stuck the book on top of the new bookcase, picked up my handbag, and nudged the cat off of the couch. "Come on, O'Ryan. Between River's tarot cards and the damned dream book, pretty soon I'm not going to trust anybody. Let's have some lunch, and then I'm going to change clothes and do some more shopping."

I'd kept my word to Pete about having groceries in the house, and I was pretty pleased with the way the inside of my refrigerator and cabinets looked. I felt that I was prepared for anything, from a quick snack to a sit-down dinner. I opted for a ham sandwich on rye bread with a glass of milk and served O'Ryan a tiny can of what the label claimed was "a grilled seafood feast in cream gravy."

A cooling shower helped to wash away the stress of the morning's encounter with Tommy Trent. I tossed the jeans and the yellow Tabby shirt into the hamper and put on khaki shorts, a green silk blouse, and a pair of brand-new leather sandals. My damp too-curly hair was unruly, but I took a cue from Daphne and messed it up a little more. It was a new look for me, and my reflection in the bathroom mirror told me it wasn't a bad one. I still didn't have a full-length mirror for the bedroom, so I couldn't get the overall effect, but what did it matter? I was only going shopping, and a mirror would be the first thing I'd look for.

I put the top down on the Corvette. The sun felt good on my face, and it didn't matter what the wind did to my hair. I popped in a CD, and with Aerosmith's *Music from Another Dimension!* blasting from the ten-speaker audio system with a bass box and subwoofers,

I shook away thoughts of betrayal and growling dogs and untrustworthy blue-eyed blondes. I had the afternoon off, and I fully intended to have the proverbial "good day."

My first stop was at one of Salem's old, established furniture stores where I knew Aunt Ibby often shopped. The full-length mirrors they offered were of good quality, and several of them seemed as though they'd blend with my other pieces, but nothing really appealed to me. I decided to stop at Jenny's to see if she had any mirrors I hadn't already seen. I pushed the front door of the shop open, noting that she was no longer locking it between customers.

"Jenny? You here?" I looked around the shop. Nobody there. I had a moment's discomfort, remembering the last time I'd entered an antique shop and called out the proprietor's name. Relief washed over me when I heard voices coming from the next room. I followed the sound and saw Jenny and a tall man standing together at the back of the room, almost in the spot where I'd found my Lucite kitchen set. Not wanting to interrupt a potential sale in progress, I stepped back, intending to wait in the front room, where there were more than enough antiques to hold my attention for a while.

"Lee? That you? Come on back," Jenny called. "Someone here you should meet."

I walked toward the two. Sunshine streaming through the window behind them made it difficult to see, and I shaded my eyes with one hand. It wasn't until I was standing right in front of them that I recognized the man. He recognized me, too, no doubt.

"Lee, this is my old friend Gary Campbell. Gary, Lee

Barrett. She's a new friend and, I might add, a darn good customer."

If he was surprised to see me, he didn't let on. He smiled, held out his hand, and said, "Always happy to meet a good customer. How do you do, Ms. Barrett?"

I went along with the charade and shook his hand. "How do you do, Mr. Campbell?" I turned to Jenny. "I don't want to interrupt you two. I was just checking to see if you have any new full-length mirrors. I can come back later." I was already backing up, heading for the exit sign.

"Oh, you don't have to hurry away," Jenny said. "We're almost finished with our business here."

"I'll come back later," I said again. "No problem. Nice to meet you, Mr. Campbell." And with that, I was out the door. It was a pretty chicken departure, I knew, but of all the people I didn't want to hang around with in a social situation, Gary Campbell probably topped the list.

I climbed back into the 'Vette, abandoned Aerosmith for some soothing Michael Bublé, and headed for Antique Row in Essex. I'd surely find a mirror there and might even pick up some fried clams at Woodman's to share with Aunt Ibby and O'Ryan.

It took a couple of hours of shopping, but I was right about finding a mirror. It was a gorgeous full-length oval one on a swivel-tilt cherrywood stand. I was pretty sure it would pass River's feng shui test, and I could tilt it so I wouldn't see my reflection when I was in bed. It reminded me of one that had been destroyed in our attic fire, so I knew Aunt Ibby would like it, too. I arranged to have it delivered, wondering if it would arrive in one of Bob's trucks. Feeling good about furniture, and not bad about life in general, at

Woodman's I splurged on two quarts of fried clams and a large order of onion rings, then called Aunt Ibby and told her I was bringing home dinner. She promised to whip up some homemade coleslaw, and I drove home along the pretty shore road, looking forward to a pleasant evening.

I was about halfway back to Salem when my phone buzzed. I don't like to answer the phone when I 'm driving, so I pulled over and looked at the caller ID. It read John Hampton, Jr. Tripp Hampton. What did he want?

"Hello. This is Lee Barrett. May I help you?"

"Lee? Tripp Hampton here. I've had a cancellation, and I wonder if you could come over about that coffee table tonight instead of tomorrow."

I wanted that cobbler's bench. But I looked over at the hot, Styrofoam-insulated fried clam dinner on the seat next to me and turned him down cold. "Sorry, Tripp. I have plans for the evening. Anyway, I don't have the truck. Tomorrow will be much better for me. All right?"

His "Certainly. That will be fine. See you then," along with a rather abrupt hang up, sounded just a bit petulant.

I think Mr. Tripp Hampton is quite accustomed to getting his own way.

CHAPTER 26

Aunt Ibby was ready and waiting when I tapped on the kitchen door. "Maralee, I could smell the fried clams as soon as you reached the back steps. What a good idea this was!"

The table was set, a frosty pitcher of lemonade and a big bowl of coleslaw at the center. She'd opened two of the screened windows, and a refreshing evening breeze ruffled the white curtains. It took only minutes to transfer my tasty treasures to colorful Italian ceramic bowls, arrange the little plastic cups of ketchup and tartar sauce beside our plates, bow our heads for a quick blessing, and dig in. Real New England fried clams on a real New England summer night in a real New England kitchen is beyond wonderful. Believe it.

At first there wasn't much dinner table conversation besides "Oh, my goodness, this is delicious" and "Why don't we do this more often?" After my second plateful, though, I began to tell my aunt about my eventful day, beginning with getting scared half to death by Tommy Trent.

"I was really frightened," I told her. "I mean, the

man may or may not have killed his wife, but he was definitely angry. He was glaring at me, waving that index card, and I was alone there with him, with nothing between us but a cardboard box full of bar accessories."

"My dear child," she said, reaching across the table to take my hand. "I'm beginning to regret suggesting that you apply for that position. It didn't occur to me that you might be in danger."

"I probably wasn't," I admitted. "Daphne showed up and scolded him as though he was a naughty puppy, took the card from him, and quietly led him away."

"Remarkable," she said, letting go of my hand and helping herself to the last onion ring. "So you have the card back? Did you tell Pete about all this?"

"Yes. He's going to call me tonight. I don't know what to think about Tommy finding the card and claiming he'd never seen it before, and I know the man doesn't like me one bit. I guess Pete will figure it out, though."

"I'm confident that he will," she said. "You've had quite a day."

"Oh, that's not the half of it," I said. "I'll make some coffee and tell you the rest."

I helped straighten up the kitchen, declined her offer of dessert, and we took our coffee cups into the living room. I told her about Mr. Pennington giving me the rest of the day off and about my dropping in at Jenny's shop to look for a mirror.

"Did she have one you liked?" my aunt asked.

"I didn't stay long enough to find out," I said. "Guess who was in there with Jenny?"

"I can't imagine. Don't tease."

"Gary Campbell, the man who ran into me outside of Shea's shop."

"Oh, dear." She put a hand over her mouth. "Did he recognize you?"

"He pretended not to, and I pretended I didn't recognize him. It was all quite civil, and very, very weird. I left right away and went to Essex to check out the antiques shops there."

"Essex. So that's how this excellent dinner appeared. But did you find your mirror?"

"I did. I think you'll like it. It reminds me of the oval tilt mirror we lost in the fire. They're going to deliver it tomorrow. Will you be here?"

"I will. Any more surprises during your day?"

"I turned down an invitation to go over to your friend Tripp Hampton's place tonight, which I guess was a surprise to him."

She laughed. "I guess a young man-about-town like Tripp doesn't get turned down very often. What was the occasion?"

"He has that cobbler's bench coffee table for me, that's all. I'm going over there tomorrow evening with the truck to pick it up."

"Nice of him to offer. He saw my request on Face-book, you know."

"I know. Thanks for that. Mr. Pennington will be pleased."

"Any word about the cash register?"

"No. I was going to ask Jenny about interceding for me with Mr. Campbell. But there he was in her shop. I got tongue-tied and just bolted."

"I don't blame you. It must have been awkward."

"The whole day's been like that. I made contact with

all three of the blond men River says I'm supposed to beware of."

"Three blond men," she repeated. Then she began to hum the tune to the old nursery rhyme "Three Blind Mice." "Three blond men," she sang. "Three blond men. See how they run. See how they run . . ."

I laughed and joined in. "They all ran after the farmer's wife. Who cut off their tails with a carving knife. Did you ever see such a sight in your life, as three blond men?"

Our laughter at the silly song, combined with the good meal, relieved the tension of the day, and by the time I left my aunt and headed upstairs to my own suite, I felt really good. O'Ryan waited for me on the third-floor landing and followed me inside. I had smuggled a couple of fried clams in a paper napkin for him and put them in his bowl. He hunched down, the way he does when he's really pleased with his food, and made short work of the crispy treat.

I'd just about decided exactly where in my bedroom to put the new mirror when my phone buzzed, announcing Pete's promised call. "Hi, Pete. I'm glad you called."

"Told you I would. Now, tell me exactly what happened with Trent. You said everything was okay, but you didn't really sound convinced of that."

"I know," I said. "He calmed down as soon as Daphne showed up, but he shot a pretty evil look my way when he was leaving."

"He didn't leave the building for quite a while. We had his car staked out."

"He stayed for the rehearsal. He was really excited about Daphne's performance. Whistled and clapped, as though it was opening night."

"I've made arrangements to have another talk with Daphne at the station tomorrow, after she's through at the school." He paused. "So, is she really that good in the part?"

"Actually, she is, Pete," I said. "Are you going to ask her about the index card? If it really was in Tommy's drawer in the first place?"

"Yeah. And if it wasn't, how did she get hold of it?"

"I'd sure like to know the answer to that myself. By the way, I ran into another gentleman I didn't expect to see today. Gary Campbell."

"No kidding? Where was he?"

"At Jenny's."

"Did he recognize you?"

"I'm sure he did, but he didn't let on. Neither did I."

"Must have been awkward. What'd he say?"

"Neither of us said much more than 'How do you do?' Then I beat it out of there. Jenny's probably still wondering what's wrong with me."

"Makes sense that he'd be there, though, with Jenny doing the appraisal on Shea Tolliver's stuff."

"I know. How's that coming?"

"Slowly, I guess. There are so many small items in the shop, and each one has to be authenticated and valued. I don't think Campbell will be able to take over the place for at least a couple of weeks."

"I'm still hoping I can get the cash register for the play. I didn't get a chance to ask Jenny to see if Mr. Campbell will let us borrow it."

"Got most everything else?"

"Yeah. Pretty much for the first play, anyway." I paused for a second before telling Pete that Tripp Hampton had called me.

"I told you he was hitting on you," Pete said. "What'd he want?"

"He wants to give me a cobbler's bench coffee table for the play. And he's not hitting on me." I smiled. "He's not my type, anyway. Not at all."

"Glad to hear it. I should be out of here pretty soon. Can I stop by and get that card?"

"Of course," I said. "If I had known you were coming, I would have saved you some fried clams. O'Ryan just snarfed down the last one." I looked around for the cat, who was sitting on the windowsill, his nose pressed against the glass, his tail switching. "Now I think he wants me to open the window. The downstairs door is unlocked. Just come on up. See you in a little while. Bye."

I moved the cat aside, unlocked the window, and checked to be sure the screen was solidly in place. "Can't have you falling out the window, boy," I said. "Or sneaking out onto the fire escape."

O'Ryan gave an offhanded little "mrow," flattened his ears, and moved to the left side of the windowsill. He seemed intent on something in the yard below. I leaned toward him, trying to see what had him so interested, but couldn't detect anything out of the ordinary happening down there. Fading evening light gave a rosy look to Aunt Ibby's garden, where the cooling breeze set the taller plants and bushes into languid motion. I was about to turn away when I spotted two cats, a gray one and a tabby, sitting on top of the tall wooden fence marking the boundary of our property.

"So that's it. You have a couple of friends hanging out in the yard. You know you can use your cat door and go outside and join them if you want to."

He gave a slight shake of his head, then lay down, sprawling his full length along the sill. I wasn't surprised when he didn't attempt to leave his perch. After we'd brought him home from WICH-TV, he'd become pretty much an indoor cat, rarely venturing outside of our yard.

I busied myself around the kitchen, making a fresh pot of coffee, in case Pete wanted some, then sat down next to the window to wait for his promised arrival. O'Ryan immediately hopped down from his roosting place and ran for the front door, so I knew Pete was on his way. Sure enough, I saw the gleam of his headlights as his car entered the driveway. The fence-sitting visiting cats scattered, and I headed for the living room. I unlocked the door and stood at the head of the stairs, ready to greet Pete, while O'Ryan scampered down two flights and accompanied him all the way up, with much mrowing and purring and other cat conversation.

By the time they entered the apartment, Pete had picked the big cat up, and was holding him in his arms when he leaned over to give me a peck on the cheek. "What's up with the cat? He's not usually this glad to see me."

"Who knows? He's his own cat, that's for sure. Makes up his own rules. Maybe he's just apologizing for eating that last fried clam. I made coffee." I took his hand. "Come on out to the kitchen."

"So what were you doing all the way over in Essex? I'm sure it wasn't just for the seafood."

"I was shopping for a full-length mirror for my bedroom," I said as we entered the kitchen. "I thought I'd find one at Jenny's, but when I ducked out of there because of Mr. Campbell, I thought about the shops in Essex." I poured coffee for both of us.

"Did you find one?"

"I did. And I'm sure it'll fit in with River's feng shui guidelines."

"That's most important," he said, not even trying to hide his smile. "Wouldn't want you to mess that up. Now about the card. Tell me again about how that scene with Trent went down."

So I did. I told him how scared I was and how I'd thought about whether or not I'd be able to bean Tommy with a chrome cocktail shaker if I needed to. Pete's jaw clenched, and his hand tightened around his coffee mug. He relaxed, though, and almost smiled when I described how tiny Daphne had shaken her finger at Tommy, snatched the index card, and led him away as though he were an errant kindergartner.

"Definitely an odd couple," he said. "Is he that crazy about her, or does she have something on him?"

"Don't have a clue," I said, "but they sure looked lovey-dovey after the rehearsal. Want to see the card now?"

"Yes, please."

I'd hung my purse over the back of my chair. I reached into the outer pocket and produced the index card. "It's a little the worse for wear, but here it is."

Pete grasped it by the edges and held it up to the light. He pulled a plastic envelope from his inside pocket. He slipped the card into the envelope and put it in his jacket pocket. "Probably not much in the way of fingerprints left on it, but we'll check everything."

"Aunt Ibby is worried about me," I told him. "She thinks I'm in danger at the school." I watched his eyes. "Am I?"

"Nobody's safety is ever guaranteed," he said, "but do I think the Tabby is an unsafe place for you to spend your days? No. There are always people around. We've instructed the security guard to keep an eye on you, too." He smiled. "I'm more concerned about you driving around in that bucket-of-bolts truck Pennington gave you."

I returned his smile. "I'm getting so I like it," I said. "Although I do love my Corvette, having just two seats is pretty limiting. I can throw all kinds of stuff into that truck bed."

"Are you planning to use it to pick up that new mirror?"

"No. I'd probably break it. Don't need seven years of bad luck! I'll leave that delivery to the professionals. It'll arrive tomorrow sometime. Aunt Ibby will be here to sign for it."

"Does that shop use Bob's Delivery, too?" Pete asked.

"I didn't ask. Why? Is it important?"

"Just wondering. On this case we don't know yet what's important and what isn't." He had his serious cop face in place again. "Bob's name has turned up a couple of times in this investigation so far. That's all."

"I see," I said, even though I didn't. "Want a sandwich?"

"That sounds good. And some more coffee?"

"Sure. Roast beef or turkey breast? White or whole wheat?"

"You've been shopping. Roast beef on white please."

I poured the coffee and built the sandwich, adding some pickles and chips. "Did you say that Gary Campbell has an alibi for the time Shea was killed?"

"Yeah. There are e-mails between the two of them covering about a week. They'd agreed that if he repaid the money he took—it was only a couple thousand dollars—she'd take him back into the business."

"That must have been the money they found on him that day. Two thousand dollars. He must have been taking it to her when he found her body."

"Looks that way. Seems Campbell was at his bank over in Peabody, withdrawing the two thousand, at around the time Shea was being hit over the head. Got him on camera, and the serial numbers on the bills match the money he had on him when we arrested him. The bank teller says that Campbell told him he was going to pay an old debt. Seemed real happy about it."

"So I don't have to be afraid of him, then?"

"Probably not." Pete sipped his coffee. "You say he didn't let on that he knew who you were?"

"Didn't even blink when I walked in. Jenny introduced us, and that was that."

"And you left right away?"

"As soon as I could without being rude. Now, do you mind if I ask you a question?"

"Of course not. Shoot."

"Okay. Can you tell me why you wanted the number from the dog license?"

Pete colored slightly. "I'll tell you, but you'll think I'm getting soft."

"No I won't. Tell me." I leaned forward, watching his eyes.

"Well, ever since the night I unwrapped that license and realized that someone had cared enough about a dog to keep the tag so carefully, I've thought about that dog."

Here's a side of the man I've never seen before. I like it.

"You have? I've thought of him, too."

"When you mentioned that Helena had a dog named Nicky, I just wanted to know if it was the same dog."

He gave an embarrassed shrug. "To have a name to go with the tag. That's all."

"Was it the same dog?"

He smiled then. "Yep. A twelve-year-old male schnauzer named Nicky."

"The dog in the picture. I'll give you the license tag if you'd like to have it," I said.

He waved the suggestion aside. "No, that's okay. It's safe where it is." He finished his sandwich, asked for another cup of coffee, and leaned back in his chair. "Now, tell me about this phone call from Hampton."

"He's helping me out with a prop for one of the plays, you know, and I agreed to go over to his place with the truck after work tomorrow to pick it up."

To pick up some kind of a coffee table, right?"

"A cobbler's bench coffee table. For the play. He wanted me to come over tonight instead of tomorrow."

"So he's changed the time?"

"Tried to. But I'd already bought dinner and told Aunt Ibby that I was on the way home. Besides, I didn't even have the truck."

"So what did he expect you to do? Go all the way back to the Tabby to get it?"

"I guess so. But I just told him I had other plans for this evening and I'd see him tomorrow."

"He agreed?"

"Yeah." I thought about how Tripp's attitude had seemed to change. "But he seemed kind of annoyed about it."

"He's probably used to having his own way."

"That's exactly what I thought. Was he like that back when you first met him? When Helena died?"

He shrugged. "I don't remember him that way. He was really broken up about her death. They were pretty close. Poor guy had lost his mother when he was practically a baby. Then his dad died, and then Helena. She was all the family he had left. That kind of trauma can change a man."

"I suppose so. Aunt Ibby likes him, and she's a pretty good judge of character."

"I agree. Has your aunt met Daphne yet?"

"No. Why do you ask?"

"You seem to like her, and I just wonder what your aunt's reaction to her might be."

He made a good point. I had decided I'd introduce the two as soon as an opportunity presented itself. Maybe Aunt Ibby would like to attend a rehearsal of *Born Yesterday*. It occurred to me that Pete might like to watch Daphne as Billie Dawn, too. I admitted that I wanted to know what *he* thought about the petite and very curvy blonde. He certainly had arranged for plenty of interviews with her.

Stop it! I told myself. *He's with you every chance he gets. And she's no more his type than Tripp Hamilton is yours.*

I pushed the thought away and served Pete a big slice of angel food cake with fresh strawberries and whipped cream.

The way to a man's heart . . .

CHAPTER 27

The next day at the Tabby started out really well. I worked up my courage enough to phone Jenny and ask her if she'd check with Gary Campbell and see how he felt about lending us the cash register. She called me back within minutes and said that he'd be happy to, and that all he asked for in return was a mention of Tolliver's Antiques and Uniques in the program. He'd decided to keep the name of the shop as it was, in honor of Shea.

I hurried to Mr. Pennington's office to deliver the good news. "Now the set will look the way I've pictured it from the beginning," I told him. "I can pick up the cobbler's bench this evening, that is, if it's all right with you that I use the truck after hours."

"Certainly, my dear Ms. Barrett." He came around the desk and clasped my hand in a hearty handshake. "I want you to know how very pleased I and the entire board of directors are with your attention to detail in each of our plays. The cobbler's bench and the authentic shoe forms for *Hobson's Choice*, and the minks, the vintage bar, and the gilded telephone for *Born Yesterday*—they are sheer perfection."

"We still have a way to go for *Born,* sir," I said, "and I haven't done a thing for *Our Town* yet, but I'm glad you're satisfied so far. I'm new at this, you know, but I'm really enjoying it."

"I'm very sorry about the unpleasant disruption you experienced yesterday morning," he said. "I trust that the young man involved has apologized to you for his bad behavior, as he assured me that he would."

"Um . . . no. Haven't heard from him. Frankly, I'd rather he just kept his distance from me." That was an understatement. It would suit me just fine if I never saw Tommy Trent's mean face again.

"Sometimes we just have to let bygones be bygones," he chided gently. "Tell me, my dear, how is the truck running? Any problems with it?"

"Not at all," I said, glad of the change of subject. "As a matter of fact, I really enjoy driving it. It handles quite easily, and I like having all that room to carry stuff. My own car is pretty short on extra space."

"I know. That big engine takes up a lot of room. I was quite fond of fast cars myself back in my youth. Used to love the auto races."

"I do, too," I said, remembering Pete's recent invitation. "I'm planning to go up to New Hampshire later this month for the Sprint Cup."

"Ahh, youth!" he said. "These days my social life is quieter, but still satisfying. Well, then. I must be off to Costume to settle a squabble over wigs. Carry on."

Thus dismissed, I headed for my office. I needed to straighten out my accounts. I had spent some of my own money at yard sales but had charged almost everything else to the card Mr. Pennington had given me.

It was time to balance my meager books and see what, if anything, I had left to spend on props. I still needed to visit a Home Depot to gather boards and ladders to form the spare scenery for *Our Town,* and I still needed some incidentals for *Born Yesterday.*

I was surprised to see one of those pink WHILE YOU WERE OUT telephone message slips on my desk. The school switchboard had taken a call for me from, of all people, Gary Campbell. I sat down to read the scribbled note.

> *I'll be in your area this afternoon and would be glad to deliver the cash register.*
> *Please call to confirm.*

His name and telephone number followed.

Now what? I'd be glad to have the cash register delivered. That way I didn't have to worry about damaging the pricey artifact in transit. But would Gary Campbell and I continue to pretend we'd never seen each other before? It promised to be an awkward situation. Nevertheless, I was determined to have the vintage beauty. I crossed my fingers and punched in the number.

"Hello. Tolliver's Antiques and Uniques. Gary speaking. How may I help you?"

So he's already taken over as manager of Shea's shop.

"Good morning. This is Lee Barrett at the Tabitha Trumbull Academy of the Arts. I received your message about the loan of a cash register."

Let's keep this thing on a formal, businesslike basis.

"Well, good morning to you, Lee Barrett. Thanks for returning my call. Jenny tells me that you'd like to use the old register on the set of *Hobson's Choice.* Most appropriate."

His tone of voice was warm, friendly, and he sounded as though he was smiling. I decided to try to match his tone. "You're familiar with the play? Not too many people are. It's sort of an old-timer."

"Had to read it for an English course I once took at BU," he said. "I'm looking forward to seeing it performed. I presume you'll arrange for tickets for me, along with a mention in the program."

"I'm sure that can be arranged, Mr. Campbell," I said. "What time would you like to meet?"

"I can be there at around one o'clock. Where will you be?"

"Come around to the back of the building. You'll see a pair of large doors marked 'warehouse.' Just ring the bell, and I'll open them. We can take the freight elevator right up to the theater." That sounded a little bossy. I tried to soften it. "Thanks very much for letting us use it. It plays into the script perfectly."

"The part where Hobson reaches into the register to steal some drinking money?"

"Exactly," I said, still surprised by his familiarity with the story. "The ringing of the register giving the old man's theft away is just the touch I wanted."

"Stealing a little here and there to get drinking money is something I understand," he said, the smile gone from his voice. "But that was a long time ago. One o'clock it is, then. I'll look forward to seeing you, Ms. Barrett." A click, and he was gone.

I sat there for a moment, just staring at the phone. What was all that about stealing to get drinking money? Was that what had become of two thousand dollars of the antique shop's cash?

I certainly wasn't going to discuss that topic with Mr. Campbell. I looked at my watch. It was already noon. I had just about enough time to grab a bite of lunch and then find a dolly to move the heavy cash register into the freight elevator and then to the stage in the student theater.

The diner was expectedly crowded at that time of day, but I was lucky enough to find a seat at the counter. Even luckier, I sat down right next to Herb Wilkins.

"Herb," I said, "I'm going to need a dolly to move a heavy stage prop. Do you know where they're kept?"

"Sure. But I'll move it for you if you want. Where is it?"

"It isn't here yet," I told him. "A guy is going to deliver it to the warehouse later today. I'm sure between us, we can manage it."

"Okay. There are a couple of dollies in a big closet just to the left of the elevator. Can't miss it."

"Thanks, Herb."

I gulped down my egg salad on whole wheat, drank most of a glass of milk, and headed for the warehouse. He was right about the location of the dollies. The closet yielded several, all probably left over from the long-ago days when the building was a department store. I selected the sturdiest-looking one and wheeled it over to the wide double doors. I'd hardly arrived there when the bell jingled, announcing that someone was outside. If it was Gary Campbell, he was ten minutes early.

It was, and he was. He stood there, smiling, with the cash register in his arms. It was clearly too heavy to carry, and I hurried to push the dolly in his direction.

"Oh, Mr. Campbell. That thing must weigh a ton. Put it down here, please."

"Thanks." He stooped and lowered his weighty bronze burden onto the dolly, then stood wiping his brow with the back of his hand. "If I'd tried lifting it up before I agreed to this, I might have had second thoughts."

"I'm sorry," I said. "I would have sent a couple of our stagehands over to get it if I'd known it was a problem."

"Just kidding," he said. "No problem at all. Glad to help out. Where do we go from here?"

"Just wheel it into the freight elevator." I opened the screened metal door and stood aside as he silently did as I'd directed. Then I stepped inside the elevator. "Hang on to something," I said as I pushed the button marked ONE. "I'm new to this, and sometimes she stops with a jolt."

We clanked our way upward, landed with the promised jolt, and both remained on our feet.

"Where to now?" he asked, pushing the dolly out onto the school's spacious main floor.

"I'll call for the stagehands to take it inside the theater," I said, gesturing toward the student theater entrance on the opposite side of the building. The theater had been built to resemble an old-time movie house, and the marquee overhead already displayed COMING SOON. HOBSON'S CHOICE in lights. I pulled my phone from my jeans pocket, called Mr. Pennington, and asked for one or two men to come down and help with the cash register.

"They'll be here in a minute," I told Gary Campbell. "The director says that the cast is rehearsing onstage right now. Would you like to go inside and see how it looks so far?"

"I'd like to very much," he said.

I pointed to the side door marked STUDENT ENTRANCE. "Just go ahead in. I'll wait for the stagehands, and I'll join you in a few minutes."

Again, he silently did as I'd asked, turning to give me a brief wave before he headed down the carpeted ramp to the theater. I watched his retreating back and wondered how long we were supposed to keep pretending we didn't recognize each other. I was sure that the moment we collided on Shea Tolliver's front steps was as firmly and permanently etched on his memory as it was on mine.

CHAPTER 28

I made my way slowly along the center walkway of the nearly empty theater, aided by the tiny, downward-focused lamps at the end of each row of seats. Ahead, stage lights illuminated what looked remarkably like an early twentieth-century cobbler's shop. Onstage, the action had ceased while the cash register was being carefully, almost reverently, put into place on one of Trumbull's Department Store's old oak counters. As my eyes adjusted to the darkened interior, I spotted the blond head in aisle ten. The man knew how to choose a good seat, I thought as I slid in beside him.

"It's going to look perfect, don't you think?" I whispered.

"Huh? What's going to look perfect?" The low tone was gruff, and I knew even before I turned to look at him that I wasn't sitting beside Gary Campbell. I started to get up, but Tommy Trent grasped my wrist. "Wait a minute. I've been looking for you."

"Me? Why?" I squeaked.

His whisper was harsh. "The old man said I should apologize. So I apologize. Didn't mean to scare you."

I snatched my wrist away and stood up. "Apology accepted," I muttered and hurried toward the comparative safety of the stage, where I could at least see lights and people.

Gary Campbell was in the aisle seat in the first row, his attention riveted on the placement of his cash register. It took a moment for him to notice me standing there, but he quickly moved over one seat and motioned for me to join him. He pointed to the stage. "You were so right. It really completes the set, doesn't it?"

"It looks perfect," I said for the second time—but this time to the right blond.

The actors resumed their places, and the rehearsal continued. After a few minutes I told the antiques dealer that I had to get back to work, invited him to stay and watch the performance, thanked him again, and then hurried out via the student entrance. I didn't want to encounter Tommy Trent again if I could help it.

I went straight up to my office, this time leaving the door that separated me from the rest of the Theater Arts Department wide open. It was a little bit noisy out there, but I was content to sacrifice silence for security.

I didn't like this feeling of—might as well call it what it was—fear. I'd almost always felt safe at the Tabby—even when some pretty creepy things were going on. But now I found myself constantly looking over my shoulder, avoiding the old store's still-vacant stockrooms, and trying to stay within sight of other people. I wanted to tell somebody about Tommy Trent. But what could I say? That I'd sat next to the man by mistake and he'd apologized for frightening me the day before? Big deal.

I tried to concentrate on my bookkeeping project. It

wasn't all that complicated. I added up the credit card slips and made out an invoice for the things I'd paid for with cash. Amazingly, I still had nearly a hundred dollars left in my budget. I tucked the copy of *Our Town* into my purse and headed for Mr. Pennington's office. His door was always open, but I knocked, anyway.

"Just checking on what we'll need for the Thornton Wilder play," I said after entering. "As I remember it from college, the set consisted of mostly boards and sawhorses, some artificial flowers, and a couple of tables and chairs. I think you said you viewed it that way too. I'm planning to take a spin down to the Home Depot to see what I can find."

"I see it as a simple set, just as you do," Mr. Pennington said. "You might check with Scenery and see if they have measurements for you."

I did as he suggested, and although the Scenery people hadn't prepared any useful measurements, they had raided the old store's window-display department and had come up with a couple of arched trellises, complete with plastic vines and flowers. I was sure I could round up some tables and chairs, including the ones I'd recently borrowed from my aunt. Herb Wilkins had scrounged some weathered-looking boards and a Roman pillar of sorts, all of which might work for the Tabby's version of Grover's Corners, New Hampshire.

I drove the truck to the Home Depot on Traders Way and picked up a few likely looking pine boards and a couple of closeout wooden window frames, which might come in handy, and, amazingly, returned to the Tabby with a small balance still remaining on the credit card.

I off-loaded my day's gatherings, pulled the Corvette

into the warehouse, and headed for Winter Street in the Ford. I planned to check in with my aunt to see if my mirror had arrived, change into something more presentable, and get to Tripp Hampton's before it got dark. The mirror was in Aunt Ibby's front hall, looking as beautiful as I remembered it. We carried it upstairs, one of us on each side, and positioned it in the bedroom. I tilted the mirror so that it reflected the kitchen door instead of the bed, hoping River would deem it proper *bagua,* and pulled on clean jeans and a white cotton sweater.

"I'm off to get the cobbler's bench," I called to my aunt as I headed out the back way to the truck. "I'll be right back. Want me to pick up something for supper?"

"No. You brought the food last night. My turn," she said.

As I backed out of the driveway, I heard a soft meowing coming from the garden. The two cats were back, and this time they'd brought along a friend—a black cat wearing a collar. They looked cute, sitting there on the fence all in a row.

Looks like O'Ryan has himself a little fan club going on.

I followed the route Daphne had shown me earlier and arrived at the mansion at about 6:45. A tad early, but I took a chance that Tripp wouldn't mind. I figured I had a couple of hours before sunset, and I'd already decided that I didn't want to be there after dark. The gray-stone mansion—Rockport granite probably— loomed ahead as I drove slowly along the curving driveway. I parked the truck in front of a massive dark brown door, its hinges, doorknob, and shield-shaped knocker of bright polished brass. That sounds as though the place was intimidating or even scary, but it wasn't at all. Lilac bushes, heavy with fragrant blossoms, crowded

around tall, narrow windows, and yellow forsythia vied
for attention with puffy pussy willows surrounding an
artfully constructed koi pond, complete with waterfall.
The whole effect was totally charming.

I pushed the doorbell, expecting to hear some chim-
ing melody similar to those at the house on Winter
Street. Instead, a sound something like a Chinese gong
issued from inside the mansion, and within a minute
or so, Tripp Hampton opened the door. He wore swim
trunks and had a striped towel slung across his shoulders. His blond hair was wet, and he was barefoot.

"Lee. You're early." He smiled, but the tone was
vaguely accusatory. "Daphne and I were just taking a
swim. Come on back to the pool, and she can entertain
you while I change."

He turned and walked swiftly along a maroon carpeted hall that led past several beautifully furnished
rooms. I followed his wet footprints on the soft, deep-
piled rug until we emerged in a glass-enclosed room
with an Olympic-sized pool at its center. I felt my hair
frizzing in the steamy, chlorine-scented humidity,
and the long-sleeved cotton sweater began sticking to
my skin.

"Hey, Daph," he called to the girl in the pool. "Lee's
here early. Get her a glass of wine or something while I
change!"

Daphne swam with strong, easy strokes from the far
end of the pool and lifted her bikini-clad self onto the
edge closest to me. "Hi, Lee. Tripp should have told
you to bring a bathing suit. Great pool, isn't it?"

"Great pool," I echoed.

"Helena had it built. Takes up the whole back of the
house. This used to be some kind of a ballroom, but

she had them make it all out of glass." She pointed upward. "Even the ceiling."

"It's amazing," I said. "But, Daphne, I've got to get out of here. My clothes are sticking to me."

"Oh yeah. Come on. I'll get you a glass of wine, like Tripp said."

I followed her small wet footprints into an adjoining room that looked like an ice cream parlor. White hair-pin-backed metal chairs with pink- and white-striped cushions surrounded small pink tables. I sat, glad of the air-conditioning, while Daphne positioned herself behind a long white counter, a wine bottle in each hand.

"What kind of wine do you like? We've got all kinds."

"I don't really care for any. Thanks," I said. "I'll take a Pepsi, if you have it. What a cute room this is."

She popped the cap from a Pepsi bottle and carried it to the table, then took the seat opposite me. "We used to have all kinds of ice cream and syrups and cherries and whipped cream and all that good stuff in here. But ever since Helena died, it's just booze and mixers." She gestured toward a long shelf laden with liquor bottles. I thought it was a shame to repurpose such a charming space that way, but didn't say so.

I sipped from the bottle and turned toward the glass wall overlooking the pool. "Guests with kids must have loved this place. A pool and ice cream cones, too."

"They did. And Helena loved the little kids, even though she never had any of her own. The first hus-band was too old, and Tommy sure didn't want any. So Tripp was her only child. Him and that little dog, Nicky." She smiled. "That dog. She used to dress him up. He even had a tiny orange life preserver of his own for when she used to take him out in that boat of hers."

"Helena had a boat?" I'd become more and more

interested in this woman, who had once owned my bureau . . . and had lately been appearing to me in shiny surfaces. "I hadn't heard that about her."

"Yeah. A neat little speedboat. She used to take me for rides in it sometimes." She paused, eyes downcast. "Before . . . well, before she caught me and Tommy doing things brothers and sisters don't usually do."

I didn't know how to respond to that bombshell, so I didn't say anything. But she wasn't through with what River called TMI—too much information.

"She saw us through this glass wall," she said, pointing toward the pool. "One day—"

Tripp chose that minute to reappear, interrupting Daphne's narrative, thank God. He'd changed into chinos and a blue chambray shirt with rolled-up sleeves. "Ready to see the cobbler's bench now, Lee? Just follow me. It's in one of the small TV rooms." He looked at the bottle of Pepsi in my hand. "Jesus, Daph, don't you know enough to give our guest a glass?"

"This is fine," I said. "I like the bottle. Nice and cold."

I hoped to save Daphne from more criticism, but Tripp's words didn't seem to bother her at all. She just smiled, said, "Sorry," wiped down the bar and the table, and headed back to the pool. "Next time bring a bathing suit, Lee. See you tomorrow at work."

Tripp opened a side door, and I followed behind him. "That Daphne," he muttered. "Cute as hell, but dumb as a brick. I've made it kind of a project—almost a hobby—to try to make a lady out of her." He laughed. "My Henry Higgins to her Eliza Doolittle."

"She's doing awfully well in the play," I said, feeling as though I should come to her defense. "Everyone loves her in the part."

"Really? I haven't been to any of the rehearsals, although she's invited me. I don't want to run into that murdering son of a bitch she's sleeping with. You met him yet?"

"Mr. Trent? Yes. We've met."

This house seemed to be full of corridors and side rooms. As I followed Tripp, I realized that without a map I'd never be able to find my way back to the pool, or to the front door, for that matter. I quickened my step to keep up with him. "I feel as though I should be dropping bread crumbs," I said, "like Hansel and Gretel in the woods."

"Didn't do them much good," he said. "They wound up at the witch's house, anyway, remember? Come on. I won't let you get lost." He grabbed my hand and pulled me toward him. I began to wish I hadn't come here, cobbler's bench be damned.

I pulled my hand away. "Just lead on," I said, getting behind him again. "I can keep up with you."

He gave me a long look with those narrow blue eyes. "You think so?"

CHAPTER 29

We arrived at what Tripp had described as "one of the small TV rooms." By most anybody's standards, the room wouldn't be called small, and neither would the very large wall-hung television set. The furniture was large in scale, too, with a long and very comfortable-looking couch flanked by two matching chairs. In front of the couch was the object of my visit—the cobbler's bench coffee table.

"It's absolutely perfect," I said. And it was. It was larger than I'd expected, and it had the slight depression where the cobbler could sit, the separated sections for tools and nails, and just the right amount of wear. "It's so kind of you to let us borrow it. I promise we'll take good care of it and I'll return it just as soon as the play is over."

"No problem," he said. "Do you think between us we can carry it out to your truck? It's fairly heavy."

I put both hands under one end and lifted it a couple of inches. "Not too bad," I said. "I'm sure we can manage."

"I used to have servants for this kind of thing," he

said, a frown creasing his forehead. "No more. Had to let them all go."

"Uh-huh," I said. "Well, let's head for the truck, shall we?"

"All right." He positioned himself at one end, and I took the other. "One, two, three, lift!"

I picked up my end, and with Tripp walking backward and me facing forward, we moved crab-like into a long corridor.

"We can stop and put it down every so often, you know," he said. "Just say when."

The corridor walls were lined with framed photographs. Some were of men and women in old-fashioned clothing and formal poses. Others were of a more recent vintage. "This is quite a portrait gallery," I said. "Are these people all your relatives?"

"They're mostly Hamptons, but there are some of Helena and her folks, too. Want to stop for a sec? My hands are starting to hurt. This thing is heavier than it looks."

I was glad for the break. My hands hurt, too. We put the table down, and I turned to study the nearby pictures. I found myself eye to eye with a black-and-white likeness of a pleasant-looking old gentleman. I moved a little closer. It was the same man I'd seen in the mirror, the same man whose picture, marked GRANDPA, I'd found in my bureau. I was sure of it.

"Who's this?" I asked. "He's quite friendly looking."

"That's Helena's grandfather," he said. "I never met the old gent. Helena told me she used to spend her summers with him when she was a little girl. Ready to get moving again? We're almost there."

I picked up my end of the table, and we resumed our slow and awkward pace through this seeming maze of corridors, past doorway after doorway, most of them with doors closed. "We don't use this part of the house much anymore," Tripp said. "Lucky I remembered which room the table was in." Again the frown. "It's hard to maintain a place this size without servants." He gave a genteel shrug. "Daphne does most of the dusting and vacuuming. She's a good kid."

"Yes, she is," I agreed. "I like her, too."

We rounded a corner, and I recognized the entry hall and the front door. "Back where we started," I said. "The truck is parked right out front, and I'm sure this will fit nicely in the truck bed. I brought some big quilted furniture covers, so I'm sure it will ride safely enough back there."

Once outside, I dropped the tailgate, and together we lifted the table into the Ford, wrapped it tightly with quilts and bungee cords. I offered Tripp my hand.

"Thanks again, Tripp," I said. "You don't know how much I appreciate this. I'll see that you get tickets to the play, and if you like, we'll include a mention in the program."

He held my hand a moment longer than necessary and flashed the perfect smile. "If you really want to show your appreciation, you'll invite me over to your place sometime soon. I'm dying to get a look at what you found inside Helena's bureau. Did you say there was a notebook?"

I withdrew my hand from his and closed the tailgate. "There is," I said. "I guess she wrote it when she was quite young. I haven't had a chance to read it yet, but it appears to be some essays of the 'what I did on my summer vacation' variety, along with a few poems."

"Oh." The smile faded a bit. "Anyway, it would be

interesting to see what she thought was worth hiding in all those secret compartments."

"Sure. As soon as all this play business gets over with, Aunt Ibby and I will be happy to have you come over to our house again soon."

"Just let me know when. By the way, your hair looks great that way."

"Thanks," I said, self-consciously running a hand through the tousled mess on my head, and climbed into my truck.

Daylight was fading fast, and a pale moon peeked through the trees beyond the gray mansion. I turned on the headlights and started for the Tabby. I drove slowly, trying to avoid shifting the table around while I navigated the curving driveway. As I passed the narrow road leading to Daphne's cottage, I wondered if she was there or at Tommy Trent's apartment or still in the mansion, swimming or dusting or vacuuming. Maybe those innocent pursuits were what she'd meant when she'd told me that Tripp liked having her around. I felt a little embarrassed about what I'd thought. I wondered, too, if she'd met with Pete and answered his questions about the index card.

The lot behind the Tabby's warehouse was empty when I arrived. I opened the wide doors, backed the Corvette out, and pulled the truck inside. I planned to get a couple of stagehands to move the cobbler's bench onto the set in the morning. I'd left my handbag in the truck, along with my phone, when I went inside the Hampton estate, so I grabbed them, closed the warehouse doors, and climbed into my own car. I checked for missed calls and found two. River North and Pete Mondello had each called. River's call was first, so I called her back.

"Hi, River. You called?"

"I did. Nothing important. I was just wondering if Pete found anything interesting in the velvet jewelry box."

"If he did, he hasn't told me about it," I said. "But guess where I've just been."

"I give up. I don't do psychic, just tarot."

"I was at the Hampton mansion, picking up a cobbler's bench for one of the plays from Tripp Hampton."

"Isn't he one of your blue-eyed blonds?"

"Please! None of them are *my* blue-eyed blonds. But, yes. He is. And now that you mention it, I've run into all three of them today!"

"That's too weird! Tell me about it."

I told her about Gary Campbell agreeing to lend the cash register, and how I'd sat down right next to Tommy Trent by mistake, then kept my appointment with Tripp Hampton.

"Hmmm. Three blond men," River said.

"Don't tell me you're going to sing it."

"Huh? Sing what?"

I laughed. "Aunt Ibby sings, 'Three blond men,' to the tune of 'Three Blind Mice.' I thought you might be about to do the same thing."

"I would have if I'd thought of it. What do you think of them? The three?"

I thought about that for a moment. "You know, I don't really care for any of them."

I told her about the swimming pool and the maze of rooms in the mansion, and about the picture gallery where I'd recognized the man called "Grandpa."

"There's some other stuff I'll talk to you about later," I said, "but I'm on my way home right now."

"You be careful," she said. "Talk to you soon."

I was going to return Pete's call, but I was all alone in the empty lot, except for a cat sitting on top of the Dumpster, and I decided to wait until I was safely home.

CHAPTER 30

Aunt Ibby was still experimenting with recipes from Tabitha Trumbull's collection, and the evening's offering was a creamy corn chowder sprinkled with crispy bits of salt pork, served with tiny oyster crackers. As I ladled a second helping from the ironstone soup tureen, I repeated the story of my day, much as I'd related it to River.

My aunt shook her head as I described the encounter with Gary Campbell in the antiques store, and tsk-tsked as I told about my surprise at sitting next to Tommy Trent in the dark theater. She had never seen the pool or the ice cream parlor at the Hampton mansion but remembered the gallery of pictures lining the corridors of the sprawling place.

"You're quite sure the old gentleman in the picture you saw today is the same man in the picture you found in your bureau?"

"It's the same man." I was confident of that. "I saw that man in the mirror in my bureau, too. Tripp says that he's Helena's grandfather and that she used to spend summers with him. I think the notebook we found is Helena's childhood accounts of those summers. I'm going to start reading it tonight."

"Good idea. I've been curious about that notebook myself. Old documents can be a treasure trove of useful information."

"Like Tabitha's recipe book?"

She smiled. "Exactly. I'll take care of the dishes. You run up to your apartment and start reading that notebook."

"I will," I said. "I've been so busy with my hunt for props, I've been neglecting a lot of the things I've wanted to do personally."

"Is the prop hunt nearly finished?" she asked.

"Except for some miscellaneous items, I think so, and thanks for dinner. Your recipe book is sure to be a best-seller."

"It's Tabitha's book, not mine." She smiled. "And by the way, what's wrong with your hair? Looks like you combed it with an eggbeater."

I laughed. "I know. It's the humidity. See you in the morning."

O'Ryan was already in the apartment, sprawled across the windowsill once again. I sat in the chair closest to him and pulled the phone from my purse, then punched in Pete's number. "Is your fan club out there again, boy?" I peered over his head toward the fence where I'd last seen the cats, but didn't see any of them this time.

Pete answered on the first ring. "I called a long time ago. I've been worried about you. Is everything all right?"

"I'm sorry, Pete. Didn't mean to worry you," I said.

"I went to pick up that coffee table and left the phone in the truck."

"How'd that go?" he asked. "I wish I'd gone with you. I don't trust that guy as far as you're concerned."

"It was okay. Daphne was there, too. The main concern I had while I was in the place was finding my way out again. It's like a darned rabbit warren!"

He laughed. "I remember. When we were doing the investigation of the murder, the chief marked the way to Helena's room with pieces of blue tape."

"Good idea. Better than dropping bread crumbs."

"Hansel and Gretel? Wicked witch stuff?"

"Sure. This is Salem, after all. Want to hear about the rest of my day? I ran into Tommy Trent at the school again."

"You did? His car's been in his driveway all day. We didn't see him leave the house."

"Probably took a cab with Daphne, I imagine. Anyway, he apologized for scaring me," I said, "although he didn't sound as though he meant it."

"What was he doing? Watching Daphne's performance again?"

"No. Oddly enough, he was down in the student theater, watching a rehearsal for *Hobson's Choice*. I sat next to him, thinking he was Gary Campbell and—"

"Wait a minute," Pete interrupted. "Why'd you think Gary Campbell would be there?"

"Didn't I tell you? He decided to let us borrow the cash register. Brought it over himself and stayed to watch them position it on the stage. It looks perfect."

"Lee, I thought we'd agreed on something." His serious cop voice was back. "You're supposed to keep me—the department—informed about where you are and what's going on."

"You knew where I was," I said, annoyed. "I was at the school all day, and then I went over to Tripp's house, then came home here. You knew all that."

"I knew you went to school, and I knew you went over to Hampton's place. Had a tail on you." He sounded more annoyed than I did. "But I didn't know you'd been hanging around with a couple of murder suspects when we weren't watching."

"You had me followed?" I didn't know exactly how to react to that, whether I should be mad because I didn't know about it or happy because it made me feel safe. Then the rest of his words began to register. "Murder suspects? Trent and Campbell?"

"Trent's already admitted to one murder, and Campbell stands to profit from Shea Tolliver's death. Besides that, everyone is interested in the damned pink diamond, and that includes your friend Hampton."

My redhead's temper began to flare. "Tripp Hampton is *not* my friend, and everyone knows by now that I don't have the diamond. Anyway, you said that you think Daphne and Tommy have it stashed away somewhere."

"You weren't listening. I said the chief thinks that. I don't."

"But the chief is usually right. You said so yourself." I knew that this conversation was deteriorating rapidly into a verbal food fight, but I couldn't seem to stop it. "You told me Gary Campbell was at some bank when Shea was getting hit over the head."

Pete's cool, calm cop voice was back. "Take it easy, Lee. It's just that I worry about you. I can't be with you every minute, so I need to know what's going on."

"I'm not totally helpless, you know! I don't *need* you to be with me every minute."

"I know you don't. I didn't mean that the way it sounded. But until we get this case figured out, I have to suspect everyone. Maybe Campbell is just an innocent antiques dealer. Maybe Daphne is just a dumb blonde and maybe Hampton is just a rich mama's boy and maybe Tommy Trent has found Jesus. But until I know for sure, I need to know you're safe." He paused and rubbed his forehead. "Hell, Lee. I sound like an ass. It's just that when I think about anything happening to you, it makes me crazy. I'm sorry."

I felt a warm rush of tears as the tension fell away. "I'm sorry, too. What's the matter with us?"

"Shhh. Let's not be sorry about anything. I have tomorrow night off. Want to do something? Take our minds off all this?"

"I'd love to," I said, "and I promise I'll let you know if anything unusual happens at the Tabby. I mean it."

"Good girl," he said. "Good night. See you tomorrow."

O'Ryan had left his perch on the windowsill in favor of the chair opposite mine. He sat upright, ears forward, golden eyes fixed on mine. I returned his stare, trying hard not to blink. This was a cat game he liked to play sometimes, one he almost always won. This time he blinked first, which pleased me. He jumped down from the chair and disappeared into the bedroom. I turned off the kitchen light and started to follow him but paused in the darkness to look out the window. The three cats, illuminated by the moonlight, were back on the fence.

I changed into pajamas, took off my make-up, retrieved Helena's notebook from the bureau, and turned on my cute new reading lamp. I climbed into bed, and a loudly purring O'Ryan curled up beside me.

"Pete just wants to protect me," I told the cat. "I shouldn't have been such a witch."

"Mrrow," said the cat, cuddling a little closer.

"You want to protect me, too, don't you?"

"Mrrup," he said, licking my cheek.

"You let me win the blinking contest, didn't you?"

He didn't answer, but I knew he had.

I opened the composition book to the first page and began reading. It was, as I'd suspected, a little girl's journal recording a summer vacation. The page wasn't dated, but I guessed from the handwriting and the occasional misspellings that the author was probably around ten years old.

Grandpa took me fishing today in his boat. He said now that I've grown taller, I should be able to cast better, and he was right. We both caught some flounder, but I caught two more than Grandpa. Then he showed me how to cook them. Grandpa's stove isn't like ours at home. He puts wood in it, and when the top of the stove got hot enough, we put our fish in a big frying pan. It was so good. Grandpa says someday we won't be able to come here and use this cabin anymore, but he says we should enjoy it while we can, and I said I will always come here in the summer, even if we can't use the cabin anymore. Tomorrow we are going to plant some pansies. Grandpa says it was Grandma's favorite flower.

The words were followed by a little rhyme.

Grandpa and me in his boat in the sun
Catching big flounder was lots of fun.

I stared at the page for a few minutes, thinking about the happy little girl who'd written about her summer adventures, then put the composition book on my bedside table, set the alarm clock, and turned out the light.

"Good night, O'Ryan," I said to the sleeping cat. "I'll read some more soon." In the darkness a silly tune played softly in my head.

Three blond men.
See how they run.

CHAPTER 31

Breakfast at the diner had become a regular ritual, and since I'd become acquainted with most of the summer theater staff and players, I rarely ate alone. Jenny was a regular patron, too, and Gary Campbell even showed up occasionally. On the morning of the opening of *Hobson's Choice,* I shared a booth with Daphne, Jenny, Mr. Pennington, and a tall, slim girl named Amanda, who played Maggie, Hobson's oldest daughter.

"You nervous, Amanda?" Daphne asked. "On account of opening night?"

"A little bit," the actress admitted. "I worry about forgetting my lines or missing a cue. Don't you?"

"It's my first play ever." Daphne stirred sugar into her coffee vigorously. "I don't know how I'll feel when there's an audience."

"From what I've seen in rehearsal, you both have your lines down perfectly," I said. "Don't they, Mr. Pennington?"

"Indeed they do." The director smiled at each actress.

"Gifted young women, each with a great future on the stage. Mark my words."

"I carry my script around, reading it every minute I get," Amanda admitted. "I bet you do, too, Daph."

"Nah. Can't read mine." She tapped a finger below one long-lashed eye. "Bad eyesight. Rupert—Mr. Pennington—reads all my lines into a little tape recorder for me, and I memorize them that way."

"Cool," said Amanda. "Whatever works for you, I guess."

Daphne's revelation surprised me. "Isn't there some way . . . Can't your vision be corrected?"

"Oh, sure. But I'd have to wear glasses." She wrinkled her perfect little nose. "That's not happenin'!"

"The child is quite vain, I'm afraid," said Mr. Pennington. "But with a talent such as hers, we allow for small peccadilloes."

"That's why I can't drive a car," Daphne said. "I know how, naturally, but they won't give me a license unless I get some glasses. Bifocals, for God's sake!"

I remembered the TV clip of her at the wheel of Tommy Trent's Mercedes. "But don't you drive Tommy's car sometimes?"

"Only once. His car was still in the garage at Tripp's place. Excuse me. Tripp calls it the 'carriage house,' but it's a garage. Anyway, somebody had to go pick him up from jail. And I still had the keys." She shrugged. "Tripp wasn't about to do it, so I had to. Drove real slow, and as soon as we got away from the cameras, Tommy took over. Didn't you ever wonder why I didn't have a car of my own?"

"Well, yes. But it was none of my business," I said.

Daphne smiled. "You rich girls. So polite all the time."

By then Amanda had excused herself, saying she

had to get back to the set. Whether that was true or whether Daphne's tales of astigmatism and incarceration had scared her off, I couldn't tell. Meanwhile, Jenny hadn't contributed much to the conversation at all. A lined yellow legal pad, covered with scribbled words and scrawled numbers, was propped against the stainless-steel napkin dispenser in front of her. She leaned back in the booth, put her pencil down, and rubbed her eyes with both hands.

"What a pain in the butt this is," she said. "Some of it doesn't make a darn bit of sense."

Mr. Pennington's tone was sympathetic. "Are you having problems resolving the inventory of the antiques store?"

"Oh, I'll get it done, but Shea had so much stuff! Lots of smalls. Way more categories than I carry over in my place." She picked up the pencil. "First, I have to count everything, like a regular inventory."

"Do you research every article?" I asked.

"Shea had most everything in the shop marked. That's a big help. I have to determine the insurance value of each piece, and that takes some research, but in the end, the item is worth whatever the customer is willing to pay for it."

"A lot of work, but interesting, I'll bet," I said.

"Interesting but confusing." She turned the yellow pad toward me. "Look at this. Fourteen-inch brass candlesticks, four hundred dollars for the pair."

"Yes," I said. "The Victorian brass candlesticks. I saw them when I bought my bureau. Thought about buying them, until I read the price tag. Beautiful things."

Jenny dropped the pencil. "Wait a minute. I was confused because I couldn't figure out why she priced a single candlestick as a pair. You say you saw two of them? Then where the heck is the other one?"

Shea died from a blow to the back of the head with a heavy object.

"Excuse me," I said. "I need to make a phone call."

I used the diner's front door and stepped out onto Essex Street, speed-dialing Pete's number as I walked. I crossed the parking lot, opened my car door, and turned on the air conditioner. The Corvette offered the most private space I could think of, and I didn't want anyone at the Tabby to overhear my conversation. He answered on the second ring.

"Pete, they've never found the heavy object that was used to kill Shea, have they?"

"Not yet. Why?"

"The papers just said it was a heavy object," I said. "Like what?"

"The ME said it was something smooth, rounded. Sort of like a baseball bat but not wood. Why? Have you heard something?"

"I think so. I was just in the diner with Jenny, and she says there's a brass candlestick missing from Shea's shop, but the mate to it is still there. I remember seeing the pair when I bought the bureau, but now there's only one."

"What did they look like?"

"They were tall. More than a foot, I'd say, with round bases and regular tops—you know, the part where you put the candle. But the middle part was shaped a lot like a baseball bat, only thinner." A picture was growing in my mind. "Pete, what if whoever killed her swung the candlestick so that just the middle part hit her?"

"Is Jenny still there?"

"I don't know. I came outside to call you."

"I'm coming over. If Jenny's still there, will you ask her to wait for me? I'll be there in five minutes."

"Okay."

I hurried back into the diner. Jenny was still there with Mr. Pennington and Daphne, but Gary Campbell had joined the group.

Awkward.

I pasted on a big smile and stood beside Daphne. "Still room for me? I think I have time for some more coffee."

"Sure, hon. Sit here." Daphne scooted over closer to Mr. Pennington and made room for me.

I nodded to Gary Campbell. "Good morning, Mr. Campbell," I said. "How are you?"

"Well. Thank you, Ms. Barrett. And you?"

"Fine. Thanks." The polite inanities over with, I turned to Jenny. "Jenny, if you have a few minutes, Detective Mondello would like to speak to you about that missing candlestick. He's on his way." I watched Gary Campbell's eyes, which shifted from me to Jenny and back, and then finally he looked out the window, just in time to see Pete's Crown Vic pulling into the parking lot.

"I always have time for the handsome detective," Jenny said with a wink. "But I don't know how I can help. Look, this booth is getting kind of crowded. Come on, Lee. Let's you and me and the cute cop grab another booth. Come on over to the shop later, Gary."

I stood in the aisle while Jenny gave Gary Campbell a gentle shove. He stood, and she got up and followed me. I motioned to Pete and then pointed toward a small booth beside the back window of the diner, and he hurried to join us there, pausing to nod a brief hello to the group remaining at the table. As soon as we three were seated, Pete began to speak in low tones.

"Jenny," he said, "Lee told me about the single candlestick you found. Is it still in Shea's shop?"

"Was last time I saw it," she said. "It was in the back part of the shop. The room behind the beaded curtains."

"Is that where you saw *both* candlesticks, Lee? In the back room?"

"Right. I remember them because they were so pretty. I considered buying them, but I'd just spent a lot on the bureau, so I didn't make an offer. They were marked four hundred dollars for the pair."

Pete let out a soft whistle. "For candlesticks? Wow."

"Well, as Jenny says," I told him, "the item is worth whatever the customer is willing to pay for it."

"I get it," Pete said. "Can you arrange to go over to Shea's shop with me now, Jenny? I'd like to borrow that candlestick. And, Lee, I'd like you to come, too, to make sure it's the one you remember as part of a pair."

I nodded my agreement, but Jenny frowned. "You mean you want to take it out of the store?"

"Yes."

"It's okay with me, but you'd better ask Gary. After all, the stuff all belongs to him now, doesn't it?"

We all turned and looked toward the table Jenny and I had just vacated. It was empty. Everyone had left the diner, including Gary Campbell.

Jenny, Pete, and I climbed into Pete's car and headed for the Bridge Street shop. "I have Campbell's contact number," Pete said. "I'll call and confirm with him. Shouldn't be a problem. I don't think there'll be any need for a warrant." Pete was still on the phone, waiting for an answer, when we pulled up in front of Tolliver's Antiques and Uniques.

Gary Campbell had arrived ahead of us and was inserting his key into the lock on the front door. Pete hurried out of the car and reached the shop's front step just as Gary pushed the door open. Jenny and I followed, leaving a discreet distance between us and the two men.

"I'm sure Gary won't mind if Pete needs to borrow the candlestick," she whispered. "But he'll give me a receipt for it, won't he? I have to account for every little thing. The man watches me like a hawk. He lives right upstairs from the shop now, you know."

"I'm sure there won't be any problem," I whispered back. "Shall we go on in?"

Pete motioned to us from the open doorway, and we hurried inside. The shop felt different. Even smelled different. The air conditioner had been turned off, and the musty odor of old furniture and fabrics permeated the place. Jenny dropped her purse on the counter and hurried toward the thermostat.

"Jeez, Gary," she scolded, moving the round dial. "I told you to leave the air conditioner on to dehumidify and cool the place. The old wood can't take temperature changes, and this place is as hot as a two-dollar pistol. You should know better."

"Just trying to save a few bucks. There'll be no money coming in until you finish counting all this, you know, but the bills keep right on coming."

Pete cleared his throat. "Mr. Campbell, this shouldn't take long. I've asked Ms. Barrett to identify a brass candlestick as one of a pair she saw here on the day Ms. Tolliver died. Jenny says that she's been able to locate only one of them. If the remaining candlestick is the one Ms. Barrett remembers, I'm asking your permission to borrow it."

"How much is it worth, Jen?" Campbell asked, turning toward the appraiser.

"According to Shea, about two hundred dollars."

"You'll provide a receipt, of course?" Campbell faced Pete. "Or, considering our temporary dearth of cash, perhaps the department would prefer to buy it."

Pete frowned. "I'll sign a receipt . . . or I can just get a warrant and take it, anyway. Doesn't matter to me."

Campbell nodded. "That's what I figured. Oh, well, let's take a look at this thing." He gestured toward the beaded curtains. "Jenny? Ms. Barrett? After you."

Jenny and I parted the beads, with Pete and Gary Campbell following close behind us. Jenny pointed to a long shelf filled with what looked like hundreds of shiny brass candlesticks. She reached toward the last row of the display.

"Let's see. Which one is it?" she said.

"Excuse me, Jenny," Pete interrupted. "Let Lee find the one she remembers from that day. Then we'll see if it's the one with the missing mate. Okay?"

"Sure. You're up, Lee." Jenny stepped aside.

It took only a few seconds for me to recognize the tall, graceful shape. I pointed to it, realizing that it had lost its charm for me as soon as I'd visualized the rounded curve of the thing smashing into Shea's head. I hoped that moment had been brief.

"That's the one," Jenny said. "Are you thinking that maybe the other one—the missing one—is the murder weapon?"

"I don't know." Pete reached for the candlestick, then hefted it in his right hand, as though judging its weight. "But it seems to be a distinct possibility. We'll need to photograph this one, take some measurements. Shouldn't take too long." He nodded in Gary Campbell's direction. "I'll sign a receipt and return this ASAP."

Campbell shrugged. "Guess it'll have to be all right. Jenny will make out a receipt for it with a full description. And, Jen, be sure to include the value, in case they lose it or damage it or anything, so we can collect the insurance." He parted the beaded curtains, and we followed him into the front of the shop.

Jenny rolled her eyes in my direction, took a pad of receipts from under the counter, and began to write. When she was done, she showed the narrow slip of paper to Campbell, who read it, nodded, and passed it to Pete, along with a pen.

"Just put your John Hancock right there, Detective," he said. "Take the damned thing and let me and Jenny get back to work. I'll drive her back to her store when we finish up here."

Thus dismissed, Pete and I headed back to his car, Pete carrying the candlestick as casually as though it really was a baseball bat. He held the passenger door open for me and, as soon as I was inside the car, handed me the candlestick. "Hang on to this, will you, babe? I wouldn't want it to roll around in the backseat and get dented or anything."

I didn't want to touch it, but I did as he asked, holding it by its base, upright in my lap, trying not to look at it. "Are we going to take it right down to the station?" I asked.

"I called the chief, and he's anxious to see it. I'll just take it in, and then I'll drive you back to the Tabby. Will they mind if you're a little late?"

"Not at all. I'm just making lists, figuring out what else I need to find for the plays. Does the chief think this . . ." I lifted the candlestick a couple of inches. It was heavier than it looked. "This thing really could kill somebody?"

"I never know what Chief Whaley is thinking." He smiled. "But I think you could be right about it. Did I ever tell you you'd make a good cop?"

I laughed. "Yes, you have. Many times. But I don't want your job, thank you. If the mate to this one really *is* what killed Shea, now you have to find that one, don't you?"

His serious cop face returned. "It would be a big help, that's for sure."

He lapsed into silence, and I looked out the window, watching the familiar Salem scenery pass by. We passed the new commuter rail station and turned onto Washington Street, headed for the police station. I glanced down at the candlestick as we passed the Tabernacle Church. Sunshine glinted on the polished brass surface. I tried to look away, but already the tiny cloud and the pinpoints of light had appeared. I saw Shea Tolliver then, her face distorted because of the candlestick's curved surface, but recognizable all the same. She smiled, almost laughing, and held her hand toward me, a gold chain dangling from her out-stretched fingers. At the end of the chain, the beautiful pink diamond sparkled.

CHAPTER 32

I closed my eyes, willing the vision to go away. What did it mean? Had Shea found the necklace, after all? Was that why she'd been killed? If that was true, then somebody else had it now. But who?

I felt the car pull to a stop and opened my eyes. We'd arrived at the police station. I dared to glance at the candlestick as I handed it to Pete. Only a candlestick. No vision.

"I'll just run in with this," he said, taking it from me. "Be right back."

I nodded, attempted a smile, but didn't say anything as he walked away. What could I say? "Oh, Pete, by the way, Shea found the necklace, and somebody else has it now. I know because I saw a vision in a candlestick."

Yeah, right. That'll go over well.

The necklace must have been in Helena's bureau all along, I thought. Probably in the blue velvet jewelry box. But why would Shea take the necklace and leave the jewelry box? It didn't make sense. And did the vision in the brass candlestick mean that I was apt to see things in just any random reflective surface? That could become a problem. A big one. The thoughts buzzing around in my head became more and more disturbing. I was relieved when Pete opened the driver's side door and climbed in.

"How'd it go?" I asked, as we drove in the direction of the Tabby "Did Chief Whaley think it might be important?"

"Sure did. He said to tell you, 'Thanks.'"

"Wow. Kind words from the chief. That makes my day." I meant it. I'd made a really bad impression on Pete's boss the very first time we met, and there'd been little improvement since. "Are we still on for tonight?"

"Far as I know, I still have the night off. What would you like to do?"

"Want to see a play? It's opening night, and I've got free tickets."

"If that's what you'd like to do. It's the one about shoes, right?"

I had to laugh at his casual summation of the Harold Brighouse comedy. "It is. It's about shoes and people and love and life. I think you'll like it."

"Okay." He sounded doubtful. "If you say so, but I warn you, I'm not much for plays. The last time I saw one, I was in high school. Our English class went to Boston to see *Julius Caesar.* Didn't like it."

"This one's nothing like that, I promise. Oh, oh! Tickets. That reminds me. I promised Tripp Hampton tickets because he loaned us the cobbler's bench. I'd better call him right now."

Pete raised one eyebrow but didn't say anything as I took out my phone and punched in Tripp's number.

"Hampton residence. Tripp Hampton speaking."

"Good morning, Tripp. This is Lee Barrett. I just remembered that I'd promised you tickets to *Hobson's Choice.* Tonight's opening night. I'll leave a pair of tickets for you at the box office. Of course, if you prefer another performance, just let me know. The show runs for seven nights."

"Thank you, Lee. I don't happen to have other plans for this evening, so I'll be delighted to attend." He sounded pleased. "I trust the cobbler's bench worked out for you?"

"It looks great. Completes the set nicely. You'll see. Bye now."

"Oh, Ms. Barrett? Lee? I trust you'll be there tonight?"

"Yes, I will." We were just pulling into the Tabby's parking lot. "It's time for me to get back to work now, Tripp. Enjoy the play. Bye."

"I hope to see you there," he said. "Really looking forward to it."

"Is the Hampton heir going to be there?" Pete asked after I'd hung up.

"He says he will. You don't like him much, do you?"

"Can't say I do. Do you?"

"Not crazy about any of them."

"What do you mean, 'them'?"

I realized that I hadn't told Pete about River's tarot warning to be wary of a blue-eyed, blond man. I gave him the condensed version, leaving out the "cruel or brutal" part. "The problem with the warning," I told him, "is that I've met three blue-eyed blonds lately."

"Three of them? Let's see. Gary Campbell for one. And Hampton has blue eyes, too, doesn't he?"

"Yep. He sure does."

"Who else? Somebody at work I haven't met yet?"

"Tommy Trent is the third one." I was surprised that Pete hadn't figured that out.

"You can't count him," Pete said. "He's not really blond. Daphne colors it for him. Didn't you notice that his hair was brown when he got out of prison?"

"No. But now that you mention it, he was wearing a hat. But he's blond now. I wonder if that counts. I'll ask River."

Pete shook his head and smiled. "You do that. I'll see you tonight. What time?"

"Curtain's at eight," I said. "How about six thirty? I'll fix us a quick dinner at my place."

He leaned in for a fast kiss. "Sounds good. See you then. And, Lee, be careful. Of everyone, blond or not."

I went directly to my office. It would be relatively quiet there, and I needed to think about what I'd seen in the candlestick. I'd had enough of these visions to know that even if I didn't understand them at first, they'd turn out to be spot on. I was pretty sure—no, I was convinced—that Shea Tolliver had found the pink diamond. And I was just as sure that someone had taken it away from her. But how could I tell Pete that?

I sat at my desk, trying to concentrate. I was still nervous about being alone in there, so I'd left the door to the Theater Arts Department ajar. I could hear the cast of *Our Town* going over their lines. Because the set for that play was so minimal, they could rehearse just about anywhere in the building, and sometimes they even used my nearly empty second-floor TV Production classroom to go over their lines. I was glad they'd chosen to work right next door to me on this particular day, though, and the barely audible hum of stage conversation was comforting.

I tried hard to think of some way to tell Pete that

Shea had found the diamond and probably had been killed for it, without revealing the secret of how I knew about it. I spent nearly an hour plotting, then discarding, schemes that would put him on the right track without confessing that I was a scryer.

I have to tell him.

The ringing of the office phone jarred me out of my fruitless contemplation. It was Jenny.

"Hi, Lee. Sorry to bother you, but I'm dying to know. Is the other candlestick the murder weapon or not? Did Pete tell you?"

"I don't know anything more about it," I said. "These things take a while. They'll weigh it and measure it and compare it to the . . . you know . . . the wound." I paused. "Even then," I added, "Pete doesn't tell me much about police business."

"No kidding. It looked to me like you two were pretty tight."

"About a lot of things we are," I admitted. "But we don't tell each other everything."

We sure don't!

"Yeah, well, sometimes that's best, I guess. I know you're busy. I'll let you get back to work."

"You're busy, too. How's the inventory going? Mr. Campbell seems quite anxious to get the shop open."

"I know. The bills keep coming, even when you aren't selling anything." She sighed. "And I keep coming up with these little roadblocks—like the missing candlestick."

"Something else missing?"

"It's the darnedest thing. Did you notice the silver coin display in a glass case in the back room?"

"Nope. Sorry. I didn't. That room is pretty crowded."

"Tell me about it! Well, there was a nice complete set of Benjamin Franklin half-dollars there. They minted them only from nineteen forty-eight to nineteen sixty-three, you know."

"I don't really know much of anything about coins," I said.

"A complete set is worth more than just a bunch of individual coins."

"I should think so."

"Shea had it priced as a set, but wouldn't you know it? There's one missing, so that changes the value and messes up my appraisal."

I didn't need to ask which half-dollar was missing, and I knew exactly where that 1951 Ben Franklin was.

CHAPTER 33

"Somebody probably offered her enough money for just the one to make it worthwhile to sell it. I'm sure she meant to replace it later." Jenny sighed again. "Oh, well, I'll figure it out. Let me know if you hear anything about that candlestick, will you?"

I promised to keep her informed and returned to thoughts of my own problem. I realized that Jenny had handed me the answer. I dialed Pete again.

He answered right away. "Anything wrong? You okay?"

"I'm fine. Don't worry. But I think Jenny has just given us another clue."

"I know you like clues, Nancy Drew. What is it this time?" I heard the smile in his voice.

"I'm serious, Pete," I told him. "Listen. Jenny's found something else missing in the shop. A Benjamin Franklin half-dollar."

Cop voice back. "Nineteen fifty-one?"

"I'm betting on it. I think Shea found something in that compartment in the bureau, took it out, and looked around for something small to replace it. That's why the tissue paper from the dog license was torn. She wrapped the coin in one half of the tissue paper and put it in the bureau in place of the . . . whatever."

"You're thinking 'the whatever' is the diamond."

"I am. You?"

"Could be. Could very well be. Nice going, Lee. Did I ever tell you—"

"That I'd make a good cop? Couple of times. I saved the torn tissue paper. I'll show you when you come over tonight."

We said our good-byes, and I leaned back in my chair, relieved. I'd managed to plant the idea that Shea had found the diamond, and I'd done it without saying anything about candlestick visions. Dodged a bullet on that one. For now.

I pulled my prop lists from the top desk drawer and ran a finger down the vertical row of checked boxes. Too many boxes were still without check marks. Most of it was small miscellaneous stuff—ashtrays, footstools, lamps, artificial flowers and plants, cups and plates. My budget was down to less than a hundred dollars, so it was time to "beg, borrow, and steal," as Aunt Ibby had predicted. I also knew that my aunt had much more "miscellaneous stuff" than anyone needed, and I was pretty sure some of it was squirreled away in our rebuilt fourth-floor attic.

I told Mr. Pennington I'd be out of the office for a while, phoned Pete, and left a message that I'd be at the Winter Street house. I exchanged my car for the truck once again and headed for home.

Although the top floor of the house had been completely restored after the fire, I hadn't ventured up there at all. Too many bad memories from that Halloween night when Aunt Ibby and I had confronted a killer there. I backed the truck into the yard, then tapped on my aunt's kitchen door.

"Home already, Maralee? Is everything all right at the school?"

"No worries," I said. "I'm home to check out the stuff in the attic, if you don't mind. Might be something in there we can use onstage. Want to come up with me?"

"You're more than welcome to anything up there. You go ahead. I'll join you in a few minutes." She pointed to the ticking oven timer. "I'm trying out another of Tabitha Trumbull's recipes."

"Smells good, whatever it is. I'll see you in a few. I have some more news about the pink diamond."

The enclosed stairway to the fourth-floor attic room was not far from the door to my apartment. Even so, I'd avoided it for months. I'd just turned the glass doorknob and started up the stairs when O'Ryan pushed his way through the kitchen cat door and dashed ahead of me. The smell of new wood was pleasant, and thankfully, there wasn't a whiff of smoke.

"What do you think, boy? It's a lot different from the last time we were up here, isn't it?" I said when we reached the attic room.

O'Ryan inspected the edges and corners of the long room. Unlike the attic I remembered, which was jampacked with castoffs, this new space was relatively bare. But what I saw held theatrical possibilities. There was an old kitchen chair and a small stepladder, which would do for *Our Town,* a clear plastic box full of ashtrays—nobody we know smokes anymore, but the people in suite 67D probably did—and at least half a dozen stacked cardboard boxes marked ODDS AND ENDS. It looked like a good haul of props for no money.

The cat, tail twitching, walked to a window overlooking the garden far below, hopped up to the sill, and sat there, looking outside. The window frame was brand new and didn't resemble the old one—the one Aunt Ibby and I had, not so long ago, climbed through to get onto the flat roof below and escape from a killer.

I bypassed the cardboard boxes and headed over to the cat, then leaned over his head to see what he was looking at. It was another cat, a black one wearing a red collar, who'd somehow made its way up onto the roof and now sat there, looking in at us.

I heard footsteps on the stairs behind me and called out, "Aunt Ibby? Is that you?"

"It's me, and I can hardly wait to hear what you've learned about the diamond. Has it been found?" She appeared on the top step and hurried into the room.

"Not exactly, but I think I've discovered something new about what's become of it."

"Really? Here. Sit down and tell me everything." She sat in the old chair and motioned for me to sit on the top of the little stepladder. O'Ryan had left his post by the window and had returned to his position in front of the cardboard boxes.

"First, I guess I'll have to tell you . . . there've been some recent changes in my gazing ability."

She frowned. "In addition to seeing things in the new mirror?"

"I'm afraid so. Apparently, some other shiny surfaces can show me, um, things."

"Things?"

"The old display shoe at the Tabby still works, for instance, so I know the visions aren't limited to just one object anymore, like Ariel's obsidian ball or the tarnished mirror."

"Yes, I suspected that when the new mirror in the bureau offered you scenes. But your ability to turn these pictures on and off whenever you want to seems to have grown, too. Isn't that true?"

I nodded. "Right. But today I saw . . . something . . . on an unusual surface." I told her about the candlestick missing from the inventory of Shea's shop, and about my remembering that I'd seen the pair when I'd bought the bureau.

She leaned forward. "Did you tell Pete about this? A heavy candlestick like that could be used as a weapon!"

"I called him the minute Jenny told me about it. He came to the Tabby right away, and he and Jenny and I went to the shop to check it out."

"Does Pete think the mate to it could be what killed Shea?"

I shrugged. "He took it back to the police station with him. They'll have to run tests."

"I understand," she said, "but what did you start to say about seeing something? On an unusual surface? Not the candlestick!"

"Afraid so. It was a little bit distorted, but I saw Shea Tolliver. She was alive and smiling, and, Aunt Ibby, she was holding the pink diamond necklace."

"So Shea found it in the bureau, after all! Maralee, you have to tell Pete about this. Someone must have killed her for it." She frowned. "But how can you tell him such a thing? He wouldn't believe it, would he?"

"I don't know whether he would or not. I know I'm not ready to tell him that I . . . see things. But Jenny found something else missing." I told her about the half-dollar and my idea that Shea had just looked around the shop for something small enough to fit in the space where the necklace had been, and had grabbed the Ben Franklin coin.

"Well," my aunt said, "she owned the bureau fair

and square, along with everything in it. The necklace belonged to her, no doubt. As they say, 'Possession is nine points of the law.'"

"Anyway, I told Pete about my idea that Shea had switched the half-dollar for the necklace, and I think he agrees with me. So I didn't have to tell him about . . . you know."

"I do know, my dear. But if that young man cares about you as much as he seems to, it would be dishonest of you not to tell him about this 'gift' of yours. I'm sure you'll find the proper time and place to do so."

"I hope so," I said. "But it won't be today. We're going to the opening of *Hobson's Choice* tonight. Will you and Mr. Pennington be there, too?"

"Wouldn't miss it for the world." She stood and motioned to the pile of boxes. "Now back to business." She picked up a small willow clothes basket. "Take whatever you want. You should be able to fill this up."

"Thanks. O'Ryan and I will sort it out. Afterward, maybe we'll have time for a bite of that great-smelling Tabitha treat you were baking. What is it?"

"Tabitha called it Louise's Bread Pudding. I don't know who Louise was, but she used marmalade and toasted almonds in her bread pudding."

"Yummy. We'll hurry with the sorting," I promised. "Will there be whipped cream?"

"Absolutely. If you want this little stepladder, I'll carry it downstairs for you." I nodded. She picked it up, gave a little wave, and disappeared from my view.

"All right, then, cat," I said, lifting the top box from the pile. "Let's get started." O'Ryan sniffed at the box, batted at it with one paw, then hopped up onto the chair my aunt had just vacated and watched as I pulled the folded flaps apart. "So this is just going to be a spectator sport for you, huh? Okay. You relax. I'll do the work."

The articles in the boxes had all been carefully wrapped in newspaper. I unwrapped and inspected each one, putting things that might be useful props in the willow basket and rewrapping the others and returning them to their boxes. I even found a couple of items I could use in my apartment. One was a small framed watercolor of a bowl of fruit—just what River had said I needed for the kitchen. Time passed quickly as I sorted and repackaged the assorted castoffs, all under O'Ryan's watchful gaze.

The last cardboard box in the pile, unlike the others, had been tightly sealed with packing tape. As I picked at a corner of the sticky binding, O'Ryan jumped from the chair and landed with a thud on top of the flat, slim box. He stood there, legs slightly apart, all four feet firmly planted, the golden eyes fixed on mine.

"Get down from there, you silly boy," I scolded. "We're almost finished here. Don't you want some nice whipped cream?"

He shook his head from side to side. No question about it. The witch's cat didn't want me to open that box.

"Scat," I said. "Get away from there." O'Ryan hunched down, not breaking his unblinking stare, and gave a low growl. I was surprised. He'd never growled at me before. "What's wrong, boy?" I reached out to pat his head, but he shook my hand away. I heard a scraping noise behind me and turned toward the direction of the sound.

The black cat was scratching at the window, and it was no longer alone. A gray cat with a star-shaped white blaze on its forehead stood beside the black one. The gray cat tipped back its head, opened its mouth, and gave a long, loud, bone-chilling yowl.

"Okay," I said. "You and your friends win. Let's get out of here." I put the basket under one arm, picked up the kitchen chair by its ladder back, and clattered my way down those stairs in a hurry, O'Ryan right behind me. As soon as we reached the third floor, I ducked into my apartment, then closed and locked the door. I plopped the basket on the kitchen table and shoved the chair behind the counter. Seconds later, the cat strolled calmly through the cat door, approached his bowl of kitty kibble, and began munching away, as though he and his feline pals hadn't just scared the bejesus out of me. I was glad no one else had been in the attic to witness my unceremonious departure, and I was in no hurry to go back up there anytime soon, either.

"No need to be greedy," I said, "The ladder and chair and the basket of tchotchkes will do just fine for now."

The cat looked up from his bowl and gave me an up-and-down nod.

"You agree?"

Another nod.

"Maybe there's something hazardous or toxic in that box, and you don't want me to get hurt."

O'Ryan gave me a blank, ordinary cat look and then turned his full attention to the kibble. The conversation was over.

CHAPTER 34

"Find anything else useful among the castoffs?"
Aunt Ibby asked when I returned to the downstairs
kitchen.

"A few little knickknacks," I said, sitting at the round
table. "Mr. Pennington says he likes realism on the sets,
and he thinks the small incidental pieces are important."

"You would have had so much more to choose from
in the old attic," she said with a tinge of sadness. "It
looks quite bare now, doesn't it?"

"It does," I agreed, picturing the long, almost empty
space, with its new wood smell.

She shook her head. "Nothing left except memories
and that one box of things the flames didn't touch. Did
you find anything interesting in that one?"

*A box of things the flames didn't touch? The box O'Ryan
doesn't want me to touch?*

"One box had so much tape on it, I didn't want to
bother with it," I lied. "Do you know what's in it?"

She laughed. "I've never opened it, either. Our old
handyman, Bill Sullivan, told me he'd packed up a few

things that hadn't burned with the rest. 'Nothing valuable,' he said. It seems a heavy old mirror in a gilt frame had fallen onto one small pile of stuff and had protected it all from the fire." She placed a round brown-glazed bowl of bread pudding on the table. "Doesn't this smell good?' She placed a smaller matching bowl of whipped cream beside it. "Help yourself."

"Did Mr. Sullivan tell you exactly what's in the box?" I asked, keeping my voice level and taking a big spoonful from each bowl.

"'Mostly paper things,' he said. Greeting cards, your old report cards, theater programs. Bill thought they might have some sentimental value, that's all. So he packed them up. He was such a thoughtful man, Bill was. May he rest in peace." She looked down at the table. "Oh, and there was a scribbly old book." She smiled. "That's what he called it. A scribbly old book."

I knew what it was. And I knew why O'Ryan didn't want me to open the box. The "scribbly old book" was the witch Ariel Constellation's spell book. It had originally been the property of Bridget Bishop, the most notorious of the Salem witches and the first one to die on Gallows Hill in 1692. I'd deliberately thrown it into that raging fire, hoping the evil damned thing would be destroyed forever. I should have known better.

Saved by a falling mirror. Why am I not surprised?

I decided then to leave the book exactly where it was—safe, for the time being, from falling into the wrong hands. I was pretty sure that there was no point in trying to destroy it again. Having made that decision, and having taken a vow to stay away from the attic as much as possible, I felt a little better.

"You're too quiet," my aunt said, frowning. "Don't

you like the bread pudding? Too much marmalade? What?"

"It's perfect," I told her. "I'm just savoring. Don't change a thing."

Her smile returned. "I think I'll save the rest for an after-theater treat for us to share. That is, if you two don't have other plans." We'd already decided that we'd all ride to the theater together in Mr. Pennington's big Lincoln.

"We don't," I said. "And you know how Pete loves your cooking. Speaking of food, I need to pick up a couple of things at the grocery store. Pete's coming over for a quick dinner before we go to the play. I'm thinking lasagna and a salad."

"Are you going to take the things you found in the attic back to the school now?"

"Yes. Where's the little ladder?"

"In the back hall. I'll come upstairs with you and get the basket, if you can manage the chair."

Between the two of us, and with O'Ryan supervising, we secured the chair and the stepladder in the truck bed and put the willow basket on the front passenger seat. I started the engine.

"I'll see you later," I said. "Oh, I almost forgot. I promised O'Ryan some whipped cream. Will you give it to him please?"

She promised that she would, and I drove carefully back to the Tabby, steadying the basket with one hand, steering with the other, and trying to sort out the kaleidoscope of thoughts tumbling around in my brain. The distorted picture of Shea showing up on the polished surface of the brass candlestick, Helena Trent appearing on the toe of the giant black pump, Helena's grandpa in the mirror of Helena's own bureau, and the little gray dog named Nicky chasing sticks on that long, empty beach. What did it all mean?

I looked at the round clock in the dashboard and wondered if River was awake. I needed to talk to somebody who'd understand what was going on in my head, and that field was extremely limited. At this point, River was it. I pulled my phone out of my pocket and dialed her, and she answered right away.

"River," I said, "I'm so confused. Do you have time to come by the school for a little while? You can bring the cards if you want."

"Really? I think this is the first time since the day we met that you've actually asked for a reading. I'll be there!"

She was right about that. She'd offered to read the tarot for me many times, and occasionally I'd agreed, but my asking her to bring her cards was surely a first.

I knew River lived fairly close to the school. She and two other witches shared an apartment over on Lynde Street, right near the old dungeon where they used to keep witches awaiting trial back in the late sixteen hundreds. As a matter of fact, the apartment had previously been Ariel Constellation's home, and the three considered themselves lucky to have rented it.

I pulled into the warehouse and loaded the stepladder, the chair, and the wicker basket onto the freight elevator and rode up to the third floor with a minimum of bumps and jerks. I was actually getting quite good at this. I carried the basket over to my desk and left the larger pieces in the elevator. I'd barely had time to sit down when River appeared.

She was dressed in her full tarot-reading regalia— an outfit she wore only for the kind of readings she did for corporate meetings, birthday parties, state fair appearances, and the like—all of which paid handsomely. Her long, black velvet dress had an Elvira-like neckline, and her silver lamé turban sported a huge red stone at its center. I recognized the red velvet cape as one of several that Ariel had kept at the TV station. I'd worn some of them myself. River's waist-length black braid had bright crystal stars woven into it, and silver high-heeled sandals completed the picture of a most glamorous, but far from authentic, Salem witch.

"What's the occasion?" I asked, getting up and closing the office door. "All this elegance isn't for my benefit, I trust?" I asked, half wishing that it was.

"On my way to the Old Gentlemen's Home, believe it or not, for a ninety-first birthday party—no charge for the old gents—and I thought they'd like the outfit."

"That's so cool," I said. "Pencil me in for my ninety-first, will you? Meanwhile, please sit down. I don't know if I need a reading or just someone to talk to about my weird life."

She'd already pushed aside my pile of scripts and file folders and placed one tarot card on the desktop . . . the Queen of Wands, which she always chose to represent me. She bowed her head. "May only the higher forces surround this seeker while this reading takes place and may the truth of the matter concerning her be revealed." She sat up straight in her chair and placed the deck of tarot cards facedown on the desk. "Okay. Do you want to talk first or just ask questions as we go along?"

"Talk first, please," I said. "There's so much going on that I don't understand. The gazing thing . . . it's expanding somehow."

"Expanding? What do you mean? The pictures are getting bigger?"

"No. They're just showing up on more surfaces. It's not just the shoe or the mirror anymore. I've even seen one in a candlestick. Why is it happening?"

"Hmmm." She handed me the deck. "Shuffle the cards and concentrate on *why*. Then, with your left hand, cut the cards into three piles and put them face-down."

I did as she asked, concentrating on the various surfaces and the scenes I'd witnessed. I looked at the three piles of cards. "Did I do it right?"

She smiled. "There's no wrong way to do this. Relax. Tell me what's going on that's got you so freaked out."

I began to talk . . . thoughts coming so fast, it would have sounded like mindless babbling to anyone but River. As I spoke, she silently—almost in slow motion—placed cards faceup in a neatly spaced pattern. I talked about the dog Nicky and about the grandfather in the doorway. I told her about Helena facing me, weeping, holding something in her arms, and about seeing Shea in the candlestick that might be the mate to the weapon that had killed her. I realized that my cheeks were wet with tears as I described the lonely beach, the voice calling me to follow, the little dog growling. All the while, River arranged the cards, their colorful pictures facing up.

I talked, too, about things that weren't a result of gazing. I told her about little girl Helena planting pansies because they were her grandmother's favorite flower, about the maze of corridors in Tripp Hampton's house, about Tommy Trent's angry face, and about Daphne needing glasses.

After a while the tumbling thoughts and the tears

stopped. The room was silent except for the *slap, slap* of the cards. I leaned back in my chair. I felt empty, exhausted, but somehow calm, even peaceful.

River smiled across the desk. "Feel better?"

I returned her smile. "Yes. Thanks for listening. But what does it all mean?"

She began the reading, starting with the card she'd placed on top of the Queen of Wands. "This is the moon. It's the card of the psychic. It means you may be developing powers you've only recently discovered in yourself. You can control the visions, no matter where they appear." She tapped the card with her forefinger. "This can be a good thing, a very good thing, but it can also mean unseen peril, and misfortune to someone you know."

I nodded, pointing to what appeared to be two dogs on a path between two towers. "And the dogs? What do they mean?"

"One is a dog, and one is a wolf. They mean that you must travel between those towers of good and evil to reach your goal. But don't worry. Mother Moon is watching over you."

She continued, moving cards, explaining symbols and the things they might mean in my life.

She smiled as she pointed out that the Knight of Swords, which she interpreted to be Pete, was watching over me, too. That one made sense.

A card called the Fool told me that I had an important choice to make. *Great. I have several. Do I tell Pete about the scrying? Am I going to sleep with him or not?*

The High Priestess card meant that I shouldn't talk about something that was supposed to remain secret. *Okay.* Did that mean Bridget Bishop's book should stay where it was?

The Empress symbolized the realization of a creative project. *An easy one.* The plays would turn out well.

The fact that the Priestess and the Empress were close to the Fool apparently meant that someone else would make the important choice for me. *See? Back to square one.*

But I did feel better, and by the time River left in a swirl of red velvet, with a promise to meet me for lunch on her next day off, I really believed that I could control the visions, no matter where they appeared, and I resolved to leave the box in the attic unopened for now. I didn't much like the idea of someone else making an important decision for me, but since I didn't know which decision that might be, it didn't make much sense to worry about it.

Most of the things in the wicker basket went to the *Born Yesterday* set; a couple of pairs of men's shoes went to *Hobson's,* with an unspoken question as to where my maiden aunt had obtained them; and the stepladder and kitchen chair were set aside for *Our Town.* There didn't seem to be much more for me to do at the Tabby that afternoon, so I secured the truck, picked up my car, and drove to the grocery store for pasta sauce for my lasagna.

A play opening in Salem is a dressy occasion, much as it is in most cities, and I'd decided on a Chinese-inspired emerald-green silk dress with a mandarin collar and side slits. With the lasagna bubbling away in the oven and the salad crisping in the refrigerator, I showered, shampooed, and took extra care with my make-up. Then I slipped on the emerald dress, consulted my new full-length mirror, and messed up my hair just a little bit.

CHAPTER 35

Pete was right on time, as usual, and on that particular evening, in a light gray suit with his jacket unbuttoned over a black turtleneck, he could easily have graced the cover of *GQ*. The lasagna was hot, the salad crisp and pretty, and I was—if I did say so myself—looking good in Chinese silk. I could tell that Pete thought so, too. The kisses we exchanged before dinner helped me answer two of the questions that had been on my mind that day. Yes, I was going to tell him I was a scryer, and yes, I was going to sleep with him—and not necessarily in that order.

But . . . not tonight. Dinner was ready, there was an eight o'clock curtain, and my aunt was apt to knock on the door any minute to tell us that Mr. Pennington had arrived. Anyway, we needed to talk about the Ben Franklin coin and the missing pink diamond. There was no news yet about the missing candlestick, but we were both pretty sure it was the murder weapon. We hurried through the meal, not giving the lasagna the admiration it deserved—as it was every bit as good as Aunt Ibby's. I loaded the dishwasher, then put Pete to work making coffee, while I, avoiding temptation, went into the bedroom alone and brought the two halves of torn tissue paper, the coin, and the dog license back to the table.

"See what I mean about the torn paper?" I said. "I can almost see Shea finding the necklace. She's amazed, and she stashes it, still in the tissue paper, someplace nearby, then looks around for something to put in its place so that whoever bought the bureau wouldn't think something was missing. She grabs the coin out of the case right next to where she's standing, tears the tissue paper that was on the dog tag in half, and fills the empty half of the compartment that way."

"Good visual," Pete said with a grin as he poured the coffee. "You make it sound like a movie!"

You have no idea how visual I can be.

He picked up the pieces of tissue paper, fitted the torn edges together, then rewrapped the coin and the dog license. Nicky's license.

"I think you may be right about Shea finding the necklace, and it could have gone down just the way you described it," he said. "Any thoughts about who has the necklace now?"

"Nope. Not a one." I picked up the tissue-wrapped coin and tag and headed back to the bedroom.

"Need any help in there?" Pete had started to follow me when O'Ryan dashed from the living room, down the hall, into the kitchen and pushed his way through the cat door.

"That must mean Mr. Pennington has arrived," I said. "We'd better go downstairs."

O'Ryan was right—no surprise there. Pete and I joined my aunt and my boss, and the four of us piled into the Lincoln. As we pulled away from the curb, I waved to O'Ryan, who watched us from the bay window in Aunt Ibby's living room.

Downtown Salem might not look much like Broadway, but with a couple of rented searchlights sending bright beams into the sky, the flashing marquee, and the line of well-dressed first-nighters lined up in front of the Tabby's student theater, it was pretty impressive. Once we were inside, a uniformed usher led us to our seats. The houselights were on, and I looked around to see who I might recognize.

My aunt was seated beside me. "Looks like everybody who is anybody is here," she whispered. "Look. There's the mayor and his wife, and isn't that Tripp Hampton over there with a pretty blonde?"

I looked to where she pointed, and nudged Pete. "There's Tripp Hampton," I said. "With Daphne."

"Saw them," he said. "Gary Campbell's here, too, with Jenny." He nodded toward the couple a few rows ahead of us, their heads bent over a play program.

I wasn't surprised by Gary Campbell's choice of a theater date, but Daphne being Tripp Hampton's escort was a shocker now that her boyfriend was free. Was it possible that Tommy didn't mind Tripp playing Henry Higgins to Daphne's Eliza Doolittle? I turned in my seat and looked toward the back of the theater, halfway expecting to see Tommy Trent's angry face, but the houselights had dimmed and the curtain rose on the Tabby's first play of the summer.

By intermission the success of *Hobson's* was assured. Pete and I and my aunt and Mr. Pennington headed to the lobby. A discreet cash bar had been set up, where a

tuxedoed bartender served wine and soft drinks. A
beaming Mr. Pennington mingled with the crowd, and
Aunt Ibby, as usual, was surrounded by friends. Pete
and I carried our wineglasses to the far edge of the
long lobby, where I happily eavesdropped on the
enthusiastic comments of passing patrons. Pete, his
cop face in place and his back to the wall, stood close
at my side, watching the crowd.

"Oh, there you are. Hi, Lee! Hi, Detective!" Daphne,
splendid in a gold, all-over sequined mini with matching four-inch-high heels, enveloped me in a Juicy
Couture–scented hug. "The play is good so far, isn't it?"
She frowned. "Wish we could have got front-row seats,
though, so I could see better."

Tripp Hampton, in black Armani, stood back for a
moment, looking at her much the way a proud daddy
might look at his cute four-year-old. Then he stepped
forward, right hand extended, first to Pete and then to
me. We all spoke the expected greetings, commented
on the actors' performances, the attractiveness of
the set.

"The cobbler's bench looks absolutely authentic,
Tripp," I said. "Thank you again so much for lending it
to us."

"My pleasure," he said.

"Tripp," Daphne said, all dimples and smiles. "Want
to get me a glass of white wine?"

"Of course. Refill, Lee? Detective?"

"No thanks," I said. We each lifted our glasses.

"We're fine." Pete tapped my glass with his.

Tripp headed for the bar, and Daphne squinted,
watching his retreating back. "I'd get it myself except
I didn't bring any money," she said. "I'd like to get a

closer look at the cute bartender. Love men in tuxes. Do you have one, Detective?"

Pete laughed. "Not me. I rent one when I need it."

Tripp returned and handed Daphne her glass with a flourish. "Cheers, dear."

She favored him with a dimpled smile. "Tripp has one. Looks good in it, too. One time he took me to a black-tie thing where all the men wore them. What a feast!" She laughed the silvery little giggle she'd perfected as Billie Dawn. "The only problem that night was, I didn't have the slightest idea who I was dancing with most of the time. They all looked alike to me!"

The five-minute-warning buzzer sounded. I looked around the lobby, hoping to see Gary Campbell so I could thank him for the loan of the cash register. Not only did it look good onstage, but its loud ring also brought hearty laughter from the audience every time the old man dipped into it for drinking money. I remembered what Campbell had said about knowing what that was like. When we all trooped back into the theater for the last two acts, I saw that he and Jenny were already in their seats, and resolved to thank him later.

We watched while Maggie swore to Will that she'd wear her brass wedding ring forever, and cheered when old man Hobson got his comeuppance. The place erupted with applause. A standing ovation for the cast and three curtain calls! Mr. Pennington was ecstatic. Again, I searched for Gary Campbell but couldn't spot him in the crowd.

The mood was still celebratory when we arrived back at the house on Winter Street, and Aunt Ibby's latest creation from the Tabitha Trumbull cookbook to be, served with hazelnut-flavored coffee, was received with enthusiasm. It was after midnight when Mr. Pennington and Pete left, and while my aunt and I dealt with the dishes, something nibbled at my mind. It was something Daphne had said.

"Aunt Ibby," I said, "want to do a bit of research for me?"

"Love to. Research is my middle name." Her face lit up, and she rubbed her hands together. "What do you need?"

I smiled at her eagerness. "Do you think you could dig up some newspaper accounts of any big society events that happened in Salem on the night Helena was murdered?"

"Sounds intriguing! I'll go to the library and get on it first thing in the morning."

"I'd appreciate it. Thanks."

She hung up her dish towel and turned off the kitchen light. We headed for the front stairs together, O'Ryan trotting along behind us. "Want to give me a hint about what I'm looking for?" she asked.

"I'm not even sure myself," I admitted. "It may be nothing. May be something."

We'd reached the door to her second-floor bedroom. "Good night, then, Maralee. Sweet dreams."

I climbed the stairs to my own apartment, O'Ryan scampering ahead of me. I heard his cat door open and saw the flick of his yellow tail as he went inside. By the time I opened the door, he was already sprawled out along the windowsill.

"That seems to be your favorite perch lately," I said. "Are your friends in the yard again?"

Leaving the kitchen light off, I knelt beside the

window and looked in the direction the big cat faced. The bars of the fire escape blocked the view from that vantage point, so I stood and looked through the panes at the top of the sash. The moon had paled, but the back fence was still visible. At first I didn't see the lone cat sitting there, black as the night sky.

CHAPTER 36

Things were upbeat at the Tabby's diner when I stopped in for morning coffee. Newspapers were in evidence all over the place as actors and directors, stagehands and volunteer staff members searched for reviews of the previous night's opening performance. The *Salem News*, the *Boston Herald*, the *Boston Globe*, and a few tabloids I'd never heard of were spread out on the counter and on most of the tables.

Mr. Pennington called to me from a booth tightly packed with players from the cast of *Hobson's Choice*. "Ms. Barrett. Do come and join us. The reviews are stellar! Look. The *News* even mentions the excellent set design."

I stood at the edge of the table and looked at the paper, pleased that my efforts had brought positive editorial notice. There was clearly no room for me to join the happy group, but two seats at the crowded counter behind me were vacated as I stood there, and I hurried to claim one. As I slid onto the round red stool, a man captured the one next to me, and we bumped elbows.

"Well, Ms. Barrett, we literally keep running into

each other, don't we?" Gary Campbell rubbed his arm. "You okay?"

"I am," I said, relieved that we were finally acknowledging that collision on the steps of Shea's shop. "You?"

"Smacked my funny bone, that's all. Can I buy you a cup of coffee?"

"You don't have to do that," I said.

"I'm not so broke, I can't afford coffee," he said, smiling.

"Thanks," I said. "I looked for you last night. I wanted to thank you again for the cash register. Did you and Jenny enjoy the show?"

"Very much. The old man got a laugh every time he opened it to grab his booze money, didn't he?"

"It added a lot to the story. And thanks, too, for being so gracious about the candlestick."

He shrugged. "It's nothing. Glad to help out when I can."

"You're very generous." As soon as I said the words, I remembered what River had said about the blue-eyed, blond man. *He can be generous, but he can be cruel or brutal.* What had he said to Shea that was cruel enough for a judge to issue a restraining order? Had they really reconciled, agreed to go back into business together? I sipped my coffee and looked at his reflection in the Coca-Cola mirror behind the counter. He was still smiling.

"I understood how the old man felt, though," he said.

"The old man?"

"In the play. When he was stealing from the company to support a bad habit." He turned and faced me.

"I used to steal. Out of that same cash register. For almost the same reason." The smile had disappeared.

What the heck are you supposed to say to an admission like that? I was saved from having to say anything when Daphne's reflection appeared between us in the mirror. "Hey, Lee! Did you see the reviews? Awesome, huh?"

"Wonderful. Mr. Pennington is so happy."

"I know. I wonder if the papers will say such good stuff about my play."

"I'm sure they will. Daphne, you know Mr. Campbell, don't you?"

"Sure." She faced the man, squinting. "Can I sit with you guys?"

"Here. Take my seat," I told her. "I have to get up to my office. Thanks for the coffee, Mr. Campbell."

"You're welcome. Please call me Gary, Lee."

I left the diner through the doors leading to the Tabby. When I looked back, the two were in animated conversation.

On the third floor, the *Our Town* actors were going over their lines in front of the old S&H Green Stamp redemption center, while one of the stagehands ran a vacuum cleaner over the rug on the suite 67D stage. Once again, I left my office door ajar, finding the sounds of activity soothing. I cleared the top of my desk, putting a few folders into the file cabinet. As I arranged the bound scripts into a neat stack, I noticed one of River's tarot cards. I turned it over and found myself face-to-face with the Knight of Wands . . . that blond, blue-eyed mystery man. I turned him facedown again and smiled as I texted River, telling her she was no longer playing with a full deck. She texted me back, telling me to keep him as a reminder to be careful. I taped old blue eyes to the wall beside me.

I read through the property lists on the back page of each of the remaining scripts, checking off the things we'd decided to use and crossing out the ones the director thought unnecessary. I looked up from my work when I heard the office door swing open. This time Tommy Trent didn't look angry, but he didn't look particularly friendly, either.

"Please don't close that door," I said as he started to push it shut.

"Oh, sorry." He opened the door halfway. "That better?"

"Yes, thank you. What do you want?" My phone was close at hand.

"I took my car to the car wash today," he said.

"Oh?"

"Had a full detail. They vacuumed the whole inside."

"Uh-huh." My hand crept closer to the phone.

He pulled a wrinkled sheet of paper from his pocket. "They found this under the front seat. It's got your name and address on it. First the card in my bureau drawer and now this. What are you trying to prove, lady?" He shook the paper close to my face. I recognized the name on the heading.

Bob's Moving and Delivery.

"I've never seen it before," I told him, "but I know it was stolen, and I know that the police are looking for it. If somebody put it in your car, that somebody is trying to get you into trouble."

"One thing I don't want is more trouble," he said. "I've had enough of it." He put the paper on my desk. "If the cops need it, they can have it. Call them if you want to. Maybe they can figure out how it got into my locked car. I'm calling my probation officer." He reached into the breast pocket of his shirt. "Something's going on here that can land me back in prison."

My mind raced, and my first thought was Daphne. She'd claimed she'd found the index card, and I knew she had access to Tommy's car. Gary Campbell had been in the shop with Shea's body. Had he taken the index card from the register? Were Daphne and Gary working together? Was that a chance meeting downstairs in the diner, or had they arranged it?"

I almost blurted out, "What about Daphne?" when the door swung open all the way. Pete stood in the doorway, and my aunt Ibby was right behind him.

"Put your hands where I can see them, Trent," Pete ordered. "What are you doing here?"

Tommy put his phone down and spread his hands out flat on the desk. "I found something in my car that I thought might belong to Ms. Barrett here. Has her name on it." He jerked his head in my direction. "She'll tell you."

I walked over to where my aunt waited in the doorway, and stood beside her. She squeezed my hand.

"That right, Lee?" Pete stepped closer to the desk and looked down at the crumpled work order.

"That's right," I said, "and I'm pretty sure that's the paperwork somebody took from Bob's, isn't it?"

"Looks like it. You say you found this in your car, Trent? Let's step outside, and you can tell me all about it."

Aunt Ibby and I moved aside as Tommy Trent and Pete left the office.

"Good heavens, Maralee," she said. "What on God's green earth was that all about?"

"It's pretty much what Tommy Trent said. He found that paper with my name on it and wanted to know what was going on."

"Pete seemed to know Trent was here."

I smiled. "Pete's keeping an eye on me. But what are you doing here? Is anything wrong?"

"Not at all. I did as you asked and learned a few things about the night Helena died." She reached into her handbag and pulled out a sheaf of papers. "I thought we might go to lunch together so I can show you what I've found."

"Good idea," I said, grabbing my purse. "Let's get out of here."

I closed my office door as we left, and looked around for Pete and Tommy in the Theater Arts Department. "Pete must have taken him outside to see what he has to say about the work order."

"Did you believe what the man said about it, Maralee?" my aunt asked. "That he found it in his car and didn't know how it got there?"

"You know something? I did believe him. Strange, isn't it?"

"Not so strange. If he'd stolen it, he'd hardly carry it up here and show it to you, now would he?"

"That's probably what Pete's thinking. So if both the index card and the work order were planted on Tommy, who did it? And why?"

"I'm sorry to say it," she said, "but little Daphne comes to mind."

I sighed. "I thought of that, too."

Aunt Ibby stopped at the head of the stairs leading

down to the second floor and looked around the huge space. "This used to be Trumbull's furniture department, you know. And over there was the beauty parlor. And I think over there, where those actors are, was the place where Mother used to cash in her Green Stamps." She shook her head as we started down the stairs. "Things change."

CHAPTER 37

The diner was still pretty crowded, so we opted for Rockafellas just down the street, in the old Daniel Low Building, because Aunt Ibby loves the way they do Caesar salad. We each ordered the salad and raspberry iced tea, and my aunt again pulled the sheaf of papers from her handbag.

"There were several of what you might call 'society events' going on in Salem the evening that Helena died," she said. "And the *Salem News* had reporters at most of them. I cross-checked the reports with the articles about the murder, trying to narrow it all down to what I thought was of the most interest to you." She pushed several pages across the table to me. "See what you think."

The top one showed a photo of Tripp Hampton posing next to a large painting he'd donated to a charity auction sponsored by the North Shore Patrons of the Arts. "I remember reading that he and Daphne attended that auction together." I checked the date at the top of the page. "This paper came out the next morning, before they found Helena's body."

"That article is quite extensive," Aunt Ibby said. "It was apparently an A-list party, and extremely well attended."

"Must have been," I said. "It says here they raised well over a million dollars."

"Read on," she said, sipping on her iced tea.

I skimmed through the report on the event, which had taken place at a private home. The reporter had been seriously impressed. The story fairly bristled with adjectives. Hundreds of *wealthy* guests. *Fabulous* music. *Exquisite* hors d'oeuvres. *Beautiful* women, all in *gorgeous* gowns. *Handsome* men, all in black tie . . .

I stopped reading and looked across the table at Aunt Ibby. "Bingo," I said.

"Find what you were looking for already? That didn't take long."

"Mr. Pennington has told you about Daphne's poor eyesight, hasn't he?"

"Yes, indeed. He says the poor child is probably legally blind, but she still refuses to wear glasses."

"That's true," I said. "And last night she mentioned that Tripp Hampton took her to a party once where all the men wore tuxedos."

"Could be the charity auction."

"She said all the men looked so much alike, she didn't know who she was dancing with half the time." I looked again at the picture of Tripp. "She and Tripp were pretty much each other's alibis on the night Helena was killed."

Aunt Ibby nodded. "You're thinking Tripp could have left the party, and she wouldn't have noticed."

"Uh-huh. And he could have mingled enough and posed for enough photos that among over a hundred guests, it wouldn't be hard for him to slip away for a little while. Did you happen to find the address where the party was held?"

"The Garland mansion," she said. "It's right over near the Hampton place, and it's even bigger."

"Walking distance?"

"Maybe, for a young person. One thing, though, Maralee."

"What's that?"

"Was Pete with you when Daphne mentioned the men in tuxedos?"

I remembered Pete saying he always rented a tux if he needed one. "Yes, he was there."

"Then I'll bet he already has all this." She picked up the pile of papers and put them down again. "I'll just bet he does."

I knew she was probably right. Not much gets by Pete. "All the same, I'm going to tell him about it."

"You do that, dear." She picked up the check. "Lunch will be my treat."

"Thanks," I said. "This must be my lucky day. Gary Campbell bought my coffee this morning."

"Gary Campbell? The cash register man?"

"And the candlestick man. *And* the man I saw leaving Shea's shop."

We walked back to the Tabby, where Aunt Ibby had left her car in the guest parking lot. I looked around but didn't see Pete's Crown Vic or Tommy Trent's Mercedes.

"I don't have a lot to do today," I said, "so I'll be home early. Want to look at Helena's composition book with me?"

"Can't think of anything I'd rather do," she said, climbing into the Buick. "I've been curious about it from the beginning."

After Aunt Ibby drove off, I went over to the student theater, where a cleaning crew was at work, guaranteeing that everything would be in order for the evening performance of *Hobson's*. I checked out the stage set, moving a chair here, a pair of shoes there. It was important that all the props were exactly where the actors expected them to be. Onstage, reaching for something that should be there and finding nothing is unacceptable.

Reaching into a secret compartment where there used to be something and now there is nothing is unacceptable.

I was more and more convinced that Shea'd thought about that when she'd removed something from the bureau. That it had to be replaced so that it wouldn't look as though she'd removed something valuable—like the pink diamond.

By three o'clock I'd run out of things to do at the Tabby. I called Pete and left a voice mail telling him I was leaving for home, then called my aunt to see if she wanted me to pick up something for dinner.

"Don't bother," she said. "I'll whip something up. Hurry home. I'm dying to read Helena's story."

I was growing impatient to read it, too. I wanted to learn more about Grandpa and about where the cabin was.

I was just pulling into the garage when Pete returned my call. "You left work early. Anything wrong?"

"Nope. Just ran out of things to do. Aunt Ibby and I are planning to read Helena's journal," I said. "And I have a couple of ideas about the night Helena was killed that I'd like to tell you about. Why don't you join us when you get off?"

"You've got me curious now," he said. "More clues?"

"Don't laugh," I told him. "One of these days I'll turn up something important."

"Hey, I'm not laughing. You're the one who figured out the candlestick angle. Did I ever tell you . . ." He trailed off teasingly.

"Yeah, I know. I'd make a good cop." It was my turn to laugh. "Really, come over if you can. Aunt Ibby's cooking."

"Okay. I can come for a little while. I'm taking my nephews to hockey practice at around nine."

"And, Pete, by the way . . ." I paused, not sure whether or not I should ask the question on my mind.

"You'd like to know what happened with Trent today, wouldn't you?"

"Uh-huh. If it's all right for you to tell me."

"I headed over there as soon as I got the word that his car was in the Tabby parking lot."

"I was so relieved when I saw you in the doorway," I said, "and thankful."

His voice became gruff, in a tender sort of way. "I don't want creeps like Trent anywhere near you."

"I wasn't as frightened as the last time he appeared in my office," I admitted. "He didn't seem to be angry with me—just confused about the work order being in his car. He says it was locked."

"I know. He told me the same thing. And he'd already called his probation officer about it, and about the index card, too. We think he's telling the truth this time, Lee. Somebody's messing with him."

"I believed him, too," I said. "Did he tell you who else might have keys to his car?"

"Nobody that he knows of. But it's not hard to get duplicate keys made for an old model like that."

"Are you thinking Daphne?"

"She has access, no doubt. I can't tell you anything more." The cop voice was back. "I'll call you when I'm on my way over, okay?"

"One more thing," I said. "It might be nothing, but Gary Campbell told me he used to take money out of that old cash register for the same reason old man Hobson did in the play. For drinking money."

"Must be what the two thousand dollars he was returning to Shea was for."

"Must be. See you later."

I climbed out from behind the wheel, locked the Corvette, glad that I knew where both sets of *my* keys were, and hurried through the garden to the house. I glanced over at the fence, wondering if any of O'Ryan's cat friends might sit there during the day, but there were no cats in sight. I let myself into the back hall, where something smelled good. I tapped on Aunt Ibby's kitchen door.

"It's me," I called. "I'm going up to my place to change. Be right back down."

"Okay, dear," came the answering voice. "I'm making Tabitha's corn chowder again, using heavy cream this time."

It didn't take long for me to shower and change. Helena's notebook was still on my bedside table, where I'd left it after my first reading. Tucking it under my arm, I left via my kitchen door and headed down the two flights to what I still thought of as home.

Did the grown-up Helena always think of her grandpa's cabin as home, even though she had a mansion of her own?

As I entered the living room, O'Ryan looked up from his favorite perch there, a needlepoint pillow on the window seat in the bay window, blinked a couple of times, and went back to sleep. "I guess I'm definitely cat staff now," I muttered. "No big greeting at the door for me anymore."

"Are you talking to me, dear?" Aunt Ibby appeared, wiping her hands on her apron. "Did you bring the notebook?"

"Right here," I said, lifting Helena's composition book with both hands. "And I was just complaining about O'Ryan taking me for granted these days."

"Yes, he rules this roost, no doubt. Why don't we take the book into the kitchen? Light's better in there, and I can keep an eye on my chowder."

I followed her into the bright, cozy room and pulled one of the captain's chairs up to the round table. "Sit next to me so we can read it together." I handed the book to her. "Start at the beginning."

Aunt Ibby and I began reading Helena's story, starting with tales of idyllic days spent fishing, picking wild blackberries, swimming, learning to operate a motorboat—all in the company of Grandpa. There was no mention of other children, and we got the impression that Grandpa's cabin was in a remote place.

There were postcards of Marblehead Harbor and Salem Willows pasted onto the lined pages here and there, as well as movie ticket stubs and brochures from several North Shore historic sites, which indicated "field trips" taken with Grandpa.

Although the journal pages weren't dated, they seemed to cover activities from several summers. The handwriting and sentence structures changed subtly as Helena's story progressed. The prose was broken up occasionally with a short rhyme. At about the midpoint in the volume, an undated newspaper clipping noted the passing of Arthur Cole at the age of ninety-four. Mr. Cole had been preceded in death by his wife, Mildred.

The account mentioned a daughter Sarah and a granddaughter Helena. Written across the top of the clipping in pencil was the word *Grandpa,* and on the facing page was a browned and brittle pressed flower between two squares of waxed paper.

"What kind of flower do you think it is?" I asked.

"Looks like a pansy. A purple one," my aunt said. "Helena's grandmother's favorite flower."

"Of course, that's what it is," I said, feeling a tiny sting of tears. "This is so sad."

Pete called at just about that point in our reading, so we closed the notebook and cleared the table to make room for dinner. When he arrived ten minutes later, bearing a bottle of wine, a box of chocolates, and a large package of kitty treats, O'Ryan and I met him at the front door, and then the cat led the way to the kitchen.

"Want to give me a CliffsNotes version of what is in Helena's book?" Pete asked as Aunt Ibby ladled the creamy corn chowder into our bowls and sprinkled crispy bits of fried salt pork on top.

"We're only about halfway through it," I said. "We just got to the sad part, where her grandpa dies."

Pete poured chardonnay into Aunt Ibby's second-best crystal wineglasses, while I sliced French bread. "Grandpa being the gent in the picture in the bureau?" Pete asked.

"Must be. She spent summers with him when she was a little girl, according to Tripp," I said.

"Around here?" Pete asked.

"I think so. They visited Marblehead and the Willows and fished for saltwater fish, but she doesn't say exactly where the cabin is . . . at least so far in her story."

"You said you have some ideas about the night Helena was killed. Want to tell me about that?"

"When Daphne told us about the party where all the men wore tuxedos, it made me wonder about something I'd read about Helena's murder."

"Made me wonder, too," he said. "Made me wonder about some people's alibis that seemed airtight at the time. Now . . . maybe not so much."

"Did you—the police—know back then about Daphne's eyesight problem?"

"No. She hides it so well, I don't think anybody would notice it unless she told them."

"Will you . . . is this . . . I mean, is it a reason to reopen the case?"

"Not my call," he said. "I typed it up and put it on Chief's desk. May be something. May be nothing. He still thinks Trent and Daphne have the diamond stashed somewhere."

Aunt Ibby started to clear the table, and I got up to help her. "Let's get on with Helena's story," she said. "Leave the dishes in the sink. I want to learn more about that girl."

We three sat there at the round table, with the notebook centered between us. Aunt Ibby read aloud, and we took turns looking at the handwritten pages and the items Helena had pasted in. The writing on the pages following the obituary notice was noticeably neater, clearly written by a more mature hand.

Nicky and I took a boat ride to the island today. He looks so cute in his new life preserver. Everything is so different out there now. The last of the cabins is gone. There weren't many people around, so I don't think anyone noticed when I dug the little hole in the dirt

behind the chimney and planted Grandmother's
pansies. I planted the yellow ones this time. I hope the
trustees don't mind that I do this once in a while.

Pete pointed at the paragraph. "She must have been
talking about Misery Island. Don't you think so, Miss
Russell?"

"I think you're right, Pete. There used to be cot-
tages, even some good-sized houses, on the island. All
gone. Just a few chimneys, some stairways, cellar holes.
It's a nature reserve now, and quite a lovely one.
There's a ferry service that takes people out there."

"I suppose an island that size has a nice beach," I
said, remembering my vision of Helena and the dog.

"It does," Pete said. "Misery's just a short boat ride
from Salem Willows. Want to go some time?"

"I'd love to. Daphne told me that Helena had a
speedboat. She told me about Nicky's life preserver,
too. It's nice about the pansies, isn't it?"

"It is," my aunt said. "Helena was an awfully nice
person."

"An angel," Pete murmured. "That's what everybody
says about her. An angel."

"I know," I said. "Even Tommy Trent calls her that."

"He still claims he didn't do it, you know. He admits
he married her for the money, though." Pete shook his
head. "He even admits he stole about a million dollars
from her to pay his gambling debts. It's hard to believe
anything a rat like that says."

Aunt Ibby turned the page.

"Oh, dear, look at this. It's another obituary. John
David Hampton, Jr. She lost her grandfather and
then her husband. He was only seventy." She made a
"tsk-tsk" sound. "He was survived by his wife, Helena,

and one son, John David Hampton the Third. Poor Helena. Here's another of her little poems."

Dearest John, I know you're watching from above
But how I'll miss your faithful love.
You called me the sparkling gem of your life.
My greatest treasure was being your wife.
Love forever,
Helena

The very next entry was a wedding announcement engraved on heavy cream-colored stock. It announced the marriage of Ms. Helena Hampton to Mr. Thomas Trent. Another pressed flower was pasted onto the facing page.

"Must be from Helena's wedding bouquet," Aunt Ibby suggested. "A white rose, I think. You can still smell the fragrance."

"She should have quit when she was still ahead," Pete grumbled.

The following several pages held candid photos. Helena and Tommy on a cruise ship. Helena and Tommy at the top of the Eiffel Tower. Helena and Tommy at the Grand Canyon. Helena and Tommy and Daphne at Disneyland. Helena and the little dog Nicky posing in front of a Christmas tree.

"Did you notice there are no pictures of Tripp? Didn't they get along?" my aunt wondered aloud.

"Maybe he was away at school," Pete said. "He sure was broken up when he found out she was dead. Cried like a baby."

"Really?" I was surprised. "He doesn't strike me as a very emotional type."

"He was away at school a good deal of the time," Aunt Ibby said. "Maybe Helena and Tommy didn't want him around." She picked up the notebook and dropped her voice. "You know I don't like gossip, but there's a rumor going around that Tripp may be in some serious financial trouble at the investment firm." She aimed a questioning look in Pete's direction.

He smiled. "I don't deal in rumors, Miss Russell. Let's read some more."

Aunt Ibby returned his smile and turned a page. "Oh, no!" she exclaimed. "That poor woman."

"What is it?" Pete and I each leaned closer.

"She had to put her little dog down. Look here." She pointed. A receipt with a veterinarian's name on it was pasted onto the page. "It's a bill for euthanasia for a male dog named Nicky, aged twelve years."

CHAPTER 38

Pete shook his head. "What a run of rotten luck. I guess it's true, what they say. 'Money can't buy happiness.'"

"I'm so sorry for Helena," I said, feeling the sting of tears behind my eyes. "I feel as though I know her a little bit."

"Yes," Aunt Ibby agreed. "This notebook is extremely personal. I think we all do know her a little bit now. She had to deal with a great deal of sadness, didn't she?"

"And then to die the way she did," Pete said, teeth clenched, cop voice activated. "It's not fair."

"Sometimes life isn't," my aunt said. "Look. Here's a nice long poem on the next page. Maybe it'll sound a happier note." She turned the book toward us as she read so that we could see the staggered lines.

Look Both Ways
How can I tell what's right and wrong? What's truth
  and lie?
How can I judge between scream and song? Between
  you and I?

I don't know you. You don't know me. We're strangers.
We shared a bed, good times, bad times, dangers.
I've lost a partner. I've lost a friend. I've lost my trust.
What burned so bright, seemed so right, has turned to
        dust.
How could you? How could she? Why was I so blind?
So now ends the you and me, as I try to be fair, to be
        kind.
I haven't told you yet what I saw through the glass
        today.
I'll tell each of you tomorrow. Then you both must go
        away.
Next time I'll look both ways.

"Oh, my God. Helena must have written that after she caught Tommy and Daphne in the swimming pool." I pushed the book away. "She never saw it coming."

"She caught them in the pool? How do you know that?" Pete asked.

"Daphne told me. After that, Helena threw Tommy out of their bedroom. Told him to pack up his stuff and find another place to live."

"That's what Trent claims, too. Says he was in a guest room on the other side of the house, packing, when she was killed." Pete looked at the book again. "Nobody believed him. No wonder. What a creep. Imagine doing it right in his wife's house. In the pool, for Christ's sake."

"Do we have to keep reading?" Aunt Ibby asked. "There are only a few pages left, but I'm getting depressed. How about we have some nice chocolate ice cream and save the rest of this for another day?"

I would have kept right on reading, but ice cream

won. Aunt Ibby marked where we'd left off with a Salem Public Library bookmark, closed the notebook, and handed it to me. Chocolate ice cream was served, and the conversation turned from murder and deception to plans for a picnic on Misery Island. It was decided that Aunt Ibby and Mr. Pennington would join Pete and me for the excursion via ferryboat on the following Sunday, Pete's next day off.

After Pete left to pick up his sister's kids, and after Aunt Ibby and I had taken care of those dishes, I carried Helena's notebook back up to my apartment. I planned to read it through again from the beginning. There was something about the last poem that had really hit home.

When I'd thrown Ariel's spell book into the flames, I'd been sure it was the right thing to do. But that book had survived somehow since 1692. It had once belonged to Bridget Bishop, easily the most notorious of the Salem witches and the first one hanged at Gallows Hill. Because of the things Ariel had done, and because of everything I knew about Bridget Bishop, I'd been thoroughly convinced that the book was evil. Say what you will, and believe whatever you want to about witches, but Ariel and Bridget Bishop were the real deal, and not in a good way. I knew, too, that River and her roommates, all of them far from being evil, were still searching in Ariel's apartment, looking for that same book.

But had I looked both ways? Was it possible that the magic in those ancient pages held good spells, as well as bad ones? Who was I to judge? Anyway, I knew in my heart that if Bridget's book held enough magic to preserve it from a fire of that magnitude, there wouldn't be much point in trying to destroy it again. When I got upstairs, I made a phone call.

"River? It's me. Tomorrow's Saturday, and since we both have the day off, want to come over to my place for lunch? There's something I need to tell you. And something I need to give to you, too, if you want to accept it."

Was I doing the right thing? Or was passing the spell book along to River just a way to get it out of my house and off my conscience? Whatever it was, River happily agreed to join me the next day, and I hung up feeling just a little bit lighter in the conscience department.

O'Ryan had followed me upstairs, as he usually did when he thought it was bedtime. I donned pajamas, but I wasn't anywhere near ready for sleep. I put on a fresh pot of coffee, gave the cat a few of the kitty treats Pete had brought over, plumped up my pillows, and turned on my reading lamp. I'd just settled down with Helena's notebook propped against my knees, mug of coffee on the bedside table, when I realized that I could see myself in the oval mirror. River had specifically warned me against that.

Bad feng shui.

Grumbling just a bit, I climbed out of bed, turned the mirror to the right, fluffed up the pillows again, and got back into bed. Before picking up the book, I checked the mirror. Now it reflected the kitchen window and the big yellow cat sprawled out full length along the windowsill. *Much better.* Maybe this place was beginning to feel like home, after all.

The pages after Helena's sad poem held a variety of pasted-in items. There was a blue ribbon marked BEST OF BREED and a photo of Nicky wearing a little white sailor hat, being held by Helena, who was wearing a matching one. A short nonsense poem was printed beneath the photo.

Picky little Nicky, Mommy's pretty pet
Dress him up with ribbon bows, costumes, hats, and yet
He'd rather dress like Mommy as he runs to meet his dad
Picky little Nicky, truest friend I ever had.

A colorful packet that had once held pansy seeds shared a page with a ticket stub from the Misery Island Sea Shuttle. A folded copy of an official-looking deed assigned a parcel of land, with all buildings, improvements, and appurtenances, to the trustees of reservations. A crude hand-drawn map took up a whole page. I smiled when I saw it.

"I feel even more as though I know you, Helena," I said aloud. "I'm not much of an artist myself."

O'Ryan, hearing my voice, jumped down from his windowsill perch and joined me on the big bed.

"Come on, cat. Let's look at the picture together."

There was a shape, which looked to me like an upside-down elephant, surrounded by wavy lines, which I guessed represented water. At the top of the page she'd printed 42°32'55"N 70°47'53"W.

"I can look it up later," I told the cat, "but I'm sure this is the latitude and longitude of Misery Island. Think so?"

O'Ryan said, "Mrrit," which could mean anything, but in this case I took it to mean "Yes."

I pointed to a little house-shaped drawing, complete with smoking chimney, close to the southern edge of the island. "And I'll bet this is Grandpa's cabin."

O'Ryan nodded.

Just behind the cabin was a small, curvy-edged,

roundish form. "What do you think that's supposed to be?" I tipped the notebook left, then right. "I don't get it. Do you?"

Out snaked a yellow paw. He lifted the page so that the edge of the previous page peeked through, displaying the seed packet.

"Of course. It's a pansy. Helena and her grandfather planted pansies behind the cabin, and Helena kept up the tradition." I patted his head. "Good eye, O'Ryan. And look at this one." I pointed to a stick figure with four legs and a tail. "That must be Nicky. Cute."

O'Ryan yawned, gave my hand a pink-tongued lick, curled up beside me, and closed his eyes, showing no interest in the dog—or maybe dogs in general.

"Okay. Time for sleep, I guess." I put the notebook on the bedside table and turned off the reading lamp. As I rearranged the pillows and snuggled under the blankets, I glanced again at the oval mirror, where the outline of the open kitchen window was dimly reflected. I thought for a moment that I saw a gray cat sitting on the fire escape outside, but the image quickly disappeared. I was about to close my eyes when the little cloud and the pinpoints of light danced across the mirror and the woman began to take form.

I sat bolt upright and kicked off the covers. This was no small vision. Because the mirror was of the full-length variety, the vision was, too. Helena—because this was surely Helena—appeared to be life size. I scooted down to the foot of the bed, closer to the mirror. She was smiling and held the little dog in her arms. She wore jeans and a black turtleneck. Around her neck was the pink diamond pendant on a leather thong. Then she pointed to the dog's collar. An identical pendant sparkled against the gray fur.

I gasped. The scene in the mirror changed. Helena was still there, but this was the weeping Helena I'd seen in the giant patent-leather pump at the school. She held something in her arms, as she had before. She extended both arms toward me so that I could clearly see the small metal coffin. Then she grew smaller and smaller, until she faded away and I was once again looking at my own kitchen window.

Two Helenas. A small coffin. And two pink diamonds. *Just try to go to sleep after that.*

I finished the pot of coffee and watched *Tarot Time with River North* on WICH-TV, including the night's feature movie, *Zombie Apocalypse,* all the way to the end.

CHAPTER 39

I was up early on Saturday morning, even though I'd had little sleep. Aunt Ibby wasn't in her kitchen yet, so I picked up the morning papers from the front steps, started the coffee, and fed O'Ryan. I was anxious to tell her about the full-length-mirror visions.

My aunt appeared in bathrobe and bunny slippers and joined me at the kitchen table. "You're the early bird," she said. "Is everything all right?"

"I think so," I said. "I found out last night that the new mirror, the oval one I bought in Essex? I can see visions in it, too."

"Visions? Like the ones in the mirror in the bureau? Or in Ariel's obsidian ball?"

I nodded. "Like those. Only much, much bigger."

"What did you see?"

"Two different visions. Both of Helena. One of them was almost exactly the same way I saw her in the black shoe."

"Was she crying?"

"She was, and she was carrying something in her arms."

Aunt Ibby leaned forward, her hands clasped together. "This time, could you see what it was?"

Thinking about it brought tears to my eyes. "It was a small metal coffin," I told her. "I'm afraid it was her little dog, Nicky."

"No wonder she was crying. You say there were two visions. What was the other one?"

"It was even stranger. She showed me *two* pink diamonds. One was on the dog's collar. All the visions I've seen have had good reasons behind them, and this one must be important, as well."

She poured us each a cup of coffee. "Let's think about what she's shown you so far. It started with the scene on the beach, didn't it? Where she threw the stick to the dog?"

"Right. And later I saw the old man and the cabin."

"Between what you've seen in the various surfaces and what we've learned from Helena's notebook, everything is connected to the old cabin on Misery Island, her grandfather, and Nicky the dog."

"Right," I said, excited. "And there's a map in her notebook that ties those three things together. Wait a minute. I'll show you." I ran all the way up the two flights of stairs to my apartment, grabbed Helena's book, and was back in the kitchen in minutes. "Here. Look at this." I turned to the bookmarked page and put it on the table in front of her.

She studied the map without speaking, turning it this way and that, just as I had.

"Are you trying to figure out what the curvy, round

thing is? O'Ryan knew what it was right away. A pansy."

"Of course. I can see it now. There's the grandfather's house, the place where they planted the grandmother's favorite flowers, and the little dog Nicky." She snapped her fingers. "Maralee, could you see where Helena was when she first showed you the dog's coffin?"

"She was on a long, empty stretch of beach, all alone."

"Well, then, do you think she might have buried Nicky out there, too?"

"That's just the kind of thing she'd do," I said. "That explains that. Thanks, Aunt Ibby."

"You're welcome, dear. Want a blueberry muffin with your coffee?" She stood, opened the freezer, and removed a package of muffins. "I made them."

"Love one," I said, then frowned. "But why does Helena want us to know where she buried her dog?" I was pretty sure I knew, but it seemed too crazy to be believed.

She popped a couple of muffins into the microwave. "Maybe River would have some ideas."

"She's coming over for lunch," I said. "Maybe between us and her deck of cards, we'll figure it all out."

By lunchtime I'd done a little housework in my apartment, made some sandwiches and a pitcher of lemonade, and carried the still unopened cardboard box down from the attic. This time, although he'd accompanied me up to the fourth floor, O'Ryan hadn't attempted to prevent me from picking the thing up, and thankfully, there were no cats yowling at the window.

I'd told River to call me when she was on the way so that I could go downstairs and unlock the back door. She called just before noon.

"More news about Helena," I told her. "More puzzles to figure out. She drew a map and I think it's important. Maybe you can figure it out. Got cards?"

She laughed. "Yep. Playing with a full deck today. See you in a minute."

I disarmed the alarm system and unlocked the downstairs door, then ran back up to my kitchen, set the table, and waited for my friend.

The bell chimed "Bless This House," and I opened the door.

"Thanks for inviting me. I'm starving," she said. "Skipped breakfast. Dying to know what's new about Helena." She looked around the living room. "Wow. New furniture since I was here last. Looks good. Move that lamp, though. It's interrupting the energy. Never mind. I'll do it." She unplugged the floor lamp and moved it to the opposite end of the couch, then stood back to admire her handiwork. "There. That'll work."

"Don't know what I'd do without you to keep my *bagua* straight. I even found a picture of fruit and hung it where you told me to." I laughed. "Come on. I'll feed you and tell you what Helena showed me last night."

Once we were in the kitchen, River nodded her approval of the new watercolor, then looked at the long, still rather dusty cardboard box I'd placed on the counter. She raised an eyebrow but didn't say anything.

"Later," I said. "I'll tell you about that later. First, have lunch, and I'll show you what I've found in Helena's notebook."

The sandwiches were all of the vegetarian variety, since the last time River had shared a meal here, I'd noticed that she'd fed all the pepperoni on the pizza to the cat. After we'd polished off the plate of sandwiches, and as River nibbled on one of Aunt Ibby's sugar cookies, I carried the notebook from the bedroom and put it on the kitchen table, opened to Helena's map.

I pointed out the symbols one at a time. "That's the latitude and longitude of Misery Island. I looked it up," I said. "You know the place?" She nodded. "There's the grandfather's cabin, and behind it is the place where she and the old man used to plant pansies every summer, because they were her grandmother's favorite flower."

"Got it," she said. She touched the stick figure. "And that's the little dog. Nicky. The one the license belonged to."

"Right. Now, here's the part about the vision I saw last night. It was in the new full-length mirror, so everything was life size."

"Wow. Scary, huh?"

I thought about that. "Not so much. It was mostly sad. Some of it was the same vision I saw in the shoe, when she was carrying something in her arms. This time I could see what it was. A small metal coffin, just about the right size for a small gray dog."

"Nicky died."

"Yes. And there was more. I saw Helena and Nicky together, and, River, they were both wearing pink diamond pendants."

"Are you thinking it's possible that there were actually *two* of them? Two diamonds?"

"Maybe. Or maybe it's some kind of symbolism. I don't know." I pushed the notebook toward her. "There's a poem in there about looking both ways. Maybe that's why she showed me two." I shrugged. "The receipt from the vet for putting Nicky down is pasted in the book, too. Look through it. Take your time."

She leafed through the pages, pausing to read the poems and to examine the pasted-in items one by one. Finally, she leaned back in the Lucite chair. "I don't know what it all means," she said, "but I don't have to read your cards to tell you what you need to do next."

"I need to go out to that island," I said.

"Yep. As soon as you can."

"Pete and I are going tomorrow. Want to come with us?"

"Wish I could. But I need my sleep. I have to work tomorrow night."

"On Sunday? Why?"

She made a little pouty face. "Special edition of *Tarot Time*. Mr. Pennington's idea. I'll be doing readings for the whole cast of *Our Town*. A little extra promotion for the play. But it's okay. The station's paying me double. But you said you have something to give to me? If I want to take it?" She looked again at the dusty box on the counter. "Is that it?"

I nodded. There was a lump in my throat. Would my friend hate me when I told her the truth about what I'd done to Bridget Bishop's book?

I cleared away the dishes, wiped the dust from the top of the box, and put it on the table in front of her. "You don't have to open it, now or ever, unless you want to," I said, then sat opposite her and took a deep breath. Once I began speaking, the truth came spilling out. I told her how I'd discovered Bridget Bishop's spell book in the pocket of Ariel's purple cape. I'd been wearing that cape when Aunt Ibby and I were trapped in the attic of our house with a murderer, who'd set the place ablaze. I'd read about what malicious things Bridget Bishop had done back in 1690, and I knew, too, what vile things Ariel had learned to do. As far as I could see, none of it was good. I'd seen my chance to end the evil, and as my aunt and I escaped the raging fire, I'd thrown the book back into the consuming flames.

"The fire didn't burn it," I said. "Probably didn't even singe it. It's back, and I'm sure it's in this box. I know you and your friends have been searching for it ever since Ariel died. I may have been wrong. Maybe there are good spells in it, too. Maybe something to benefit today's world. It's up to you now, and I hope you can forgive me."

I watched her face. She reached for the box and touched it lightly with one finger, then looked at me. "It's a big responsibility, isn't it? You may have been right about it in the first place. I don't know. Some say that certain people in Salem just had it in for Bridget because she was pretty and she used to wear a scarlet corset over her black dress, something like a bustier, I guess, and she worked as a barmaid." She patted the top of the box. "On the other hand, a lot of people testified against her in the trial back then. Some of the things they said she did are kind of hard to explain. People who had crossed her seemed to have accidents—bad ones. And they said she could change shape, and they knew that she controlled cats and birds." She shrugged. "I'll take it with me, but I'm not going to tell the others about it yet. I'll see what the cards tell me. She stood, and picked up the box.

"The cards never fail. And, Lee, there's nothing to forgive."

Together we traced our steps back through the living room and with the box under her arm, River started down the stairs. She paused and looked back at me. "I have a feeling your trip to Misery Island will answer some of your questions." She lifted the box a few inches. "And don't worry about this. I'll take good care of it."

CHAPTER 40

Did I do the right thing? I could only hope so. At least it was one less puzzling item on my mind. I still had gazing problems, not knowing what reflective surface was going to spring a vision on me at any given moment. I still didn't know which, if any, of the blue-eyed, blond men I was supposed to beware of. My quandary about how much to tell Pete about my so-called gift and when to tell him hadn't improved one bit, either.

Aunt Ibby had made reservations for the four of us on the Misery Island shuttle boat for Sunday. "I'll pack a lunch in our old wicker picnic basket," she said. "It will be such fun."

"Do you think there'd be room in the basket for a small pansy plant?" I asked. "I'd like to put one out there for Helena's grandmother."

"That's a kind and loving idea, Maralee," she said. "Let's do it."

"Good. I'll take a ride over to the nursery and pick one out."

"As long as you're going over there," she said, "why

don't you pick up a nice variety of them for our garden, too? I love pansies. They have such sweet little faces."

I bought a whole flat of pansies in an assortment of happy colors, along with a small trowel for planting the purple one I'd selected especially for Helena's grandmother. Then I made a copy of Helena's map and put it in my purse.

Aunt Ibby and I spent some of the afternoon planting a row of pansies along the path leading to the house, while a couple of O'Ryan's cat friends sat on top of the fence, watching us.

"Are there more cats in the neighborhood than usual," my aunt asked, "or am I imagining it?"

"I think they've always been around," I said, "but our handsome boy seems to have acquired a fan club of sorts." I told her about how O'Ryan liked to stretch out on my kitchen windowsill and watch them. I didn't mention the black and gray cats who'd been at the attic window, though. Too creepy.

Sunday dawned bright and clear, a perfect day for a boat ride and a picnic. Aunt Ibby and I rode with Mr. Pennington in the Lincoln, and Pete met us at the Willows Park Pier, where we joined a dozen or so fellow adventurers. The ocean was calm, sunlight sparkled on deep blue water, and the waves made a pleasant *slap-slap* sound on the twin hulls of the shuttle boat. On the way to the island, I showed the map to Pete.

"It's a pretty rough drawing," he said, "but if you want to see if we can find the place where that cabin was, I'm game."

I couldn't tell him about the metal coffin in Helena's

arms, though, so I kept silent about that. And how on earth could I explain about the two diamonds? He smiled about my sneaking a purple pansy aboard in the picnic basket, and as soon as we'd docked, and my aunt and Mr. Pennington had selected an appropriate place to picnic, Pete and I set out to follow a trail to where we thought the site of the cabin might be. It was easier to find than we'd thought. Pete simply showed the map to one of the island guides.

"You see where your map has a picture of a house with a chimney?" the man asked, pointing at Helena's drawing. "Well, the house is long gone, of course, but some of the chimney is still there. Can't miss it." He nodded toward the pansy in its little peat pot, which I had tried unsuccessfully to hide behind my back. "Another lady used to come out here once in a while to plant those behind that chimney. Long time ago. Haven't seen her in years. You folks have a nice day now."

Pete and I followed the guide's directions and found ourselves alone on a high bluff overlooking a long stretch of beach. I pointed to a tree-covered, much smaller island a short distance away. "What's over there?" I asked.

"Nothing, really," he said. "They call that 'Little Misery Island.' At low tide you can walk to it."

"No thanks," I said. "Let's just concentrate on this one." A crumbling, but still recognizable, brick chimney stood at the edge of a grassy area, and clumps of wild rosebushes bordered what must have once been the grandfather's yard. I stopped to look at a low granite step marking what could have been the doorway where I'd first seen the old man in my dream. But naturally, I couldn't tell Pete about that, either.

It will be such a relief to be able to tell him everything—if that day ever comes.

Pete walked to a spot behind the chimney, stooped down, and pushed the long grass aside with his hands. "Hey, Lee. Come here. Look at this."

I knelt beside him and looked at where he pointed. An oblong piece of granite, much smaller than the step I'd just discovered, was embedded in the dirt. "What is it?" I asked.

"Look closer," he said. "There's a name scratched into it."

We spoke the name in unison. "Nicky."

"She buried her dog here," Pete said. "The dog whose license we found in your bureau."

"Yes," I said. "She loved this place. And she loved that little dog."

"Want to plant the flower here? Where Nicky is?"

"I think that's where Helena used to plant them," I said, handing him the trowel.

Afterward, we walked slowly hand in hand along the trail leading back to the shore where Aunt Ibby and Mr. Pennington waited.

"So there you two are," Mr. Pennington called as we approached. "Ready for some lunch?"

Aunt Ibby had spread a red-and white-checked tablecloth on the sand and had placed the wicker picnic basket at its center. My aunt was protecting her fair skin from the noonday sun with a wide-brimmed white picture hat, and Mr. Pennington wore a classic straw boater. The scene was worthy of a Renoir painting. So was all the rest of that beautiful afternoon.

By the time the shuttle came back to pick us up, our tummies were full, our skin was a little bit sunburned, and best of all, our curiosity about Helena's map was somewhat satisfied. We'd found her island; we'd found her childhood summer home. We'd even found her dog. But we hadn't found her diamond, and if Tommy Trent was telling the truth, we hadn't found her killer yet, either.

At the dock Pete and I said a reluctant good-bye as I climbed into the Lincoln with my aunt and my boss, while Pete headed to the police station to work the night shift. The rest of the day stretched before me. Aunt Ibby and Mr. Pennington planned a drive to Marblehead to visit friends. They'd invited me to come along, but I'd declined, saying something polite, if not exactly truthful, about catching up with my laundry.

Alone in the big house, I was restless. I read the Sunday *Globe*, took a bath, and washed my hair. I even threw a small load of clothes into the washer. I heated up a can of soup for dinner, rearranged the books in my bookcase, watched TV for a while, and finally fell asleep on the couch.

It was dark when I woke up. I knew it must be late, because the regular programming was over and an infomercial about an exercise bike was on. I went into the bedroom, knowing I should get undressed and go to bed, but by then I was wide awake. I picked up Helena's notebook and opened it to the bookmarked page—the one with the picture of happy Helena and Nicky in matching sailor hats. I read again the little nonsense verse.

Picky little Nicky, Mommy's pretty pet
Dress him up with ribbon bows, costumes, hats, and yet
He'd rather dress like Mommy as he runs to meet his dad
Picky little Nicky, truest friend I ever had.

I looked at the photo again. Helena wore the diamond pendant, and Nicky wore an ordinary collar. The pose was exactly like the one in the vision I'd seen in my mirror, except in the vision Nicky wore a diamond, too.

All right, Helena. I think I know now what you're trying to tell me.

I looked at my watch. One thirty in the morning. Could I be right about this? Was the missing diamond around the neck of a dog long buried on Misery Island? I looked at the page in Helena's notebook again. No mistake. Helena was a trickster. Tripp had told me so. Loved puzzles, games, mysteries. The little rhyme, the drawing on the page added to what the vision had shown me. . . . I knew I was right.

I paced back and forth between the bedroom and the kitchen.

I didn't want to wake Aunt Ibby at this hour, and I couldn't very well tell Pete about what I'd seen in the mirror. But River was at the TV station tonight. She'd be wide awake, just winding up her show. I put Helena's notebook on the table and sat in one of the Lucite chairs, reached for my phone and speed-dialed my witch friend.

Please answer, River. I have to tell someone about this. Voice mail. Damn!

"River, I know exactly where Helena's diamond is, but I can't tell Pete yet, because . . . you know why . . . but it's all here in Helena's journal. Come over as soon as you get out of there. Don't ring the doorbell, though. I'll turn off the alarm and unlock the back door. Come on up, but be quiet. I don't want to frighten Aunt Ibby so late at night."

I hung up, then leaned back in my chair. I peered out the window. It had become kind of a habit to look for the cats on the fence. They weren't there. Maybe they showed up only when O'Ryan was on the window-sill. Where was O'Ryan, anyway?

I was sure River would be on her way over the minute she got my message. At two o'clock I tiptoed down the back stairs, disarmed the alarm, and un-locked the door. I'd just turned to climb the stairs when the door swung open behind me. I started to turn as an arm went around my throat and something pressed against my face. *Rough. A towel? That smell.* I remembered it from high school chemistry class. *Ether? Chloroform?*

Then I drifted, floated, slid into soft, soft blackness.

Awareness came back slowly, so slowly. Throat burn-ing, head throbbing. I squeezed my eyes shut tight, trying to think, to reason.

There's motion. I'm moving. I'm lying down, but I know I'm not in my bed.

I opened my eyes, trying to focus, trying to under-stand what was happening. A car. I was lying in the backseat of a car. Why? Where was I going? I tried to speak, but only a weak croaking sound came out. The car jolted to a stop, and the towel thing was on my face again. The smell was back, too. A voice then, with a faraway sound. "Coming around, eh? Back to la-la land for you, my snoopy little friend." I welcomed the soft blackness.

When I awoke again, there was no softness, no darkness. Bright light made me blink. Water cascaded down my face. I wanted to wipe it away, but my hands wouldn't move. I sat upright in a chair, hands tightly bound behind me, as Tripp Hampton lifted another bucket of water from the pool and dumped it over my head.

"Tell me where it is, Lee, and I might let you go."

Still groggy, I struggled to speak. "What do you want? Why are you doing this?"

"You know what I want. The goddamned diamond. The real one. Not this piece of crap." The pink gem sparkled under the lights. He held it toward me, and it swayed back and forth hypnotically on its fine gold chain before he whirled and threw it into the far end of the pool.

"But . . . but . . . Shea had that one. She found it in Helena's bureau. You mean you . . . the candlestick . . . It was you!"

"Of course it was me. You mean, you hadn't figured that out, too? I gave you too much credit. I knew you'd pegged me for dear old Mom's tragic passing. I saw it in your face when Daph made that crack about the tuxedos. Then I heard you talking to the cop about it." He smiled, but it wasn't the charming toothpaste ad smile I'd seen so many times before. It was a mean, self-satisfied, evil smirk, and it, more than the cold water soaking into my clothes, made me shiver.

He went on. "It was so easy. I swiped Daphne's keys to the Mercedes, ran down to the carriage house. I knew Tommy always kept his gun locked in the glove box, so I put on *my* gloves and took it. Just walked right into Helena's room, aimed the gun at her, and told her to hand over the diamond." The smile disappeared. "She laughed out loud. Called me a silly boy and turned her back. I don't like it when a woman turns her back on me. Remember that, Lee."

He moved close to me then, bending so that his face was close to mine. His breath was fetid; the blue eyes were mere slits. "So I shot her." He shrugged. "Didn't have time to search thoroughly, but I was positive the diamond was in her room someplace. I went back to the carriage house, put the gun right where I'd found it, and ran back to the party. Slipped Daph's keys back into her purse and danced the rest of the night away before Daph and I drove home." His laugh was high pitched and eerie.

"Slept like a baby till noon the next day. Why not? I knew Helena was dead and Tommy would get blamed for it. Perfect. And I could take my time searching the house." He stood, grinning down at me. "Oh, well, enough conversation. You told the witch you know where my diamond is. I need it now. Where is it? Where did Helena, that conniving trickster, hide it? I know she put the answer somewhere in that bureau of yours. There's no other place it could be."

"You heard me talking to River? How?"

He laughed. "Simple. I bugged your phone. An ingenious device. Anyone can do it. Is your daughter dating a no-good jerk? Is your spouse cheating? Are your kids buying drugs? Bug the phones. My phone buzzes every time yours rings." He stood up straight. "I haven't got time to wait any longer for an invitation from you to see what's in those secret compartments. I need that diamond. I need that money, and I need it now. I'm not like Tommy Trent. Prison would kill me."

"Prison? So it's true? You've been stealing from your investors?"

"Huh! Bernie Madoff is a two-bit piker compared to me. I need money. Lots of it. I have appearances to keep up. I'm John David Hampton the Third. But I have to put it all back, or the bastards are going to turn me in. I've been trying to pay it. Selling my things.

Humiliating! But it's not enough. Tell me where my diamond is."

Keep him talking. Stall. Someone will come. Someone has to.

"What about Shea?" I asked. "Did you think she had it?"

"Oh, she had what looked like a pink diamond on a chain, all right. Showed it to me. Then she laughed. Said she'd bought the bureau fair and square and everything in it was hers." His lips stretched in an ugly sneer. "Then she turned her back on me. Big mistake."

"Tell me something, Tripp," I said, trying to keep my voice from quivering. "Why did you take the index card with my name on it? And how did you get it into Tommy Trent's bureau?"

"Pretty smart, huh? I'm no dummy, Lee. I had top marks in school, you know. I was pretty sure that the card had the name of whoever bought Helena's bureau." He laughed again. "Lucky you, Lee!"

"I know you're smart," I said. "But I don't understand about the card and the work order winding up with Tommy. Was he helping you?"

His face grew red. "Tommy? Helping *me*? That moron? Of course not. I put the card under the drawer liner when I went to check out the apartment, to be sure darling Daphne would be safe there. Then I picked the very simple lock at Bob's and grabbed the folder I wanted. Planted it in the Mercedes. Easy stuff. You can learn more at private school than calculus and Western civilization, you know."

"You wanted Tommy to go back to jail. Why?"

"That simpleminded oaf would undo all the progress I've made with Daphne. She's almost ready for polite society. She's my creation. All my doing!" He leaned down again, his face close to mine. "And I intend to keep her. Now, tell me where my diamond is, Lee. Right now."

"Why should I? Are you planning to kill me?"

"Of course not. What kind of gentleman would do a thing like that? No. But if you don't tell me, I'm going to kill your cat. See?" He reached behind the chair and lifted a cat carrier so that I could see the limp form of O'Ryan, his eyes closed, lying inside. "Oh, don't worry," Tripp said, shaking the carrier. "He's not dead . . . yet. It took only a little whiff of chloroform to knock him out. But the pool water will revive him, just before he drowns." Tripp giggled. A hideous sound. "I know you'll do anything for the stupid animal, won't you? Just like Helena. She cared more for that stupid dog than she ever did for me."

I strained at whatever was binding my hands. It felt sticky. *Duct tape,* I guessed, and the water Tripp had poured on me was beginning to loosen it. *Stall him,* I thought. *River will know something's wrong when I'm not there. She'll call Pete.*

"Well?" He held the carrier over his head. "Shall I throw it in? Or are you going to tell me where my diamond is?"

"Wait! Don't hurt O'Ryan," I yelled. "I'll tell you."

Again the sick smile. "Hollering like that won't do you any good. Daphne can't hear you. She's sleeping with good old Tommy tonight. No one can hear you." Again Tripp lifted the carrier, shaking it back and forth. I saw O'Ryan's legs move. The big cat was waking up. "Where's my diamond?"

"Okay. I know where it is, but I don't know how you're going to get to it."

Might as well tell him the truth. What harm can it do now?

I kept straining at the duct tape and spoke slowly. "Do you know where Helena's grandfather's summer place was, Tripp?"

"Yes. Yes, of course I do. It was on that godforsaken island. Misery. Well named."

The tape was loosening. I kept talking. "That was a very special place to Helena. She used to go out there every summer to plant pansies. Do you remember that?"

"She tried to make me go with her. I hated that boat of hers. I was glad when Tommy sold it." He laughed out loud, and it was then that I heard the tinkling sound of glass breaking.

I spoke louder then, and more rapidly, to cover the cracking noise, hoping he hadn't heard it, too. It had to mean someone else was there. I talked about Nicky dying and about Helena buying a metal coffin for him.

Tripp put the carrier down beside the chair and leaned closer to me. "Get to the point, damn it."

I'd worked one hand loose. "She put the real diamond in the casket with the dog. That's where it is now. In Nicky's metal casket." Behind my back, I picked at the remaining tape with my free hand. It was then that I saw the first cat. It was black, and it came silently through a small jagged opening in the glass wall. Then came another. And another. I kept talking, and the cats kept coming. "The casket is buried on the island," I said. "You'll see a chimney."

Tripp's eyes were focused on me now. I described the granite step, the wild rosebushes, everything I could think of, to hold his interest, to tell him exactly how to locate the grave. I felt the last of the tape give. Both hands were free, but I kept them behind my back.

I tried not to look at the parade of cats, tried to keep Tripp's attention on me.

O'Ryan's yowl was long and loud. The cats silently surged forward, and Tripp saw them then. His eyes widened, and his mouth formed a silent O. He backed away from me, from the carrier, making a whimpering noise. I reached down and released the latch on the carrier door, and Tripp made no move to stop me. Through the opening in the glass wall, they kept coming. Gray cats, tabby cats, Siamese cats, white cats, bobtail cats. There must have been hundreds of them. O'Ryan stepped out of the carrier and joined them as they crept soundlessly, eyes glowing, ever closer to the man, yet not touching him. I heard a splash when he fell in the water. I looked back as I ran for the door leading to the ice cream parlor. Rows of cats surrounded the huge pool on every side, mutely watching the screaming man as he flailed about. A black cat wearing a red collar separated from the rest and raced ahead of me through the pink and white room and out into the maze of hallways.

The black cat stopped, turned, and looked at me. A voice called, "Follow me, Lee," just as it had in the dream. I ran, following the cat through the labyrinth of corridors and hallways. Here and there I spotted a tiny bit of blue tape along the baseboards. We reached the mansion's entrance hall, and I twisted the knob on the massive front door and stepped out into the summer night and freedom. The black cat stood in the doorway, watching me as I ran down the curving driveway to Daphne's cottage.

CHAPTER 41

Daphne's door was still unlocked. I let myself in and looked around. I didn't dare to turn on the lights. What if Tripp had climbed out of the pool and was looking for me? I saw a faint glow coming from somewhere beyond the living room and followed it. There was a small night-light shaped like a crucifix over Daphne's bed. Next to the bed was the pink Princess phone she'd told me about. I called 911.

Things moved fast after that. Sirens blared, and a parade of police cars proceeded up the long driveway. As soon as I saw the flashing lights, I went outside and waved one of the police cars down.

"I'm Lee Barrett," I told the uniformed officer. "Tripp Hampton is in the main house. He's in the pool. He killed Helena Trent and Shea Tolliver."

"You're soaking wet, miss. You'd better get in the cruiser." He held the door open for me. "We've been looking for you for an hour."

An hour? Have I been gone only for an hour?

I sat shivering in the backseat while the officer used his radio. "Detective?" he said. "I've got the lady you're looking for. She's right here in my backseat. Here. I'll let you talk to her." He handed me the microphone.

"Lee? Are you all right?" Pete's voice broke.

I was so relieved to hear him that I began to cry. "Oh, Pete. It was Tripp." Tears rushed down my cheeks. "He used chloroform. He was going to kill O'Ryan. I got away when he fell in the pool."

"The pool? Is that where he is now?" His cop voice was back. "You sure?"

"That's where he was when I got out of there," I said. "Be careful. He's crazy."

The officer stayed with me in the cruiser. Even turned on the heater, although the summer night was warm. After a while my teeth stopped chattering and the shivering stopped. Staccato voices sounded over the radio. I heard the sirens again, and red, white, and blue lights flashed past, heading away from the mansion.

"What's going on?" I asked. "Did they catch Tripp?"

"Yeah. Detective Mondello's on his way over here now to get you."

Just then Pete opened the cruiser door and pulled me into his arms. For a long moment, neither of us spoke. "I love you so much," he whispered.

"I love you, too," I said, realizing that this was the first time we'd spoken those words to each other.

"You're cold." He took off his jacket, then wrapped it around my shoulders. "Lee, it was the damnedest thing. The man was fully clothed, shoes and all, and was swimming around in circles in that pool. He fought us when we tried to help him out. Didn't want to get out of the water."

I waited for him to say something about the cats. The hundreds of cats.

Pete shook his head. "Damnedest thing I ever saw.

All alone in there, just swimming around in circles. Anyway, when we got him out of the water, and he'd settled down some, he started talking. I told him he was under arrest for kidnapping, read him his rights, but he kept right on talking."

"What did he tell you?" I asked.

"We were right about him slipping away from that charity thing and sneaking home. He killed Helena, all right, but the surprising thing is, he says he killed Shea Tolliver, too." He led me to his car, and gently helped me into the passenger seat. "Come on. I'll take you home. River is still at your place, and your aunt is frantic with worry. I'll fill you in later. I have to get back to the station. Hampton will calm down and get himself lawyered up pretty soon, I'm sure." He hit the siren, and we headed for home.

"Pete, I need to tell you something. I know where the pink diamond is." I blurted it out. I didn't give him a chance to respond, just kept talking. "It's on the island. Helena buried Nicky there in a metal coffin. The diamond necklace, the real one, is tied around his neck. There's a fake one, too. The one Tripp killed Shea for. He threw it in the pool."

"How do you know all this? Never mind. Here we are." We were in front of the Winter Street house. "We'll talk later. I'll come back as soon as I can. Wait for me, okay?" He left the Crown Vic's engine idling, and together we hurried up the steps. Aunt Ibby and River rushed outside to greet me. Pete gave me a fast kiss, ran back to the car, and sped away without his jacket, siren blaring.

Once inside the house, everyone talked at once.

"Maralee, your clothes are wet." My aunt threw her

arms around me. "What happened? Where have you been?"

"When I got here and found the back door wide open, I knew something was wrong," River said. "I ran upstairs and saw that you weren't there, so I called the cops and banged on your aunt's door until I woke her up. We've been worried sick ever since."

"It was Tripp Hampton," I told them, sitting on the living-room couch, where my aunt wrapped a warm knitted afghan around me. "He was waiting outside the door when I unlocked it. He had a rag with chloroform. He took me to his house. He took O'Ryan, too. . . . O'Ryan! He was going to drown O'Ryan. I have to look for him!" I started to get up, and my aunt put a calming hand on my arm.

"Shhh. O'Ryan is fine. He came in through the cat door a few minutes before you got here. You say Tripp took you both all the way to his house?"

The cat strolled into the living room, glanced at the three of us without curiosity, and curled up on his favorite needlepoint cushion.

"Yes, he did," I said. "All the way to his house."

"O'Ryan must have hitched a ride home, then," River said, "to have made it here before you did. And you were riding in a police car."

"Maybe one of the other policemen drove him home and let him out. Yes. That must be exactly what happened," I said, knowing in my heart that it wasn't.

"How did you get away from Hampton?" River demanded. "And why did he grab you in the first place?"

"My phone was bugged. He heard me tell you that I know where the diamond is. And he's been listening to my conversations with Pete, too. He wanted the diamond. He said he needs money so he won't go to jail for stealing from his investors, and—"

"Slow down, Maralee." My aunt spoke softly, gently, the way she used to when I was little and got too excited about something. "Take a deep breath and start at the beginning." She put a cup of hot tea in my still shaking hands. "There now. You're safe here, and O'Ryan is safe, too. Take your time and tell us what happened."

I did exactly what she told me to do. I took a deep breath and a sip of hot tea and began to feel warmer, better, safer. I looked across the room at the cat, who appeared to be dozing, eyes squeezed shut, ears flattened, and I knew he was wide awake, listening.

Do I tell them about the cats, O'Ryan? The hundreds of cats who came and saved our lives?

I started at the beginning, as Aunt Ibby had instructed. I told them about how Tripp had knocked me out and how he had O'Ryan in a cat carrier and had threatened to throw him in the pool to drown him if I didn't tell him where the diamond was.

River interrupted. "So where *is* it? You still haven't told us."

"It's on Nicky. Helena's little dog. She buried him on the island. He's wearing the diamond necklace. It was all in a poem she wrote in her notebook after he died. She said he was running to meet his dad—that means her first husband—and she dressed him up in the diamond necklace John Hampton had given to her. That's where it is now. Out on Misery Island, in Nicky's coffin."

"My goodness. Did you tell Tripp Hampton that?" My aunt clasped her hands together.

"I did. I had to tell him if I didn't want O'Ryan to

drown. I kept talking. Stalling for time. I knew you'd call for help, River, when you found me missing. I knew someone would come."

"But you got away. How?"

"It's a pretty wild story," I said, "and I don't think I can tell anyone except you two." I pulled the afghan close and took another sip of tea. "Nobody else will believe it, anyway, but I sure wish I'd had a camera with me."

So I told them. I told them every crazy, impossible bit of it. How I'd worked my hands loose and freed O'Ryan from his carrier. How I had heard glass crack and had watched while cat after cat had silently padded into that long room, and how they'd crowded around Tripp Hampton until he backed into the pool.

"And the cats kept coming," I said. "Hundreds of cats. All kinds of cats. I swear, every cat in Salem must have been in that room."

My aunt and my best friend stared at me. Was it disbelief I saw in their eyes?

I kept talking. "After Tripp fell in the pool, one of the cats, a black one with a red collar, led me through all those confusing halls and corridors, straight to the front door. I ran then, down the path to Daphne's cottage, and called 911."

"I've seen that cat before." Aunt Ibby spoke hesitantly. "A black cat with a red collar. I've seen her sitting on our back fence."

"Yes. I've seen her on that fence, too," I said. "And on the roof, outside the attic window, too. She was there when O'Ryan and I were up there looking for things to use in the plays."

"You never told me about that." Aunt Ibby refilled my teacup.

"She was with another cat that time," I said, recalling the scene. "A pretty gray one with a star-shaped white blaze on her forehead."

River sat forward, looking as though she was about to say something, then settled back in her chair, a smile flitting across her face.

"I told you there seems to be a lot of cats around here lately." My aunt shook her head. "A lot of cats."

"So, did Pete say anything about them?" River asked. "A roomful of cats isn't something you see every day."

"Not a word," I admitted. "They must have all gone away before he got there."

"Uh-huh," River said. "Anyway, did you tell him where you think the diamond is?"

"I did."

"Really? Didn't he want to know how you figured it out?" my aunt asked.

"Yes. But he was in a hurry to get back to the station," I said. "He said we'd talk later."

"Looks like now's the time, Maralee." Aunt Ibby patted my knee. "Now's the time to tell the truth about how you know . . . things."

I sighed. "You're right. I'm going to tell him."

"Good," Aunt Ibby said. "And I'm going to make some more tea. Be right back." She headed for the kitchen, and River moved onto the couch, beside me, and began to speak in a tone so low, it was almost a whisper.

"Those cats," she said. "I believe you about the cats. I believe they were there."

"Thanks, River. That means a lot."

"I kind of doubted it at first," she said. "After all, you'd been through a terrible experience—being chloroformed and all. But when you mentioned those *particular* cats, the black one with the red collar and the gray one with the star on her head, I understood." She nodded confidently. "I understood exactly what was going on."

"You did? You do?" It was my turn to be puzzled. "What *was* going on? Tell me. Please."

"Remember what I told you about Bridget Bishop when you gave me the box with her spell book in it? About how she dressed?"

"A red *bustier*." I smiled. "Not proper dress for a Puritan lady."

"And do you remember Ariel Constellation's beauty mark, which she was so proud of?"

I nodded. "Sure. A star on her cheek."

River leaned back against the couch cushions and folded her arms. "Well?"

It was like one of those long, silent moments when you almost expect to hear crickets chirping. Or like the lengthy pause in conversation while Mr. Pennington waits for someone to come up with the correct movie title. I could actually hear the grandfather clock in the front hall ticking.

Then I got it.

"Bridget Bishop with the red collar. Ariel with the star."

River offered a high five. I tapped her hand. "Right," she said. "Bridget had control over cats. The court said so in sixteen ninety-two. And O'Ryan was Ariel's familiar. Between the three of them—the black cat, the gray one, and O'Ryan—they called all those cats together to save you." She looked over at the sleeping cat on the needlepoint cushion. "And to save him."

"Amazing."

"Not so amazing when you consider today's date," she said. "June tenth. Bridget Bishop's birthday."

Pete came back to our house, as he'd promised. By then the sun had come up, and it looked as though it was going to be a beautiful summer's day in Salem. River had left for home, and I'd taken a hot shower but, still feeling chilled, had climbed into my trusty old gray sweats. Aunt Ibby bustled around in the kitchen, making breakfast for the three of us.

Pete told us all he could about what had transpired at the police station when they'd arrested Tripp Hampton on the kidnapping charge. "Looks like there'll be more charges later on," he said. "It's a pretty sure bet that he killed both his stepmother and Shea Tolliver. Then there's the matter of swindling millions from investors." He shook his head. "What a mess he made of his life. Smart guy like that. Good education. Fine family."

"And it was all for a piece of jewelry," my aunt said.

"Apparently," Pete said. "Lee says the necklace is buried on Misery Island, with Helena's dog. That right, Lee?"

I nodded. "It's all here in her notebook." I'd brought the notebook downstairs with me, knowing that Pete would want an explanation for how I could be so sure Helena had buried the gem with Nicky. I opened the book to the page with the picture of Helena and her dog wearing twin sailor hats. I read the poem about "picky little Nicky" aloud and explained about the dog wearing the necklace like his mom and running to meet his dad; hoping that would be enough evidence to justify my insistence that the gem would be found with poor Nicky's remains.

It wasn't.

"You said that she'd buried the dog in a metal coffin," Pete said. "How do you know that?"

I thought about lying to him. I could have said that maybe I'd seen something about it in one of the newspaper clippings, or that perhaps Daphne had mentioned it once. I caught Aunt Ibby's eye but couldn't read anything there. O'Ryan looked up from his red bowl of kibble and gave the tiniest nod.

"After breakfast," I said. "After we've eaten this delicious breakfast, which Aunt Ibby has so kindly prepared for us, if you'll come upstairs with me, I'll explain about that—and about a lot of other things."

So that's what I did. We sat together at the Lucite table in my kitchen, and I tried to explain about scrying, explaining that it was a real gift that some people have. Yes, for the first time in my life, I actually called it a gift. I told him about the terrible vision I'd seen in my Mary Janes when I was five. I told him about the obsidian ball and the things Ariel had shown to me in that smooth black surface. I told him how Tabitha Trumbull had appeared to me in the giant patent-leather pump, and I told the truth about why the mirror in my bureau had frightened me. I talked about Helena and the grandfather and the little gray dog and the small metal coffin a tearful Helena had held in her arms, and I described the vision of Shea I'd seen in the brass candlestick.

When I finished, I watched his face, realizing how much I loved this man and realizing at the same time that what I'd just shared with him might very well end our relationship.

"You're a scryer," he said.

"Yes, I am. Some people would call me a gazer. Same thing."

"You see these things, these visions, whether you want to or not?"

"I'm learning to control it. I can turn it on and off."

He smiled then. "Like a TV set."

"Something like that."

"A gift like that could come in handy sometimes, I suppose." He leaned forward, his elbows on the table, his chin resting on his fists.

"It has. Sometimes," I said. "At first I really hated it. Scared me to death. Now I'm kind of getting used to it. I've wanted to tell you about it so many times, but I've been afraid."

"Afraid?"

"Afraid you'd think I'm crazy. Afraid you wouldn't ever want to see me again." I felt tears welling up. I hadn't fully described the horror of some of the scenes I'd witnessed or the astonishing wonder of some of the others. I hadn't even told him about the hundreds of cats who'd probably saved my life just a few hours ago. I wasn't at all sure I could. Not yet.

"Okay," he said, reaching across the table and taking both of my hands in his. "Listen to me. I don't think you're crazy. I think you're the most wonderful, beautiful, caring woman I've ever known, and I love you. Please, from now on, do you think you can tell me when you see . . . something? Even if it's bad stuff?"

Can I promise such a thing? Am I ready to share that much of myself?

"It would be a big relief to be able to do that," I said finally. "I promise I'll try."

"I understand," he said, squeezing my hands. "I'm still trying to wrap my head around this amazing gift of yours, this new aspect of you. Thank you for trusting me."

"I do trust you, Pete," I said and let the tears of relief flow. "And I love you, too."

He stood, crossed to my side of the table, and gently pulled me to my feet. "Don't cry." He wiped my wet cheeks with his finger, and his kiss was gentle but insistent. "You're exhausted. Get some rest. I'll call you tonight."

He held my hand as we walked together to the door. He stepped out into the hall, then turned back toward me, smiling.

"Oh, about the Sprint Cup races next weekend. Do you still want to go?"

"Of course I do."

"Great. I'll call up there tomorrow and get us a couple of rooms."

"Pete . . ."

"Yes?"

"Just get one room."

EPILOGUE

Tripp Hampton is still awaiting trial on kidnapping, two counts of murder, and several felony charges, including money laundering and fraud. Federal marshals have seized his assets, including the Hampton mansion. His lawyers are pursuing an insanity plea. He complains about a black cat that, he says, sits outside the barred window of his seventh-floor cell at night, watching him.

Pete got permission to exhume the body of Helena's dog, Nicky. The pink diamond necklace was around his neck, just as I'd said it would be. Nicky was quietly reburied, with just Pete and me and an island guide in attendance. Because Helena had deeded the property on Misery Island, with all "buildings, improvements, and appurtenances," to the trustees of reservations, the court ruled that the diamond belongs to them. The money the organization will realize from the sale of Helena's necklace will go a long way toward preserving New England's historic heritage.

O'Ryan's back fence fan club still visits sometimes on warm summer nights, but we haven't seen the black cat with the red collar or the gray cat with the white star marking again.

Mr. Pennington and Aunt Ibby are still "keeping company," and *The Tabitha Trumbull Book of New England Cookery* is due to be published next year, with all proceeds going to the Tabby's scholarship fund.

Daphne's run as Billie Dawn in *Born Yesterday* was so successful that she's been invited to reprise the role with a Boston theater company, and there's a rumor going around that she and Tommy may be headed for Los Angeles soon for a round of interviews with a major movie studio.

The summer play season was entirely successful, and Mr. Pennington has offered me a new teaching contract at the Tabby. I'm looking forward to the start of classes in the fall, when I'll welcome students to a class on television performance and production.

Pete and I have relaxed into a relationship that gets more comfortable every day. We're at the point where we finish each other's sentences and laugh at the same silly things. We've gone out to the island several times and always remember to take along a pansy plant for Helena's grandmother and, of course, for Nicky. I haven't had any more visions lately, scary or otherwise, and I'm getting so that I can pass a mirror without flinching. I've been helping Pete with picking out some new furniture for his apartment, and he's even bought a few small antique pieces from both Jenny's and Gary Campbell's shops. River has offered to check everything for proper feng shui when we're finished.

But I'm sure Pete's *bagua* is great, just like everything else about him.

From *The Tabitha Trumbull Book of
New England Cookery*
(Recipes adapted and edited by Isobel Russell)

Joe Frogger Cookies

In 1798, in the seafaring Barnegat section of old
Marblehead, Massachusetts, a black man named Joe
Brown opened a tavern in a saltbox house at the edge
of a frog pond. Joe's wife, Lucretia, served the drinks,
and Black Joe's Tavern soon became popular as a place
where a thirsty man in from the sea could count on a
glass of good homemade beer or a taste of honest rum
at a fair price.

It was said that Black Joe made the best molasses
cookies in town, and people called them "Joe Froggers,"
after the plump little frogs who lived in the pond.
Fishermen liked them because they never got stale and
hard, and Marblehead women regularly packed them
for the men to take to sea. Joe claimed that what kept
them soft was rum and salt water, but he wouldn't tell
how he made them.

When Joe died in 1834, people thought that was the
end of Joe Froggers. But one day Lucretia shared the
secret recipe with a fisherman's wife, and before long
most of the women in Marblehead were making them.

Served with a pitcher of cold milk, Froggers became the town's favorite Sunday night supper.

3½ cups all-purpose flour
1½ teaspoons ground ginger
1 teaspoon baking soda
½ teaspoon ground cloves
½ teaspoon ground nutmeg
¼ teaspoon ground allspice
1 cup molasses*
1 cup light brown sugar
½ cup vegetable shortening
⅓ cup hot water
2 tablespoons rum
1½ teaspoons sea salt
Waxed paper, for rolling out the dough

Mix the flour, ginger, baking soda, cloves, nutmeg, and allspice in a large bowl until well combined. In a separate large bowl beat together the molasses, brown sugar, and shortening. In a small bowl, combine the hot water, rum, and sea salt.

Add the dry ingredients and the water-rum-sea salt mixture alternately to the molasses-sugar-shortening mixture and mix well to make a dough. On a cutting board, roll out the dough between two sheets of waxed paper until ¼ inch thick. Refrigerate the rolled out dough on the cutting board for at least 2 hours.

Preheat the oven to 375°F. Grease 2 baking sheets.

Remove the top sheet of waxed paper. Dip the cookie cutter in flour, then shake it and cut the chilled dough into 2½- or 3-inch rounds.** (Old-timers claim that originally Froggers were the size of a luncheon plate!) Gather up the dough left after cutting, put a

fresh sheet of waxed paper on top, and roll it until
¼ inch thick and cut some more rounds. Place the
rounds on the prepared baking sheets, and bake for
10 to 12 minutes, or until they are a little bit dark
around the edges and firm in the middle. Check on
them after about 9 minutes of baking.

Cool the cookies on the baking sheets for 5 minutes,
then remove them to wire racks to cool completely.

Makes about eighteen Froggers

*Aunt Ibby uses Grandma's Molasses, Bacardi rum,
Crisco shortening, and Atlantic Saltworks sea salt.

**A 14½-ounce vegetable can with both ends cut out
makes a nice 2½-inch cookie cutter and results in
3½-inch cookies after baking.

Love Lee? Want to know how it all began?
Be sure to read the first two books
In
The Witch City Mystery series

CAUGHT DEAD HANDED

And

TAILS, YOU LOSE

Available now
From
Kensington Books